Gary N Dyck

THE PHOTOGRAPHER'S WILL

Limited Special Edition. No. 12 of 25 Paperbacks

Gary N Dyck is an artist, photographer and writer with a passion for travel and adventure. As a young man, he went to university with the goal of becoming a writer but discovered that the best education for writing isn't found in the classroom. It is found in living. His writing reflects his deep connection to the land and the often-twisted relationships that fashion humanity.

This book is dedicated to my father-in-law. If he were alive, I'm sure he would hate every bit of it. I dedicate it to him anyway because without him I would not have my beautiful wife. Although my father-in-law inspired parts of this book, the storyline is not based on his life.

Gary N Dyck

THE PHOTOGRAPHER'S WILL

AUSTIN MACAULEY PUBLISHERS™

LONDON * CAMBRIDGE * NEW YORK * SHARJAH

A CIP catalogue record for this title is available from the British Library.

ISBN 9781528981781 (Paperback)
ISBN 9781528981798 (ePub e-book)

www.austinmacauley.com

First Published (2020)
Austin Macauley Publishers Ltd
25 Canada Square
Canary Wharf
London
E14 5LQ

Many thanks to my beautiful wife, who puts up with all the time I spend inventing other realities.

Preamble

As a writer, I choose topics, characters, and conflicts that help me tell the thousand stories that spin around in my head. I intend no slander against any nationality, gender, orientation, religion or person. This book is fiction. The characters are most definitely fiction. Any resemblance to real people or real situations is purely coincidental.

Prologue

They met over beers at Hooters. Well, Karl drank beer. Rudy drank Coke and Ricky sipped orange juice the barmaid promised was organic. They had little in common and, truth be told, they despised each other. Yet the brothers came together from the far reaches of Canada to say things in person that they didn't dare say over the phone or by email. Together they laid out a plan to murder their sister.

Ricky

Ricky felt extremely uncomfortable with the topic. His sister Addy was the best of them. The one child of Hans Ulfert that wasn't totally screwed up. Adelheid was six years his senior, and he just turned 30. For his birthday, Addy sent him a birthday card with a picture of a bouquet of pink roses on the cover and a $100 gift card to Rad Hourani, a boutique in Montreal where he lived. She wrote in the card in purple ink, "Hoping this next year is the best one ever. Love, Sis."

Her husband Jack wrote in it too, and it sounded like he meant it. "I hope you can come to stay with us at Christmas. We have room. Love, Jack."

Ricky sat in the same room as them twice in the last 10 years. Once when his grandmother died nearly a decade ago and last fall when they were together for his mom's funeral. "Good times," he said out loud.

Addy included with the card a photograph of her family. "Who does that nowadays?" he asked himself. "Everyone posts everything online." But he saw her point. It is not like any of his siblings considered each other Facebook friends. A fridge magnet held the picture in place, and he smiled every time he opened the fridge door.

Ricky did like Addy's kids, and they liked him. Riley was cuter and more precocious than any 10-year-old girl should be and her eight-year-old brother, Cody, played rough and tumble. *Playing with them was the one bright spot, the one good thing, at Mom's funeral*, Ricky thought. *And Addy's kids don't have German names.*

Just after Riley was born, Ricky's older brother, Karl, told him, "Heinrich, Dad demanded that Jack and Adelheid rename their kid Wilhelmina after Mom. Guess what? The fools wouldn't do it."

Apparently, Jack stood his ground and Ricky's dad let everyone know that he wrote Adelheid and Jack out of his will. Karl thought this was the best thing ever. Ricky felt sorry for them.

Yes, good old Dad, Ricky thought. *Had his kids exactly three years apart. Gave them all German names. First Adelheid, then Karl, himself and Rudolf. Seriously, who the hell gives their kids names like that and demands everyone at school call them by their real names?*

"Karl got away easy. How can you screw up that name?" he complained to himself. "The kids called my sister Heidy or Addy when Dad wasn't around. And Rudolf? Rudy wasn't the usual first pick of things to call him. Most often the kids called him Red Nose. And then there is my name. Heinrich. I got called Heiny for years."

Ricky felt proud of Addy for standing behind Jack. He admired Jack too. They were the only people ever to stand up to the old man.

"It is a real shame that we have to kill Addy," Ricky whispered. "She's done more for Mom and the old man than the three of us put together."

Rudy glared at him with such hatred that Ricky wondered if Rudy planned to kill him too.

"There is no other way," Karl stated calmly.

"Who isn't afraid of Rudolf Ulrich Ulfert?" Ricky said to himself. His very large and scary brother stood seven-feet tall and was built like a redwood tree. His head looked twice the size of a normal man's. His unkempt beard and hate-filled eyes took away any thought that he might be a giant teddy bear.

Rudolph stared with hatred across the table at Ricky and pumped his massive hands into fists the size of a melon. Then he lifted his thigh-sized left arm and flexed the muscles into definition. "I bench press 225 kilograms and I can break you in half. If you chicken out, Ricky, I will kill you. And I won't do it fast. First, I'll tear off all your appendages and shove them up your ass. Then I'll…"

"Shut up, Rudolf!" Karl ordered. "Heinrich will do his part. He wouldn't be here if he wasn't willing."

Rudy's hate-filled face, as he glared at Karl, was like seeing the face of the Devil as he discovered Christ rose from the grave. *Not that Karl is anything like a Saviour*, Ricky thought. *No, Karl is very much like my father. Manipulating, scheming and evil. An absolute control freak, yet all wrapped up in a charming personality.*

Ricky never would call his brother Rudolf to his face. God, Rudy hated that name. But Karl did it and got away with it. Karl always used their proper names, just like their old man. And Ricky knew from the way Rudy turned purple with rage, yet never punched out Karl's teeth, that Karl held something over on him.

Smiling Karl. All the while holding a very sharp axe over Rudy's gigantic neck just waiting for an opportunity to take him out. Karl the expert blackmailer. Karl, Ricky's father incarnate.

A scantily clad and very busty waitress came by and Karl ordered another beer. His third.

"And bring one for my brother," he said as he pointed at Rudy.

"No! I drink Coke," Rudy hissed at Karl.

He barely got the words out when Karl said, "On second thought, bring us each a pint."

12

Rudolph

Rudolph felt embarrassed to sit at the same table as Heinrich. He hated Ricky's tight jeans with the bling on the back pocket. He despised Ricky's black shirt with the pink trim on the collar and the pocket. He abhorred Ricky's pink sapphire earrings. Most of all, he loathed Ricky's eyelash extensions.

Normally, I would never be caught on the same side of the street with anyone of Ricky's persuasion, Rudolph thought.

Just then, Karl said to the barmaid, "We're brothers. Supposedly, we all have the same mother and father. Do we look like brothers to you?"

The barmaid tipped her head slightly to one side, her long auburn hair dangled to her bare and shapely midriff, and she looked at each of them. She smiled at Karl and answered, "You're all kinda different, but you do all have the same nose. And your hair is the same sandy-brown colour. Yes, I'd say you are brothers."

Karl smiled from ear to ear as he extended his little finger to touch the side of the waitress's hand.

Rudy turned red and pumped his fist because he wanted to knock Karl into next week. Then he heard Ricky snicker. Rudy turned his hatred towards Ricky and began to rise, but Karl put his hand on Rudolf's massive wrist and the giant sat back down.

"Ricky is definitely the result of defective sperm," Rudy hissed. Rudolph would have blamed his mother for having an affair nine months before she gave birth to Ricky, but Rudolph couldn't see how that could happen. His father controlled every second of his mother's life, absolutely every second, even when he was out of the country.

Rudy remembered how Hans Ulfert, his father, was totally at a loss when the doctors diagnosed Wilhelmina with inflammatory breast cancer. He could do nothing to control deadly disease. Hans demanded that the doctors perform a miracle. He threatened to sue them if his wife died. He promised them money if they would save her. And he changed doctors and hospitals until he ran out of options.

Hans Ulfert called the doctors so many times they refused to take his calls. At every hospital, he created such a fuss they banned him. The Foothills Medical Centre got a restraining order to keep him off their property.

Rudolf didn't doubt his father threatened the hospital staff. *The old man was like that. After all, I would have done the same thing*, Rudy thought. *Otherwise, the staff do nothing for you. Dad's actions just prove how much he really loved Mom. And I was Mom's favourite. Her baby.*

When Rudy's father called him useless, his mother reassured him. When his father threatened, "You won't get a dime from me," his mother opened her purse strings and promised him that he would get the lion's share in the end.

Why did you have to die first? Rudy asked in his mind as if he whispered to his mother. Then he added, *Damn you for leaving!*

He hoped his mom's last will and testament spoke of how much she loved him and how she set aside money for him. But the lawyers never read her will. Everything that was hers passed to Hans.

Rudolph always figured that the old man would blow a gasket and drop dead. Mom would be around forever. She loved him unconditionally and Rudy took her for every penny he could grab.

It wasn't wrong of me, Rudy thought. *She owned more than she could ever use anyways. Besides, every penny I took left one less for Karl. Karl the clone. Karl the spitting image of the old man. Hans Karl Ulfert the second.*

However, Karl liked his beer. A lot. He drank 24 beers every day and carried a bulging midriff to show for it. Rudy knew Karl lost at least four jobs for drinking at work, yet he would find a job somewhere else in less than a week. Karl the greasy, smooth-talking, used-car salesman. Lying through his teeth while smiling like Jesus.

Rudy saw Karl glance his way. He knew that Karl saw his clenched fists and defined arm muscles, yet Karl brought his eyes back to the barmaid's voluptuous breasts as he smiled at her.

The brothers met at the beginning of happy hour and now the place began to fill, yet the barmaid wasn't in a hurry to leave. *She pretty much ignores Ricky and me,* Rudy thought with jealousy. *Obviously, the slut is attracted to Karl's clean-shaven face, his businessman haircut, and his perfect smile. Yes, Karl the womaniser. He could talk himself into bed with anyone.* Rudy put his Coke glass down hard and Karl jumped. Rudy smiled to himself, *Karl pretends he is not afraid of me, but I know better. One day soon I'll make him pay for thinking he is untouchable.*

Rudy turned his gaze to Heinrich. *Now he is afraid of me,* Rudolf thought. *Skinny Heinrich. Weak. Small. Effeminate. Heinrich the bum screw. Heinrich the son my father hated. Heinrich the boy chaser. It would have been better if he had never been born. On the bright side, no matter what the old man thought of me, he always thought less of Heinrich. Why Ricky is here today is beyond my understanding. What could the fairy offer?*

Yet Karl called them both and they came. At their own expense too. Ricky flew in from Quebec and Rudy flew from Calgary.

Karl

When Karl moved his family to the West Coast, Heinrich already lived in Montreal. The brothers both wanted to get as far away from their father as possible. Ricky left in disgrace so moving east was no big deal. Karl, on the other hand, pretended the coastal weather was necessary for his wife, Ursula's, health.

As the barmaid turned to leave the table, Karl reached out and ran his hand down her orange shorts. She smiled as she looked back over her shoulder and winked at him.

Karl married Ursula Steyr one week after her 19th birthday. She was a pretty bride, a German bride with blonde hair and blue eyes, and eight-months pregnant.

Karl smiled as he thought about how she acted head-over-heels in love with him. Now she just looked hard, no doubt filled with bitterness from all his broken promises. The seething anger never left her eyes. But she took good care of the kids and always made sure they never went hungry. And she never left him. She could never leave him. She gave birth to his three children. Besides, she'd never get a dime from his inheritance if she left him because she signed the prenuptial agreement that the old man's fancy lawyer wrote.

Their daughter Angelika was eight, Torsten just turned six and Ulrich four. True German blood. True German names. And his father could not be happier. When Ursula gave birth to their daughter, Karl told his father, "We'll name our daughter Wilhelmina, after Mom."

Hans answered with some venom, "No. Adelheid gave birth to the first girl. Wilhelmina is her daughter's real name. Someday Adelheid will change her daughter's name."

"I wouldn't hold my breath, Dad," Karl remarked, just to keep the anger going. "Then what name would you like us to choose?"

"Name your daughter Angelika, your mother's middle name," Hans ordered. And they did.

When Karl' sons were born, the old man started trust accounts for each of them because they carried the family name. Ursula complained to Karl that it wasn't fair to Angelika. "Your old man is loaded. You'd think he'd give money to all his grandkids."

"Life is not fair," Karl answered just like he'd heard his father say a thousand times. "At least some money is coming towards our family now," he continued. "If we play this right, all of the inheritance will come to us someday."

Karl noticed that Ursula seemed discontent with someday. The illusive someday did not make him happy either. That was the reason his brothers sat together at a back table in Hooters. Karl put his plan in motion.

Getting my brothers here was easy, Karl thought as he smiled at them. *I just phoned and told them the truth. Well, my version of the truth. I told them both that when Dad had the heart attack, guess who was the first one to the hospital? Adelheid. She drove down from Edmonton like a bat out of hell. You know she is there for just one reason. She is making a grab for the money.*

Heinrich answered him, "The old man wrote Addy out of the will years ago. If she made a trip to see the SOB, it is because she still hasn't figured out that he really doesn't give a shit about anyone. Especially her. Besides, the old man wrote me out of his will too. Whatever you think she is up to has nothing to do with me."

"I need your help, Heinrich," Karl answered. "And in exchange, I'll give you half of my share of the inheritance." Karl heard Ricky suck in his breath. Karl knew his brother swallowed the bait, hook, line and sinker. He knew Ricky would be on the next plane to Vancouver.

Convincing Rudolf was even easier. "Your sister is making a grab for the money. Dad told me that she saw his account books and knows exactly how much money the old man gave you to settle your divorces. And for the lawyers when those girls accused you of rape. And the payouts to the families. And for child support. Dad told me that Adelheid told him that he should never give you another penny."

Karl knew all the right buttons to push and he pushed them one after another. He could imagine his giant brother's face turning red as a newly painted barn and then purple like an eggplant. Before he took a rage-filled breath, his face would turn as black as coal. Karl held the phone at arm's length.

"I'll kill her!" Rudolf screamed.

"Yes," Karl replied when he brought the receiver back to his mouth. "That is exactly what we must do."

After he hung up the phone, he said, "Rudolf the Neanderthal. Big and dumb. Thinks only with his dink. His kind manage to survive only because they leave a baby in every woman they screw. Rudolf must have at least 10 kids already and he never paid a dime supporting one of them."

And he thought, *As much as the old man had his faults, he always said, 'Being a father is the ultimate responsibility.' Rudolf never comprehended that sentiment. What a Neanderthal.*

Karl looked at his brothers' faces and smiled like this was the best day of his life. He lifted his glass and proposed a toast, "To Adelheid, the best sister we ever had."

He watched his brothers lift their pints of West Coast brew and click their glasses together as if sealing their oath.

"To Addy," Ricky said with tears in his eyes.

"May she burn in hell," Rudy chimed in with hatred in his voice.

Karl's smile reached his blue eyes as he swallowed the golden-coloured liquid. Ricky made a face like he just swallowed skunky-tasting horse piss, but he never set the beer stein down. And a look of determination settled across Rudy's face that made Karl wonder what Rudy just decided.

Hans

Hans Ulfert's heart attack came on suddenly. Totally out of the blue, at least to him.

On Thursday afternoon at a quarter to four, he finished the photoshoot in the magnificent studio in his home. He found the shoot challenging because the Premier sat for the portrait. It was not that he couldn't use lighting to make the Premier look softer and more trustworthy, the problem was the Premier's aid and secret service agents. They insisted on being in the studio.

First, they wandered around touching things, and then the Premier's squirrelly little aid had the audacity to tell Hans that the shadows were too severe under the Premier's chin. Hans lost it on him.

"I scared the crap out of him," Hans laughed to himself as he turned out the photo lamps when he returned to the studio after escorting the Premier out the front door. "The little shit of an aid literally hid behind the burly secret service agent as I told him in no uncertain terms where to go and how fast to get there."

Hans put all the equipment away, even though he needed it all out again in two days. "Who knows how much dust might settle on it," he said to himself as he pulled the lens filters and portrait lens of his Hasselblad H5D and put them each in the proper padded spots in their aluminium cases.

The camera cost more than $50,000 without the lens. Of course, he wiped down each piece of equipment with a lens cloth first. Dust. The bane of any photographer.

"I'll reprimand the cleaning staff again," he told himself. "And maybe I'll hire another company anyways."

He scheduled the cleaning staff to come in the next day. Every time he did a photoshoot in the main studio, the cleaning staff did a complete clean of the change rooms and the big studio. That included vacuuming the big studio's walls, sets and three-metre high ceiling. They'd wash and polish the marble floors too.

"Most of tomorrow will be a colossal waste of my time," Hans complained to himself. However, he would supervise the cleaning staff every moment they worked in the studio. Hans trusted no one.

Because of the people in the studio today, Hans went room to room making sure they left nothing out of place. When he flipped the light switch on in the woman's change room, he noticed it right away. He saw a finger streak on the marble makeup vanity where the security agent's hand skimmed the polished grey marble while he made sure no assassin hid there. Hans swore in German.

After he left the change room, he made sure that the studio two door and the office door were locked even though no one went into them.

He walked across the marble floor of the studio, turned on a bank of air filters that sat against the west wall, and walked out the wide studio door into his living quarters. The door clicked closed and he heard the bolt slide into place. Then he tried the handle just to be sure.

In the great room, Hans sat in his over-stuffed, sable-brown leather armchair reading the Calgary Herald cover to cover. He reached for his coffee without looking at the custom-made, red-coloured, cherry-wood end table.

When his hand found no coffee and remembered that Wilhelmina, his wife, died a year previously.

He sighed, got up and walked to the two-storey-high windows and looked out across the manicured lawn, the gazebo and water feature, and professionally maintained flower gardens of his two-acre yard. The tree-lined Bow River wound through the valley below him.

He fought the city to build this place. The city's planning department told him that his proposed Goslar-castle-style house, with arches and turrets, did not fit in with the neighbourhood. They told him he could not build one house in the middle of two lots. And they told him his house could not be more than one storey high as it would block his neighbours' view. They told him lots of things, but he fought City Hall and won. Mind you, not without threats, bribery, and a half-dozen lawsuits.

Hans smiled remembering how he made the contractor rebuild the six-foot picket fence around the bottom of his property four times so that, when he measured, each board was exactly the same distance apart at the top as at the bottom. In the end, the contractor used a plane and power sander to make every board as straight as an arrow on all sides. *If the contractor would have done that to start with, he would have saved a lot of time*, Hans thought. *And to think that he wanted to reuse the boards that he pulled down. When the rich and famous come to me for a portrait, do I tell them we can reuse something I've already taken? No! A true craftsman would never do that. I taught him a thing or two about business.*

Hans remembered his coffee and shouted towards the hallway that led to the kitchen, "Maid, bring me my coffee."

His voice echoed off the pastel-yellow walls of the great room and from the second-floor Bavarian-style balcony above him and to the left. For a moment, he stared up at the designs cut into the white-painted slats of the balcony, and he pictured his wife standing there like a queen surveying her castle.

He shouted again, "Bring my coffee now!" Hans liked the sound of his voice. It sounded like a German general shouting commands. However, no one answered his order. Over the years he hired several maids and three different butlers, but not one of them lasted more than their first day on the job.

"No one met my high standard," he reasoned. He walked through the massive room, past the long hallway and almost to the entranceway. There he turned left into the short hallway that led to the massive kitchen with its stainless-steel appliances. He opened the white cupboard door and chose a coffee mug then spent a minute turning the remaining blue and white peony-patterned mugs so all the handles faced the same way. He made sure that the distance between each mug looked exactly even. "How hard is that?" he shouted at the air. "I'll have a word with the manager of the cleaning staff. Again!"

Hans put a K-cup into the coffee machine and put the Meissen china mug under the spout and pushed the button. The machine hissed and groaned as he waited impatiently. Like a German soldier on parade, he marched from the kitchen side of the room into the dining room with its gold and crystal chandelier. As he stared at the gold filigree on the sea-blue walls, he drummed his fingers on the red-coloured, cherry-wood dining table. Hans remembered the look of joy on Wilhelmina's face when the Dutch furniture builder delivered it. "Now my dream kitchen is complete!" she said.

"Speed it up," Hans yelled at the coffee machine as it hissed and groaned.

The coffee tasted mediocre at best, and it wasn't hot enough. "Wilhelmina knew how to make coffee," he complained loudly as if his dead wife might be listening in from the next room. "And she always used fresh ground Kona coffee beans and pre-warmed the coffee mug. This stuff is shit!"

He gulped it down anyways, becoming angrier with each swallow. He glanced at his yellow-gold and diamond-encrusted Rolex, although he already knew the time. He expected the caterer to arrive precisely at 5:30 with his supper. It was 15 seconds past 5:30.

"Wilhelmina always had supper ready on time!" his jowls jiggled like Jell-O as he shouted at the three-metre-high, sea-blue coloured kitchen walls with the white cornice where the wall met the ceiling and a white chair rail in the dining room.

Hans carried extra weight and looked somewhere between paunchy and jolly, except no one would describe him as jolly. He held the coffee cup in an outstretched arm and, for a moment, debated lobbing it at the chandelier above the dining room table. Hans set the cup down hard and swore. He glanced out one of the tall thin windows to see if the caterer pulled into the driveway. He swore again and marched to the great room.

At 5:32, he phoned Krueger's Wiener Schnitzel Haus and gave Deitfried, the owner, a piece of his mind. Hans stomped around the great room shouting into the receiver. He marched the length of it and almost back to the kitchen hallway when the first wave of nausea swept over him. Sweat suddenly poured from his forehead like it did in the humidity and hot sun of Vietnam. His chest felt tight like someone cinched a corset around his lungs.

His angry words suddenly went from a booming tirade to a whisper, like all the air in the room vanished. In mid-sentence, Hans Ulfert's body hit the hardwood floor with a thud.

Deitfried Kruger listened to Hans Ulfert's rants many times. At least once every few weeks. Deitfried put up with the abuse because the photographer spent at least $100 every day on goulash, spätzle or schnitzel. Normally the rant lasted at least five minutes and, today, it barely started and then everything went quiet. Deitfried Krueger heard Hans's doorbell ringing.

His son texted him 30 seconds later, 'Dad, no one is home. What do I do with the food?'

Deitfried called 911.

At 5:48, Rudy's home phone rang. Raven, his live-in lover, glanced at the call display and said with some concern, "Rudy, it's the Calgary City Police."

Rudy did not pick up. He wracked his brains wondering who saw him do what. Then his cell phone rang, also from the police. He let it go to voicemail.

He played back the cell-phone message, "This is an emergency message for Rudolph Ulfert. This is Constable Fred Harmond of the Calgary City Police. It appears that your father had a medical emergency. EMS is at his house, but is unable to get in. Frazer Alarm company gave us your name and number as a person with access. As soon as you get this message, please call me and please hurry to your father's house."

Rudy called Constable Harmond. "This is Rudy Ulfert. I'm on the way."

Rudy grinned like a boy who didn't cover his eyes during a game of hide and seek. For years he waited for this day. He planned for this day. If he believed in prayer, he would have prayed for this day.

On the way across the city, he stopped to celebrate at the golden arches. He ate three double cheeseburgers and drank a super-sized Coke. He did not do the drive-through, and he did not hurry.

He put on his concerned expression as he reached the driveway of his father's massive, stone, castle-like mansion with its hand-carved stone gryphons. Then he laughed when he saw the bewildered emergency responders, huddled around the now battered, wooden, 3-metre-high, arch-shaped castle door, with its black cast-iron studs. He knew that behind the medieval-looking wooden planks was a high-security, anti-breach metal door.

He turned into the cobblestone driveway that might be described as circular because, from the front of the house and to Rudy's left, the cement-edged cobblestone sidewalk framed half of a circle around a 15 metre in diameter circular fountain and continued to the street. Behind the sidewalk, to Rudy's left, he saw the perfectly manicured lawn and flower gardens. To Rudy's right side, red and grey cobblestones covered the entire parking-lot-sized yard like a European town square.

The ambulance driver parked against the sidewalk facing the street, the police parked their car in front of the door, and a fire truck parked close to the house, in front of the kitchen, dining room and office. Decorative cast-iron bars enclosed the kitchen and dining room's eight narrow, two-metre tall, arch-shaped windows preventing anyone from breaking in.

Rudy knew the one small, cast-iron, grate-covered window high up in the wall provided light for the office. On the left side of the arched entrance, decorative metal grates covered ten windows near the top of the stone wall in the ballroom-sized great room.

Around the entire fortress-like mansion, the top of the wall was a crenellation, the saw-tooth look of blocks of stone called merlons, where archers might hide or defenders might pour boiling oil down on attackers. Once, Rudy saw his father walking around the top of the wall, yet his father never gave him permission to go up there. His father never disclosed the location of the access to the roof. Actual castle watchtowers formed the corners of the mansion complete with narrow arrow-slits so soldiers could shoot at any angle down at the hoards.

From where he drove in, Rudy could see the top floor of the living quarters rising above the wall and to the right of the entranceway. On the front side of the living quarters, ornate ironwork covered the arch-shaped windows of the library, games room, oratory, and master bedroom.

Rudy knew the bedrooms were on the opposite side of the living quarters and their windows faced the river valley. The bronze living-quarter's roof turned green from oxidisation two years previously. To the left of the entranceway, the bronze roof formed a steep cone like the steeple of a church. A German flag flew from a pole on the top of the steeple.

As Rudy drove past the fire truck and parked in front of one of the three oversized, medieval-style garage doors, he thought, *If ever I have to make a last stand against the cops, I want to do it from this fortress.* Rudy got out of his customized Ram 250 and swaggered as he walked up to the imposing-looking entryway.

He loved how the emergency responders' faces showed awe and fear at seeing a giant walking towards them. Then, with gigantic fingers, Rudy inserted the massive key and entered the passcode into the keypad. Then he slowly turned the key. He pushed the heavy door inward.

He stepped out of the way, and police officers and emergency medical services staff rushed past him only to find that they were in the entryway. Another door barred them from the house, and it needed a security code too. Rudy waited as they got out of his way and he slowly and carefully entered the access code. Then everyone rushed to his father's aid.

The old man lay face down on the dark, reddish-coloured, cherry wood floor in the palace-like great room. Rudy guessed his father died as he fell because Hans's nearly bald head looked as white as a soccer ball. His pale ears looked like they belonged on a china doll. His legs were splayed and his arms were out to his sides like he did a spread-eagle face plant.

Rudy covered his smile by putting his gigantic hands over his mouth.

Paramedics put a stretcher on the floor beside the photographer, tucked in his arms and rolled him onto the stretcher. Hans's head flopped over and he stared wide-eyed at Rudy. Blood seeped from Hans's nose and his mouth looked unnaturally red from the blood that ran from where his tooth pierced his lip.

Rudy jumped when he saw his father try to raise a hand toward him. He saw Hans struggle to say something as the paramedics picked up the stretcher. His father's lips moved, but no words came out.

His father did not mouth 'I love you' or even 'Help me'. Hans Ulfert said, "Don't you dare."

This time Rudy did not hide his smile. He did dare. And he would.

Addy

Adelheid got the call while she read a bedtime story to Cody, her eight-year-old son. At mid-sentence on the first page of the *Adventures of Jimmy Skunk*, Jack brought the phone into Cody's bedroom. It annoyed her that Jack didn't just take a message. She counted her time with Cody as precious. It didn't help her feelings towards Jack as she saw the disappointment spread over Cody's face. Jack saw it too and tickled him under the chin. This brought a smile back to Cody's impish face as the child pulled the covers up so only his smiling eyes showed.

"Who is it?" Addy whispered to Jack.

"It is the Foothills Hospital in Calgary. They won't tell me why they are calling," he answered with his finger over the microphone as he handed her the phone.

"Hello," she said into the phone, hoping that it was just a fundraiser call. She hoped somehow someone got her name from another charity that promised not to share her personal information. She hoped the churning feeling in her gut was due to her second helping of pot roast at supper.

"Is this Adelheid Penner?" the man asked.

"Yes," she answered curtly.

"Is your father's name Hans Karl Ulfert?"

"Yes," she answered timidly, afraid of what might come next.

"This is Dr. Vandenberg, a heart specialist here at the Foothills Medical Centre. Your father appears to have suffered a major coronary earlier this evening. He is in the intensive care unit here at the Foothills. He is asking for you."

"A heart attack? Is he going to be all right?"

"I'm not saying that he is dying, but your father really is not doing well. He is very weak and things could go either way. If you want to see him alive, I'd suggest you hurry."

Jack tried to convince Addy to get some sleep and leave at 5:00 a.m. the next morning, but she tossed some clothes and shoes into an overnight bag, went online and booked a sub for her class at school, and drove out of Edmonton less than an hour after receiving the call. She set the cruise control in her blue Chrysler minivan for 112 kilometres per hour and cried until she reached Red Deer an hour and a half later.

In that time, she emptied almost an entire box of tissue, and soggy tissues covered the floor like a tissue-flower art project she did with her kindergarten class. She did not cry because she shared a close relationship with her dad. She cried because her father asked for her.

She was the oldest of his children. The only girl. She remembered a few things that someone would call quality time with her father. For the most part, when he wasn't off somewhere in the world taking pictures, he worked in his studio or locked himself in his darkroom in the basement.

During her growing up years, her father doted on Karl, his oldest son. No one else mattered. When she became a teen, Addy thought her only value came from the chores she did around the house.

I'm not naive enough to think that my father has had a change of heart, she thought. And then she chuckled at the pun. *But he never asked for me in years. Maybe, just maybe, I could hear him say the words every child needs from her father. Maybe he will tell me he loves me. Maybe he will say he loves my kids too.*

The black and white police car followed the ambulance out of the circular driveway, past the life-size, carved-limestone statue of a nude woman reclining at the edge of a circular pool of koi. The statue was a replica of the one at the Herrenchiemsee Palace fountain in Germany. When the emergency vehicle reached the two and a half metre tall cedar hedge that surrounded the top of the property, they turned right with their sirens blaring and lights flashing.

Rudy watched the red fire truck with the white stripe down the centre, back up and then drive out of the yard. With lights going and siren wailing, it stopped traffic and turned left.

As Rudy turned to step back inside, he noticed the insulated, red, delivery box from Kruger's Schnitzel Haus on the cobblestone sidewalk at the left side of the massive doorway. He unzipped the lid and, instantly, the smell of gourmet food wafted into the air. He put his hand on the stainless-steel lid. "It's still hot," he exclaimed.

He picked up the box and carried it into the house. "I would have preferred pizza," he said out loud as he took the metal trays out and set them on the countertop in the kitchen. "But I won't turn down a free meal on the old man. May God burn his soul."

He took a large Meissen dinner-plate out of the cupboard and loaded it up. And he grabbed some genuine gold-plated cutlery. Rudy sat in his father's sable-brown leather chair in the great room and stared out at the river valley as he ate chicken cordon bleu and sautéed asparagus even though he had just eaten three burgers. His old man would have a fit that he ate here. He didn't care. His father would be dead soon if he wasn't already.

The salty food made him thirsty and Rudy craved pop. He walked to the kitchen, but only found beer in the fridge. Rudy always kept a couple of two-litre Cokes in a mini-fridge in the stainless-steel cargo box in his truck box so he went to his truck and grabbed a bottle.

After he finished eating, Rudy piled the dishes and trays into the sink, although he did not rinse them. He could have gone into the hallway from the dining room, but he walked back into the great room and stared at all the gold.

"Before Karl comes to claim everything, I think I'll take a few of the photographs. The solid-gold picture frames must be worth thousands," he declared.

Then he walked down the long, wide hallway, past the large metal door to the studio on his left, and into his father's front office. He ignored the roll-top, cherry-wood desk and the file cabinets. Instead, he opened the cherry-wood folding closet doors to reveal a six-foot-high, gun-metal coloured, high-security Hamilton safe. The safe needed a key and a security code.

He knew where his father kept the key. He watched his father take it out of a hollowed-out book and then put it back when he was done. Rudy reached for *A Century of Coins: Canada 1867–1967*, took out the key and put it into the keyhole. He did not have to take the slip of paper out of his wallet for the combination numbers. For months, he practised turning the dial in his head.

Three full revolutions to the left to 54 and 2 revolutions to the right to 27. One full revolution the left to 31 and half a turn to the right. He stopped the dial at number 19. His giant fingers did not feel the tumblers slide into place, but he heard a click. He yanked up on the bar and the door swung open.

Rudy did not know the value of his father's coins collected over a lifetime. He saw binders full of Canadian and American coins in cardboard and plastic holders. He counted a dozen binders full of rare paper bills including Canadian 25-cent bills. With his giant forearm, he pushed the computer monitor to one side as he set an armful of binders on the desk. He paged through the one.

Rudy laughed as he made trip after trip out to his truck loading binders, trays and cases into the chrome-metal storage bin in the back of his truck. When he could fit nothing more into the box and still close the lid, he piled case of coins on the passenger seat. "The old man told Karl he would get all this someday, but now it is mine. I earned it."

On the bottom shelf of the safe Rudy found velvet cases with pure silver and gold coins. Two display cases held ancient Roman coins and one contained Greek coins. Rudy read the price tag on one Roman coin, "$120,000." He laughed.

"Dummkopf! You dare call me dummkopf?" Rudy said as if talking to his father. "Look who took your precious coin collection. And, when they read the will, no one will know what happened to the coins. They'll just assume you sold your collection to piss Karl off."

It took Rudy weeks to get the combination for the safe. First, he needed access to the house. When his father travelled to Europe, Rudy threw a bowling-ball-sized boulder at one of the picture windows at the back of the house. The shatterproof window vibrated setting off the alarm.

He sat in his truck three blocks from the house as he watched the police car go by. A moment later his father called him.

"Rudolph. Someone tried to break into my house through a back window. The alarm company says no one tripped any of the inside motion detectors. Go see if everything is okay."

"Dad, I don't have a key to your house or a code to turn off the alarm. I would love to help, but there is not much I can do for you," he answered. "But I'll head over there right now."

The day after his father returned from Copenhagen, Hans gave Rudy a key and the passcodes to the front doors and the alarm. That was the easy part. The hard part was setting up the cameras. Hans didn't like a single thing out of place and Rudy needed to see the dial. The safe was in the closet in the office, hidden behind folding doors. Rudy hid a micro-camera the size of a bullet in the slats in the door so that the lens aimed down at the safe's dial when someone opened the closet door. He used sticky tack to hold it in place.

"You'd have to be lying on the floor to see the camera," Rudy laughed the day he hid it.

He painted the other miniature pinhole camera gold to match the ornate frame of a large black and white portrait that hung in the office.

The portrait of his mother was stunning, and every time Rudy looked at it, his eyes locked with his mother's unblinking eyes. Rudy suspected that his father did the same thing. That is why Rudy risked setting up a camera in the open. He tried it in several spots on the top of the ornate frame and he checked the view on his laptop.

"The cleaning staff is never allowed in the office so I think it is safe right here. Don't tell Father," Rudy said to the photograph as he put the camera in place. He held his giant finger in front of his mouth and whispered, "Shhhhhh!"

His father never suspected. Rudy wanted to hide cameras in the hallway too so he could get the studio door code, but he knew that the cleaning staff wiped down every millimetre of the hallway every other day. He resorted to trying combinations of numbers every chance he got.

He started with his mother's birthday. He tried his father's social security number. Then he tried phone numbers. However, he did not know how many numbers he needed to push. Today he did combinations of six numbers. He read on the internet that there are 14 million possible combinations of 6 numbers.

The keypad contained ten rows of buttons, three across, and a row of symbols.

After two unsuccessful hours, Rudy locked the house and left. He would return. The value of whatever his father kept hidden in the studio far exceeded that of the coin collection.

When Addy arrived at the Foothill Medical Centre in Calgary at five minutes before one on Friday morning, the parking lot looked deserted. She thanked God it was early September rather than winter. A trip that should take three hours in the summer could take nine during a blizzard, that is, if you are lucky enough to make it through. She pushed the green button and the yellow machine spit out a time-stamped ticket for parking.

Not counting the staff, the few people Addy saw in the hospital lobby looked frightened and tired. She presumed correctly that she looked afraid like them.

At the information desk, a dark-haired and pretty receptionist told her, "Visiting hours ended at 8:00 p.m."

"My father had a heart attack," Adelheid answered. "I just drove down from Edmonton. Is he... is he still alive?"

"Miss, if you tell me your father's name, I could look up which room he is in."

"Hans Ulfert," she answered, embarrassed that she hadn't given that information to start with.

"He is in ward 6D. Speak to the ward nurse."

As the elevator doors opened on six, a sobbing, middle-aged woman rushed out of the elevator and almost knocked Adelheid over. The woman looked up with shock in her eyes and did not apologise as she fled from the hospital.

As the elevator door closed, Addy thought, *Death*. A cold shiver ran down her spine as she remembered the hurt and loss in the woman's eyes. Addy shuddered again and said out loud, "I can feel the Grim Reaper."

Addy introduced herself to the ward clerk as Hans Ulfert's daughter. It sounded strange to her. For years, she introduced herself as Jack's wife, and then as Riley's and Cody's mom. Only forever ago, people knew her as Hans Karl Ulfert's daughter.

Once, years ago, when she took the education program at the University of Alberta, a professor from the sciences wing asked if her name was Heidi. She answered, "Adelheid." Then he asked if she knew Hans Ulfert. She told him that she was Hans Ulfert's daughter. He smiled. His question surprised her because everyone always told that she looked the spitting image of her mother. Today she was once again her father's daughter. It felt kind of embarrassing, and yet wonderful to feel connected to her father.

"Your father experienced a major coronary," the grey-haired and slightly overweight ward clerk answered with compassion in her voice. "From what I understand, he was on the phone with a restaurant when it happened. The restaurant staff phoned for an ambulance, but Emergency Medical Services couldn't get into the house. Something to do with security. Then your brother arrived and opened the doors. The delay was... well, it was not good."

The motherly-type ward clerk put her hand on Addy's. "We're giving him thrombolytics to dissolve any blood clots. They'll do an angioplasty in the morning to try to open his blocked coronary artery. He is very weak."

When Adelheid stepped into the intensive care room, the multitude of sounds bombarded her. The heartbeat monitor made irregular beeps. The black screen with the green lines showed weak and uneven heartbeats. Alarmed, Addy looked at the Pilipino nurse who brought her to her father's room. The nurse nodded, well aware of the situation. "We are monitoring him closely," she whispered, and then she left the room.

An oxygen mask covered Hans Ulfert's pale face up to the bottom of his closed eyes. His arms and hands looked like white plastic. He looked old and one breath from dead.

Addy picked up his hand and whispered, "Dad, I'm here."

He gave her hand a squeeze and squinted at her with one eye. "Knew you'd come," he whispered in German.

She leant in close to hear his muffled words and replied, "*Ich liebe dich.*" She hoped she might hear an 'I love you' back from her father.

Instead, he mumbled, "Want me dead. Want the money."

"Who, Dad? What are you talking about?"

"*Ihre bruder.*"

"My brothers? No, Dad. They would be here if they could."

"Get their wish soon. You are…" he stopped talking and gasped for air. Then he continued, "Executor of my will. My trustee."

His words hit Adelheid like an electric shock, but she answered, "*Ja, Vater. I should go now so you can rest.*"

He clenched her hand and hissed, "Secrets! I'll burn in hell. Destroy them."

"I don't know…"

"My house," he interrupted. "Stay… there. Destroy… secrets."

"Yes, Father," she answered, with absolutely no idea if his words were drug-induced.

When she walked out of the room, the ward nurse called her over. "He had your name and number on a business card in his wallet. That is how the hospital knew how to find you." She handed Adelheid the card.

Addy recognized her father's lawyer's business card. She'd seen the name and the black and red logo on the letter the lawyer sent her after she gave birth to Riley. The letter let her know in no uncertain terms that she and any children she might have were forever written out of her father's will. It informed her bluntly that she could never contest the will.

She didn't care about the money. It hurt that her father did not have the slightest bit of love or respect for her.

Under the lawyer's contact information on the card, in her father's handwriting, it said in English, 'Adelheid Penner, my daughter. Call her in case of emergency.' Below that, she saw her phone number.

On the back of the card, written in German in very precise and tiny handwriting, it said, 'Adelheid, if you are reading this, I need your help. Whether I am dead or alive, do this for me. Find the secrets. Destroy them. Use what you would least expect.'

Written across the edge of the card, she read, "Ich liebe dich."

Addy crawled into bed in the Radisson Hotel at 2:00 in the morning, exhausted both physically and emotionally. As she drifted from consciousness to bazaar dreams, her mind churned with the strange things her father said. She awoke with every sound and lay awake from 5:00 a.m. until she got out of bed at 7:15.

In the hotel's restaurant, the XS Lounge and Grill, she ate tropical fruit and yoghurt. Addy wondered how many cantaloupes and honeydew melons actually grew in the tropics, but the choice seemed like a healthier breakfast than Belgian waffles smothered in whipped cream. She drank several cups of coffee as she watched the time crawl by.

At 8:45, she looked at the time and said to herself, "My father will be prepped for surgery. At 9:00, the medical team will insert a catheter into a vein in his ankle or his groin and carefully feed it up to his heart. They'll insert a stent into the narrowed coronary artery and expand it with a balloon so that my father's blood flow won't be restricted."

At 9:00, she said another prayer for her father and then called the number on the card.

"P. K. Parkman and Associates. How may I direct your call?"

"May I speak to Paul Parkman please?" she asked.

"May I ask who is calling?"

"This is Adelheid Penner. Hans Ulfert's daughter."

"One moment please." She waited more than a moment and Addy flagged the waitress over for a refill of coffee.

"This is Paul Parkman. How may I help you, Mrs. Penner?"

"My father had a heart attack yesterday and the doctors are performing an angioplasty even as we speak. In his wallet, the hospital staff found your business card with a note to me on the back of it. I'm hoping you know what it means?"

For a minute, the lawyer remained silent and Addy wondered if the line went dead. Then Paul Parkman said, "Well then, this is a new wrinkle. Do come in at your earliest convenience. Does 1:00 p.m. today work for you? If not, just tell me what works and I will rearrange my schedule to accommodate you."

"Yes, 1:00 p.m. works fine. See you then."

Then Addy phoned and left messages for Karl and Heinrich that their father experienced a heart attack the previous evening and the doctors were performing an angioplasty at the moment. She added that she would update them on the results.

Then she called Rudolph's number and left a message thanking him for rushing to their father's aid. If Rudy actually answered, she would ask him, "Why on earth didn't you call me to tell me about Dad's heart attack?"

By 10:00, Adelheid waited at the hospital for news of her father. They wheeled him back from recovery at 10:27. His colour looked much better than when she saw him last.

Dr. Vandenberg told her, "Everything went extremely well. The stent should prevent any more heart attacks. He is a very lucky man. It took EMS over an hour from when the 911 call came in until they could get to him. Apparently, your father is obsessed with security."

"That he is," she replied.

"EMS tried to break in, but the ground-floor doors are breach-proof and the doorframes are stone. Apparently, every window in his house is barred except for the picture windows around back. The firemen took a ladder around back and tried to break a picture window to discover they are shatterproof. I guess your father never considered what would happen if he had a medical emergency."

"He looks much more alive now than he did early this morning. Thank you."

"He'll need perhaps a week in the hospital to rest and we'll start him on cardiovascular rehabilitation. We need to teach him how to eat right, take off some weight, and lower the stress. He'll need to attend the classes for the next nine months. With some lifestyle changes, he should be around for a very long time yet."

Addy called her brothers again and left messages with the update.

Raven, Rudy's 17-year-old squeeze, heard the phone message and phoned Rudy's cell. He didn't answer so she texted him, 'Message from your sis. Father is doing fine and should go home in a week.'

As Rudy carefully welded a steel plate onto the tailgate of a dump truck, he felt his phone vibrate. When he finished welding the bead, he flipped up his visor, dropped his glove and pulled the phone from his pocket.

"God damn it!" he screamed. He picked up a two-metre-long sheet of plate steel and hurled it across the shop like it weighed nothing. It crashed into a rolling press and everyone in the shop stopped what they were doing and stared at Rudy.

"My father just had a heart attack!" he screamed at them. Everyone went back to work.

Addy sat with her father as he dozed. By 11:30, most of the effects of the anaesthetic wore off. He opened his eyes, saw her and said, "Adelheid! I wondered if I dreamt that you came last night."

"Yes, I arrived after midnight. You look better now than you did. And, Father, you said some things that did not make any sense."

Hans became silent and looked away from her. After a minute he reached for her hand and squeezed it.

"The doctor says you can go home in a week, but you'll have to cut back on schnitzel," she said with a musical laugh in her voice.

"I am 60. I don't think I will live to my 61st birthday. I'm scared, Adelheid."

"You had a heart attack. You were barely alive when they got to you so of course, you are scared. But you are on the mend now and everything will be okay," she said and kissed him on the forehead.

"I thought that no one would find out," he whispered. "But they will. I should have ended it. I should have destroyed it. I'll burn." His blood pressure rose as he spoke. Alarms rang and nurses rushed in.

P. K. Parkman and Associates took up the entire top floor of the 56-storey Brookfield Tower. The elevator door opened and Adelheid glanced at the elevator panel to be sure she arrived at the right floor. Through the open doors, she stared out at a jungle as if the elevator transported her to the tropics.

A shapely black-haired woman in a skin-tight red designer dress and wearing red stiletto high heels walked towards her on a washed-cement path. "Mrs. Penner, please follow me to the waiting room," she said. The woman wiggled her hips as she walked like a fashion-show model.

Mr. Parkman obvious hired her for her looks, Adelheid thought as she followed the woman down the path that wound through the trees and flowers. A small stream flowed under a footbridge and tumbled down the rocks into a pool of koi. Songbirds and colourful butterflies fluttered about. It reminded her of walking in the tropical pyramid at the Muttart Conservatory in Edmonton.

At the other side of the nature room, two large glass doors slid apart and they walked into the plant less, grey-marble reception area. The air felt noticeably cooler and less humid. Addy chose an overstuffed black-leather chair, but the woman said, "This way please," and led her into a huge room with loveseats, a pool table, shelves of magazines, tables with checkerboards and a television.

"Can I pour you a drink, Mrs. Penner? We have a nice 2010 Beaujolais," the woman said while lifting a decanter from the table. "But if you prefer white, we keep a Chablis on ice," she said while pointing to the clear bottle with a French label in the silver ice bucket. "Of course, we also have scotch and bourbon."

"The red wine would be lovely," Adelheid answered, feeling a little guilty for accepting a drink so early in the day. She also felt justified in drinking wine supplied by the lawyer who informed her, in no uncertain terms, she was cut out of her father's will.

Paul Parkman came to the doorway five minutes later. Adelheid stood at the floor-to-ceiling windows looking out over the city as she sipped red wine. He sized her up. She stood perhaps five-feet four-inches tall and her straight, sandy-blonde hair with blonde highlights hung to her shoulders. Her black high heels did wonders to show off her figure.

However, she did not dress like his usual clients. *Her Jessica-brand, department-store dress and bargain-store shoes match her occupation,* Paul thought. *She is a great looking kindergarten teacher.*

"Mrs. Penner," he said as he walked into the room. "I'm Paul Parkman, your father's attorney."

He held out his hand. She guessed that he neared his mid-50s by his greying hair and sagging skin. She also noticed his $10,000 suit, his Rolex, and the huge diamond in the ring on his pinkie finger. Adelheid wondered how much of her father's money supported this man's lifestyle.

"Thank you for meeting with me on short notice," she replied as she shook his hand. "But I really don't know why I am here."

"Let's go to my office," Paul said. "Then I can tell you the little I know about your father's wishes."

Mr. Parkman's office looked nothing like Addy expected. She envisioned dark wood wall panels, shelves of law books and an intimidating desk. This almost windowless office contained ultra-modern furniture. The chair looked more like a crystal sculpture than a seat; however, Addy discovered that it felt incredibly comfortable. However, the clear moulded-glass desk made Addy glad she did not wear a short skirt because she knew the lawyer had a good view of her legs. And she could tell he liked to look. Paul did not have an unkind face, but certainly not a face you would instantly trust.

"I'm sorry to hear of your father's illness," Mr. Parkman said consolingly. "How is he?"

"That is the strange part. They did an angioplasty this morning and he looks much better. The doctor says Dad will make a full recovery, but he will need to make a few lifestyle changes. He is talking crazy, though. He wants me to do something for him. Something about secrets. The only clue I have is a message written on your business card."

She passed Paul the card. He read her name on the front and flipped it over. "What does it say? I don't read German."

"Basically, it says I am his only hope. And then my father begs me to destroy the secrets."

"Your father is an interesting man, Mrs. Penner. The day he asked me to write you a letter saying you would never get a penny of his money, he handed me a letter he wrote. He asked me to give it to you when you came about the secrets. He said to tell you that you are the only one of his children that he trusts." Mr. Parkman held out an envelope.

"He shows trust in a strange way," Adelheid responded. Sadness swept over her like a wave. And anger too. Before she could stop them, tears spilt from her eyes and coursed down her cheeks. She grabbed her purse and dug for a tissue. As she wiped her tears, she told herself, "It is better when I stay in Edmonton. When I am busy with work and family, it keeps the pain away. I should stand up and walk out the door."

The lawyer patiently held his arm outstretched to her. Her hand shook as she took the brown 13 by 18-centimetre envelope from the lawyer's hand.

Sets of numbers covered the entire backside of the envelope. Black ink crossed out all but one number on the front of the envelope and the last two on the back. "What are these numbers?" Adelheid asked, trying to make her voice come out calm.

"The first number is your alarm company code and ID. The number below that is the code to your father's front door. The number on the back of the envelope is the code to the door from the front entryway into the house. As you see, he changes those numbers every few months and I update the envelope."

"What now?" Adelheid asked, her voice shaking as much as her hands.

"I'll give you some time alone to open the letter. As your father's lawyer, I'll inform you that you have no obligation to read the letter or to act upon it. I have no idea of the contents of the letter nor do I have any inkling of what secret or secrets your father refers to. However, I have protected your father's interests and now it appears that he is trusting you with things he did not share with me. Should you need the assistance of an attorney, I would be glad to help."

"Thank you," she replied.

The lawyer left the room and Addy opened the letter. She saw the large, double-sided front-door key taped to one page. On the other page, her father's precise, handwritten German script said, 'Adelheid, I'm sorry. I'm so sorry. You have always loved me and I don't deserve it. So I ask this one thing of you, destroy the secrets. Every one. Of all my children, you were the one with a real love for books. You read *Sherlock Holmes* when you were 12 so I know that you are the one to unravel the clues. The secrets are not in the front office safe. That safe holds only the coin collection. Don't trust your brothers. Hansel Karl Ulfert.'

The lawyer came back into the room. Adelheid said to him, "There is really nothing here that wasn't on the back of your business card. I guess I'll have to go to the house and see if I can figure it out."

"Then you intend to follow your father's wishes?"

"I will do what I can," she answered.

"He said you would. And he said to give you this when you said yes. This is a debit card for his chequing account. He assured me that there is sufficient money in that account to cover any expenses."

The sticky note in German stuck on the back of the card read, 'Do not hesitate to use the card for any expenses you incur sorting this out. By all means, take money for any days you miss work because of this. PIN #221B.'

Tears still fell from her red eyes as Adelheid walked to the parkade. "I've become one of those people," she said to herself. "The women you see walking down the street with tears streaming down their cheeks, mascara running like streams from a coal mine, and eyes like red spider webs. I am one of the women people turn away from because they cannot help."

She really wasn't sure why she cried. She felt sad that her father struggled with a health issue, but that wasn't it. It upset her that a heart attack suddenly reduced Hans Ulfert, the strongest man she ever met, to a frightened old man lying in a hospital bed. But those were yesterday's tears.

"Are you all right, lady?" a voice asked from a few feet away and she almost jumped out of her skin.

Then she saw him. A dirty homeless man in tattered clothes sat on a filthy old blanket. He leant against a cement pillar and with an empty wine bottle in his hand. He lifted the bottle to his dry lips, stuck his slimy tongue out from between rotting yellow teeth and tried to shake out one more drop of alcohol. Adelheid realized she must have walked right by him on the way to her appointment, yet never saw him.

"You okay?" he asked again.

"I'm fine," she mumbled as she hurried towards her car, afraid the man would try to rob her.

"You need to forgive him," the man hollered after her. "Or you will end up like me."

She locked the minivan's doors, started the engine and backed out of her parking spot in a hurry. The drunk waved an unsteady hand at her as she passed by. Adelheid drove out of the parkade without wiping the tears off her face or redoing her mascara. Her hands still shook three red lights later.

"I hate Calgary," she said to the air.

34

This city had not been her home since the day she left home 18 years previously. When she and Jack were engaged, she brought him down to meet the family, and that was the only reason she returned. Her mother loved Jack, and her dad offered no acceptance.

Their wedding took place in the Lutheran Church in Calgary, on her father's insistence. That forced everyone to travel for the wedding except Adelheid's family. In hindsight, she should have said no. In their first year as husband and wife, she and Jack visited her parents at Christmas and Easter and a weekend in the summer. They always took a hotel.

When Addy became pregnant with her first one, her mother came up to Edmonton for the baby shower. She gave more gifts than everyone else put together. You could tell that she felt very happy to have a grandchild on the way. The next day they went shopping in West Edmonton Mall. They laughed and talked and, for the first time in years, Addy felt close to her mother.

And then the baby came and Jack named her Riley. Addy's father went berserk, threatening them, demanding they change Riley's name and, in all other ways, treated them abusively.

To this day, Adelheid's kids never set foot the inside Grandma or Grandpa Ulfert's house. Addy's mother sent gifts for them with the warning not to let Hans know. Her mother met them secretly at the Calgary Zoo one Saturday the summer after Riley turned four and Cody was two. When she saw them, Wilhelmina cried.

Adelheid lost track of how many trips she'd made to Calgary after her mother became ill, yet she did not spend a single night under the same roof as her parents. They never invited her to stay and she never asked. Addy brought Jack and the kids to see her mom in the hospital just before she died. Addy did not ask her father's permission. The kids did not recognize their grandmother, not because the disease devastated her, but because they hadn't spent time together.

Now, as Addy turned into her father's circular driveway 35 minutes after leaving the city centre, the memory of the last time she arrived here swept over her like a wave of grief. Wilhelmina came home from the hospital for Christmas, and not because her cancer went into remission. Wilhelmina barely clung to life.

Maybe sending the dying home at Christmas appears like charity, but Addy believed the hospital sent patients home so they needed less staff for the holidays. The bottom line trumps all. Addy drove down on December 22nd and it snowed the entire way. The wind whipped snow across the highway like rushing water making it impossible for her to tell if she drove in her lane or headed for the ditch. She made the journey anyways to give moral support to her mother and father, to give love, and to pray.

On that trip, she bought and decorated a Christmas tree for her mother. Then she cooked Christmas turkey, complete with stuffing and all the side dishes. Two of her brothers shared the meal. Karl and Ursula and their kids stayed at the house, and Rudy arrived with his newest plaything. Yet Adelheid ended up doing all the dishes and cleaning everything up while the others visited. When Karl and Ursula headed upstairs to one of the five spare bedrooms, Addy went to a hotel.

The Christmas before that, her mother came home from the hospital after just having a double mastectomy and two weeks of chemotherapy. Addy smiled remembering the look on her mother's face as she pulled the white tissue out of a Christmas gift bag to see the chestnut-brown wig Addy gave her to cover her balding head.

"Thank you, dear," her mother said as she looked at herself in the hand mirror that Addy held for her. "I look like myself again."

"Beautiful as always," Addy replied. The next time Adelheid saw the wig, it covered her mother's head in the casket. And her mother did not look beautiful.

Today sunlight gleamed off the statue leaning into the water and made the droplets of water from the fountain shine like diamonds as Adelheid drove around the circular driveway and parked right in front of the castle-like front door. "Why me?" she asked God. "What did I ever do to deserve this?"

No booming voice resounded from heaven. Not even a whisper.

"I haven't had a proper Christmas with my kids in two years, and I've spent every long weekend for two years and countless summer days away from them. I don't need this. I don't want this!"

In her mind, she heard the homeless man's words, "You need to forgive him." Adelheid realized why she tears still coursed down her cheeks. She held on to anger like a dog with a bone.

"I should just walk away!" she shouted. Yet she held the key and the code for the door and instructions from her father. And twice in his own handwriting, he said he loved her.

"I don't doubt he wrote that just to get me to do this for him. Manipulating bastard that he is," she said to God. "Whatever I am to get rid of is something he doesn't possess the desire to do himself. This has nothing to do with me."

But Addy got out of the car and walked to the incredibly tall, arch-shaped door framed by figures of knights carved into stone. Apparently, the locals called her father's house, the German castle. She ran her finger over the deep indents in the wooden door planks where EMS tried repeatedly to batter down the door. "I bet it looked like invaders trying to breach the castle's defences," she said out loud.

Then she realized something. "My father sees himself as a baron," she exclaimed as she put the extremely large key into the keyhole. Addy read the code as she punched numbers into the stainless-steel keypad, the only part of the door that looked modern then she turned the key to the right. As if on its own, the door swung into an entranceway the size of Cody's bedroom.

Addy walked in and glanced up at the glass ceiling far above her. Above the door behind her, she could see the stone walkway where soldiers might hurl down stones or shoot arrows at any invader who made it through the outer door. Looking up to her right she saw the section of the house that contained the bedrooms and library. Huge wooden beams held up the roof. Up to her left, the roof over the great room climbed towards heaven like the Tower of Babel.

At her feet, European cobblestones, just like the driveway and courtyard, covered the floor. Her father paid a German artist to paint the entranceway walls to look like a German park in the spring with apple trees in bloom. Between a couple of ornate metal-work park benches, half of a real fountain protruded from the wall and poured water into a trough. Goldfish swam towards her, looking for food.

To her right side, a real apple tree grew in a garden space. It actually looked more like half of an apple tree because it had been pruned to grow flat against the wall. The mural behind the tree showed painted branches covered with pink blossoms. The real tree's green leaves and large red apples did not match the mural.

Addy stood there in dismay. The keypad for the alarm wasn't screaming. "Maybe Rudy forgot to set the alarm when he hurried to follow the ambulance to the hospital," Addy reasoned.

As she again took in the opulence of the entryway, the strangeness of this house overwhelmed her. She did not grow up here. Her father was probably just as famous a portrait photographer when she was a child, but his wealth came later. Or maybe he just decided to spend some of his money as he got older. When she lived at home, they lived in a modest two-storey house in Rosedale and her father rented a studio downtown. Hans started building this mansion the year she married Jack.

Addy walked the length of the room and stood in front of the breach-proof, metal, exterior door from the entryway into the house in the left-hand wall. This door didn't need a key and a code both, so she put the key back into the envelope and punched in the numbers into the keypad. She heard the lock motor snarl as the deadbolt slid back. Addy took a deep breath and stepped into the house.

The size and opulence of the great room took her breath away like it did every time. The white cathedral-like ceiling stood almost three stories above her with multiple arches meeting in the centre. Straight ahead of her, arch-shaped stain glass windows started four metres off the hardwood floor and extended towards heaven like colourful arrows pointing to God.

To her right, massive two-storey windows provided an amazing view of the perfectly manicured lawn, the precise and spectacular garden and, beyond that, the Bow River Valley. A couple of times during her previous visits she saw the stunning view of the city lights at night from these windows.

To her left, suits of armour stood like knights defending their king. On the wall behind them hung ancient tapestries depicting great battles. Golden statues and historic displays lined the floor below the stained glass.

Her father did everything for show. Clients would come in through the front door, even though he could bring them into the studio from the side of the house. Arriving this way, they'd see the massive great room with its 12-metre high ceiling and the Bavarian-style balcony where the second floor overlooked the great room. And they'd see the spectacular view of the valley.

They would admire the stunning, large-format portraits of kings, sheikhs, and movie stars on the walls in golden frames. The clients would then go into his ultra-clean and ultra-modern studio like stepping from medieval times and into the future. They'd expect magnificent results, and Hans Ulfert never disappointed.

Adelheid took it all in and then turned right. She walked past the short hallway that led to the kitchen and walked towards the windows that overlooked the river valley. One-third of the way through the great room, she turned right into a long, wide hallway. White and dark grey marble blocks in a checkerboard design covered the floor. Lighted portraits in gold frames lined the walls like some great gallery.

She saw the mahogany doors on the right-hand side, but only one door on the left. Half-ways down the hall, leaning against the wide stainless-steel studio door, she saw a half-full, two-litre of Coke. "Rudy!" she swore. "He already tried to break into the studio."

She walked past portrait after portrait. At the studio door, she tied turning the handle even though she could tell that Rudy did not succeed. Then she picked up the pop bottle and carried it with her to the office.

She stopped in the office doorway and stared at the portrait of her mother. She always loved this picture, taken the day her mother turned 29. In spite of her father's faults, he did have a way of capturing a look in his subject's eyes that seemed to reveal their soul. Her mother looked vividly alive. Her mother's eyes glowed with life. They made Addy smile because the eyes said, 'I love you'. Anyone could tell she felt loved and gave love wholeheartedly.

That Addy stared at her mother's naked body came as an afterthought. "You were hot, Mom," Addy said to the picture. "And I am glad Cody is not here to see you like that."

Yes, Hans Ulfert often said Adam and Eve were God's ultimate creation and nudes are the highest form of beauty. Addy grew up with photographs of nudes hanging on the walls and her father's hardbound picture books of nudes on the coffee table. Black and whites and full-colour editions.

"I'm not a priss," she said out loud as she reminded herself that she paid her tuition at university by posing nude for the drawing and painting classes. Just because she was not ashamed of her body didn't mean that she slept around. Jack was her only lover, and how she wished he stood here with her.

She did not wander around naked in front of her children and no nude photographs adorned her home. Adelheid definitely did not want her children exposed to the images she grew up with.

She took her eyes away from the picture and stepped in. Shelves full of photography books and magazines lined the walls and surrounded two grey file cabinets. On the large, dark cherry-wood desk covered with a sheet of glass, the phone and the computer monitor were pushed to one side like someone tried to make room to set something down.

That's odd, Addy thought. *Dad never leaves anything out of place. He is the epitome of German obsessive-compulsive disorder. OCD to the extreme. Everything in its place and a place for everything.*

Then she saw on the floor under the desk, and partially hidden by the computer's electrical cord, a coin in a square protective cardboard cover. Dust covered the cord, but she found none on the coin. She picked it up and examined the 1921 silver Canadian five-cent piece that looked smaller than a dime. The price written in pencil on the cover read, '$160,000'.

Addy turned to her mother's portrait and said, "This is part of Dad's coin collection. Remember how he started Karl collecting coins when Karl turned nine? And how pissed off Dad got when Karl took the coins to the corner store and bought Slurpees with them? I'm glad he didn't give Karl this one."

She looked at her mother's smile and said, "We can laugh about it now. Not then. Dad screamed and yelled at the store clerk and demanded that he hand over the coins. As if that would happen."

Addy remembered how Karl's interest in collecting coins waned after her father announced that someday his entire coin collection would go to Karl. Addy said to the portrait of her mother, "When I see Dad later this evening, I'll ask him why he dropped this coin."

Addy tapped down the space bar on the computer and the screen lit up. She opened the folder window and did a quick look through the computer files. There were no business files or business photographs on the computer. She only found pictures of coins, places her father travelled, and a few family memories. The document files were about coin collecting.

She dug through the filing cabinets and found cards and school projects she and her brothers made for either Dad or Mom. She found the first black and white photographs she developed when her father still kept a darkroom in the basement of their old house. She found her father's files on how each of his children advanced in their photography skills. Addy even found the certificate she won for a Grade Nine photo contest.

There were no secrets in these file cabinets. Addy scanned the room and noticed an odd set of books in a room dedicated to coins and photography. There, amongst the hardbound photography books, her eyes landed on *The Complete Adventures of Sherlock Holmes* by Arthur Conan Doyle.

Rudy Ulfert left the welding shop at noon on Friday. He told the foreman he felt sick, and he didn't have to put on an act. He hadn't slept all night and now his head ached like someone had clubbed him.

"Go home," the foreman said. "You look like hell."

But he didn't go home. He drove straight to his father's mansion.

"I have two choices," he said to himself as he drove. "I can keep the coins and he'll find out and write me out of the will. And then my old man will probably call the police and I'll end up in jail. But if I put the coins back, he'll know for sure that I took them and brought them back. He'd give them straight to Karl, write me out of the will, and probably phone the police anyways."

Rudy came to the same conclusion he'd come to as the sun peaked over the horizon. He would go to the house, break down the studio door and find something he could use to blackmail his father.

"Anyone who keeps that many doors locked is hiding something," he said to himself as he drove. "I know of at least one thing he wouldn't want public. I'll find it; use it to protect myself, and then milk the old man dry."

At the end of a long row of two and a half metre tall cedar shrubs, he turned into his father's driveway. There, right in front of the mansion doors, he saw Addy's blue minivan. He knew it was hers because he read the big bold letters of the bumper sticker, "If you can read this, thank a teacher."

"Shit! Shit! Shit!" Rudy screamed as he stepped on the gas, made a loop of the driveway, and turned right onto the road. "What the hell is Adelheid doing here? How did she get into the house? What is she taking?"

Rudy drove around the hill-top road four times. With every pass, he saw the minivan and each time he became more desperate. He half-ways hoped that he would catch her loading his dad's things into her van so he could threaten to call the police on her.

He wouldn't really call them. No police. He'd confront her, threaten her, accuse her of being a thief, and run her off the property. He needed her gone. He drove one more loop of the upscale neighbourhood and saw the van still parked there. It didn't look like his sister planned to leave anytime soon.

"I have no choice," he reasoned with himself. "My sister is forcing me to do this. It is her fault."

He drove to the hospital. He needed to end this before he lost his inheritance and before his father found out he stole the coins. He needed to end this before his father came home from the hospital.

Rudy parked his customized half-ton truck three blocks from the hospital in a tree-lined residential area. "The security cameras won't catch me," he said to himself as he tucked his shoulder-length mullet up under his cowboy hat. Raven went to a lot of trouble to track down and buy the over-sized white Stetson for him for Stampede week. Now he would use it to hide his face.

"Yee-haw," he said as he looked at himself in the truck's side-view mirror.

When he was a quarter of a block from the hospital, he noticed a couple of the house-keeping staff smoking as they stood in the shade. He quickened his pace. The Filipino man glanced at his watch, said something to the woman, and they each took a final drag and butted their cigarettes out. The man opened the emergency exit door. With the toe of his shoe, rolled the apple-sized rock away from the door jam, and the hospital workers went in.

Rudy grabbed the door handle and yanked it open just a millisecond before it clicked closed. He made his way down the pale mint green hallway and took the first stairs. The stairs and walls were unpainted grey cement and the handrail was painted the same pale green as the main-floor hallway.

He met only one person as he climbed the stairs. On the fourth-floor stairwell, a pretty Japanese nurse sat on a step talking on her phone. Rudy heard her say very intimate things to her lover but, when she heard Rudy's footsteps coming up the flight below her, she turned towards the wall and whispered. At the sixth floor, Rudy walked onto the floor and down the hallway scanning the room numbers.

"Can I help you find someone?" an orderly asked.

"I'm looking for 6D," he replied. "My mother is on 6D."

"This is 6C. Go to the end of the hallway and turn left."

Right at the beginning of the next hallway, Rudy saw the nurses' station for 6D. Two nurses sat at the desk and another stood behind it checking the label on a bag of blood hanging from a stainless-steel pole. He hurried past, when one of them called to him, "Can I help you?"

Rudy realized he would never find his father's hospital room, never mind sneak in and out. He felt like someone kicked him in the gut. "I'm here to visit my father, Hans Ulfert," he answered. "He had a heart attack yesterday."

"Your father is in room 6255. He is very weak so I suggest you don't visit for long."

As Rudy walked to his father's hospital room, he smiled and said to himself, "I'll be short and to the point. I have nothing to lose. I am backed into a corner and I know it."

Hans did not feel happy when he saw Rudolph walk through the door. His giant of a son terrified him ever since Rudolph turned 13. Rudolph grew to almost two metres tall and developed arms the size of tree trunks. As a teen, Rudolph won many wrestling and weight-lifting trophies. After high school, he earned a spot on the Canadian Olympic weight-lifting team. Hans never felt prouder. Proud, until Rudolph raped one of the gymnasts.

Hans would have disowned him right then and let him go to jail, but then the media would have dragged his own name through the mud. It cost a fortune to keep it all quiet but may have cost him more to let it go public. Besides, Wilhelmina loved the boy. Her forgiveness towards him seemed endless. And because Rudolph lived in Calgary, Wilhelmina often invited him over for meals. They saw a whole string of young women hanging on his arm and Wilhelmina loved them all. And not one of them left the house without a gift.

Rudolph gave them at least six grandchildren, each with a different mother. It broke Wilhelmina's heart that they had no access to any of them. But for six of them, Hans paid a lump sum to cover 18 years of child support. No, Hans did not want a visit from Rudolph.

He called his giant son only once since Wilhelmina died because someone tried to break into the house, so he gave Rudolph the key and passcodes to the main house. Rudolph smirked as Hans handed over the front door key. He knew that trusting Rudolph was a mistake, but what else could he do? He needed someone close with access to the house.

"I heard that you saved my life," Hans said as a greeting.

Rudolph stood at the foot of his bed. "I rushed right over when I heard from the police that EMS couldn't get into the house," he lied. "You looked pretty bad. Do you remember what you said to me?"

"No. The last thing I remember was phoning the Schnitzel Haus. Then I woke up here."

"You told me not to dare," Rudy said casually. "But I did."

Hans's face turned even whiter as the blood drained away. His mouth started to form the word 'no' when Rudolph lunged at him, grabbed his ankle and squeezed like a vice.

"I know all your secrets," Rudy hissed with as much venom as he could. "And I will make you pay for what you have done. I should kill you right now." And Rudy squeezed even harder to let his father know that he could snap bones with his bare hands.

Alarm bells rang and nurses rushed in. "Something is wrong with my father," Rudy told them. "He turned pale and started thrashing. Please help him." Rudy smiled as he left the room. "Now I know the old man really does have something hidden. And I will find it."

Adelheid took the two-volume *Complete Adventures of Sherlock Holmes* from the shelf and opened the cover. There, on the flyleaf of the first book, she read a message from her father. "To Adelheid on your 12th birthday. I know your mother already gave you a gift, but I thought you might enjoy some new detective stories. If you keep reading books like this, soon you will know all my secrets. Happy Birthday! Dad."

The words stunned her. As a child, she spied on her father from behind the divan while he read the newspaper. She dusted the doorknobs with baking powder, her version of fingerprint dust. And he left clues like muddy footprints in the hall and a single key on the floor, a key that didn't fit any locks in the house.

Addy smiled at the memories. She and her dad about drove her mother crazy. One time Hans hid a treasure and Adelheid discovered it. A dozen clues led her to a coffee can full of quarters in the basement on a shelf. 'Don't tell your mother or your brothers,' the note in the can said. 'Spend it on whatever you want.' She bought a Ralph Lauren tie for her father for his birthday.

Clues her father never intended to leave led her to Hans's secret stash of scotch, a secret she never told her mom. And Adelheid discovered that her father bought Karl a new bike for his birthday and hid it in the garage. The key on the floor fit the bike lock.

She remembered asking, "Daddy, have I discovered all your secrets?"

He answered, "Almost all of them. But there are still a few more. And some I hope you never find out."

They played the game for years and, until this moment, she thought it only a game. She turned the page. There, at the bottom of the page in the publishing information, someone circled the date in pencil. She flipped back to the flyleaf. Twelfth was circled. She never remembered circling it and had ignored the pencil mark to read the words from years ago.

Starting with the first adventure, *A Study in Scarlet*, she now turned page after page looking for circled numbers.

Rudy felt genuinely pleased with himself. For the first time in his life, he succeeded in intimidating his father. "I made him cower," Rudy laughed as he waited for the elevator. "I made the old man shit the bed. He pissed himself in fear of me. If he ever threatens to take me out of the will, I'll pick him up with one hand and threaten to tear him apart piece by piece."

The blood clot in Hans's vein measured only two millimetres across. When Rudy clamped his hand around his father's right ankle, he squeezed into the bloodstream the clot that formed to stop the vein from bleeding after the angioplasty. It raced up the femoral artery and reached Hans's heart before Rudy finished his threats.

Had the doctors not inserted the stent, the clot may have lodged in the coronary artery causing a heart attack right then or, perhaps, years down the road. Instead, in just three heartbeats, the blood clot reached Hans Karl Ulfert's brain. Hans's blood pressure forced the clot into a capillary where it lodged depriving of blood flow to the part of the brain on the opposite side of the clot. Without oxygen, the brain cells began to die. As Rudy threatened him, Hans Ulfert suffered a stroke.

Blood pumping into the blocked capillary instantly ballooned the capillary walls like water from a garden hose pouring full-blast into a party balloon. First, the aneurysm put pressure on the brain and then it burst. Hans's heart pumped blood into his brain cavity.

If Hans Ulfert would have been able to talk, he would have said, "My head feels like a horse just kicked me. I can't see from one eye. Everything is blurry from the other. My whole right side feels numb. And I just messed myself."

But Hans Ulfert could not speak. His brain told his mouth what to say, but his brain seemed unconnected to the rest of his body.

He could hear a nurse calling his name. "What is going on, Mr. Ulfert? Talk to us," she pleaded. He tried to speak yet only managed to chew on his tongue. The other nurse barked orders and Hans heard people come running in. As they loaded him on a gurney, the nurse said to him, "Mr. Ulfert, we are taking you to the operating room."

Adelheid held a sheet of printer paper in her hand as she walked out of the office. She hoped the string of 10 numbers and 1 character she found was the door code. "It sure would have been simpler if you just gave me the code," Addy complained as if talking to her father. "Why did you have to make this so complicated? Why did you make me search through 983 pages?" She found the last number, one, circled on the last page of the last story of volume two.

She noticed that her hands shook as she stood in front of the studio door. "I really do not want to do this," she said to the air. "I'm afraid of what I might find out about my father." Yet she knew, once she did her part, she could go home. Home to Jack. Home to peace.

Just as she reached her finger towards the number one, her cell phone rang. She jumped. She read the call display, "Foothills Medical Centre."

As she answered, "Hello," she hoped the call was from her father telling her not to search for secrets.

"Your father appears to have suffered a stroke a few moments ago," the nurse said. "Perhaps even an aneurysm. We are rushing him down to OR to do surgery to relieve the pressure on his brain. There is no point coming here until we have him stabilized. We'll keep you informed."

Addy immediately wrote a text and sent it to Jack. She wished that she knew her brothers' cell phone numbers so she could text them too. They had no idea how hard it was to repeat the same message three times for answering machines. 'Dad just had a stroke and perhaps an aneurysm. The doctors may operate. Pray for him. That is as much as I know for now.'

As she dialled Heinrich's number, she realized that Ricky would be off work by now. She hoped he would answer. She wanted to talk to a person. She wanted to feel that she wasn't all alone.

Ricky listened to the messages from Addy as soon as he got in the door after work. He carried no love for his father. Since he left home 12 years ago, he'd only been in the same building with him twice. Both times in a church for a funeral. Not just any church. The church. Both times he said to his father, "I am sorry for your loss."

His father did not reply either time. Hans never spoke one word to him and never even looked his way. How could he? Not that Ricky hoped for reconciliation. He wasn't looking for love or acceptance. The hope for those things died long before Ricky reached junior high school. He expected common courtesy.

Hans Ulfert embodied the epitome of public graces and courtesy. He moved among the rich and famous as one of their own. When it came to his own family though, he showed no courtesy. He offered no grace. He gave no forgiveness. He never compromised. And he never said 'I'm sorry.'

The phone messages from Addy stirred up these memories. When Ricky got the first call saying that the old buzzard suffered a heart attack, Ricky rejoiced. He felt glad for two things; that Adelheid considered him family, and that the old man would soon meet his Maker.

A year before, when Ricky's mother lay dying, Adelheid phoned to say, "Mom is asking for you."

"Dad wants me there?" Ricky asked with disbelief. "He told you to call me?"

Adelheid paused and then answered, "No. He does not want you here. Mom wants you here. She begged Dad to call you."

"Let me guess. Hans Ulfert, our famous father, refused. He refused to give his dying wife her wish. He refused even to tell me the doctors diagnosed my mother with terminal cancer."

"I'm sorry," Addy replied.

"Don't be sorry. It is not you who needs to be sorry. Addy, you are the only one in the family who talks to me. You are the one that gave me the news and let me know her condition all along the way. So tell me this, do you honestly believe our illustrious father will ever let me in the same room with Mom?"

"I'm sure he will let you. He let me. I've even been to his mansion," she replied.

"So now you are one of the family again. How is that working for you?" Ricky regretted speaking those words even as they spilt from his lips. He could hear Addy crying. "Sorry, Sis. I am glad for you. Truly I am. I'm glad that you could see Mom. Tell her that I love her and would be there if I could."

Through her tears, Addy managed to say, "You could see Mom when Dad goes home for the night."

"Check with the staff if I am even listed as family. Besides, the bastard probably got a restraining order to keep me away."

She checked and let Ricky know he was right on both counts.

Ricky knew better than to fly across the country in the hope that his father would let him in the same room with his mother. Ricky knew a secret, and Hans Ulfert did not Ricky spilling the beans. Hans wanted Wilhelmina to pass into eternity believing that her husband was a saint. And he got his wish.

"Why are you so afraid of me?" Ricky asked the air as if talking to his father. "No one would believe me even if I told them. You made sure of that."

Ricky admitted to himself that Addy's second message about the old man making it through the surgery disappointed him, and not just a little. He hoped to dance and shout on hearing the news that Hans Ulfert died. "If there is a hell, Father, you will burn forever. Sooner or later, you will burn."

Ricky just poured a glass of Classique St-Jacques white wine when the phone rang. He took a sip as he read the call display, swallowed, and answered on the third ring. "Bonjour, Addy. What is the news?"

"Hi, Ricky. The hospital phoned me just now to say that it looks like Dad just had a stroke. They are rushing him down to the operating room in case he needs surgery. Please…" Addy's voice trailed off.

"Please what?"

"I was going to ask you to pray."

"God never answers my prayers. If he did, the old man would have croaked years ago. I learnt as a child that Hans Karl Ulfert is more powerful than God. Dad did whatever he wanted and God did not intervene."

"I'm sorry," Addy said. "I didn't mean to upset you."

"I live on the other side of the country and I speak a different language just so that I don't have any reminders of home. There is nothing in my life remotely connected to my father. Nor do I want there to be. And then you call and I feel giddy at hearing your voice, and I smile at the memories of the fun we had together. Then you talk about our father and all the grief comes up like sewage from an overflowing toilet." At that point, Ricky started to cry.

"I'm sorry," Addy said again. "Would you prefer not to hear from me?"

"No, Addy, I want you to call. Even if it hurts. Someday soon we will talk, and the heartache won't be driving the bus. Sometime soon the old man won't be around to haunt us. We will be free."

Addy said goodbye and hung up. Tears spilt down her face. She wanted to say, "I don't know if we will ever be free." She knew saying those words would not help her or Ricky.

Addy wandered down the hall towards the kitchen. "Just this morning, it looked like Dad would make a full recovery," she said to herself in disbelief. "God," she prayed, "Why is this happening?"

In the kitchen, sunshine illuminated tan-coloured quartz countertops, white cupboards, and sand-coloured porcelain tiles. The room looked beautiful except for the stainless-steel catering pans stacked in the sink with gravy and who-knows-what-else dried on.

"Rudy!" Adelheid exclaimed. "They rush Dad to the hospital while you stay here, eat his food and try to break into the studio."

As she scrubbed the chafing trays with the cleaning pad, trying to steel her nerves for going into the studio, Rudy drove by. She would not have noticed him for the position of the window above the sink allowed only a very narrow view of the road, except she stared longingly at the traffic going by and wished she was driving home.

A custom-painted, blue Ford 250, with lots of chrome, turned into the driveway, then quickly made the circle and turned right onto the avenue. She could not swear on a Bible that she actually saw Rudy's face, but she knew her brother custom-built his truck with an extra-tall cab, extra wide doors, and so the driver's seat sat back in the crew-cab section.

Addy dried her hands and went straight to the front door. With a few searches of the internet on her cell phone, she learnt how to reprogram the code for the lock. She did the same for the lock between the entryway and the house.

Ricky stood in the shower for an extra ten minutes. He deep-conditioned his shoulder-length, sandy-blonde hair. Last week, his hairdresser put in highlights and cut it the same style that Addy wore in the picture she sent him. It pleased him that his hair grew out from the pixie cut he wore a year previously. His body shape did not please him. He hoped to have his bottom ribs removed next spring so that he would have a figure. And after that, he would have other surgeries.

Ricky sighed. "At the rate I'm saving money, it will be 15 years before I can afford a sex-change operation."

Addy marched down the wide hallway determined to open the studio door and get this ordeal over with. The keypad made a beep with each button she pushed, lit up with a green glow, and Addy heard the mechanical sound of the deadbolt sliding back into the lock.

"Lord, give me strength," she prayed out loud as she turned the doorknob. She pushed the metal door open and cool stale air rushed over her like she opened a crypt. The windowless room appeared pitch black, and the light from the hallway shone like moonlight on a black sea. Goosebumps erupted on her bare arms.

Adelheid gave her arms a rub and took a tentative step forward while frantically running her hand up and down the wall looking for the light switch.

The motion-activated sensor detected her movements and the room lit up like noonday on a white-sand beach.

She heard herself expel a breath and realized she'd been holding it. Then the door slammed closed behind her with a thud that echoed off the walls. Addy's heart pounded as she whirled to run and she heard the deadbolt lock motor hammer the bolt into place. She took a couple of deep breaths, told herself to calm down and turned to take in the magnificent studio.

Her father told her many times over the years of the studio he would build. Now she stood in his dream studio, bigger than two gymnasiums, and it looked exactly like she imagined it. She wandered throughout the marble-floored room admiring the many photosets, each one like an elaborate stage set with walls and furniture or bridges and cobblestone streets. Regal-looking chairs sat on carpet or marble in front of backdrops that showed the inside of palaces and parliaments. Without a doubt, her father took the background pictures himself then printed the scenes three metres wide and three metres tall.

Her father went to great expense to recreate exact replicas of beautiful places from all around the world. Addy saw a piece of the Eiffel Tower complete with a walkway and the backdrop of Paris below it. She recognized one set as part of a State Room in Buckingham Palace. A tropical set, with a black-sand beach with palm trees and the backdrop of Mauna Kea volcano in Hawaii, made her feel like sun tanning. Around each set, her father mounted lights on stage frames and poles so he could get the mood and the exposure exactly right.

Addy's meandering brought her back near the doorway where she came in and she sat on one of the two baby-blue love seats in the little cluster of furniture. On the coffee table between the love seats and an overstuffed black-leather chair, she saw one of her father's more famous hardbound collections, *Portraits of the Famous*.

She could imagine her father sitting on the edge of the chair talking to clients as he pointed to portraits. To a man, he would say things like, "You have such noble features. It is an honour for me to take your picture. It will hardly be like work at all. Now, look at this portrait of the Duke of Edinburgh. With the right lighting, we could do something better than this for you."

To a woman, he'd say, "My dear, you are absolutely lovely. Your face was meant to be in photographs." He would page through the book and find a portrait of a woman 10 years younger than his client and say, "This portrait will pale in comparison to the one I will do of you." And he wouldn't be lying.

"You are a great salesman, Papa," Addy said to the empty chair. She gave him credit, as much as he pushed sales, he made each portrait a work of art, and no two looked similar. Many of the sets he built, he used for just one photoshoot.

Just because he built elaborate sets, did not mean that her father did not travel to photograph clients. In fact, his clientele included dictators. Famous people are not necessarily good people. Some couldn't leave their countries so Hans Ulfert went to them. He used to joke that his name topped every terrorist watch list. He also joked that government agencies approached him to pinpoint the location of certain of his clientele. One thing Addy knew for certain, her father hated border guards digging through his equipment.

Addy walked to the poster display, just on the other side of the loveseats. She flipped through poster-sized portraits in metal frames mounted on a pole. It reminded her of looking for a poster to put on the wall of the basement suite she shared when she went to university. Back then, the poster she liked cost $9. It showed a silhouetted couple hugging each other as they watched the sunset. She did not buy it because she could not scrape enough together even if it were half price.

A huge bank of air filters created a breeze as they hummed, making Addy feel cold. She looked down at her pantyhose-covered feet and wished that she put on socks. She walked over to the air filters, found the power bar, and flipped the switch to off. Suddenly, the room became very quiet and her footsteps echoed off the far wall. She could hear her heart beating.

She wandered the remaining sets and admired the details in the props, but never found anything the slightest bit alarming. She opened the metal case for her father's camera, certainly an upgrade from the film camera she remembered as a kid. She found no secrets in this studio.

Excluding the door where she came in, she passed six doors. On the only door on the right-hand side of the room, her father painted 'emergency exit' on the high-security, anti-breach metal door. Addy noticed her father added two heavy steel bars across the door to ensure no one could breach it.

In fancy script in gold paint, her father painted either '*schöne männer*' or '*atemberaubende frauen*' on the side-by-side, white, wooden change room doors. Addy translated out loud as she walked straight across the studio from the hall entrance towards the change rooms, 'handsome men' and 'gorgeous women'.

Adelheid checked out the women's change rooms first. In this immense room that could easily accommodate a large wedding party, she found make-up mirrors and full-length mirrors with amazing lighting. She checked out the wardrobe closet and then sat on one of the chairs with green velvet cushions just to experience it. The marble counter contained several sinks with gold fixtures, and even the toilet stalls contained marble toilets with gold toilet-paper holders.

"I wish I had a bathroom like this at home," she said looking at herself in the makeup mirror. She noticed she looked exactly as she felt, sad and lonely.

Addy checked for hidden cameras, not that she expected to find any. When her father wasn't doing portraits, he shot nudes. He didn't need to hide cameras hoping to catch a glimpse of someone in the raw. Addy found nothing alarming in either changing room.

"One odd thing is the showers. Who showers at a photoshoot?" Then she remembered that her father shot models with body paint for several big-name magazines.

She stepped back into the studio, turned right and walked to the door labelled 'raum drucken'. She translated, 'print room', as she walked in. Here she discovered a set of rooms. In the main room sat an HP Designjet Z6800 Photo Production large-format printer, stacks of photo paper, and bottles of colour. Paper cutters of various sizes sat on the counter, and framing material hung in racks on the far wall.

From that room, she found an ultra-high-tech photo lab, complete with a darkroom. She thought it interesting, in this age of digital, that her father still did some things the old-fashioned way. The third room contained reams of paper, and the fourth room held chemicals and ink. Addy went cupboard to cupboard, opening each. She saw nothing the least bit out of the ordinary.

Back in the main print room, Addy tapped the space bar on one of the two computers on the countertop. The screen lit up. She opened the 'My Computer' tab and searched through folder after folder of portraits of handsome men and beautiful women. Addy recognized some of the faces from movies.

After browsing through every folder, Addy tapped the space bar on the keyboard for the second computer. A screen came up that read 'Password required'. She typed in 'nudes'. The machine responded with 'Password required'. She tried 'Nudes', with a capital N, and then tried 'AdamAndEve'. When she typed in 'Adam&Eve', the screen lock vanished.

As she expected, there were many folders of people standing in the nude. She did not go through every file but chose some at random. *They are all very professional*, Addy thought. *There is nothing actually sexual about them. Well, other than they are not wearing clothes.*

She was about to log out of the computer when she noticed a file folder labelled 'New Folder'. Obviously, her father hadn't named it. She clicked on it and there were dozens of folders inside, all labelled. Many of the names she recognized as royalty, political figures, and movie stars. She chose a file labelled Princess Marilia and double-clicked the mouse.

The pictures that popped up on the screen showed a woman on a bed, posing in the most sexual ways. And the look in her eyes said, 'Make love to me'.

Addy opened two more folders. She tried to rationalize that these were works of art. The superb lighting and the focus on certain body parts looked amazing, but the eyes alone appeared erotic. Try as she might, Addy could not call these images anything except pornographic. Very good porn.

She could see how it might happen. A wealthy client asks him to take some erotic pictures as a gift to their lover. It really isn't a huge leap from taking pictures of nudes so her father agrees in order to keep his client happy. Soon his reputation spreads among the rich and famous as the photographer to go to for that special gift for a lover.

"These are not the kind of photographs I want my brothers looking at," Addy said to herself. "Can you imagine what Rudy would do with them? He'd sell these to some tabloid. Karl would probably contact the clients and demand money with the threat of selling the pictures. Ricky? Baby brother, I hope you would do the right thing."

With that, Addy right-clicked on the parent folder, scrolled to 'delete' and clicked.

"Yes," she said to the computer, "I am sure I want to delete that folder and all its contents." And she clicked the mouse again. Then she emptied the computer's trash bin.

Doctors drilled a small hole in Hans's skull and blood shot out like a fountain. They removed a cookie-sized piece of Hans's skull with a tiny circular saw in order to reach the bleeding capillary. They carefully separated folds in his brain, found the broken vein and pinched it closed with a very tiny neurovascular clip. The doctors placed the bone back over Hans's brain and sowed his skin back together. They saved his life.

After deleting the more sexually explicit files from the computer, Addy looked for the backup hard drive. She knew that her father would not have all his files on one computer in case it crashed. She did not find one.

Back in the studio, she walked past the change rooms to the white painted, metal exterior-type door marked 'studio zwei'. She tried to turn the doorknob of studio two but found it locked. She knew right away the code she used for the main studio door would not work. This lock did not have any symbols keys.

She tried the code anyways leaving out the symbol. The door remained locked. Next, she tried the code for the front door, and then she entered the code for the door from the entryway into the house. Nothing.

She walked to the steel door on the far right, closest to the emergency exit, labelled '*büro*'. As Addy tapped in the studio code into the office keypad, it lit up and the lock made a beep for each number. As she pushed the last number, she prayed that the lock would open. The lock made a prolonged beeping sound as the keys flashed red. "If this is a game, Dad," Addy complained out loud, "You could have at least shared the rules with me. You do know that I can just call a locksmith?"

She felt frustrated as she walked towards the hallway door. Addy glanced at the portrait book on the coffee table and ran to it. She turned page after page, looking for numbers or pencil marks. Nothing.

"Maybe I don't care if the whole world finds out your secrets!" she shouted. Her voice echoed off the walls making her feel very alone.

She texted Jack, 'Wish you were here. This place is very lonely. I have a story to tell you about the rich and famous. I'll call you tonight.'

Addy just put a k-cup into the coffee machine when her cell phone rang. "This is the Foothills Medical Centre. Your father is back from recovery. The doctor would like to meet with you to discuss the prognosis."

"I can be there in 30 minutes. Does that work for the doctor?" she asked, as she pulled the German china mug out from under spout.

"I'll let him know."

In the entranceway, Adelheid sat on one of the black, cast-iron park benches as she put on her high heels so she could walk out to the car and get her to-go cup. She looked up at the sky which had been cloudless and blue when she went into the mansion. Now dark clouds billowed up into the heavens like giant indigo mushrooms.

Just as she grabbed her to-go cup off the minivan's console, a hailstone the size of a golf ball skimmed her hair and crashed down into the windshield. The impact left a hand-sized star in the centre of the windshield. Lightning flashed and immediately the ground shook with the thunder. A second later, three more hailstones hit the van. Addy slammed the van door closed, held her hands over her head as she dashed for the house as fast as her high heels would let her.

Just as she reached the open doorway, the sky turned black like someone switched off the sun. Giant hailstones pelted the ground and bounce five metres into the air. It looked like a Biblical plague and it sounded like a freight train rumbling over the house. Addy heard windows break and immediately covered her face with her hands. But no glass fell.

A minute later, the hail stopped. Addy looked up at the unbroken glass roof above her and saw the sky became blue again. She turned to look outside. The sun shone brightly on a carpet of golf-ball-sized hailstones and her minivan looked like an army of blacksmiths attacked it with their hammers.

"Oh no!" she exclaimed.

Addy walked carefully down the driveway trying to keep her balance as she surveyed the house. "This is like walking on marbles," she said as she tried to make sure the point of her high heels was on cobblestone before she stepped forward. Her toes were against ice. "Icy marbles! Why on earth I brought the most impractical shoes I own is beyond me," she complained.

She walked by the three garage doors made of planks of wood and covered with cast-iron studs like the mansion's front door. They were made to look like draw-bridge doors. Then she walked by the stone-block, watch-tower corner of the house.

From what she could tell from looking up at the house from the far side of the castle, three of the upstairs windows on the west side of the house were cracked. A hailstone punched a hole through one of the master bedroom windows. She wanted a better look but knew better than to walk onto the wet grass in her heels. She thanked God that the main-floor windows were shatterproof.

"I don't have time for this," she complained while shaking her fist at the sky. "Why me, God?"

Addy went back into the house and found a roll of packing tape and a box of black plastic garbage bags in the three-car garage. She carried them upstairs to the 1,000 square metre master bedroom at the end of the hall. This room went from the front to the back of the house. Picture windows from floor to ceiling made up the back wall, except for the door to the watchtower. Hardwood panels with solid-gold crown moulding covered the walls and an enormous stone fireplace graced the west wall. Frescoed scenes of saints and angels covered the arched ceiling like a European cathedral.

A European craftsman built the custom-made Cherry wood four-poster bed with a canopy. The bedroom furniture that wasn't custom-made was Louis the 14th. Addy saw a gorgeous Roman tub to the left of the doorway, near the his-and-hers bathrooms. There were three walk-in closets the size of her bedroom.

Glass shards covered the floor near the broken window and a hailstone the size of a baseball slowly melted into the Persian carpet that covered the hardwood. Addy was glad she kept her heels on.

Last time she walked into this room, her mother looked a frail shadow of the woman she used to be, and hardly more than skin and bones. And looking into Wilhelmina's once beautiful, sparkling eyes seemed like staring into an empty shell. Addy fed her mother chicken soup and helped her get to the bathroom and back to bed. Addy could not remember a sadder time.

Addy would have cried at the memory except her mouth hung open in shock. Hundreds of pictures of her mother plastered the bedroom walls, all of them extremely sexual. Pictures with her mother's legs spread apart. Pictures with her bent over. And pictures her father could only have taken while they made love.

Most of the photographs were from their first ten years of their marriage, but there were some up to the time her mother got cancer. "Oh, Mom," Addy said to the picture that her father took while Wilhelmina straddled him. "I know you loved Dad, but I really don't want to see this."

She had to admit that some of the pictures were fascinating. "So this is what Jack sees when we make love," she said. But she turned her attention to the storm damage.

Addy pulled out her phone and took a picture of the hailstone with a two-dollar coin beside it. And another of the broken window. She retook the window shot because the first picture showed provocative images of her mother on either side of the window.

She picked up the hailstone and made her way through the glass to the bathroom. She set it in the sink. She grabbed a towel off the towel rack and used it to wipe down the wall and floor where the rain poured in. In a few minutes, she taped the garbage bag over the hole. She would clean the glass off the floor later.

She left for the hospital without filling her to-go cup with coffee.

The nurses' station on 6D let the brain-trauma doctor know that she arrived. Just a few minutes later, a very handsome young doctor walked up to her. He had dark hair, olive skin, and the bluest eyes she'd ever seen. "I'm Doctor Goldstein, your father's surgeon. Well, brain surgeon that is. I'd be absolutely no good at heart surgery." And he smiled.

"I'm Adelheid Penner. Hans Ulfert is my father."

And Addy thought, *You'll never be good at heart surgery because you break too many hearts just with that smile.* And she smiled and said, "I hope I didn't keep you waiting. I got caught in a hailstorm. I'm sure my car is totalled."

"Hail? It never hailed here at all. Well, let's step into the conference room and I can tell you how your father is doing." He led her around the corner and into the first room in the A-wing.

The conference room was no bigger than a regular hospital room. It had a small closet, a washroom, and the connections for oxygen. Definitely an afterthought. Four yellow, hardback chairs sat on a woven-hemp, indoor-outdoor area rug that covered most of the floor.

She sat and Doctor Goldstein sat down facing her. "Your father suffered a brain aneurysm. Aneurysms really are not that uncommon and can happen in various parts of the body. The vein wall is weak for some reason and balloons outward. A person can have one for years and not know it."

Addy nodded that she understood so the doctor continued, "Sometimes these bursts. If they are very tiny, the body stops the blood flow to that part of the vein and the body absorbs the blood. In the brain, we call this TIAs which stands for the transient ischemic attack. Each one causes a small amount of brain damage as the oxygen no longer reaches some of the brain cells. Some people refer to this as having mini-strokes. However, the body is amazing and looks for new ways to get blood to those areas and starts building new brain cells."

"I've heard of that," Adelheid commented.

"What happened in your father case was a vein burst in his head and not one of the tiniest veins. Blood pumped into the brain cavity putting pressure on the whole brain. And a substantial section of the brain did not receive oxygen. Fortunately, the nurses recognized the symptoms and rushed him to surgery."

"I'm glad you were here, too," Addy said.

"I did a craniotomy, found the vein and clipped it off. Your father will live. However, he has suffered severe head trauma. The chances of a full recovery are very slim. The brain is an amazing thing, and miraculous things can happen, however, the majority of people with similar trauma need some sort of assisted living."

Addy replied, "So you are saying that he will need to move into a nursing home?"

"Not necessarily. Depending on how severe the damage is, perhaps a family member can take care of him. What we know right now is that he will need at least three weeks in the hospital. We'll start him on a rehab program as soon as we can to teach him how to walk with a paralyzed right side. And then he will need to come here for rehab at least four days a week for the next few months to try to reconnect or rebuild some brain pathways."

Addy's head spun with the information. "Brain damage? Paralyzed right side? Rehab for months?"

"I know this is a lot for you to take in, but there is one more thing. Please follow me." The doctor led Addy down the hall a few doors.

Tubes and wires from monitors and machines seemed to be attached all over Hans Ulfert's body, even more than the last time she saw him. Bandages swaddled his head and a small tube drained pink fluid from his brain cavity. The doctor motioned her closer and lifted the sheet off of Hans's left leg.

From just above his left ankle to almost halfway to his knee, the skin looked black and blue. Addy could clearly see bruises the shape of a thumb and four fingers. Giant-sized fingers.

"Rudy!" she gasped.

"Just so you are aware, we called the police. We can't have people coming into the hospital and injuring the patients," the doctor said. "The person who did this identified himself as Hans Ulfert's son. The police will want to talk to you."

Rudy drove by his father's cobble-stone driveway. A block later he flipped a U-turn and drove back to his father's three-acre snob-hill property. He saw broken cedar branches littering the sidewalk, and the flowerbeds looked like someone took a whipper-snipper to them. Hailstones still melted in the shady spots.

None of the neighbours' yards looks like they got any hail, Rudy thought. *It just goes to show that the old man's money can't protect him.* And he laughed.

Rudy carried a 10-kilogram sledgehammer in his hand as he swaggered up to the battered front door. "And let's just see if he can keep his secrets from me."

Rudy balanced the sledgehammer on its head, slid the door key into the slot and punched in the door code. The keypad did not respond or allow him to turn the key. This did not surprise him because his giant-sized fingers often punched more than one button at a time. He re-entered the code, being slow and deliberate to make sure he got the code right. Still nothing.

He tried a third and a fourth time. He tried turning the key hard until he thought it might break off. Then it dawned on him. "Adelheid!" he screamed in rage. "Do you honestly think you can keep me out?"

He lifted the massive sledgehammer like it weighed nothing. He swung it high and was about to bring it down hard on the door handle. He planned to do what EMS couldn't. At that moment his phone rang. He set the hammer down, leant the handle against the door, and pulled out his phone. The call display said, 'A. Penner'.

"What the hell do you want?" Rudy snarled into the phone.

Adelheid tried to remain calm as she answered, "Hi, Rudy. This is just an update that Dad made it through surgery. Apparently, he had an aneurysm in his brain shortly after you were here to see him, but it looks like they caught it in time. He will recover."

"Why would you give a shit if he recovers? He doesn't give a shit about you. Why don't you just go home? Nobody wants you here. Especially our old man."

"And Rudy, the police asked me if I knew where you were. They have some questions for you."

"About what?" he demanded.

"Something to do with the bruises on Dad's ankle. I said that if you weren't at work or at home, then they should drive by Dad's house."

Rudy hung up. He ran to his truck and drove away, leaving the sledgehammer leaning on the front door.

Although Adelheid's voice remained calm as she spoke to Rudy, she wailed with anguish after he hung up. "Why does he hate me so much?" she asked. "What have I ever done to deserve this?"

Adelheid finally ate supper at 8 p.m. that night. She sat alone in the hotel restaurant eating blackened salmon and a Caesar salad. She sipped pinot grigio and took bites of supper between sending texts to Jack.

'I wish you were here, Jack. It would be great to have this meal with you.'

She thought, *Jack would tell me I look beautiful. I'd answer that I look cried out. Then he'd say something witty to make me smile like, 'If you are all cried out, then all that is left is laughter and fun.' I miss Jack. I feel beautiful when I am with him.*

"Excuse me, miss," said a male voice from the table beside hers. She looked up from her phone and the middle-aged man continued. "I see that you are alone and I am alone. If I joined you for supper, neither of us would be alone."

"Thanks for the offer," she replied. "But I am not in the mood for visiting."

"You are very beautiful," he said. "We wouldn't have to make small talk. We could go straight to my room. Or yours."

"I'm not interested," she replied and turned her chair so her back was to him.

"What can I do to make you change your mind?" he asked.

She ignored him.

"You look like you could use some cheering up and I guarantee that I can put a smile on your face."

Addy took her wine glass in one hand and the dinner plate in the other and walked out of the restaurant. In her room on the eighth floor, she phoned Jack.

"Some ass in the restaurant wouldn't take no for an answer," she told him. "He kept hitting on me. I finally picked up my food and walked out. Just hearing him talk to me that way made me feel dirty like I did something wrong. So I decided something, Jack. I'll visit Dad in the morning, and then come back to the hotel and check out."

"Then you are coming home tomorrow. We can have a movie night with the kids and, once they are in bed, we can open a bottle of wine."

"Sorry, sweetheart, but I can't leave here yet. What I am saying is that I can't spend another night in a hotel. I'll move into the mansion until I know Dad is through this rough spot. Besides, I need to find out which company looks after Dad's house insurance so we can get the broken windows replaced."

"Now that it is the weekend," Jack said, "I don't imagine that you can arrange any of that until Monday. With luck, maybe you can come home Tuesday night."

"School just started and I've already missed two days. You know how important those first weeks are in getting the children excited about learning. Never mind encouraging the ones that have never been away from their mothers. I just have to be back at work by Wednesday."

"How is this for an idea," Jack suggested. "I can bring the kids down there tomorrow morning. We could all stay at your dad's house overnight. He is not there so he can't object. I'll take the kids to Heritage Park for the afternoon and we could spend the evening with you."

"No, Jack. There are things here that they should not see. As much as I want you here, and I want to see Riley and Cody, you need to keep our children away from this place."

"That bad?"

"I've seen stuff that I don't want to see. But it's not that. I have the strangest feeling when I am there like there is something just below the surface. Like there is some great evil just waiting to take shape. I feel like some power is working against me."

"Then I don't want you there. Just walk away. "

"I can't. He is my dad."

Ursula Ulfert listened to a weeks' worth of phone messages while working in the kitchen. She set down the box of frozen pizza in the only spot on the kitchen counter that wasn't covered in crumbs and dried-on spills. She tore open the cardboard tab, removed the Hawaiian pizza and put it into the oven of her avocado-green stove. She groaned at seeing the dirty dishes piled in the sink and opened the dishwasher to discover it was full and no one turned on the wash cycle. She opened the cupboard door under the sink to grab the dishwasher powder to find the garbage can overflowing. Trash tumbled onto the floor. Ursula poured the powder into the dishwasher, started it, and scooped up the garbage with her hands. Then she lifted the garbage bag out of the can and carried it out.

"I should just keep walking," she said, but she put the lid back on the trash can, sighed, and turned around. Back in the kitchen, she washed the dishes in the sink by hand. When she opened the avocado-green fridge, she discovered it contained no food.

"I'll give Karl hell when he gets home," she said to herself. And then she remembered it was Friday evening. "I'm not expecting Karl to come home anytime soon. If at all," she admitted. "He'll come in Saturday afternoon claiming that he went for a drink with the boys and got a little carried away so he slept over at George's house. Or Chuck's place. Or Dan's. All the people she never heard of. The smell of sex and perfume on his clothes would give him away."

Karl gave her endless reasons to leave him in their eight years of wedded bliss. She would have left him ages ago if it were not for the money. Not his money of course. He worked shit jobs. She stayed for the family money. She stayed because Karl was the pride and joy of his millionaire father.

Ursula worked as a sales rep for Petco, a company that sold a wide variety of pet food, animal medicine and pet accessories to retailers. She serviced all the stores and veterinary clinics in Vancouver that were north of the Fraser River. She travelled every two or three months to products shows in Calgary, Toronto or San Francisco. At 27-years-old, she pulled in $80,000 a year.

With her income, she made the mortgage payments on this 1971 split-level on 26th Street East, North Vancouver. And she bought the kids clothes and put the food on the table. And paid for the birthday and Christmas presents. Her wage covered the utilities and everything else. They lost their first house, the beautiful house they bought with the down payment that Karl's father had given them as a wedding present. Karl was supposed to make the payments, but Karl's money went into booze.

The answering machine kicked into the next message. As she heard her own voice leaving a message for Karl, she grumbled, "He could at least check for messages."

She threatened to leave Karl once. She told him, "I don't care about the money. All I want is a husband who is faithful." He swore up and down that he never slept around. He begged her to stay. To this day she still thought he begged because he didn't want to disappoint his father. His stingy, selfish father.

Unless they actually stayed in her father-in-law's house, they never saw a penny. So they made the pilgrimage to Calgary every year and stayed for at least a week. They'd visit the zoo and the planetarium or, if they travelled there in July, they took in the Stampede. Sometimes the family would do a day trip to Banff National Park or the dinosaur museum in the Drumheller badlands. And the kids loved their grandpa. They were too young to see what a self-centred scrooge he was.

All in all, it did make for a cheap vacation and they never left empty-handed. One year they left with a new minivan. Last year Karl's father put $20,000 in an RSP for them. "A guilt offering," Karl complained, but he never refused the money.

Ursula could probably stay at her father-in-law's house when she made business trips to Calgary, but she never did. She made a point of not letting Hans know. That way she didn't have to answer awkward questions. He really only wanted to see the grandkids anyways.

After hearing the message reminding her that Torsten, her six-year-old had a dentist appointment on Saturday, Ursula heard a voice that she seldom heard. "This is Adelheid. Dad had a heart attack last night. He is not doing well. He is in the Foothills Medical Centre in the heart unit's intensive care section on 6D. They are doing an angioplasty right now. I will update you when I have news."

Ursula felt giddy with the news. "Karl's father is dying!" she exclaimed as she danced around the kitchen with the empty home-bake-pizza box in her hand. "Soon, Karl will get the lion's share of the money, and I'm out of here."

Torsten asked, "Grandpa is dying?"

"And what do you mean you are out of here?" Angelika, her eight-year-old, asked.

Ursula forgot completely that the kids hovered around her. She hoped they missed her when she was away, but she suspected that the prospect of pizza kept them in the kitchen. No doubt Torsten would stare at the pizza through the oven door for the entire 20 minutes it took to bake.

"I'm a lion," Ulrich, her four-year-old, growled. "Roar!"

Ursula picked up Ulrich and said, "Yes, you are a lion. Do you know what that makes me?"

"The mama lion!" Torsten shouted.

Ursula growled and Torsten fled down the hallway towards his bedroom laughing hysterically. Ursula chased him with Ulrich in her arms, both growling like hungry lions. At the bedroom door, Ursula put Ulrich down and he ran towards his brother growling, his hands raised like claws.

When Ursula turned around to go back to the kitchen, Angelika stood in the kitchen doorway with her hands on her hips and a look of determination on her face. "What did you mean when you said you are out of here?" Angelika demanded.

"Your grandpa is leaving almost all his money to your daddy. That means we can buy a new house on an acreage and you can have your very own pony."

"Really? A pony?"

Ursula guessed the promise of a pony would keep Angelika occupied for a long time. *The thought that Hans Ulfert would die kept me hanging on to this marriage for years*, she mused. *And the prenup? There are ways around it. I am the mother of Karl's three kids. That should garner me alimony for years.* But more than that, Ursula controlled the money already. *Once the millions are in the bank, I'll siphon off a fortune into my own account. Then I'll walk away.* She smiled at the thought.

"When will Grandpa die?" Angelika asked. "That lady said he was doing fine and should be home in a week. What is frog nosis?"

Ursula realized that there must have been another message from Adelheid. She hit the play-message button once more, skipped forward and stood there listening to the end of all the messages. Angelika stayed in the room listening too. As she did, she unbuttoned the bottom half of her blouse and tied the corners together.

Ursula turned to look at her when the phone messages finished playing and saw her daughter's bare belly and the shirt tied up western style. "Undo that right now. Just because you are a cowgirl, doesn't mean that you are suddenly grown up. You are not a Dallas Cowboys' cheerleader."

There had been three more messages from Adelheid. One saying that the doctors inserted the stent and Karl's father was doing great. Another said that he suffered a stroke and needed an operation. Her final message said Hans survived a brain aneurysm, but his prognosis did not look good.

After Riley and Cody got into their PJs and brushed their teeth, Jack read to them. He knew he did not read with a beautifully melodic voice like Addy. And he had no idea how to put expression into each sentence as she did. He enjoyed hearing her read as much as his children did.

But he read to his children anyways. Not every night, but at least three times a week from the time Riley was six months old. Now that they were older, he read novels to the kids. Usually animal stories like *Black Beauty* and *Call of the Wild*. Some of the books took months to finish. He would sit in the middle of his bed with Cody leaning on one side of him and Riley on the other.

When Addy read to them, she read to them separately. Cody first because his bedtime came first. Cody would crawl into his bed and pull the cowboy blankets up to his chin. Addy would sit on the edge of Cody's bed and read *Sugar Creek Gang* and *Hardy Boys* books. For Riley, she'd read Nancy Drew or something from the Enid Blyton's *Famous Five* series. She read them books from her own childhood, the stories that taught morals and showed that actions brought consequences, good or bad.

Addy used the one-on-one time to ask questions and to gauge what was going on with each child. Jack told her, "You can read our children like a book and I am always amazed that you can spot trouble a month in advance."

Today Jack read the chapter out of *Red Fox* where the fox got its foot tangled in the Oregon grapevine and just as the farmer's boy and his dog Bowser step into the clearing. Cody and Riley stared wide-eyed in anticipation. Jack stopped reading and put the bookmark in. "Bedtime," he said.

"No, you can't stop now!" Riley exclaimed. "What happened to Red Fox?"

"Please, Dad? Please, please, please, please read some more?" Cody begged.

Jack often ended reading with a cliff hanger as a way to judge if the children were into the story. It also made it easier to get them into bed next time.

"Mom isn't here. She'll never know if we stay up past our bedtime," Riley argued. "Besides, it is Friday night." Cody shook his head in agreement.

"So," Jack said, "You are telling me that if your mom isn't watching, then you don't have to obey the rules?"

"Well, no," Riley answered. "That is not what I'm saying. It's just... well, maybe you could tell Mom that we stayed up a little later so you could finish reading the chapter."

Cody shook his head in agreement and said, "Yes, Daddy."

"So you are telling me it is okay to break the rules as long as someone else gets in trouble for it? For even thinking that you get a zerbert!"

Riley laughed and tried to roll off the bed, but Jack put his face against her waist, lifted her pink flannel pyjama top just enough to show some of her stomach and he blew on her belly making farty-zerberty sounds. Riley screamed with laughter.

Cody scrambled to get off the end of the bed, but Jack caught him by one foot and dragged him back onto the bed. "You are not getting away, young man." Cody tried rolling onto his stomach, but Jack rolled him over and blew a big wet zerbert on his stomach as Cody laughed hysterically.

Both Riley and Cody hugged Jack. "I love you, Daddy," Riley said.

Jack kissed them both on their foreheads.

"When is Mom coming home?" Cody whined.

"Grandpa is very sick. She wants to help him," Jack answered. "She is hoping to be home on Tuesday."

"Tuesday!" Cody exclaimed. "That is four more days."

"So the sooner you go to bed, the sooner Mom will be home."

"Not really," Riley stated. "The time until Mom gets home is exactly the same whether you sleep or not."

"Then maybe, to pass the time, you want zerberts until your mother gets here."

Both Cody and Riley screamed with laughter and ran out of the master bedroom. "I'm going to catch you!" Jack hollered after them as he chased them as far as the bathroom door. They ran laughing to their rooms.

"I love you, Dad," Cody called from his room.

"I love you too, Son."

"I miss Mom," Riley called.

"I miss her too," Jack answered.

He missed Addy more than his children or wife could know. He fell in love with Addy the first moment he saw her. That she didn't have any clothes on may have contributed to his feelings. Jack chuckled at the memory.

Riley asked him once, "How did you meet Mom?"

He answered truthfully, "I met your mother when I took an art class at university. She was the model, and everyone in the class had to draw her."

"Do you still have your drawings? Can I see them?"

"That was a long time ago. I'd have to find them," he answered, even though he knew exactly where he kept the drawings.

Jack remembered the art classes like yesterday. The beautiful woman would strike a pose and stay there, not moving for an entire hour. Over the weeks, he studied every feature of her face, her neck, and her shoulders. Yes, all of her. A few minutes before class would end, she'd slip on a white bathrobe and walk into one of the offices and close the door behind her.

Six weeks into the semester, she stood in front of him in the line-up at the cafeteria. He didn't need to see her face to recognize the model. She wore blue jeans and a pastel-green tee shirt. She wore her blonde hair up in braids.

He tapped her on the shoulder and said, "Hi. My name is Jack."

"I won't sleep with you so don't even ask," she replied as she turned around. "And don't tell me I am beautiful. I've heard all the lines before. And I don't pose for private lessons." And she turned back and shuffled forward in the line.

"I didn't ask to sleep with you. And don't tell me I am handsome. I've heard all the lines before. And no, I don't pose for private lessons either. Did I mention my name is Jack?"

Addy whirled around with the recycled-plastic-grey food tray held high and poised to hit him over the head with it. When she saw his terrified face, she lowered the tray.

"Wow! It looks like you are lethal with a cafeteria tray. Where is campus security when you need protection?" Jack said as he feigned looking for someone to rescue him.

"Sorry," she said. "I must have sounded rude. And perhaps looked a little crazy too. It is just that I get pestered all day long."

"I just wanted to ask if I could join you for lunch. No obligation. Perhaps, if I sit with you, no one will pester you."

"I study while I eat," she stated to put him off. She did not want company.

"So do I," Jack answered.

They sat facing each other across the table and read textbooks and scribbled notes as they took mouthfuls of cafeteria food. She ate a salad while he ate macaroni and cheese. They never said a word to each other.

After a half-hour, Addy said, "You're right. That is the longest I've gone without having to chase some guy away. I have to run to class now, but perhaps we could have lunch together again. Tuesdays and Thursdays, I'm here right at noon. Mondays and Wednesdays, I'm here at 11:35."

Of course, Jack waited for her the next day. She carried her tray with her salad and glass of tap water over to the table where he sat. "Hi, Jack," she greeted him. "Will you be my guardian again today?"

"Only if you promise not to hit me with the tray."

"Only if you promise not to hit on me."

So they sat together the second day in a row and Jack stole glances at her perfect face. Today, she wore her hair parted down the middle and it hung down like shimmering golden curtains. At one point she looked up and saw him looking at her. "What are you thinking?" she asked.

He wanted to say, "You are breathtakingly beautiful and I could stare at you forever." Instead, he answered, "I wondered what you think about when you pose? You seem so focused."

"I try not to think about all the guys and some girls too, that take the class just to see me naked. I actually get embarrassed. Sometimes I think about my father. He is a photographer and I often posed for him. But mostly I think about God."

"God? You spend the time praying?"

"Why are you surprised? When you are standing naked in front of a crowd, it feels like you have nothing to hide. Nothing to hide from people or from God. No pretences. No self-righteousness. You should try it."

"I don't think I could stay in one spot that long without moving. Besides, no one would want to see me naked."

"You'd be surprised. There is a shortage of people who model nude. They pay $200 an hour and you get art credits towards your degree."

"And it sounds like you get a lot of unwanted attention."

"Yes, that is the downside. I'm working my way through university and modelling pays a lot better than working in the cafeteria. Well, I should get to class now."

"I still don't know your name. My drawings are titled 'female nude'. I don't suppose you want me calling that out across the cafeteria."

"Adelheid. But you can call me Addy." And she smiled.

"I'll see you in art class, Addy."

"Undoubtedly," she said. And she winked at him and walked away. He stared at her perfect backside until she walked out of the room.

Jack chuckled at the memory. And he found himself grinning like he did that day in the cafeteria. Thinking about Adelheid still made his heart do flip flops.

Two things happened that afternoon in the art class. Addy came in, dropped her bathrobe, and fixed her eyes on Jack. Usually, she picked a point in the distance or faced sideways. Today she stared into his eyes. Several people followed her gaze and turned to look at Jack.

And Jack stared back for several minutes and then started to draw. The instructor, a middle-aged woman with greying hair that hung to her waist, wandered around the room giving advice. Jack described her as a left-over hippy. Today she stopped behind Jack and watched him draw. After 30 minutes, she asked Jack, "May I?"

She called the class to attention and said, "Your assignment is to draw a nude. I hope by now you know drawing is about replicating a shape. Art is about capturing a feeling or an emotion." She lifted Jack's drawing pad and announced, "This is art."

Jack had drawn only Addy's face. Looking into the eyes of the drawing was like staring into Addy's soul. She looked beautiful and strong. Childlike and fragile. She looked completely exposed as if Jack stared into the dark places of her mind and she had not turned away.

Adelheid blushed as she put on the bathrobe and slipped into the office while everyone stared at the drawing.

Because it was Saturday morning, when Addy arrived at the hospital at 8:30, cars already filled 80% of the football-field-sized visitor parking lot. She felt glad she arrived when she did.

Her father was awake and saw her come into his room. The left side of his face smiled and it made the grey stubble on half his chin bob up and down.

"You gave us a scare," Addy said as a greeting. "But you survived an aneurysm. You are a fighter. You are a survivor." She realized as she said the words that she gave the same sort of encouragement to her father as she would give to five-year-olds. Short sentences. Loads of encouragement.

He stretched out his left hand to her and she took it. He lifted her hand to his chubby mouth and kissed it and then held her hand tight against his breast. He struggled to say something. It sounded like 'Wilhelmina'. Then he smiled the half-smile again.

"Yes, Dad," Addy replied. "This is your daughter Adelheid. I'm here to take care of things. I love you."

His grey eyes showed his confusion. Then he shut them. Two seconds later, he opened his eyes and stared at her and smiled with half his face. This time Addy knew he said, "Wilhelmina."

The right side of Han's face drooped. His right eye looked like a slit and drool spilt from the right corner of his mouth. Addy noticed the new head bandages, and a tube from his skull drained pink fluid to prevent pressure from building upon his brain.

"I'm here, Dad," she said and wondered if there was any point in correcting him. His right eye closed and his left eyelid drooped. His grip on her hand relaxed as Hans Ulfert began to snore.

The charge nurse stopped Addy before she left. "Does your father have a living will? He isn't able to give us express, informed consent for his medical treatment."

"I really have no idea," Addy replied. "But Dad does have a lawyer and a will, so I imagine he has a living will too. I'll find out."

"We will need a copy of it. And we'll need a copy of the medical power of attorney for whoever is helping make medical decisions."

"I'll ask about that, too," she replied.

"Thank you," the nurse said. "It makes our jobs a whole lot easier when we have direction."

Addy heard the compassion in this woman's voice and saw the genuineness of her smile. Addy gathered up the few bits of encouragement like treasures, convinced she would burst into tears otherwise.

The sunshine helped. The early-September day felt like summer, and Addy soaked in the rays as she phoned P. K. Parkman while leaning against her van. As she expected, the lawyer's office was closed so she left a message.

"This is Adelheid Penner. My father, Hans Ulfert, had a stroke last night." The tears welled up and Addy took a couple of deep breathes before she continued. "Anyways, the hospital is asking if he has a living will and someone appointed as the medical power of attorney. Do let me know as soon as possible." And she left her cell phone number.

When Addy checked out of the hotel, she paid for it with her father's debit card, and she felt guilty. She came down on her own volition. It didn't seem right to use his money; however, she followed his wishes.

When she turned into her father's circular cobblestone driveway, she noticed the giant sledgehammer leaning against the massive front door. "Rudy!" she exclaimed. "Am I supposed to phone the police about my own brother?"

Addy unlocked the door and struggled to lift the head of the sledgehammer high enough to move it. She set it down immediately inside the entryway.

Karl came home Saturday morning just before 11:00. Angelika met him at the screen door and said, before he opened it, "Mom is pissed at you. And I'm pissed at you. Where have you been?"

Torsten did not look up from the cartoons on TV, but said, "Hi, Dad. I'm not pissed."

"Don't talk like that," Karl scolded. "And what are you angry about Angelika?"

"Grandpa is dying. Well, maybe he isn't. Soon, we'll be out of here and I'll get a horse. Or else not. And Mom wants to know where you were last night."

If Ursula felt angry, she didn't show it. When they walked into the bedroom, Karl rehearsed his rebuff to her tirade although he thought of nothing new. Same excuses. Same lies. He steeled himself to ignore her screaming and her threats.

Instead, she greeted him by saying, "Your father had a brain aneurysm yesterday. They did surgery and he survived. Your sister says his whole right side is paralysed."

"So is he dying?"

"Your sister says it is touch and go."

"Let's hope it is go," he said. And he reached for Ursula and she stepped into his arms.

She ignored the smell of yesterday's beer and a recent cigarette. She pretended she didn't smell the cheap department-store perfume. She kissed him on the neck and said, "Yes, and soon."

Angelika tiptoed down the hall and stood to one side of the open bedroom door. She waited for the screaming to begin. When it didn't, she stepped into the doorway to see her father kissing her mother on the mouth. One of his hands squeezed her bum.

"I know what you are going to do," Angelika exclaimed. "You are going to have sex."

"Young lady, you watch too much television," Ursula said. And she closed the door on her daughter and turned the lock. "Have a shower, Karl, then come to bed."

Addy carried her suitcase up the long set of stairs to the second-floor bedrooms. She remembered helping her mother walk up here one step at a time, and stopping to rest every few steps. Wilhelmina fought for air and fought to stay upright.

"Dad, you should have installed in a chair lift," Addy said out loud. "Of course it would have been a big expense for something that Mom would use so seldom, but it would have helped her." A tear trickled down Adelheid's cheek. She said, "For a place I've never stayed, I sure have a lot of bad memories here."

Adelheid chose the suite farthest from her father's room and put her suitcase on the bed. The room was three times the size of her bedroom at home. She walked to the picture window and looked out at the valley. Then she opened the German-style balcony door, took a few deep breaths and prayed, "God, help me get through this."

Back inside she checked out the full bathroom. Then she went to the bed and opened her suitcase. She took out her knee-length black dress with the white floral design. She bought it at Sears as one of the January clear-out specials. She paid $24.95.

The dress looked wrinkly and she decided to hang it up in the closet. When she opened the closet doors, there were six empty hangers and on the seventh hung a white Ralph Lauren bathrobe. That gave her an idea.

She really hadn't planned to stay in Calgary this long so she did not have any clean clothes. Addy stripped, put on the housecoat and carried all her dirty laundry to the finished, walk-in laundry room next to her father's bedroom. She remembered putting in the sheets and blankets from her mother's bed when her mother threw up because of the chemotherapy.

"This laundry room is a far cry from carrying laundry down to the basement at my house," she said as she put her jeans, socks, tee shirt, bra, underwear and dress into the machine.

She crossed the hall into the games room. One would not shoot pool in this room. Her father designed this room for playing chess and at least ten chess sets showed games in progress. He ordered each chess set to be custom made, some created of gold and silver, some ivory, and some carved stone, beside each stood a time clock. Obviously, Hans Ulfert played chess masters from around the world.

From that room, Addy crossed into the library, a room until that moment was forbidden to her because the door always remained closed when she visited. More than 10,000 books filled the shelves from floor to ceiling and the sight overwhelmed her. Many were in German, but English first editions also lined the shelves. Glass display cases held the most priceless books. After a half-hour of paging through books, she went downstairs.

Addy walked into the office and said, "Hi, Mom," to the portrait in the most cheery voice she could muster, just like she had done when cancer, chemo, and God knows what else the doctors prescribed ravaged her mother. "You'll never guess. You and I are wearing exactly the same outfit today."

Addy stared at the portrait imagining that she could hear her mother's laugh. "I miss you, Mom. I am sorry I wasn't around more. I'm sorry things were the way they were."

Addy wiped a couple of tears then opened one of the filing cabinet doors. Just as she remembered from yesterday, she saw a file folder in that drawer marked INTAC Versicherungsgesellschaft. She took out the insurance policy and, from the phone on the desk, called INTAC Insurance. She explained how her father ended up in the hospital and then hail damaged the windows and possibly the entryway's glass roof.

The insurance agent said, "We can send a claims adjuster over on Monday afternoon. I'll open a file today; however, we will need to see your power of attorney to act on your father's behalf."

"Is that the same thing as medical power of attorney?" Adelheid asked. "I've asked my father's lawyer for one of those."

"No, that is not what you need for house insurance. You'll need a power of attorney so that you can make financial decisions for him. The lawyer will know what you need. You can fax or email me a copy, but do show the adjuster the real one."

"The lawyer's office is closed today. I may not have this until Monday morning. I'll send you a copy as soon as I have it in hand."

She hung up, turned to her mother's portrait and said, "I have no idea if Dad has medical power of attorney, never mind a regular one. And if he does, there is no reason why he would have named me. He disowned me before I left home. He only let me back into his life, and yours, when you were sick. And I think it you had something to do with that."

Her mother's all-seeing eyes seemed to look into her soul. Her face still smiled but Addy could, for the very first time, see that she posed a question behind the smile.

"Mom," Addy said as she choked back some tears, "some things happened that I never told you about. Some things, to this day, I can't understand. I guess I never told you because I did not want to hurt you."

Addy wiped her tears onto the sleeve of the housecoat, looked back into her mother's eyes and said bluntly, "Dad tried to rape me. It happened during a photo-shoot in his studio downtown when I was 16. As he took pictures of me in various stages of undress, with all the lights out except for the photofloods, he told me I was the most beautiful woman in the world and that we were creating the most amazing art together."

Addy stared at her hands for the longest time, looked back at the portrait and said, "You know I modelled nude for him. Did you know he paid me? For years, he did. He said the payment made it a confidentiality agreement. He told me that because he paid me, he owned the photographs and could do what he wanted with them. I was never to speak of them to anyone. Including you. It was a dad and daughter secret. He said modelling was my way of earning some money. You are still smiling." Addy said to the portrait, "So I'll tell you what happened. I stood naked under the spotlights and Dad came over to position me so that the light looked right. He stood behind me and ran both his hands up my belly and over my boobs. He lifted my long hair over my shoulders and then he kissed me on the neck. I started to pull away and he told me again how beautiful I looked, and then he walked back into the dark behind his camera.

"I know what you are going to say. I wondered at the time. Maybe he accidentally caressed me. Or perhaps I misinterpreted my father's affection, so I stood there staring into the spotlights while he gave me direction on how to stand, how to tilt my head, then to give him a sexy-pouty look. And I did just what he said.

"No, Mom. That wasn't what made me flee from home the moment I could. There is more to the story. I stood there giving Dad the pouty look and he walked out from behind the spotlight completely naked. Not naked like the Michelangelo statue of David. He had a hard-on. For me.

"No, I didn't imagine it. The floodlights lights were on. I'm sure he recorded the whole thing with video. He reached for me. I knocked his hands down and screamed at him that he should never to touch me again. Ever.

"He just reached for me again and said that sex between consenting adults is a wonderful thing. That there is nothing dirty or immoral about it. That he could make me feel loved in ways I couldn't begin to imagine.

"I ran. I scooped up my clothes and ran out of the studio into the women's bathroom in the storefront. I locked the door behind me and got dressed while he stood on the other side of the door and threatening me.

"He said no one would believe me. He said even the mention of the incident could mean that you would leave him. That you would leave us kids.

"I'm sure you remember that day. When we came in, Dad told you he found drugs in my clothes. You cried like your heart had broken. I never did drugs, Mom. Never!

"So I tried my best never to be alone with him. I refused to go back into his studio. I'm sure you remember that. I did not want to be his assistant, his receptionist or his model. Definitely not his lover. He told me if I didn't come back, he wouldn't pay a cent of my university. I told him to screw off and you know the rest of the story. I left home the moment I could get away."

Addy was surprised at herself. She managed to relate the whole story without breaking down into a puddle of tears and snot. It helped that her mother smiled encouragingly through the whole thing. It helped that her mother could not actually hear the awful truth.

"I should have told you when you were alive, Mom," Addy said to the portrait. "Then you may have understood why I acted the way I did. Then maybe you may have understood how I could hate my own father.

"So why am I here then? Why am I trying to help the person who tried to abuse me? Why am I trying to help my millionaire father who never gave me a dime for education? Who never gave a present to either of my kids? Who told all sorts of lies about me? I guess that just shows how twisted I really am. Perhaps I am trying to please him out of love for you. Thanks for listening, Mom," Addy said to the portrait. "I'd love to hear how things are with you, except that I have to check on the laundry, and then get Dad's bedroom cleaned up so that the insurance adjuster won't see poses of you that I'm sure you would rather not share."

Addy walked down the long hallway lined with framed photographs of famous people. *It is just not normal to hang pictures of strangers in your house, even if it is to promote sales*, Addy thought. *Normal people have photographs of family, the grandkids, their pets, or even the places they've been on holidays.*

She climbed the long flight of stairs to the upper level and walked past the black and white photographs of nudes that lined the hallway. The washing machine whined, still on the spin cycle so Addy walked to her father's room. She sighed when she realized how much glass lay scattered across the floor. Then, looking at the walls, she unconsciously pulled the top of her housecoat together so no one would see her breasts because the sexual nature of the myriad of photographs struck her again.

"OK," she said to the room. "Let me clarify what I said earlier. Normal people hang pictures of their loved ones with clothes on. And perhaps famous photographers display pictures of nudes. What's in this room is way past normal, way past even liberal, modern-thinking normal."

Theoretically, the bedroom closest to her father's room was a guest suite; however, this is where her mother kept her shoes. Her mother loved shoes and loved buying shoes and, at one time, hundreds of pairs lined the shoe racks in the walk-in closet, all sorted by colour and style. Her father installed full-length mirrors at angles so Wilhelmina could see what she looked like wearing various shoes. As Addy walked into the shoe room, she hoped her father hadn't thrown out all of her mother's shoes.

To her joy, none of the shoes were missing. And none were dusty so, no doubt, the cleaning staff minded this monument to her mother. Addy picked a pair of dark-brown Romikas, carried them to the cream-coloured high-back chair and sat down. She slipped the European-made shoes onto her feet and they fit her like they were made for her because she wore the same size shoes as her mother.

Tears welled up in her eyes. She remembered her mother sitting here before one of her medical appointments. Adelheid said, as if her mother were in the room, "When I brought you pair after pair of practical shoes to try on, Mom, you told me you wanted to wear heels. You always did have class, but heels to see the oncologist? You asked me to bring the grey snakeskin ones, and I think you would have worn them except your feet were too swollen from the chemotherapy."

Addy wiped a tear away, just like she had that day. "I was down on my knees right there when you ran your fingers through my hair, brushed my cheek with your hand and told me you loved me. It meant a lot, Mom. I kissed your hand and told you I loved you too. And you said you knew, but I don't know if you knew how much."

Addy wiped away another tear. "I wanted to go with you to the appointment. You know I volunteered to take you, but Dad said no. I just wanted to spend time with you. I think you knew Dad would separate us. You wanted to spend time with me too 'cause you didn't stop me from bringing you a lot of shoes you had no intention of trying on. Then you slipped me a roll of $20 bills. 'Buy your children birthday presents from me,' you said."

Addy looked down at her feet and realized, of all the shoes to choose from, she picked the brown Romikas, the very same shoes she slipped onto her mother's feet for her trip to the cancer specialist. "These are comfortable shoes, Mom. Like you, I chose them for doing something I do not want to do."

Back in her father's room, Addy pulled down picture after picture. It took most of an hour and a huge pile of photographs filled the bed. In the process, she'd made a stack of pins on the dresser like a metal haystack. *I'll toss the photos under the bed, for now*, Addy thought. *That way they'll be out of sight when the repair people come, and Dad can put them back up if and when he comes home.*

She lifted the beige-coloured brocade dust ruffle to discover white plastic storage bins under the bed. She pulled one out and popped it open and immediately felt sorry she did. The enlargements in the bin were of her dad and mom making love. Various positions. Some of the photographs were from the old house. Some shot in the old studio. The more imaginative ones were shot on some of her father's sets in this house and it appeared that her parents were going at it in some very public places.

"Really, Dad? Really, Mom? You needed more pictures of yourself? You were afraid you might forget who you were married to?"

Addy closed the red plastic interlocking lid and pushed the bin back underneath the bed. She did not want to see what the other bins held. She picked up as many photos as she could from the bedspread, carried them into the bathroom, and put them into the marble Roman tub. It took five huge armfuls and three trips picking up the photographs that spilt out of her arms along the way.

In the bathroom, she washed her hands and arms up to her elbows and she still felt dirty. She wished she could wash the images out of her mind. She took the phone out of the housecoat pocket and sent a text to Jack. 'Sweetheart, I miss you.'

Jack answered back immediately. 'L U 2. Riley and I are doing laundry. Cody is collecting the garbage and will sweep the kitchen floor. Then I'll take them to a movie. Wish you were here.'

She responded, 'Tell the kids I have a load of laundry in here, have seen a pile of garbage I should throw out, and I am about to clean up the floor. Doing chores at my own house is definitely better.'

Addy got down on her knees and picked up shards of glass, dropping them into the garbage can that she got from the bathroom. As she did this, she thought about Jack. How she missed Jack. How she wished he was here to put his arms around her and tell her that everything would be okay and that she would make it through this.

She met him in while in her second year of university, her first year in the Teachers' Ed program. He was in his second year in Communications Studies, his third year of university. Addy chuckled at the memory. Jack came up behind her in the cafeteria line and tapped her on the shoulder. She told him to buzz off in no uncertain terms.

"Mom," she said to the air, "the very first thing I said to Jack was, 'I won't sleep with you.' I could not have been more wrong." Addy found it wonderful to tell her mother the things that she never shared before. Her father robbed so much of their mother-daughter time.

"Instead of just saying hello in return like a normal human being, I tried to hit Jack with my cafeteria tray and only the look of terror in his eyes saved him. I'm sure I traumatized him. For the next year, he prefaced almost everything he said with 'I hope you won't hit me.' Poor, Jack!

"I ended up eating lunch with him. Not that I wanted to, but I wanted to show him I wasn't completely off my rocker. He never said a word, no doubt afraid that I would bean him with the tray. He never even looked up. He studied the entire time. I never said a word either. Finally, I told him that I'd be back the next day. As if the university provided anywhere else to eat!

"We ate lunch together every day for a week before he asked me out. That is if you want to call helping him do homework a date." Addy laughed out loud at the memory and realized that it was the first time she laughed since she left home on Thursday night.

"He said, 'Please don't hit me, but I was wondering if you could help me with an assignment. I need to shoot a video and I need an actress. Please don't be offended, but you'll need to keep your clothes on.'

"We hadn't spoken much in the week of eating at the same table, and I wouldn't have said yes, except Jack was the only guy I met that saw beyond my body. Besides, when he was with me, the other guys left me alone. Maybe I said yes because he stood six-feet tall and his muscular farm-boy arms made me feel safe.

"He came by my place, a wretched, tiny, and probably illegal basement suite, in his beat-up old Toyota and explained the video plot as we drove to Hawrelak Park. 'The assignment is to take a children's story and tell it as if it was written for grownups. I chose the Red Riding Hood. All you have to do is adlib the lines. Act natural. We'll shoot a scene in the woods and then go out for supper.'

"It freaked me out to think about going into the woods with a stranger, but he always acted ever so polite in the time that I had known him. And truth be told, I hadn't eaten a restaurant meal in more than a year. He reassured me that it was all on the up and up.

"I had my doubts and he knew it. In fact, he counted on it. I put on the red hood and cape that he had rented from a costume shop. He set up the camera on a tripod, clipped a microphone to my collar, and punched the record button.

'Where is your costume?' I asked him.

'I don't look like a wolf to you?'

'You are way too handsome to be a wolf.' Then I blushed down to my toes.

'Thank you for saying so. After supper, we'll go back to my place to film the bedroom scene.'

"'I'm not going to sleep with you so scrap that idea right now. I know you've seen me naked almost every day this week and now you want more? If you think I'm letting you put your ice-cold paws on me, you have another thing coming. I don't do bedroom scenes! I am through with the acting and I'm through with you. I want you to take me back home right now. And, for future reference, wandering around the woods in this red costume isn't my idea of a fun date.'

"Then Jack threw his arms around me, gave me a kiss on the forehead, and said, 'You were absolutely perfect. And I was kidding about the bedroom scene. I have reservations at the Sawmill for supper for 8:00.' And he started packing up the camera.

"Mom, believe me when I tell you that I was in shock at the kiss. And he put the camera away like I wasn't even there.

'What do you mean that I was perfect?' I stammered. 'You were expecting me to freak out?'

'I actually expected you to hit me,' he replied.

"Mom, Jack had cameras all the time. He was a little like Dad that way, but he never took a picture of me naked. He never asked if he could. He never filmed us having sex. Jack never laid a hand on me without my permission. He is nothing like Dad.

"Jack pleaded with me to forgive him before I said yes to the meal. The tears in his eyes convinced me that he really felt horrified that I didn't ever want to see him again. When we finally sat down in the restaurant, he asked me, 'Are you vegetarian?'

'No,' I answered. 'Whatever gave you that idea?'

'Because salad is the only thing I've seen you eat.'

'I like salad,' I answered, trying to convince him.

"'I like salad too, but the salad at the university always looks wilted like they don't keep it in the fridge. Do you like it that way?'

'Well, no. It is just that I'm on a limited budget. The other cheap meal is mac and cheese. If I ate that every day, I'd put on a ton of weight.'

'Tonight I want you to eat steak. Filet mignon. I owe you a meal for being my actress.'

'Yes, and you owe me an explanation,' I demanded.

'As I told you, the assignment is to do an adult version of a kid's story. The proviso was that, to get top marks, the acting needed to be convincing. If I told you to act that you were furious with me, it wouldn't have come across as the real deal. You were very convincing. I don't ever want you mad at me again.'

'But we didn't act out anything. I just yelled at you.'

'I'll add my lines and it will win you an academy performance.'

'Promise me that you'll let me see it before you hand it in. I already have a reputation for being crazy.'

'Deal,' he said.

"Mom, the version of the video that he showed in the class went like this. Now picture me in a red cape as Miss Ridinghood standing in the forest and looking apprehensive. You can't see Jack, only hear his voice.

Wolf: 'Where are you going, Miss Ridinghood?'

Miss Ridinghood (sounding annoyed): 'Wandering around the woods in a red costume.'

Wolf: 'Can I undo your top so I can find out what is in your goodies basket?'

Miss Ridinghood: 'If you think I'm letting you put your ice-cold paws on me, you have another thing coming.'

Wolf: 'I could wait for you in bed at your grandma's house and you could come warm me up.'

Miss Ridinghood: 'Not my idea of a fun date.'

Wolf: 'I'm a really nice guy and you can trust me.'

Miss Ridinghood: 'I'm not going to sleep with you so scrap that idea right now! You are a wolf.'

Wolf: 'So you're not going to show me your goodies at your grandma's house?'

Miss Ridinghood: 'I don't do bedroom scenes. I'm through with acting and I'm through with you.'

Wolf: 'The moral of the story is that the girl in the red cape is a real princess.'

(Scene of the wolf hugging Ridinghood)

"Mom, Jack asked me that night if I planned to go home for the Remembrance Day weekend. I told him no. When he asked me why, I told him my dad and I didn't get along and he would be in Calgary so I wouldn't.

"I expected him to say, 'You should try harder,' and 'I'm sure it isn't as bad as you imagine.' I thought he might put a guilt trip on me and tell me I should forgive and not harbour resentment. Instead, a tear trickled down his cheek and he tried to wipe it away before I noticed. He told me that he felt sorry for me. And I knew that he meant it."

Addy's cell phone rang while she vacuumed, but she only heard the whine of the Rainbow and slivers of glass bouncing down the vacuum cleaner hose like pinballs. Paul Parkman left a message. She didn't listen to it. She just called back.

"Mrs. Penner, I'm so sorry to hear the news that your father isn't doing well. He does have a living will and has a designated power of attorney. I'd have you come by except that I am out on the golf course. I'll have one of my staff go into the office and get those for you. Where shall I have them delivered?"

"I'm at my father's house. Have them call my cell. I may be in the studio so I might not hear the doorbell."

"It is important that you have those papers in hand this afternoon. Marsha will bring them by within the next hour. Perhaps if you are not doing anything this evening, we could go out for a drink and discuss your father's estate. Or just relax if you'd prefer."

"After I see the papers, I'm sure I'll have questions, but tonight won't work. Let's meet in your office on Monday."

Boundaries. She set them with her children. She set them with the kindergarten kids. Apparently, she needed to set boundaries for lawyers, too.

"What is it with men?" she asked the pinhole covered walls. "Why do they think that because I'm not in the same city as Jack that I'll sleep with them? Are all men like that? Are they instantly unfaithful the moment their wives are out of sight?"

She texted Jack, 'I love you.'

'L U 2,' he answered.

Addy picked up the heavy vacuum cleaner and realized she needed to empty the bin. "The problem with a water-based vacuum cleaner," she said to herself, "is that you have to dump the sludge. I can't put it down the toilet with all that glass." She ended up dumping it through a kitchen strainer into the toilet and dumping the glass into the bathroom trash can. The process created a gross mess. By the amount of grime and pubic hairs, Addy knew the housecleaning staff were not allowed in the master bedroom.

Muddy water spread across the bathroom floor. After dumping the trash into a cardboard box in the garage, she scrubbed the toilet bowl, washed the floor, sink and trash can. She threw out the strainer. "I'm sick of this place!" she yelled. Her voice echoed back and she felt very alone. "I'm going home soon," she told the house. "I'm going home as soon as I figure out how to get into the last two rooms of the studio." Then she whispered, "But first I'm going to put clothes on. The studio gives me the creeps like someone is watching me."

Adelheid grabbed her load of laundry out of the dryer and carried it to her room. She hung her dress in the closet, stepped into warm panties, and pulled the warm jeans up. As she zipped up the fly, she realized that the waistband was not quite dry. "Ignore it," she told herself. "You are not going in the studio without pants on." Then she carried the towels from her father's bathroom to the washing machine and started another load.

Addy walked down the hall, stood at the top of the stairs and said, "It's time." Then she walked down the stairs and into the long hallway. As she punched in the code for the studio door, she noticed that her hands shook. She took a deep breath, told her hand to cooperate, and pushed the final numbers. The lock snarled and Addy turned the doorknob. Like the day before, the studio remained completely black, but today the darkness even swallowed up the light from the hallway. Addy jumped back in fear and the door closed and the deadbolt snarled into place.

"This is ridiculous," she said out loud with her back against the hallway wall. "I am the only one in the house. No one could possibly be in the studio. All I have to do is walk forward and the motion detector will turn on the lights." Her muscles turned to ice and her willpower vanished like a stone tossed into a lake. She did not step forward to re-enter the code.

Just yesterday I walked right in there, she thought. *Today I'm shaking like a leaf. What on earth is going on? It is not like I am afraid of the dark.*

And then she realized the truth. The dark terrified her. Only since she married Jack 12 years ago could she fall asleep without fear gnawing at her. For 12 years Jack held her every night and she fell asleep with his strong arms around her.

She remembered the first time he held her. It happened during the first Christmas after they met. In mid-December, he asked, "Are you going home for Christmas, Addy?"

"No. My father is at home."

"For the whole break? Then why don't you spend the Christmas break with me on my parent's farm?"

"That sounds really creepy like you are taking me home to meet your folks. They'll think that we are going with each other... that we are serious. No offence, but I really don't know you very well, and asking me to spend Christmas break with you is a little forward. You are weirding me out."

"What are you going to do, spend Christmas break by yourself?"

"That is what I did last Christmas. It was fine," she said, trying to sound convincing. In actual fact, those three weeks were the loneliest and saddest of her life. She celebrated Christmas without a tree or presents. Even her crazy roommate left for home. She ate canned mushroom soup for Christmas dinner.

Jack carried on like staying alone wasn't an option. "The moment you feel uncomfortable, I'll drive you back from Bentley. Middle of the night. Middle of Christmas dinner. Any time you want. You have my word." His kind eyes convinced her. Besides, he never once tried to get her into bed.

On her first night on the farm, she lay on Jack's bed in his room, and he slept in the living room on the couch. No city lights shone through the window and no light from car headlights passed by. The clock said 1:17 a.m.

No nightlight lit the room and she felt too embarrassed to ask if she could leave the bathroom light on all night. The room seemed frighteningly dark and she lay there terrified. And then she heard the howling. Coyotes. Or wolves. She had no idea which. Maybe both. They sounded so close she convinced herself their noses pressed against the windowpane.

She bolted out of the room and ran down the hall to the living room. She planned to say, "Jack, take me back to Edmonton right now." By the time she got to him, she just flipped up the blanket and threw herself on top of Jack. "Hold me," she whispered. "Hold me all night long."

"What about not giving my parents the idea that we are going together?" he whispered.

She kissed him on the mouth and said, "We are going together now."

A smiled crossed Addy's face at the memory as she stared at the studio door. She stepped forward, punched in the code and then marched forward into the dark. When the lights popped on, she said, "You'd be proud of me, Jack." And she heard her voice bounce off the walls.

She wandered around the studio for 15 minutes without the slightest inkling of how she would open the last 2 doors. She jumped when her phone rang.

"Mrs. Penner, this is Marsha from P. K. Parkman. I am out front."

"I'll be right there," Addy said.

Even for a Saturday afternoon, Marsha's clothes suggested she was on the way to a high-class party. Her short, skin-tight black dress barely covered her panties, and she wore ridiculously tall stilettos. Marsha leant against her perfectly clean and polished candy-apple red Porsche convertible, keying words into her cell phone with fingernails the same colour as her car. She looked up as Addy came out of the mansion.

Marsha tossed her cell onto the dash, picked up the envelope that lay on windshield and held it out to Addy. "Mrs. Penner, Paul said you needed these papers today. He also said to tell you that copies of these papers will also go to your two brothers today, one I'll deliver, the other will go by courier."

"What about my other brother?" Addy asked.

"The directions that your father left only mention two brothers."

"I have three brothers," Addy replied.

"It doesn't really matter at this point. You are the important one. You are the one with power of attorney."

Adelheid took the large brown envelope and opened it to find two pages. Addy read the one marked medical directive.

Living Will Declaration

Of Hans Karl Ulfert of Calgary, Alberta, Canada.

Declaration made this the 17th day of May 2010.

I, Hans Karl Ulfert, am at least eighteen (18) years of age and am of sound and disposing mind, willfully and voluntarily and do hereby make known my desires that my dying shall be artificially prolonged under every circumstance.

I further declare:

If, at any time I have an incurable injury, disease or illness deemed to be a terminal condition by my attending physician, and the use of life-prolonging procedures would serve to artificially prolong the dying process, I direct that such procedures be given, and that I be kept alive regardless of quality of life or how extreme the life-prolonging measures are. I am to be kept alive at all cost. Even if I am declared brain dead, I am to be given nourishment and all the necessities of life until my body is no longer alive.

If possible, my body will be frozen in cryogenics to be revived at such time that there is a cure for my ailment or reverse of ageing.

In the absence of my ability to give directions regarding the use of life-prolonging procedures, it is my intention that my family and my physician(s) accept and honour this declaration as the final expression of my legal right to direct medical or surgical treatment.

I appoint Adelheid Elisa Penner of Edmonton, Alberta, Canada, as my true and lawful Attorney for Personal Care. Should she be unable or unwilling to fulfil this duty, I appoint Paul Parkman, my lawyer, to act on my behalf.

"Oh, Papa!" Adelheid said. "Why are you so afraid to die?"

On Saturday afternoon, Raven wandered around her small house doing chores. The baby turned and kicked constantly today. More than usual. He kicked her repeatedly in the ribs or the stomach and she couldn't get comfortable. She hated getting punched in the bladder.

She picked up one of Rudy's giant-sized shirts from the floor beside the bed. It looked grey on first glance, but really it was a very tight weave of black, grey and white threads. She would have called it a dress shirt, the kind you wear with a tie, except that it was the only kind of shirt Rudy fit into.

He needed something that buttoned down the front and she marvelled at how the buttons down the front were a hand-span apart. All his clothes were custom made. He wore short-sleeved shirts and long-sleeved shirts. Raven put the shirt on and it hung down to her ankles. Even almost at her due date, she still had room. She tossed the shirt into the laundry basket.

Rudy wasn't home so he probably went to the gym to work out. She liked it when he worked out because it seemed to mellow him. Exercising took the edge off of his temper and he seemed particularly wound up since his father's heart attack.

She met Rudy's old man once a couple of months back. Rudy took her with him when he stopped by the castle-like house to get a key for the place. Rudy's father did not invite them in. They stood in front of the gigantic castle door like beggars with their hands out.

Hans looked at her pregnant belly, then at her face and asked Rudy, "How long are you going to keep this one around? And I'm not giving you another cent for child support."

That was her whole interaction with the grandfather of her child to be. She could still see the look of disdain on his chubby face. She could see in his pale-blue, pig-like eyes that she meant less than nothing to him. And she could hear from his tone that Rudy rated barely above nothing.

At the time, Raven felt very sorry for Rudy. But months rolled by, her belly grew, and Rudy still hadn't worked on the baby room. They hadn't purchased any baby clothes or diapers or books or toys. They were within two weeks from her due date and they still did not have a crib. Her cousin, Star, donated a box of hand-me-downs.

"I could have this baby any time now," she said to Rudy, "And we are not ready." He just grunted and turned on the television.

She knew Rudy had previous live-in girlfriends. She knew he fathered some children, but had no contact with any of his exes. He never visited with his children and she thought it a blessing. No reminders of the past. No uncomfortable confrontations.

Now she began to wonder if Hans Ulfert gave her a warning. Did he tell her that Rudy did not keep children around? It sounded like he said any child support did not come from Rudy. Hans did make it clear that he wouldn't give a penny of his millions to help her or her baby.

"I love Rudy," Raven said to her baby. "Your papa is big and strong and someday you will be just like him." And she feared that might be true. And she wondered if she would be one of his exes.

Rudy hadn't gone with her to her ultrasounds. He had not gone to prenatal classes. In fact, he hadn't held her for a long time. "He is just afraid that he might hurt you if we make love," she told her baby bump. "He really does love us. When you meet your papa's father, you'll understand how Rudy can be a little uncommunicative."

Raven picked up the pill bottle of steroids from the 50-year-old, threadbare carpet, half-tucked under the sagging, second-hand orange couch. She put the bottle on top of the harvest-gold-coloured, 1970s era fridge. "Daddy will have to learn how to be a little more careful with his things. We don't want you getting into those."

Raven stripped the sheets off of the king-sized bed, her normal Saturday chore. Only now it seemed to take three times as much effort. She carried the white sheets down the worn wooden stairs to the 20-year-old, top-loading washing machine in the unfinished basement. That is when she got the idea.

Boxes, jars, bags and binders of coins lay in a pile in the middle of the cracked and uneven basement floor. When Rudy carried armful after armful of coins and ancient paper money into the house, he laughed, "Let's see who gets the last laugh, Karl. I have every one of your precious coins!"

"Can we spend it?" Raven asked him. "Can we buy a crib and a high chair now?"

"No!" Rudy snarled. "This is a coin collection. Each one of these coins is worth a hundred times its original value. Maybe a thousand times. And it is all mine."

"So this pile is worth thousands and we can't spend it? What good is it to have a knee-deep mound of money when we can't afford to buy our kid diapers?"

Rudy raised his arm to smack her so she turned and ran. He'd hit her before. Many times. And she did not want to show up at the hospital in labour with a black eye.

Today she stared at the mound of coins and said, "If I end up being a single mom, there is no way I can make it. I didn't even finish high school. Do I think my alcoholic mother wants me and a kid moving into her trailer? Not a snowballs chance in the hot place. What we need, Baby Boy, is an insurance policy."

With her cell phone, Raven took a picture of the pile of money. She took a few close-ups of some of the coins at the top of the pile. Then she moved some of the binders from off the top, set them aside, and then filled a pillowcase with jars, binders and cases of coins from the middle of the stack. She carefully put the layer she removed back on to the top of the pile and checked how it looked against the photo she took.

She heard Rudy's truck pull up in front of the house when she just passed the halfway point hauling the heavy pillowcase up the stairs. The truck's high-performance mufflers rumbled and then went silent. The pit bull barked furiously.

Raven bounded up the remaining stairs and dashed into the spare bedroom, the someday baby's room. She yanked the box of used baby clothes out of the closet, dumped them on the floor, poured the contents of the pillowcase into the box and stuffed baby clothes on top.

She stood at the top of the basement stairs with a pillowcase in her hands when Rudy came in. "Do you want some lunch?" she asked a little breathless. "I am just tossing in a load of laundry and then I can make you something?"

"I'm not hungry!" he snarled at her. "I spent the last hour and a half at the police station. Stupid pigs. I told them when my father started to thrash, I grabbed his ankle to keep him from falling out of the bed. I told them I felt terrified that he would hurt himself, maybe even break a hip. They asked me over and over again. Now the stupid hospital got a restraining order to keep me away. Well, I don't want to be there anyway!"

Raven had absolutely no idea what he ranted about, and she knew better than to ask. She went downstairs and put in a load of sheets. Her hands shook and, 15 minutes later, her heart still raced.

The doorbell rang. Rudy peaked out the front window and then opened the door because a very beautiful, black-haired woman stood there. She wore a very short, skin-tight black dress with a V-front that went down to her waist. Rudy wondered how she kept her magnificent boobs from flopping out. He hoped that they might.

He only looked up from her bust when she said, "You must be Rudolph. You match your description. I'm Marsha from P. K. Parkman, your father's lawyer. I was asked to deliver this to you." She held a large brown envelope in her hands.

"So the old man is finally cutting me out of his will!" Rudy exclaimed. "Today I join Adelheid and Heinrich as nobodies."

"I don't believe that is the case, Mr. Ulfert. This is a copy of your father's living will and continuing power of attorney. His instructions were that the moment his medical directive went into place, the firm would deliver a copy of the directives to yourself and your brother Karl. Karl's is going by courier."

Rudy took the envelope. He tried to think of a question he could ask so he could keep the woman on his doorstep. He wished Marsha would give him her phone number. He wished he could make love to her right there on the front steps. He wished Raven wasn't home so he could drag Marsha inside.

He stood there speechless as she turned and walked away. Her hips swivelled when she walked and he caught a glimpse of her bum. He did not take his eyes off her until her red Porsche 911 Carrera turned the corner at the end of the street.

Rudy had no idea what a medical directive was or what continuing power of attorney meant but, seeing he was the only one of Hans's children that lived in Calgary, he knew the papers gave him rights. He would make sure money came his way for looking after the old man.

In the front office, Addy made two photocopies of the medical directive, left the copy with her suitcase, locked up the house and took the medical directive to the hospital. Well, she tried to. She drove less than six blocks when a police car's lights came on behind her. The siren gave a little shriek as she signalled and pulled over.

"Driver's license, insurance and registration please, ma'am," the officer demanded.

Addy's heart pounded as she dug through the glove box for the insurance and registration papers. She pulled out napkins from McDonald's, her emergency supply of tampons, and the cars operating manual and piled them on the passenger's seat. She found several years' worth of registration and insurance cards and handed them all to the officer. He did not look pleased.

"Do you think I have time to sort through this? The law states that you are to keep only your valid insurance and registration in the car. Some of these are from years ago."

"Sorry," Addy said. "I'll sort through them." And she held out her hand. He did not give them back.

"I can give you a ticket for this, ma'am, but I won't. Do you know why I pulled you over?"

"No, sir. I don't."

"The windshield of your car is damaged. It is illegal to drive like that. You pose a hazard to yourself and everyone else."

"I'll get it replaced today," she offered.

"I'm writing you a ticket for driving with an obstructed windshield. I am also deeming your vehicle unsafe to drive. A tow truck will take your vehicle to an impound lot. I will call you a cab."

An hour later, Adelheid arrived at the hospital. She paid the cab fare with her father's debit card. On her father's floor, she showed the charge nurse the original medical directive and gave them a copy to keep for the files. When the nurse read it, she looked shocked. "Oh my," she exclaimed. "In all my years of doing this, I've never seen a directive like this."

"Apparently, my father wants to live forever," Addy replied.

Hans Ulfert stared wide-eyed at the ceiling when his daughter walked in. "Hi, Dad," Addy greeted him cheerily. "I'm here for a visit." He turned to look at her with wide and unblinking eyes like he stared at the most amazing sight.

"Dad, it's me. It's Adelheid. How are you doing? Are you feeling any better?" She touched his cheek with her hand. He did not respond in any way. "I'm taking care of things," she said. "You have nothing to worry about. I just brought your medical directive here to the hospital and I will make sure they do as you requested."

After a minute of silence, Addy said, "Cody and Riley said that they are praying for you. And Jack sends his love. He says you have to get better so you can play him that golf game you promised the day Jack and I got married." Hans did not even grunt.

Addy waved her hand in front of her dad's eyes. He did not blink. She walked to the left, but his eyes did not follow her. "I've got to go now," she told him. "I'll see you tomorrow."

She cried all the way to the parking lot. While searching for where she parked the car, she remembered she arrived by taxi. She took a cab to National, the nearest car-rental agency, and rented a compact.

The young man behind the counter said, "If you take it for a week, we can give you a really good rate."

"No, thanks," she replied as she pulled out her father's debit card. "I'll be heading home on Tuesday." Even as she said it, she realized that she would have to get her car out of impound and get the windshield fixed before she could leave.

Before heading back to her father's place, Addy stopped at North Hill Centre and bought a thank-you card from the Hallmark store. Then she picked up a huge bouquet form Itinerante Flowers. She wrote in the card while sitting in the parking lot.

'Dear Kruger's Schnitzel Haus staff,

You saved my father's life when you phoned 911 when he had a heart attack. What you did means the world to me and all Hans Ulfert's children. God bless you. With deepest thanks, Adelheid Penner.'

Back at the house, Adelheid put the chafing pans and other Schnitzel Haus dishes into the delivery box and loaded it into the trunk of the rental car. They almost filled the Kia's tiny trunk. She arrived at the restaurant just after 4:30 and counted two cars in the parking lot. *I'm too early for the supper crowd*, Addy thought as she parked close to the entrance.

She walked in carrying the bouquet of flowers and a portly, middle-aged woman turned from the patron she visited with and hurried to the door to greet her. The woman wore the traditional Bavarian-style clothing with a white, lacy, short-sleeved trachtenbluse, and a long grey dress with a red pinafore over it.

"*Blumen für mich?*" she asked.

"*Ja, für Sie,*" Addy replied in German. Then in English, she said, "My name is Adelheid Penner, the daughter of Hans Ulfert. Someone here saved my father's life when they phoned 911. I'd like to say thanks."

"Hans Ulfert's daughter! You are nothing like him!" the woman exclaimed. "Let me get Deitfried, my husband. He is in the back getting ready for the supper crowd."

As Addy waited, she looked around. The restaurant looked quaint with red and white chequered tablecloths covering picnic tables. Fancy German beer steins lined wooden shelves on the walls and pendant-style banners for various beers hung from ropes that went from one dark-wood rafter to the next. She could imagine this pace pack and rowdy during Oktoberfest.

Deitfried came out from the back, still wearing his apron and chef's hat. "So you are Hans Ulfert's daughter. You look just like your mother. Beautiful! And I heard that you brought us flowers."

"And I brought back your chafing pans and delivery box from Dad's house. They are in the trunk of my car. I wanted to stop by and tell you in person that I really appreciate your kindness to my father. I know that he could be difficult."

When she said this, Herr and Frau Kruger looked at each other and they both said, "Ja."

Mrs. Kruger asked, "How is he doing? We have not heard a thing."

"Not well, I'm afraid. He survived the heart attack, but then suffered a stroke and a brain aneurysm. The doctor says that he will likely live for many years, but will never be the same."

"We are so sorry to hear that, *meine lieben*. Tell him that we wish him well."

"I will," she replied, but she doubted if her father would understand.

"Have you eaten?" Deitfried asked.

"Not a thing since breakfast."

"Then you will eat here. It is on the Haus," said Deitfried and laughed. "Order anything you like. I heard that the schnitzel is very good." And he whispered, "The boss pays me to say that," as he pointed to his wife. "Maria will keep you company until it gets busy. You have been through a lot and you shouldn't be alone."

Addy found it interesting that these strangers cared about her. The owner's wife prattled away in German and Addy worked hard at trying to catch all the words and meanings. She really hadn't used German since the early days with Jack's family. Even Jack's parents' church switched to English only.

After she finished eating, the owner's son came out to the rental car with her to get in the delivery box with the pans and dishes. He looked a little afraid of her so she said in a soft voice, "Your mom told me that you delivered food to my father almost every day. Thank you." Addy guessed he still wore a smile as he carried the box into the restaurant's back door.

When she arrived back at her father's house, Addy half-ways expected to see Rudy's truck in the driveway. Or the front door smashed in. She felt pleasantly surprised to find everything as she left it. She parked the red Kia in front of the door and got out. She looked up at the gargoyles at the top of the wall and announced to the house, "Here I am again. I will unlock your secrets and then I will never come back."

The kids were in bed and Jack sat in the front room of their bi-level house watching a Saturday-night Western on TV. Addy hated cowboy movies, so watching one was a rare occasion. Addy did not grow up on the farm or even in a small town where she would have friends who lived on farms. Everything about cowboy movies seemed foreign to her.

Jack remembered the first time she set foot on a farm. It was almost Christmas and the University of Alberta would close for three weeks. He asked Addy if she was going home to Calgary for Christmas, and she wasn't. She looked so lonely and sad when she answered, that before he knew it, he asked her to come spend Christmas with his family on the farm.

Jack laughed at the memory. *If you don't think that took a lot of explaining to my mother*, he thought.

"No, she is not my girlfriend," he assured her. "She is just someone with no place to go. Besides, she is very poor, and she won't get Christmas dinner if she stays in Edmonton."

It really hadn't been a hard sell. Jack's parents were kind and generous and often brought home strangers to stay with them. However, Jack needed his mother to phone Addy and invite her. Jack thought that this silly as he already told Addy that his mother said yes to her staying with them.

Addy insisted, "Have your mother phone me."

"I like her," Jack's mom said to him even before she called Addy. "You have to respect a girl that won't head off for three weeks with a guy from school without knowing where she was going and what the sleeping arrangements are."

On the drive out to the farm, Jack warned Addy, "Perhaps you could avoid telling them that you are a nude model. They might not understand."

"Might not understand what? They don't know what nude means?" she asked with a bit of an edge to her voice.

"They might not understand how you can let people see you naked, and yet not live an immoral lifestyle."

"So you are asking me to lie to your parents? And I take it that you haven't told them you draw nudes? That you like seeing me naked? Maybe you haven't told them because they'll think you are living an immoral lifestyle?"

"You are right," he replied, properly put in his place. "Just be yourself. I like you just the way you are and I'm sure my parents will too."

On Friday evening just after 5:30, they turned off the snow-covered range road and onto the half kilometre long, tree-lined driveway. The sunset an hour earlier so the blue Christmas lights Jack's father used to decorate the barn, house, and on two of the spruce trees shone like beacons in the dark. Jack could tell his father recently ran the tractor with the plough blade down the driveway as the snowdrifts were cut off at the edge of the road.

They drove past corrals, the barn and farm machinery as Addy took it all in. Jack parked at the end of the path that, no doubt, his sisters shovelled through the snow-covered lawn. The snow in the yard glistened blue from the Christmas lights on the old bungalow-style farmhouse. Two black and white border collies ran barking around the car with their tails wagging.

Jack's mother stood in the open farm-house door smiling and waving as Adelheid got out of the car. Jack grabbed Addy's suitcase from the back seat, and Addy carried a gift bag in her left hand. Immediately the two collies competed for Addy's attention, each trying to walk beside her, and each trying to get their head under her free hand.

"Welcome here, Adelheid," Jack's mom said when they reached the door. "My name is Anna." And she gave Addy a hug. "My husband Reg is milking the cows and will be a little while. Come in. Come in!"

Over her blue floor-length, floral-patterned dress, Jack's mom wore a red apron with a cross-stitched Christmas tree. Grey streaked Anna's hair, and it was up in a bun. She stood five centimetres shorter than Addy and her round figure showed that she liked to eat.

"Thank you for your generosity, Mr. Penner. It is so wonderful to have a place to go for Christmas. And I brought you a gift." The gift bag contained a small dried-fruit and nut tray. It cost all of Addy's money, but she was not about to stay at someone's place without bringing a gift.

"You didn't have to bring a gift, but it is very kind of you," Anna said. "Thank you."

Various well-used work jackets hung on coat hooks that lined the pale-green entryway wall. Under the jackets sat an assortment of dirty gumboots and brown-stained leather work boots. The entryway smelled of manure and Addy tried not to wrinkle her nose. Grey-painted wooden stairs led to the dark basement and, close to the stairs, it smelled of onions, potatoes, and mildew.

Mrs. Penner stepped into the kitchen to give Jack and Adelheid more room.

Jack helped Addy with her coat and took her toque, too, to hang them on a hook. Jack's mother took one look at Addy and said to her, "Jack said that you were nice. He didn't tell me that you were beautiful."

"Maybe he doesn't think so," Addy answered matter-of-factly. Jack felt his face go red.

It looked like his mother was about to say something but, just then, Jack's teen-aged sisters squeezed in front of her. "I'm Rebekah," the older one said. "And this is my sister Ruth. Come with us and we'll show you where to put your things. You'll be staying in Jack's room. His room kind of became the spare room since Jack went away to school."

"Keep your shoes on," Ruth said looking at Addy's snow-covered running shoes. "I'll lend you a pair of slippers when we get to my room."

When Addy stepped into the kitchen, she exclaimed, "What an amazing kitchen! Look at all the counter space, and every bit covered with baking." It looked and smelled like a German bakery with rows of fresh-baked, double-decker buns called *zwiebach*, jam-filled Christmas cookies, and peppermint cookies called *pfeffernüsse*. Obviously, Jack's mother liked to cook.

Ruth grabbed Addy's suitcase and Addy looked back at Jack and smiled as she followed his sisters out of the kitchen. He never saw her again until supper an hour and a half later. Addy came to the table with his sisters and ended up sitting beside Jack because Ruth did not sit in her regular spot. Ruth winked at him.

Jack's father said, "Welcome, City Girl. My Name is Reg. It is a pleasure to have you in our home. Please consider this your home and us your family. And as the old adage goes, a family that prays together gets to eat, so let's say grace."

Everyone held hands and Jack reached over and held Addy's hand for the first time. Jack figured that, during the prayer, everyone at the table snuck a peek at Adelheid to see if she prayed. She did, and she said, "Amen," when the prayer was over.

Mealtime overflowed with laughter, the beef roast tasted amazing and there were only a couple of awkward questions. Jack had warned them that Adelheid's home life was painful so as not to ask personal questions. So Jack's mom asked instead, "So how did you two meet? Are you in some of the same classes?"

"Apparently, Jack saw me in one of the drawing classes," Addy answered with a smile, and she glanced at Jack's face. "He ended up behind me in the cafeteria line-up and introduced himself. Since then, we eat lunch together practically every day."

"So you are an artist?" Rebekah asked. She just turned 19 and really enjoyed doing crafty things. She made the Christmas centre-piece on the table.

"Not really," Addy answered. "Jack is though. He possesses an amazing way of seeing past the surface."

Jack smiled, and said to himself, "One question sidestepped. Three weeks to go."

After supper, Addy helped with the dishes, even though Jack's mom said that she didn't need to. When the dishes were done, they all played a dice game with six dice where you try to roll ones or fives, or three of a kind, or a straight.

Addy laughed and smiled and seemed every bit a part of the family. She learnt the game's rules quickly, how to steal points and when to fold.

After that, Jack's mom insisted on pulling out old photo albums and explaining one photo after another. Addy tried to keep all the aunts, uncles and friends straight, but after a half-hour, all the names blended together. She did enjoy seeing pictures of Jack as he grew up.

At bedtime, Addy said to Jack's parents, "It has been a long time since it felt like I had a family. Thank you." And she gave them each a hug and then headed to the bedroom. Jack wished that she'd hugged him.

"She is absolutely lovely," Jack's dad said when Addy was out of hearing range.

"And you tell me that she is just a girl from the school?" Jack's mom asked. "And you are not going out with her? What on earth is the matter with you, Jack? Get a move on."

Remembering his mother's words made Jack laugh out loud. How quickly things changed! He'd slept on the couch about an hour when Addy came running into the living room, flipped the goose-down comforter back, and jumped on top of him. She flipped the blanket back over them and lay in his arms shaking.

She quit shaking after a minute and soon fell fast asleep. Jack laid awake most of the night and only started sleeping soundly after 3:30.

He awoke when his mother flipped on the light at 5:35. His mother got up to make coffee for Reg before he headed out to milk the cows. To this day, her expression was burnt into Jack's memory. Her mouth hung open and her eyes looked as big as saucers.

"We are going together now," Jack whispered.

"Is she, umm… does she have…"

Jack whispered, "Pyjamas."

"You didn't…"

Jack shook his head, "No."

"Good," his mother whispered. "Marriage first. Maybe you should get her back to her room before your sisters wake up."

Jack shook Adelheid gently and she opened her eyes. Then she smiled a smile he hoped to see every morning for the rest of his life. "Good morning," she said in her lovely, sexy voice. "I think that was the best sleep I've ever had."

Jack wanted to say, "You are welcome anytime." Instead, he said, "I'm getting up now to help my dad milk the cows."

Jack's mother said from above them, "Perhaps you should go back to your room and get a few more hours of sleep."

Adelheid turned her head towards the voice and said in a cheery voice, "Oh, hello, Mrs. Penner. I've never seen anyone milk cows before. I think I'll get on some clothes and tag along." With that, Addy flipped back the cover, crawled off Jack, stood and stretched and walked towards the bedroom.

Jack's mother's mouth hung open. Again.

After all these years, Jack still chuckled at the memory. "Apparently, my mother's understanding of pyjamas is something flannel that covers you from your neck to your toes."

Addy wore a lacy, blue-silk, baby-doll set. The top had an open back, spaghetti straps, and the front had a cute little pink bow right between her wonderful breasts. When she lifted her arms to stretch, Jack was still lying down so had a very close-up view of the tiny matching panties.

Jack watched Addy walk out of the living room as his father walked in, her long sandy-blond hair falling to the middle of her bare back. "Good morning, Mr. Penner." Addy greeted him cheerily. "I'm going out to the barn to watch you milk cows."

Reg's expression matched that of Jack's mother's.

Jack thought at the time, *If there is one thing you can say about Addy, she isn't shy. When you are a nude model, wandering around in nothing but a little silk probably seems overdressed.*

Undoubtedly, Jack's mother thought the Devil himself walked out of the living room disguised as a very shapely and nearly naked 20-year-old woman. When his mother could speak, she said to Jack's dad, "They are going together now. We'll need to change the sleeping arrangements."

For the next three weeks, Addy slept in the room with Rebekah. And Jack moved into his old room.

That first morning on the farm, they trudged out to the barn through the falling snow. Addy wore Rebekah's gumboots and one of Jack's mother's old farm coats. She reached out a gloved hand to Jack, and they held hands until they reached the barn. Both collies tried to get between them so they ended up walking very close together.

When Jack's dad opened the barn door, steam rolled out and up into the dark sky, turning instantly to frost. Steam rose from manure piles on the barn floor. Jack closed the barn door behind them. Even though the barn wasn't heated, it seemed amazingly warm compared to outside.

Jack's dad owned two milk cows. Holsteins. Jack put some hay in the trough and closed the head-lock bar on each cow so they wouldn't back out of the stall during milking. Both Jack and Reg sat on milking stools and started a rhythm with the milk almost as if they were playing a duet.

Addy laughed hysterically as Jack shot milk from a cow's teat at the grey and orange kittens. Milk dripped from the kittens' faces and they seemed to take turns falling over as they tried to stand on their hind legs to catch the stream of milk with their tiny pink tongues. Addy tried to pick a kitten up, but it hissed at her.

"They are barn cats," Reg told her. "They aren't tame. We don't want them as pets. We need them to keep the mice population down."

Jack saw Addy's terrified eyes dart all around. "Don't worry," he comforted her, "Their mother is a very good mouser."

"Look. There is a mouse now!" Reg exclaimed as he pointed behind Addy at the straw-covered floor. Addy screamed and ran to Jack.

Reg laughed and Jack tried not to laugh. "That wasn't funny," Adelheid said indignantly.

"Sorry," Reg said, "But city girls always react the same way."

"They always run to Jack?" she asked.

"Well, you are the first one I've seen do that," Reg said. Trying to change the subject, he said, "I bet you've never milked a cow. Now is your chance. Have Jack show you how it is done." Reg suspected that she would say no. City girls always said no.

"Sounds like it could be fun. But I want you to teach me, Mr. Penner. You are much better at it than Jack." She noticed that Jack seemed a little insulted. *Good*, she thought.

"Okay," Reg said. "You will learn from the expert. I'll show you and then you try it." Addy came behind him and watched carefully. "You grab the teat fairly high up like this," Reg said. "Squeeze your thumb and pointer finger together and pull down as you tighten all your fingers. First, your right hand and then your left. Like this." Streams of milk shot alternately into the stainless-steel bucket. "Now you try."

Addy sat on the little wooden stool with her face almost against the body of the cow. She felt her face wrinkle at the smell. She reached underneath and grabbed a teat in each hand. They felt rough and that surprised her. She squeezed and pulled down. No milk came out and the cow let out a low *"moo"* and turned its head to look at her.

"You need to grab a little higher," Reg instructed.

She tried again and got two good streams of milk. After a few more tries she got a good stream with each hand. Then the milk stopped. "Uh-oh," she said. "Something is wrong. Can you take a look?"

Reg got down on his knees and leant in for a good look. Addy gave him two streams of milk right in the face. Reg scrambled backwards. Jack laughed so hard that he fell off his milk stool and Addy shot a stream of milk at his face too. Everyone laughed so loud that the dogs started to bark. Jack's mom looked out the window to see what caused the commotion.

Both Reg and Jack grinned as they came back into the house with the milk. Jack's mom scowled at Reg.

Down in the basement, Addy turned the crank on the milk separator until it sounded like a jet engine about to take off. Then Jack poured the milk from the milk pails into the stainless-steel bowl at the top of the machine. In a moment, milk poured out of the lower stainless-steel spout into a pitcher. A moment after that, thick cream poured out of the upper spout into a quart sealer.

Every day of the Christmas break, Addy learnt new things about farm life.

Maybe the conversations in German with her father and then the Schnitzel Haus staff started it, or perhaps because Addy missed Jack like crazy, but she remembered the first time she met Jack's parents. "I've got to tell you, Mom," she said out loud, "Jack's dad called me City Girl the first time we met, and still does to this day. 'Hello, City Girl,' he says smiling, and then gives me a hug.

"That is not to say that he didn't laugh at me. I earned the city-girl handle with my total ignorance of farm life. He laughed at the way I wrinkled my nose the first time I stepped into the cow barn. He laughed when I asked how he got the milk out of the cows. He held his sides with laughter when he opened the door to the other side of the barn and the great big turkey came strutting towards us, and I turned and ran.

"As we ate it the next day for Christmas dinner, he was still laughing. 'Make sure you stab it with your knife, City Girl. It might be dangerous.' And I didn't mind because I knew he loved me. In a lot of ways, Jack's dad is a lot like you, Mom. Full of love, and freely giving it to everyone around.

"Jack's mom is more like Dad. You have to earn every ounce of love and respect, and you can lose it all in an instant. She always calls me Adelheid. Never Addy. Never my dear. And when she says my name, it feels like she is somehow measuring me to see if I am worthy. With Dad and Jack's mom, it is like always walking on eggshells.

"Did I tell you that I actually watched Jack chop the turkey's head off? As Jack swung the axe down on the turkey's neck he said, 'This is what happens to anyone who scares my Addy.' And then off went the head. Blood spattered everywhere on the snow. And the dogs fought over the head... my rude awakening to farm life.

"Before he killed the turkey, Jack set out a big propane torch under the cauldron of water. The heat and flames melted the snow for an arms span around the pot and, when I stood close, I didn't feel like I was freezing to death. Jack held the turkey by its legs, plunged it into a cauldron of boiling water and held it there for a minute. Then he pulled it out and started tearing out handfuls of feathers and stuffing them in an old gunnysack. I think my hair smelled of wet feathers for a week. His did.

"I helped too. Jack said he felt proud of me for reaching into the body cavity and yanking out the guts. Believe me when I tell you that it was the grossest thing I've ever done. He kept saying, 'You don't have to help. You don't have to watch. You can go into the house if you want.' He didn't get it that I wanted to be with him.

"Besides, if I went into the house, I'd have to spend time with Jack's mom. Don't get me wrong, she is a nice person. She is just very caught up in rules and regulations. The first Saturday I spent on the farm, she seemed to make an effort to keep Jack and me apart. In hindsight, I suppose finding me sleeping on his shoulder that morning might have had something to do with it.

"We ate roast ham and sweet potatoes that Saturday evening for supper. When we finished eating and the dishes washed, Reg read the Christmas story, and we opened stockings. Yes, they had one for me, too. It contained all kinds of practical things like travel-size bottles of shampoo, some hair clips, candy canes and some socks.

"It reminded me of home. It reminded me of you. And tears trickled down my cheeks. Jack noticed and everyone else pretended not to notice. After that, Reg harnessed the horse to the sleigh and we went for a moonlight ride to the neighbours' farm and back. It would have been very romantic except Jack rode with his youngest sister and his oldest sister rode with me."

Jack still thought about Addy's first Christmas on the farm when the cowboy movie ended.

His parent's old farmhouse had one bathroom. In an emergency, one could use the outhouse behind the black-poplar windbreak. It was Sunday morning and Christmas Day and each of the women took extra-long to get ready so Jack trudged out to the frozen shitter through knee-deep snowdrifts.

Jack's mom told everyone the night before, "We'll all be trying to get ready for church so just come grab some breakfast when you get a chance." She set out a tray of cinnamon buns and coffee.

Jack told his dad, "I'll do the milking tomorrow so you can sleep in."

Reg answered, "I never sleep past 6:00 and the cows would miss me on Christmas morning. They'd probably give sour milk, but I will take you up on your offer to help."

Jack knew his father wanted some private conversation so, the next morning, Jack got up before 5:30. It is not like his dad needed the help because they only milked for their own family's use, but Jack appreciated the father-son time.

To the regular rhythm of milk going into stainless-steel pails on Christmas morning, Jack's dad said to him, "Your mother is concerned. She thinks you are taking things too fast. Friday, when you arrived, you and City Girl weren't even going together, and then you spend Friday night together under the covers."

"She was afraid," Jack replied. "She's never been on a farm and never heard coyotes."

"And Adelheid was too afraid to get dressed before she ran to you? Don't take this wrong, but your mother wonders what kind of morals she has."

"Don't worry, Dad. She is a good person. Addy just doesn't know how our family operates."

"I'm sure your mother will enlighten her," Reg said as a warning.

Jack took his second helping of cinnamon buns at 8:30 and still had not seen Addy. He heard her though, and his sisters, laughing themselves silly. At ten minutes after nine and just a few minutes before they needed to be on the way if they were going to get into the church before the service started, Addy and Jack's sisters came out of Rebekah's bedroom.

Addy wore a beautiful high-collar, knee-length, black and white Anne Klein zebra-print dress. She wore her hair in a crown-braid, and she really did look like a princess. Jack beamed and Addy blushed.

"Look, Mom," Ruth exclaimed as she spun around to show off the braids in her hair. "Don't I look beautiful? This is a four-strand braid."

Rebekah looked particularly pleased with herself and said, "Mom, Addy French braided my hair and tucked the tails up into a bun. She is going to teach us a new braid every day she is here."

"And she is showing us how to do our makeup," Ruth said.

Jack's mom said, "Your hair is beautiful," And she smiled. Inside, she complained, "I hope Adelheid is not here long enough to teach you any more city ways."

Jack's dad gave the compliment the girls hoped for, "You don't look like farm girls. Adelheid brought out the princesses you really are." His daughters beamed. "And that is a lovely dress, City Girl."

A flash of sadness crossed Addy's face and she answered, "Thank you. It was a gift from my mother a couple of years ago. Fortunately, I can still fit into it."

Jack suggested, "I'll drive my car so we don't have to crowd into one car."

"We will ride together. It is Christmas after all," Jack's mom insisted.

Then Jack's mom ensured that Addy sat in the front seat of the Impala. "You don't cram your guest into the back seat," she told everyone. So Addy sat squished between Jack's rather portly mom and Jack's skinny dad. Rebekah started to say something and Jack put his hand on her knee. She bit her lip and never finished. Ruth looked at Jack and rolled her eyes.

The drive to the church in Bentley took just over 20 minutes and no one spoke as Jack's dad tuned the radio to the Back to the Bible broadcast. Jack thought, *There is nothing like hearing a sermon on the way to church. Then you can compare the current one to the one you just heard.*

Cars and trucks filled the parking lot so they ended up parking on the street. As Jack's dad turned off the engine, Jack's mother said to Adelheid, "I don't know if you've ever been to church before, but this is a Mennonite Conference Church. They will sing some Christmas carols in German. I can translate them for you if you like. And there will be two sermons. The English sermon will be downstairs. Reg and I will stay upstairs for the German sermon. Rebekah will keep you company downstairs."

"Okay," is all Addy replied. Jack noticed his mother didn't mention his name in the plans.

The church exterior looked like a typical A-frame church built in the 1960s with unpainted exterior cinderblock walls, narrow amber-coloured windows, and a steep roof without a steeple. Jack's mom walked between Jack and Addy on their way to the front steps. As Jack suspected, when they got inside, the main floor sanctuary was already filled. Winter coats crammed the metal coat rack in the foyer and winter boots and overshoes filled the boot racks.

Luckily for them, an usher opened the balcony just as they got in the door, so the family got front-row balcony seats on unpadded wooden pews. Jack's mother arranged the seating order; Jack, Reg, herself, Adelheid, Rebekah, and Ruth. Jack glanced at Addy. If she felt upset or uncomfortable, she did not show it.

Jack watched Addy hang her coat over the pew behind her, and then look around to take everything in. The church's cinderblock walls were painted sky blue, and the steep roof above them was varnished cedar planks. On the carpet-covered stage at the front stood a giant Christmas tree decorated with multi-

90

coloured lights and red and green Christmas balls the size of honeydew melons. Mounted on the wall behind the pulpit, Addy saw a plain wooden cross.

A very serious-looking middle-aged man wearing a dark suit and a small, black clerical tie got up from his chair on the platform, walked to the pulpit and asked the congregation to stand for the opening prayer. Jack's mother whispered to Adelheid, "Pastor Heidebrecht."

When the pastor said, "Amen," they sat down and stood again almost immediately when the enthusiastic young song leader walked to the pulpit and announced the first carol. People paged through their hymnbooks to find the hymn. Jack's mother noticed that Adelheid did not pick up a hymnbook, but it didn't really matter because the songbooks were in German.

The organ played the first note and the 150-member congregation began to sing *Silent Night*. And then everyone heard an angel sing. Adelheid's voice came out strong and clear and sounded more beautiful than anything Jack ever heard. She sang harmonies he never heard before. And she sang in the most precise German without a songbook in front of her:

Stille Nacht! Heil'ge Nacht!
Alles schläft; einsam wacht
Nur das traute hoch heilige Paar.
Holder Knab' im lockigen Haar,
Schlafe in himmlischer Ruh!

Rebekah told him afterwards, "Addy kept her eyes closed while she sang, which was probably why she didn't see almost everyone in the church turn around to see where the voice came from." Rebekah also said, "Mom's mouth hung open so far that I could see all the way to China."

The congregation sang all the verses of seven carols before the animated young song leader told the congregation to sit down. And Adelheid knew the words to every verse. The pastor came to the pulpit and welcomed all the visitors, "And especially the beautiful angel singing on high," referring to Addy.

After the Sunday-school kids went to the front and sang *Away in a Manger*, the pastor told the congregation they could go downstairs for the English service with the youth pastor or stay upstairs for the German service. Jack's mother told Addy to stay so Jack stayed. Jack's sisters went to English service.

Jack's mom made an excuse that she and Reg needed to check on something and they left. When they came back three minutes later, they sat on the other side of Addy. Jack slid over and sat a respectable Bible distance from her, but he slid his hand over and they interlocked pinkie fingers.

After the service, Reg and Anna were inundated with people wanting an introduction to their guest. Jack's mom proudly introduced Adelheid as Jack's girlfriend. People from the congregation told Mrs. Penner things like, "She is beautiful!" "Breathtaking!" "A wonderful Christian girl! You must be so happy!"

The pastor's wife said, "Tears ran down my face from the first hymn to the last as if God himself sang over us!"

Adelheid replied in perfect High German, "You are so kind, but I am embarrassed you heard me. I used to sing in the choir in my church in Calgary and it felt so wonderful to sing the praises of my Saviour on Christmas morning that I may have sung a wee bit loud."

"Nonsense!" Pastor Heidebrecht said. "God gave you that amazing voice." And turning to Jack, he said, "This young woman is a gift from God. If your mother has not already told you this, don't let her slip away."

Both Jack and Adelheid blushed.

On the drive home, Ruth sat squished in the front seat between her parents and she didn't mind. Jack could see her grinning at him in the rear-view mirror. Jack sat in the middle of the back seat and Addy held his hand.

On the morning of December 31st, Adelheid said to Rebekah as they got dressed, "Your mother is trying to fatten me up. I don't think five minutes goes by without her holding out food in front of me or asking if I want something. I feel obligated to take something."

Rebekah laughed. "It is the Mennonite way," she answered. "Food equates to friendship. You can't stop by a Mennonite home without someone offering you something to eat, and you never leave hungry. It's a tradition. Besides, my mother says you are too skinny."

Addy looked at her own waistline. She wore low-rider blue jeans and a pink tee shirt. "Does Jack think I'm too skinny?" she asked alarmed.

"No, silly! He is smitten with you. You could be a model. My mother just thinks everyone should look like her. Traditionally round." And Rebekah laughed.

"Then I won't offend her by saying no? In the whole last year, I've not eaten as many carbs as I have since I arrived."

"That is why you have an hour-glass figure. My mother would be pleased if you were as big around as Betsy."

"Who is Betsy? Was I introduced to her at church? There were so many introductions."

Rebekah laughed again. "Betsy is one of the milk cows."

"I don't know anything about farming or Mennonites," Addy admitted. "It is all very strange."

"They both grow on you," Rebekah said as she reached up over her left shoulder and used both hands to bend a pretend branch. She held it in place with her left hand and, with her right, she plucked an imaginary apple and then took a bite. "Umm, they are ripe. Want one?"

Addy held her sides laughing. "I never had a sister. Now I know what I've been missing."

Just then they heard a door open. "Finally," Rebekah exclaimed. "You're lucky. You've never had to wait for your sister to get out of the bathroom. You'd think Ruth was the one seeing her boyfriend at breakfast. You go next."

"Boyfriend," Addy said to herself as she crossed the hall to the bathroom, trying to get her head around the idea. Adelheid looked into the bathroom mirror and made a startling discovery. She looked happy. In spite of staying with strangers a Christmas, sharing a bed, and being on the farm with its pungent smells and strange sights, she felt happy. "I guess this is what a boyfriend does for me," she said out loud.

When Adelheid walked into the kitchen, she saw Jack sitting at the kitchen table, stirring fresh cream into his coffee. He looked up at her and smiled. She felt as giddy as a schoolgirl as she smiled back. She walked to him and she kissed him on the forehead.

Jack's mother cleared her throat with obvious disapproval. Ruth rolled her eyes. "Good morning," Jack said to Addy as he put an arm around her waist.

Adelheid turned to Jack's mother. "Good morning, Mrs. Penner. Is that fresh cinnamon buns I smell? You must have been up half the night."

"*Portzelky*," Anna answered.

Addy recognized the word as Low German and tried to translate. "Tumbling down? Rolling over?" she asked.

Mrs. Penner launched into an explanation that really did not answer her question, but Jack's father walked in and asked his wife, "*Neuhjayrskekse* for breakfast?"

"Oh, New Year's cookies," Addy exclaimed.

"They're not cookies," Ruth told her. "More like doughnuts. Blobs of dough deep-fried and rolled in icing sugar."

"They are high in calories and high in fat, City Girl," Reg told her. "Fortunately, the fritters contain raisins. That makes them breakfast food. Like the commercial, two scoops of raisins in every batch."

Rebekah came in. "New Year's cookies? Jack, you should take one to Betsy. She'd give you extra cream for a week."

Addy tried not to giggle as she sat down beside Jack, took his hand and gave it a squeeze. When everyone sat at the table, Jack said grace. Then Mrs. Penner put a huge bowl of hot, brown, sugar-coated, raisin fritters on the table. Everyone waited for Addy to help herself first. She took the smallest one she could find, and it looked the size of a large baked potato.

"Try it," Jack's mother coaxed as everyone else helped themselves. Addy didn't know if she should use her fingers like eating a doughnut or if she should use a fork and knife.

"Don't wait for me," she said to everyone. "I usually start with coffee before I eat anything solid." In actual fact, Addy could rarely afford the luxury of breakfast.

Rebekah scrambled to bring coffee and Addy saw that everyone ate portzelky with their fingers. She lifted the New Year's cookie off of her plate and took a small bite. It felt warm, tasted sweet, and definitely coated her throat with oil. She set it down and lifted her coffee mug for Rebekah to pour.

"Not your usual breakfast, City Girl?"

Addy took a sip of black coffee then answered, "No, Mr. Penner. This is a first for me, but it is good. It is just a little sweet for first thing in the morning."

"It is not our usual breakfast either," Rebekah chimed in. "Except at New Year's."

"Luckily for you, you're here today," Jack's father said.

"The meaning of the tradition," Anna explained, "is that your coming year will be sweet and fruitful."

Rebekah added, "And well rounded."

"We usually only have these one day a year, but it looks like you made lots, Anna," Reg commented.

His wife answered, "I thought it would be nice to share some of our traditions with Adelheid. No one will mind if we eat these for a few extra days."

Jack agreed. Rebekah mouthed, "Told you," to Addy.

Addy managed to eat about half of one in the time Jack ate four. Then she couldn't down another bite.

"You can save it for when you are hungry," Jack's mom said, referring to Addy's leftovers.

Rebekah pretended to take a portzelky out of the bowl and stick it on her hips.

Addy replied, "I can't remember when I've been surrounded by so much food."

After they cleared breakfast dishes from the table, Ruth announced they would play Dutch Blitz in the living room. She explained, "Dutch Blitz is a card game with 4 decks of 40 cards numbered 1 to 10. Each person gets their own shuffled deck. You count out three cards, flip them over and see if you can put the card down on the Blitz pile in the middle. The point of it is to be the first one to place all 40 cards down in ascending order. Then you say 'Blitz'. The quickest way to learn is to play a few rounds."

Addy said, "This is sort of like building a long straight in playing cards."

Rebekah replied, "Mennonites don't usually use playing cards because the cards are associated with gambling."

And Jack chimed in, "So we bet on Dutch Blitz instead."

"Not money, mind you," Ruth clarified. "Chores. Loser does the winner's chores. Those in the middle keep their own chores."

"I have laundry. Six loads," Rebekah stated.

"I have the chicken barn which includes water, feed, and egg collection," Ruth said.

"I told Dad I'd feed the pigs, grind some oats and milk the cows tomorrow morning."

"I have nothing to wager," Addy said concerned. "And I couldn't possibly do your chores if I lost."

"You are off the hook because you are new to the game," Jack stated. "Just don't be surprised if we get a little excited."

"And, perhaps, just a little competitive," Ruth added.

Jack tossed a birch log into the fireplace, while Rebekah and Ruth pushed the coffee table against the couch. On the coffee table sat the nut tray that Addy brought and several bowls of candy. Then they sat down on the 40-year-old and thin red-brown carpet. Jack shuffled four decks of cards and passed them out. Rebekah promptly scooped up Jack's deck, reshuffled and handed it back to him. He took her deck and reshuffled.

The second Jack said, "Go," they were counting offsets of three cards, flipping them over and hoping they could put down the exposed card on the Dutch pile in the centre. After a couple of minutes, they were building on several stacks. Addy said, "A little excited? You look like machines at an assembly factory rapidly going through parts."

Suddenly Ruth yelled, "Dutch," and everyone one stopped. "Jack, you only counted two cards."

Jack's face coloured. Rebekah turned to Addy, "We like having you around, Addy. With you here, our brother actually gets embarrassed when he cheats."

"It was a mistake," Jack explained. "I wasn't intentionally cheating." He was still apologising when Ruth said, "Go," and Jack's sister resumed busily counting off cards.

"Blitz," Ruth shouted as she put her last card down.

Rebekah exclaimed, "No! I still have eight cards in my hand."

"Jack, you put down a card after I said Blitz," Ruth accused.

He claimed, "It was almost down."

"Then you can almost take a penalty."

Jack shrugged, removed the card, and everyone counted what they had left in their hands. Addy had not even counted through her deck once. Each round got faster and louder. Then they became frantic as the possibility of doing extra chores or escaping from the chores became a reality.

Throughout the game, Reg sat in the armchair by the fire reading the Mennonite Herald while keeping an eye on the game. With the noise level rising, he stood and walked out, and shaking his head, he commented, "Noisier than calves at branding time."

Jack lost. Ruth won. That is how Jack and Addy ended up in the chicken coup together. Addy wore the red farm coat she adopted as hers and the mandatory rubber boots. Infrared heat lamps hung on cords from the ceiling above galvanized sheet-metal food and water trays. Addy wrinkled her nose at the musty smell of feathers, feed and feces. Jack pretended not to notice her expression as he explained how, during winter, the laying hens were confined to the coup, egg production drops, and there is a lot more work keeping the coup clean.

As Addy went nest-to-nest collecting eggs, she asked, "Jack, what are Mennonites? From what I can tell, they believe the same things as the Lutherans, yet there seems to be a lot of non-church traditions that are not German, like the New Year's cookies. I won't even say the word in Low German for fear my father will appear and wash my mouth out with soap."

"He would do that?" Jack asked. "Not the appear-out-of-no-where part, but the soap?"

"Without a doubt," she answered seriously. And then she laughed, not because she was joking, but because, somehow, her overbearing father seemed less intimidating when she stood close to Jack.

"The Mennonite beliefs are pretty much the same as that of the Lutheran Church. The movement started by Menno Simons, a radical Catholic priest, in 1536. He objected to the way the Catholic Church kept everything in Latin. Menno Simons believed that we are all responsible to God for our own spiritual walk and that our relationship with God shouldn't be doled out by the priests. He taught that being baptized at birth into the church is not the same thing as choosing to be baptized because you believe. The Mennonites got the name Anabaptist because they promoted second, adult baptisms."

"That doesn't explain my oily breakfast," Addy stated as she put another brown egg into her basket.

"The followers of Menno Simons were persecuted for their beliefs and moved country to country looking for religious freedom. And because they were persecuted, they often lived in the same neighbourhoods or towns with other persecuted people, mostly the Jews. So besides the people who joined them along the way from what are today Holland, Denmark, Germany, Poland and Russia, there was a great smattering of intermarriage with the Jews."

"My breakfast was Jewish?"

"Absolutely. So besides the religious teachings, the Mennonites developed a culture that includes food. And the common people's language, Low German."

Jack finished filling the water trays and started filling the food troughs. The brown-coloured chickens around his feet clucked happily. However, one hen still sat on a nest. "This hen won't move," Addy said. "I'm not able to check for eggs."

"Just reach under her," Jack instructed.

Addy reached for the nest and the chicken pecked her on the back of the hand. "Ow!" she cried as she yanked her had back to safety. Blood filled the peck mark on the back of her hand.

Jack ran over to her, took her hand and kissed it. Then she leant into him, and he wrapped his big arms around her. They had just locked lips when they heard someone clear their throat.

"Mom says she needs the eggs right away," Ruth said smiling. "I can bring them in if you'd like."

Jack and Addy ended their embrace and Jack answered his sister, "One more chicken to go." Then he said, "Now watch this, Addy." Jack closed his right fist then extended his index and pinkie finger. He held his fist in front of the chicken's beak and rotated his hand back and forth. In less than five seconds, the chicken's eyes closed. "That is how you hypnotise a chicken." He picked up the sleeping bird and Addy picked up the egg.

"My hero, the hypnotist," Addy said then she kissed him. "Just don't ever try hypnotising me," she said sternly. Ruth burst into laughter.

After supper that night, Jack, Addy, Ruth and Rebekah went into Bentley for the New Year's Eve church youth service. Addy planned to put on the same dress she wore to church, the only dress she brought, but Ruth told her, "Wear jeans. And no nylons."

They arrived at the Wiebe's house, and she realized right away Ruth gave her good advice. All told, a dozen-and-a-half church youth attended the meeting, their age ranging from 13 to 25 and everyone wore jeans. Jack did introductions. There were Thiesen's and Klausen's, Neufeld's and Dyck's, Reimer's and Wiebe's, and Penner's.

Mrs. Wiebe seemed thrilled to see her. "Adelheid, you must sing for us tonight," she exclaimed. "My daughter, Martha, can accompany you on the piano. She has her Grade four Toronto Conservatory." Mrs. Wiebe looked as thin as a rake and obviously did not believe in using hair colour to hide her grey hair. She looked older than her 42 years.

"I'm really not prepared to sing a solo, Mrs. Wiebe. Perhaps if Jack invites me back at Easter, I could sing then."

Mrs. Wiebe turned to Jack. "Well," she demanded. "Invite Adelheid for Easter."

"Mrs. Wiebe, as much as I'd love to have Addy back to the farm at Easter, I'll have to ask my mother's permission first."

Mrs. Wiebe picked up the phone, handed it to Jack, and demanded, "Ask."

The landline phone kept Jack tethered by the cord and surrounded by listening ears. He dialled, hoping his mother would not answer. His mother's voice said, "Happy New Year."

"Mom, this is Jack. Mrs. Wiebe is standing beside me wondering if Adelheid will stay with us during Easter break. I told her that I'd have to ask you first before I invited Adelheid." As everyone stared, Jack listened to his mother and then replied. "Yes, Addy is standing beside me along with half the youth group." Jack listened for a moment and replied, "Yes, I will." Jack hung up.

"Well," Mrs. Wiebe demanded.

"Yes, my mother agreed that I would have to ask her if Adelheid could come at Easter." Jack hid his smirk until he and Addy walked out of the kitchen and into the front room.

Four boys, barely into their teens, sat around a crokinole board on a card table, playing a tournament. On a different card table, Mrs. Wiebe set out a Clue game but, to this point, no one started a game. A pool table and a foosball table filled most of on room in the basement. Rebekah and Addy team up against Jack and Ruth in a foosball best out of three. Jack and Ruth hammered them in the first game, but then Addy got the hang of it and she and Rebekah won the next two, although only by one point. After that, everyone played against them and Addy and Rebekah won against three more pairs of challengers.

On the kitchen table, Mrs. Wiebe set out trays of cold cuts, Mennonite sausage, and cheese. The counter held pop of every variety. While the young people played games, Mrs. Wiebe dropped dough balls into the deep fryer turning out portzelky, but she made hers only the size of golf balls. Adelheid didn't take any. The youth grazed and played until 11:30. Then Peter Wiebe announced it was time for the devotional, and everyone gathered upstairs in the living room. Addy saw that the game tables were gone and the room was ringed in black folding chairs interspersed between the couch and the armchair.

Mr. Wiebe read the Bible passage where Jesus washed the feet of his disciples. Peter Wiebe then talked for a few minutes about how we as Christians can follow Jesus' example and be the servants of others. Mrs. Wiebe carried in a rubber tub of hot water and set it on the floor in front of Jack. Martha, her daughter, followed her into the room carrying a stack of folded towels.

Jack rose from his chair, then knelt down in front of Addy. He lifted her left foot and peeled off her sock. Then he peeled the sock off her right foot. He lifted both her feet with his right hand and slid the tub under her feet. Then, as gently as if washing a baby, he rubbed her feet with water. As he did, he said, "Adelheid Ulfert, Jesus washes you clean, and I am your servant. If ever you need anything, I'll be there to help you."

Tears rolled down Addy's cheeks as Jack dried Addy's feet with a towel. When Jack sat down, Addy got down on her knees in front of Rebekah and washed her feet. With tears still trickling down, she used similar words and said, "Rebekah Penner, Jesus washes you clean, and I am your servant. If ever you need something, I'll help you."

Addy thought about the meaning of the foot-washing ceremony as she sat with her father, holding his hand. At one point, he looked at her and smiled, and then he tried to say something. The sentence came out neither in English or German, but in brain-damaged speech. Tears trickled down Hans Ulfert's cheeks as he tried again to say what was on his heart.

He squeezed her hand tight and managed to say, "I." After a pause of about a minute, he said, "Just." Addy realized her father was trying to form a sentence so she waited. "Wanted," he said.

After two minutes of silence, Hans's eyelids started to close like he was falling asleep. Addy asked, "What did you want, Dad?"

Hans's eyelids opened up, although the right side still drooped. "To say."

"To say what, Dad?"

"That... I..."

At that point, a nurse came in to take his blood pressure. In the few moments it took, Hans Ulfert fell asleep.

Back at her father's house, Adelheid wandered room to room. She felt lonely and helpless, and she still had no idea of the task her father asked of her. Instead of feeling a day closer to going home, the power of attorney papers made her realize that she was tied to her father and this house for a long time.

Finally, she decided to go back into the studio and try to find something that helps. As she pushed the first number of the keypad, she heard footsteps running away from the other side of the door and across the studio. She jumped back like she had just grasped 220 volts of electricity. Her heart pounded frantically as she ran down the hall and into the office. She slammed the door closed and locked it.

When her heartbeat began to slow, she realized that she sat crouched down against the door, holding it closed. She turned around and saw the smiling face of her mother looking down on her.

"So tell me, Mom, how can someone get inside the studio when only I know the code? And how could someone be inside the house when the alarm was set while I was away, and the alarm is set now for all windows and exterior doors? You're right, Mom. My imagination is playing tricks on me." She said the words but did not feel any less afraid.

She phoned Jack while still crouched on the floor. He picked up on the first ring. "And how is my long-distance darling doing?" he asked as a greeting.

"There is something in this house!" she answered sounding terrified.

"Someone is in the house? Hide and call 911."

"No, something. Something lives in the dark. It lives in the studio. Something evil!"

"You are freaking me out. What are you talking about, Addy?"

"I thought I heard something in the studio yesterday but, when I looked around, I never saw a thing. The studio is pretty much a big empty room with some photosets. Nothing could hide in there. And this afternoon I felt afraid to go in, but I thought about you and I marched right in. There wasn't anything frightening. But now I know something is in there."

"What did you see, Addy?"

"Nothing. I didn't see anything. You're going to think I'm crazy, but something stood just on the other side of the door. When I started to punch in the door code, it ran. I could hear it run across the studio."

"A cat maybe?" Jack offered trying to sound logical.

"Much bigger than a cat! I could definitely hear the sound of feet, not the soft paws of a cat."

"Did you see anything under the door? Feet or shadows?"

"No, the room is pitch black."

"Maybe something crawled in through one of the windows. A raccoon perhaps?"

"Jack, there are no windows in that room."

"Perhaps it got in through an air duct or something. I'm coming down," he announced. "So don't go into the studio without me."

"I'm not going back in there alone," she replied. "Not ever!"

"I'll arrange a sitter and come down as soon as I can. In the meantime, why don't you take a hotel? Just text me where you are at."

"I feel better just knowing that you are coming here. Braver. I'll stay, but if I change my mind, I'll let you know."

In spite of her words about feeling braver, Addy stayed locked in the office and crouched on the floor for an hour before the need to pee forced her to give up her safe place. She took a letter opener from the desk and held it like a sword. "Thanks for keeping me company, Mom," she whispered before quietly unlocking the door and slowly turning the doorknob.

She peeked out into the deserted hallway. She tiptoed past the studio door and softly tried the doorknob just to make sure it was locked.

She tiptoed back past the office and through the dining-room door. In the kitchen Addy grabbed a Henkel's filleting knife from the knife block. She made her way through the great room, past the hallway and upstairs like a black-ops agent on a kill mission. At every corner, she prepared herself to fight to the death with a knife in one hand and a letter opener in the other.

In the bedroom, she checked the closet, ensuite and under the bed. Then Addy barricaded the door by pushing a chair up underneath the doorknob. She tied one side of her pantyhose in a knot around the doorknob and the other side to the leg of the dresser.

Even though she checked the entire room, Addy held the filleting knife in her hand as she used the toilet. No one or nothing would sneak up on her as she sat undefended then, with the bedroom light on, Addy crawled into bed fully dressed.

She pulled the covers up to her nose and stared at the space between the bottom of the door and the grey bedroom carpet. "I'll stay awake all night," she announced to herself with her right hand firmly gripping the filleting knife. "I'll stay awake until Jack gets here."

Two hours later, while half-ways awake and on the verge of dreams, a memory drifted through her head like a phantom. She remembered the night her father came home from his two-month trip to Cambodia and Vietnam. She was 11 then, almost 12, and getting taller. Her boobs started to appear. On that hot August evening, she chose her light cotton pyjamas, the green ones with black and grey kittens printed on them. In the morning, she woke feeling cold to discover that she lay there completely naked. She saw the blanket folded at the foot of her bed and her pyjamas on the floor. She found her panties on top of the dresser.

Addy awoke with a start, her hand still gripping the filleting knife. She found her phone half covered by her pillow and grabbed it to check the time. The time display read 5:30 and a text message from Jack read, 'I'm here.'

Addy tossed off the covers, yanked the chair from under the doorknob, and then struggled to undo the knot in the pantyhose. In frustration, she sliced the hose in half with the filleting knife. Then she ran down the stairs, unlocked the first door, ran across the entryway, and unlocked and pulled open the outside castle door.

Immediately, the house alarm rang. She put in the code and silenced it. A voice from the alarm box said, "The front-door alarm was just triggered. Please identify yourself."

"This is Adelheid Penner. Hans Ulfert is my father."

"Thank you, Mrs. Penner. Your name and passcode are on our list. Is everything OK?"

"Yes, I just opened the door without turning off the alarm."

"Have a good day then."

When she turned around Jack stood in front of her. She leapt into his arms and kissed him passionately.

"I love you too," he said when his lips were free. "But I wouldn't mind if you set the knife down. I'm a little afraid that the next hug may be my last."

"Sorry," she replied. "I didn't realize I still held a knife in my hand."

"That is what I was afraid of."

"How long have you been here?"

"About an hour. I watched the sun come up. When you didn't respond to my text, I guessed that you must be asleep."

"Speaking of sleep, let's go to bed," Addy said. "You look like you could use some rest."

Addy left the bedroom door open a crack and turned out the light. She put her head on Jack's shoulder and her leg across him, sighed, and fell asleep in seconds. Jack stayed awake a little while, staring at the mangled pantyhose tied to the doorknob and wondering what frightened Addy so much that she barricaded herself in this room. He could not imagine the level of terror to cause her to come to the front door with a knife in her hand.

At 9:30, they got up and showered together. Jack brought clothes for Addy and she felt thankful to have something else to wear.

Jack discovered that the fridge contained almost nothing except beer. He found a full case of Schwarz Bier in brown bottles with white plastic corks held down by stiff wire and seven bottles of Roggenbier with the traditional beer caps. In the side door, Jack found a jar of pickled pig's feet and half a jar of sauerkraut, some blood sausage, kefir, and a half-kilo of head cheese.

"German delicacies. Blech!" Jack said in disgust. "I guess I'm not German, but the beer might be nice."

Addy used the unopened container of kefir and some over-ripe bananas to make them smoothies for breakfast.

"Not my favourite flavour," Jack complained.

"I could whip together headcheese, sauerkraut and beer into a high-protein smoothie for you," Addy laughed. Jack made a face like he might barf.

After his second cup of coffee, Jack asked, "Are you ready to go find the raccoon now?"

"Yes. Absolutely," Addy replied confidently, but Jack could see in her eyes that she did not believe a raccoon roamed the studio.

Jack found a club-sized piece of lumber in the scrap bin in the side of the garage where his father-in-law built his photosets. "This should do," he said to Addy as he walked into the kitchen with it.

Jack walked through the short hallway and into the Great Room with the chunk of wood leaning on his shoulder like he regularly clubbed things to death. He carried himself with such confidence that Addy couldn't help but feel brave.

When they turned the corner into the long hallway, Jack asked, "Why does your dad have a picture of Black Beauty?" At the far end of the hallway, facing them, hung a picture of a beautiful black horse with a flowing main running through a green field.

"You're right, Jack! I noticed the horse picture looked out of place, but I never realized that it was a clue." As she ran to the picture, Jack noticed, as she passed the studio door, Addy pushed her body almost flat against the right-hand wall.

The horse photograph was the only animal picture in the hallway and the only photograph not in a solid gold frame. Addy lifted the oak-framed picture off the hook and looked at the back. She translated German as she read it, "Adelheid. This was obvious. To play the game, you will need to watch closely to know your next move. H. K. U."

"It is not a clue," Addy said sounding slightly disappointed. "Just a clue to help find the clues."

"Then let's go kill the raccoon so you can finish the sadistic task your father gave you."

As Addy punched the keypad, she hoped Jack would hear the footsteps so he would stop looking at her like she had lost her marbles. However, they heard only the beep of the keys and the snarl of the lock opening.

Jack opened the door and walked into the pitch-black darkness. *He is not afraid of anything*, Addy thought. The lights popped on and Addy saw Jack scanning every hiding spot, like a hawk looking for a mouse.

Addy stood in the doorway and watched as Jack went set to set searching for any spot where a creature could hide. He banged on some of the sets that contained hollow spaces and Addy cringed, but nothing scampered out. He tried lifting the grates on the heat vents and the furnace air-intake ducts, but they were all secure.

"There is nothing here," he said, stating the obvious. Addy felt relieved and disappointed as she walked into the studio. "This is quite the setup," Jack said to her as he sat down on a gold throne in front of red curtains. He held the wood chunk like a sceptre.

Addy shuttered as she recalled the photograph of her parents making love on that chair. "Get off there, Jack. You really don't want to sit there."

Jack did not understand the intensity of Addy's words, but he quickly got to his feet. "Something I don't understand?" he asked.

"Many things I don't understand," she answered. "And many things I wish I had never found out."

"If you won't let me be the king, then I'm back to hunting." Jack marched over to the change rooms and entered the first one with the club held high. Addy hurried back to the safety of the hall doorway. Her left hand rested on the gold doorknob and her right on the gold deadbolt.

"There is nothing in here," Jack called after a minute. Then he went into the next change room. Nothing. Then Jack rattled the doorknob of the other studio. He walked to the office door, tried the handle and then banged on the white-painted metal, exterior-type door to reassure Addy. "Locked. Nothing can go in or out."

Addy backed out of the studio doorway and into the hallway. She said, "Then it has to be in the print room and lab area then. Be careful, Jack!"

Jack opened the white door marked 'raum drucken' in gold letters. He stood in the doorway listening and watching for movement, ready to club anything trying to run by him. Then he flipped on the light. Addy could tell by the way that he lowered the club that he didn't see any wild animals.

Jack saw counters, cupboards, large-format photo-printing machines and a printing press in the big room. He stepped in and closed the door behind him and spent a minute searching without finding any animals. In the smaller attached rooms, there were cupboards with the developer and other chemicals, trays, photo lamps, paper and other equipment for printing pictures. But no creatures.

The spacious photo lab contained modern photo-printing machines as well as traditional darkroom equipment. It did not have any space where a creature could hide.

Addy bit her lip and nervously shifted her weight from one foot to another. Then the door opened and Jack came out of the print room. "Whatever you heard, it is not here now," Jack called to her.

When they left the studio, they heard the door lock behind them. Addy tried the door anyway. "Thank you," she said as she hugged Jack. "Thank you for driving half the night to get here. And thanks for not saying I imagined it. Something was in there. Now let's get the last of the clues figured out so that we can go home."

Addy went picture to picture in the hallway looking for clues. She struggled to lift a portrait off its hook and it surprised her how heavy the picture frame was. Jack lifted it and Addy checked to see if anything was written on the back. When Jack lifted down the last one, Addy said in frustration, "There is nothing here."

"So what games did you play with your dad?" Jack asked.

"Really only some clue games when I was young. I pretended I was Nancy Drew and Dad left clues for me to follow. Dad really only played games with Karl. They'd play chess for hours. When Dad noticed me watching, he would tell me that if I wanted to play chess, I needed to..."

Jack filled in the rest of the sentence. "Watch closely to know your next move."

Addy threw her arms around Jack kissed him then dragged him into the great room. Pointing at the portraits, she asked him, "What do you see, Jack?"

"Random portraits of famous people. Who would hang those in their front room?"

"Tell me what they are from left to right."

"There is a picture of the Pope, an Arab sheikh, Paul McCartney, an old lady and I think that guy is a dictator."

"Exactly! Pope John Paul the Second who was the Bishop of Ombi, King Abdullah of Saudi Arabia, Sir Paul McCartney, Queen Fabiola of Belgium, and Muammar Gaddafi, a thief and a dictator."

"It is a chess set!" Jack exclaimed. "King, queen, knight, bishop, rook, but they are not in the right order."

"Exactly! The code for one of the doors is 25341."

"I'll bring the club," Jack said.

Addy walked into the dark studio first and Jack followed her. The lights popped on before she took two steps, and both she and Jack scanned for anything scurrying to hide.

She punched the code into the office door. It beeped with each number but did not open. Then she tapped in the code for studio two. Nothing happened. She looked devastated.

"Try reversing the numbers," Jack suggested. When she did, the motor whirred and snarled and the door to studio two unlocked.

Jack went in first and flipped up the light switch. Their living room at home could fit into this room. A king-sized bed was the photo set and various photo backdrops could make it appear as different locations from around the world. This studio contained microphones on booms and movie cameras. VHS tapes, computer disks, and portable drives filled the shelves that lined one whole wall.

They found nothing hiding under the bed.

Addy told Jack, "This is the bed in porn photos I deleted off the computer in the photo lab."

Jack turned to Addy, "Your father shot porn?"

"Yesterday, I came across sexy photos of the rich and famous. Not just sexy, I mean pornographic. I deleted them off the computer in the photo lab, but I didn't find the backup hard drive so I knew there must be more. No doubt those two computers on the counter are filled with porn. Photos and videos."

Jack looked absolutely appalled.

"After what he tried to do to me, I'm shouldn't be surprised that he shot porn movies too," she said referring to the movie cameras on tripods.

Jack could see tears fill her eyes and he hugged her. "I'm sorry you had to see all this," he said. "After all these years, you've never told me what happened."

"My father made sure we sat in church every Sunday, all sitting together for the sermon... the perfect Christian family. He prided himself that we were an enlightened Christian family who could see photographs of nudes without being filled with lust. And then my father tried to have sex with me during a photo shoot when I was 16. He had a video camera running. He usually always did when we did a photoshoot. He told me it was so he could review the lighting and positions afterwards. I don't doubt the recording of that event is here in this library."

"I'm so sorry," Jack said as he hugged her. "A father should never be like that. And I don't want to know what is on all these."

"After he tried to molest me, I tried to stay home from church, but he wouldn't let me. So I joined the choir at church so I could sit with the choir instead of beside him. I tried to never be alone with my father and, the moment I could leave home, I did. I thought every guy was just like my dad until I met you."

Jack kissed her on the forehead and wiped a tear away from her cheek. "What are we going to do with all this?" he asked.

"We shouldn't just put it in garbage bags in case someone gets their hands on it."

"At work, when we destroy recordings, we get a shredder company to send a truck. I'll see if I can arrange it for tomorrow."

"Does that mean you are not going home today?" she asked, surprised.

"I'll tell my boss that it is a family emergency. Getting this vile stuff out of this house looks like an emergency to me."

Rudy left at 7:00 on Sunday morning. Raven breathed a sigh of relief as she heard the roar of his truck fade as he drove down the alley. Rudy woke at 5:00 and spent the hours since then cursing and crashing about. He didn't get it that she needed rest. Or he didn't care.

"I need sleep," she complained to the bedroom walls. "It's hard enough getting any rest with the baby kicking and turning, never mind when Rudy is tossing and turning all night long." They shared a king-sized bed, but Rudy was a king-sized man. At the best of times, she did not get a lot of room.

She didn't ask where he was going. She didn't dare, but she really didn't have to ask. He muttered over and over, "We will kill her when I'm back. Then the money will be ours. Adelheid won't get away with taking a single penny. She won't take my money."

He left without saying goodbye. He hadn't said, 'I love you' since the day that she told him she carried their child. And he didn't say it now when he left. The way she saw it, she became his maid. Not even a friend with benefits. Just a maid.

She slept until 9:00, ate scrambled eggs, and the caught the bus to Market Mall. In her purse, she carried a single plastic page with 30 silver dimes in protective cardboard display folders. At Bowness Coin and Antiques, she walked up to the counter and asked, "Do you buy coins? Old coins I mean."

The skinny, balding, grey-haired man flipped up a magnifying lens from in front of the right side of his glasses and stared at the young and very pregnant native girl. "It all depends. People come in here all the time with pennies from the 60s thinking that they have found the Holy Grail. It has to be rare for me to be interested in it," he said dismissively.

Raven stared at the series of magnifying lenses on swivels to the side of the man's glasses as she pulled the plastic page out of her purse. "What about these? They are a hundred years old."

The store owner's eyes grew big as she set the page down on the glass countertop. "Oh my, my!" he exclaimed. "I am defiantly interested in these." He pulled one of the lenses down, making his right eye look gigantic, and he slowly examined each coin front and back.

Raven grew impatient. She needed to pee. "How much?" she asked as she shuffled from foot to foot. "How much will you give me?"

"You didn't steal these, did you?" he asked. "Not that I am accusing you of anything. It's just that I don't see coins like this every day. An 1884 ten-cent piece in very fine condition is a treat to see."

"My father-in-law died," Raven answered. "He left my husband his coin collection. Rudy said that a collection doesn't do us any good when we don't have money for a crib or baby clothes. He wants me to sell off a few coins. So how much will you give me?"

"I'll give you $500," the store owner offered.

Raven picked up the sheet of dimes and said, "Thanks. I'm going to see what Calgary Coins will give me. If yours is the best offer, I'll be back."

The man almost flew over the counter as he lunged to get his fingers on the corner of the page. "Let me have another look," he said. "Perhaps I missed something the first time around."

After a moment, he said, "Ah, yes. I never noticed you also have a 1905 dime in very fine condition. And seeing that you are pregnant and don't have a crib, I'll be generous and give you $1,000 for the lot."

If it wasn't for her full bladder, Raven would have danced with joy. The offer was more money than she had ever seen.

"I'll need your name and contact information," the store owner said condescendingly. "It is the law."

"No problem," Raven answered. And she gave the man her name, address and cell phone number.

"You mentioned that you have some more coins that you might sell?"

Raven nodded.

"Then be sure to bring them here. I want your baby well taken care of."

Norman Paplinski smiled from ear to ear as Raven left the store. The 1884 dime was worth a thousand dollars just by itself. And he just got 30 sequential dimes all in very fine condition. Without a doubt, he just made at least $15,000 in profit. And he knew the girl would come back.

Raven stared longingly at the entrance to Sears. She desperately wanted to buy a crib and a highchair. Instead, she waddled into the Bank of Montreal in the mall and opened a bank account. Her first. And in her name, Raven Big Bear. When the teller asked if she wanted statement mailed to her, she answered, "No, I'll try that online banking."

In the three-car garage, Jack found a cart his father-in-law used to move set pieces to and from the studio. Jack loaded it up 17 times with DVDs, tapes and hard drives. Each time he pushed the cart out into the wide hallway, Addy followed him out and closed the main studio door behind them. Every time she checked to make sure it locked.

On one trip out, a disk fell onto the hallway floor and Addy said, "Jack, you dropped one." The picture on the disk showed a woman having sex with two men at once. Jack noticed that Addy would not touch it. She hadn't helped load the cart either. Jack picked it up and tossed it back on the pile.

"What are you smiling about?" she asked him.

"I was thinking about you," he answered. "You could have gone down this road, but you didn't. That makes me happy."

"There but by the grace of God. But I don't think that is why you smiled. Fess up."

"I was thinking about that first art class after you spent Christmas with me on the farm. You came out in the bathrobe and just stood there for about three minutes while everyone waited. Then you dropped the robe and you were wearing a tiny pink string bikini. Then you smiled at me."

"On New Year's Eve, when you knelt in front of me and told me you would always be there for me, I decided you were the only one I wanted to see me naked. And I made you wait until our wedding night."

"You looked sexy and beautiful in that skimpy bikini, but it ended your career as a nude model."

"It took three weeks before they found another woman who would model nude. And enrolment in the second semester drawing class plummeted. The professor told me that it was your fault," Addy said. "He said you ruined me."

"My fault? They hired a frumpy middle-aged model to replace you. Certainly not someone who inspires art. But business in the bookstore picked up after you started working there."

"I couldn't have made it through university on the money I made at the bookstore. Thank you, Jack, for being there for me. And your parents were so kind and generous when you told them of my financial need. And Ruth sold her 4-H calf and gave the money to me to help with tuition. And Rebekah supplied almost my entire wardrobe for the next couple of years. I often wept because my own family was nothing like yours. And I rejoiced because I got to know something so much better."

"You have no choice in the family you were born into. You chose not to be like your father."

Addy looked down at the cart and frowned. "I've seen more vile garbage in the last two days than anyone should see in a lifetime. Let's get this out of the house, and then we'll destroy the computers."

Before moving the porn, Jack backed Hans Ulfert's white BMW M5 out into the driveway. Now, where the car usually parked, a mountain of pornography spilt across the garage floor. Jack dumped the cart on top of the pile and a couple of disks slid down and skidded across the spotless flexstone floor. He kicked them against the pile. Partially built or partially demolished photosets, and various saws, jigs, and forms for fibreglass filled the other two parking spots.

"Shred-X arrives tomorrow morning," Jack said. "They do secure shredding and they'll have a truck equipped to shred even the external hard drives."

"I'll watch to make sure that they shred everything," Addy replied. "I don't want a single piece escaping." Jack agreed.

Hans Ulfert owned an impressive set of tools, each with its own spot in the garage. Jack selected a yellow-handled Dewalt cordless drill and a 13-millimetre drill bit, and he grabbed a set of mini screwdrivers. Back in studio zwei, he unplugged the computers and used the screwdrivers to take off the outside shells.

"The inside of a computer really doesn't look like much," Addy exclaimed amazed. "Just a lot of hollow space and a few wires."

Jack unclipped the hard drive and held the silver box towards Addy. "This is where the files are stored. I'll put a couple of holes through the hard drives and then add them to the shred pile. Just as a thought though, we could easily replace the hard drives with new ones and we'd have two dandy new computers at the fraction of the cost of buying one at the store."

"As much as we need a new computer, I don't want anything in our house that had anything to do with my father. And especially not anything to do with this mess."

Addy watched as Jack pulled safety glasses over his eyes, then drilled several holes through each hard drive. Silver coils of aluminium curled off the disks and fell onto the cart and a few fell to the marble floor. Then Jack pushed the cart across the studio as they hauled the computers out to the garage.

When they came back into studio two, Addy said, "I want the bed gone. We are going to have to sell this house eventually, so let's get rid of it now."

"I'll call a trash-removal service. What about the cameras? These two are professional-grade Canon HD FX300s. They are five grand a piece. And the one on the sliding stand is a Red Dragon cinema camera. It has to be at least 30 grand. I hate to destroy them."

Addy could tell that the filmmaker in Jack hoped she would tell him to take them home. She tried to picture one of these movie cameras in his hand without imagining what her father had done. "I can't picture my father ever using them again. I'm sure he would be okay with us donating them to a charity or a church."

"Let's do it," Jack answered, sounding slightly disappointed. "I'll make sure there are no disks in them and nothing on their internal memories."

Jack's stomach growled and Addy looked at her phone and said, "It's 1:30 already. Let's grab a bite to eat and then visit my father."

At Cattle Baron Alberta Steakhouse on Sun Valley Boulevard, Jack ordered a steak sandwich and fries, the lunch special. Addy ordered a steak salad with fresh tomatoes and feta cheese. Halfway through her salad and while her plate still held three slices of medium rare steak, she saw Jack smiling at her. "What?" she asked.

"It took until just a minute ago for the worry wrinkles to fade from your forehead and for your shoulders to start to relax. You do better when you are away from that house."

"There is something there, Jack. When I am alone, I feel like I'm not alone. It is as if a monster lives there."

"And you heard this monster run away from the studio door?"

"No, Jack. I heard a barefoot child run away from the studio door."

Cold shivers ran down Jack's spine as she said the words. He did not ask her if she was sure. He could tell from her face that she meant every word.

At the hospital, Addy introduced Jack to the staff at the nursing station. Then she asked, "How is my father doing today?"

"Much better than yesterday. He is stable and they are moving him out of ICU on Tuesday morning. He says a few words, but it sounds like German. Perhaps you can tell us if he is asking for something."

When Jack and Addy walked into the room, half of Hans Ulfert's face smiled. "Yacob," he said. "Adelheid." And he lifted his left arm.

"Father," Adelheid said as she took his hand. "You are looking better today than you did yesterday." Addy saw the puzzled look on his face and added, "You had a heart attack, and then a stroke, but you are getting better."

Addy glanced at Jack and saw his shocked expression. Her description of how bad her father looked did not adequately prepare him. The powerful and demanding Hans Karl Ulfert now looked like a half paralysed, brain-damaged wreck.

"We're taking care of things," Addy said.

"We cleaned out studio two," Jack added. Hans Ulfert turned his head away from them and stared at the wall.

Addy gently shook his hand and Hans turned his face towards her. "It is all right, Vater. We found the secret and destroyed it. We still love you. We forgive you. And God forgives you. There is no sin too big for him to forgive."

Hans pulled his hand away from Addy's and turned his face back to the wall. Try as she might, she could not coax him to look at her. Eventually, Jack and Addy carried on a conversation between them about the fun things they did with Riley and Cody, and the places they'd been on holidays. After 15 minutes, they left.

On Sunday morning, Angelika woke to the sounds of her parents making love in the next room. She crawled out of bed, put her ear against the furnace duct and listened. A breeze from the open window stirred the curtains above her and gave her goose bumps. She pulled the pink Hello Kitty blanket off her bed and pulled it up to the collar of her pink cotton pyjamas.

When the sex noises stopped, she heard bits and pieces of conversation as her parents whispered to each other. She could not piece together what they were talking about so she got up off the floor, took her blanket, and crept down the hall past the closed door of her parent's room to the living room.

Angelika turned on the television, punched the mute button, and scrolled the high-number channels until she came across a movie that showed a couple in bed. She sat on the floor at arm's length from the screen as she watched with the volume just above mute. Her white cat, Snowball, rubbed against her then crawled into her lap.

Three-quarters of an hour later, Angelika heard her brother's barefoot footsteps coming down the hall so she quickly changed the TV to channel 17, the cartoon station. As he came into the room, she thought his blue and white striped pyjama made him look like an escaped convict. She smiled at him. He gave a bleary-eyed wave.

When six-year-old Torsten sat down on the beige carpet beside her, she got up and went to the kitchen. She poured sugary cereal into two white Corelle bowls. They were only allowed to eat Cocoa Puffs on Sunday, and they were allowed to eat it in the living room as long as they ate it dry. Angelika carried the bowls in and handed one to her brother.

"Thanks for the breakfast," Torsten whispered as he fed a cereal ball to the cat. "Mom and Dad are still sleeping."

She wanted to say that they were awake and doing what adults do when the door is closed. Instead, she just said, "Yes." She picked up a piece of cereal and tossed it across the carpet. The cat went flying after it, batting it back and forth, and pouncing on it a few times before eating it.

The clock read 11:03 when Karl and Ursula came out of their bedroom. Angelica noticed that they were dressed only in bathrobes, and they acted clingily. Her dad hugged her mom. Her mom kissed his neck and smiled. Even while they waited for the coffee to brew, they smooched.

"What are you smiling at?" her dad asked her.

"You," she answered. She felt happy that they loved each other. She knew her parents would never get divorced.

The doorbell rang just after 1:00 and Karl went to the door, still unshaven and wearing nothing but his blue housecoat. A bearded, 20s-something man in a brown FedEx uniform shirt and shorts said, "Special delivery for Karl Ulfert."

"FedEx on Sunday?" Karl asked. "Don't you take weekends off?"

"Not when it is a high-priority package," the man answered. "Please sign here."

Karl took the signing machine and scribbled on the green, tiny screen with the plastic stick on a string. The result looked nothing like his signature. The Fed Ex man handed Karl a brown envelope from P. K. Parkman.

Ursula stood beside him as he tore the end of the envelope open. "Were you expecting something from your dad's lawyer?" she asked.

"Not really," he answered. "Maybe the lawyer needs me to take over managing the old man's money."

Karl read out loud the short note typed on the lawyer's stationery:

"Re: Medical Directive and Enduring Power of Attorney of Hans Karl Ulfert

As per the instructions of your father, Hans Karl Ulfert, I have sent you a copy of his medical directive and the enduring power of attorney. Both of these came into effect when two medical doctors licensed to practise in Alberta declared that, due to a severe medical incident, your father is no longer capable nor will ever become capable of managing his own affairs. If you have any questions concerning these enclosed directives, please give me a call. P. K. Parkman."

"Yes," Karl exclaimed. "Now I am in the driver's seat!" He set down the letter and scanned the next page.

Ursula watched his face go pale and then contort with rage. "What?" she asked. "What is it?"

"Adelheid!" he screamed. "She got the old man to give her power of attorney!"

"That is not possible. You are his favourite." Ursula said in disbelief. "Besides, your father wrote Adelheid out of everything. We can contest this. She can't have him change things when he is on his death bed."

"She didn't," Karl said and handed Ursula the page. It read:

I hereby state that I understand the full import of this declaration.

Enduring Power of Attorney

This is the enduring power of attorney of Hans Karl Ulfert of Calgary, Alberta, Canada.

Applicable Law

I make this enduring power of attorney according to the Powers of Attorney Act of Alberta.

Revocation of Previous Powers of Attorney

I revoke any powers of attorney that I have previously given. I appoint my daughter, Adelheid Elisa Penner of Edmonton, Alberta, Canada, as my true and lawful attorney.

If my daughter, Adelheid Elisa Penner, of Edmonton, Alberta, Canada, dies, or refuses, or is unable to act or continue to act, then I appoint my son Karl Hans Ulfert to act as my true and lawful attorney.

Powers to Endure

The powers I give my attorney in this enduring power of attorney are to continue and are not to be revoked notwithstanding any mental incapacity or infirmity on my part that occurs after the execution of the power of attorney.

I may revoke this power of attorney at any time, in writing, as long as I have the capacity to do so. Unless revoked by me during my lifetime, this enduring power of attorney terminates on my death.

Effective Date

This appointment enables my attorney to act on my behalf and will come into effect only if I become mentally incapable of making reasonable judgments about my property. A written declaration from two doctors authorized to practise medicine in Alberta is to be conclusive proof that I have become mentally incapable.

Powers

On this enduring power of attorney coming into effect, I give my attorney full powers to do anything on my behalf to hold my property and to invest and manage my property, whose full powers include,

a. To negotiate with, deposit or transfer to any bank, any money and other negotiable notes and to endorse them on my behalf; to sign any cheques, draft of payment of money.
b. To have access to a deposit and to remove any documents or article which may be in any safety deposit box
c. To deal with any money received as my Attorney sees fit.
d. To file my taxes
e. To manage my land and real estate
f. To demand and receive from anyone all debts, in any form, which are due to me
g. To examine and settle any account pending between me and any other person
h. Sign all documents with relation to my property
i. Do any other act in relation to my property and financial affairs

Declaration made this the 17th day of May 2012.
Signed: Hans Karl Ulfert
When Ursula got to the last line, she said to Karl, "This is dated 2012! That was years ago. Adelheid has always been the one your father chose."

"Damn her!" Karl swore.

Karl read the medical directive and then went to the fridge and took out a beer. He fumed for an hour and drank several more beers before he picked up the phone and called Adelheid's cell phone.

"Hey, Adelheid, this is Karl. How is our father doing?"

"I saw him an hour or so ago. He knew who I was, and that is an improvement. But he never said a word after he said my name. The time before that, he called me Wilhelmina. It is not very long after stroke and brain surgery. The doctor says miraculous things can happen. We can always hope and pray."

"I see that he put you in charge of his money. How much does he have in the bank?"

"I have absolutely no idea and I don't really care. He wrote me out of his will years ago."

"But you are in charge of it all. The first thing I'd do is see what there is."

"I'm not you, Karl. My only concern is taking care of Dad. I may have to pay a few bills along the way. As of Monday, I'll have to start looking for someone to take care of him fulltime, either in his home or in a facility."

"That will cost a fortune! Everyone will take advantage of him. They'll rip him off big time."

"He is a millionaire, Karl. Money is not a problem."

"Then you have seen his accounts!"

"No, I haven't. I just know he is rich."

"Tell me you are not going through with keeping him alive for as long as you can even if he is brain dead. And I heard that cryogenics cost $300,000 US and then there are yearly maintenance fees!"

"Karl, Dad is nowhere close to dead. He had a stroke and a brain aneurysm. He definitely suffered brain damage, but the doctor said, with care, he could easily live another 30 years."

"Oh my God! 30 years! Do you want to look after him for the next 30 years, Adelheid?"

"Not really. But I can see why he picked me to do this and not you, Karl."

Karl slammed the phone receiver down and swore a blue streak.

Addy felt relieved when he hung up. Everything he said was about preserving as much money for himself as possible. He didn't care about getting good care for their father and she noticed that Karl didn't ask how she was doing. Karl only cared about Karl.

Karl paced from the living room to the kitchen and back again. Then he called Rudolph.

Raven waited in the mall at the storefront of Bowness Coin and Antiques. She stood there since 9:27 and the store didn't open until 10:00.

"This is the downside of depending on the public transit," she said to her baby bump. "You have to live by its schedule."

Norman Paplinski tried to hide his excitement as he rolled back the security grate. "Good morning," he said and smiled. "Did you buy your crib and highchair yesterday?"

"No, not yet," Raven replied. "But I will tomorrow. My husband is on a business trip to BC and should be back soon. I came by bus, and we'll need my husband's truck to haul the baby stuff home."

"Well, what brings you here so early on a Monday morning? I hope you are not here to get your coins back. I've already promised them to somebody."

"I wondered what you'd give me for these?" she asked as she held out a page of century old, silver 50-cent pieces.

The store owner dropped a magnifying lens over one eye and examined the page. "Believe it or not," he said as he looked at her through the magnifier, "These aren't worth as much as the dimes because they are not as rare. I can give you $500. And that is generous."

Norman Paplinski lied through his teeth. The specimens in front of him were superb. Although the rarity and condition of a coin determine its value rather than the face amount, before this moment he had never even seen an1890 obverse-four 50-cent piece in extra fine condition. That coin was worth $10,000 at least. The page in his hand was easily worth $30,000.

Raven looked disappointed with the price he offered, and that was exactly what he wanted. He didn't want her thinking she had enough cash. Norman wanted her to come back with more coins.

"Five hundred dollars is not as much as I hoped," she admitted to him, "but it is $500 more than I have now."

"Perhaps if you could make a list of the coins you have for sale, I could tell you which ones to bring in next. Of course, I am interested in any old coins, and I guarantee that I will give you top dollar. You do realize, of course, that I have to sell the coins so I need to leave a little room to make a profit. Otherwise, I'd just be collecting coins and, as you said yesterday, you need money to live."

Raven took the five orangey-brown 100-dollar bills and put them in her purse. "I'll bring you a list," she said, but she doubted if she would. She could barely stand or walk, so the thought of writing out lists of coins seemed overwhelming. And then she remembered her phone.

"I have a few photos," she said. "Not close-ups of individual coins, but maybe you'll see something that you would want." And she opened her phone to the photo library and held the phone out to the store owner.

"Oh my God!" Norman said out loud as he looked at a picture of a huge pile of binders, display cases, and coin pages. The knee-deep mound on a basement floor looked like it was two metres across. His mouth hung open as he scrolled through the next couple of pictures.

"Rudy doesn't want to sell very much of it," Raven stated. "The coin collection is a memory of his father."

On Monday evening, the brothers met over beers at Hooters. Well, Karl drank beer. Rudy drank Coke and Ricky sipped orange juice the barmaid promised was organic. They had little in common and, truth be told, they despised each other. Yet the brothers came together from the far reaches of Canada to say things in person that they didn't dare say over the phone or by email. Together they laid out a plan to murder their sister.

They sat at a wooden table in the back corner and spoke in whispers. When anyone tried to sit down at the empty tables next to them, Rudy ran them off.

"We could poison her," Ricky said. "Send her a bottle of Vancouver Island wine. She'd love that. Only we take a syringe of poison and push it through the cork. She'd never know."

"You watch too many movies, Ricky. And you don't think. First, Addy would notice the hole. She's like Dad that way. She notices everything. Secondly, who knows if she would drink it? Or how much. Or who she would share it with. And of course, a bottle of poison wine would have our fingerprints all over it and a drink-up note that we all signed."

"I'll do it," Rudolph volunteered. "I'll beat her to death. I'll spatter her worthless brains against the walls. Then I'll take her purse and the police will think it was a robbery gone bad."

Ricky bolted from the table and didn't make it to the bathroom before he threw up. He apologized profusely to the staff. "This is a bar," the young man with the mop and bucket said. "People hurl all the time. Just try to make it to the bathroom next time."

Ricky hoped that there wouldn't be a next time. He did not want to throw up. And he didn't want to murder his sister. And he certainly did not want Rudy to do it. "Rudy is scarcely above an animal," he mumbled to himself as he splashed water on his face. "Maybe not even that."

As he checked his eyeliner, a tough-looking man with a wild Duck-Dynasty-type beard walked in to use the urinal. The guy looked like a real Hells Angels' type with prison-type tattoos down his arms. Ricky quickly decided he had himself together and walked towards the door.

"Hey, you," the biker guy called. When Ricky turned around, the guy stood facing him and holding his penis. "Men have these things," he sneered.

"Oh," Ricky replied. "I see you bought a strap on." Ricky chuckled as he walked back into the bar. He heard the footsteps closing in behind him just as he reached the table. He turned to see the biker guy's fist flying towards his face.

It landed with a smack against Rudy's hand. The biker looked up in shock at Rudy towering over him. "Unless you want me to break you in half, I'd suggest you get the hell out of here," Rudy hissed through gritted teeth. The guy turned and ran.

A bouncer came over and asked, "Is everything all right?"

Rudy looked down at the bouncer's terrified face and small frame and snorted. "What can you take care of?" Rudy derided him. "What the hell would you do if I got into a fight?" The bouncer quickly retreated to his post.

Rudy glared at Ricky. "I only did that 'cause Karl says we need you to make this work. That is the only reason!"

"As I started to say before Ricky got a sudden urge to purge," Karl said, "beating Adelheid to death is not a good idea. Tell me, Rudolph, how many times have you been arrested?"

Rudy looked down at his giant-sized hands and mumbled, "Don't know."

"So many times that you don't remember? Or you don't know if you want to tell us? So just tell us the number of times it involved assault? And don't include the sexual assaults in the number."

Rudy face turned purple and he pumped his fists faster and faster like he was winding up to explode. Ricky got to his feet and backed away. Karl didn't seem the least bit worried.

"Take it easy, Rudolph," Karl said consolingly. "I asked you those questions so you would see that the police would come straight to your door. You would be the number one suspect even if you had nothing to do with it. And the police would find evidence for sure. They always do. We can't kill her with violence."

Karl watched Rudolph's colour changing from purple back to red, and he knew that it would take a long time before the anger that coursed through

Rudolph's Neanderthal veins to subside. Karl tried to hide his smile as he thought, *It is only a matter of time before Rudolph self-destructs. The old man can't bail him out anymore and Adelheid certainly won't.*

"How then?" Ricky asked as he sat down again. "You didn't summon me here from 3,700 kilometres away to tell me it is impossible."

Karl reached into his pocket and put two brown, thumbnail size nuts on the table. Ricky glanced at them and back up to Karl. "What are these?"

"Hazelnuts!" Rudy exclaimed. And he laughed the chortle of someone who just figured out how to get away with murder.

"Yes, Rudolph. Hazelnuts," Karl said smiling. He did not smile like Jesus now. He smiled like the prince of darkness.

"I don't get it," Ricky confessed. "How do hazelnuts help us?"

"You were only five when it happened so you don't remember. Mom and Dad invited the Geistbrechts over for supper, and for dessert, Mom served ice cream with a tablespoon of Frangelico on top. That's hazelnut liqueur. Within minutes of when Adelheid finished dessert, her face puffed up like a balloon. They had to rush her to the hospital because the swelling in her throat cut off her airway."

Rudolph jumped in. "So we get her to eat hazelnuts and she is dead within minutes. And all from natural causes. No suspicion. No police investigation."

"But how do we get her to eat hazelnuts or drink Frangelico?" Ricky asked. "She won't do it voluntarily."

"That is why we need you, Baby Brother. Adelheid certainly would not eat or drink anything from Rudolph. And likely not from me. She trusts you, Heinrich. You make a trip to Calgary, feed her some hazelnut brownies or something, and the money is ours."

"Addy will call 911 as soon as she starts to react," Ricky argued. "I don't know if I'd have the heart to stop her."

"That is where Rudolph comes in. He'll be right outside the door. As soon as Adelheid eats some hazelnuts, you'll signal Rudolph. He'll keep her from calling 911, using an EpiPen or whatever one does for allergic reactions. Once she is dead, everyone leaves."

"So where are you when this goes down?" Rudolph demanded.

"Sitting in your truck on the old man's fancy driveway, drinking your Coke and watching for danger. We are going to do this together. And we will be each other's alibi if there are any questions. We will just be three brothers meeting together in Calgary to talk over our father's failing health."

Rudolf Ulrich Ulfert stared with hatred across the table at Ricky and pumped his massive hands into fists. Then he lifted his thigh-sized left arm and flexed the muscles into definition. "I bench press 225 kilograms and I can break you in half. If you chicken out, Ricky, I will kill you. And I won't do it fast. First, I'll tear off all your appendages and shove them up your ass. Then I'll…"

"Shut up, Rudolf!" Karl barked. "Heinrich will do his part. He wouldn't be here if he wasn't willing."

116

The scantily clad and very busty waitress came by and Karl ordered another beer. His third. "And bring one for my brother," he said, pointing to Rudy.

"No, I only drink Coke," Rudy hissed at Karl.

He barely got the words out when Karl said, "On second thought, bring a pint for each of us. We're brothers. Supposedly we all have the same mother and father. Do we look like brothers to you?"

The barmaid looked at each of them and answered, "You do all have the same nose. And your hair is the same sandy-blonde colour. I like the blonde streaks in yours," she said to Ricky. "Yes, I'd say you were brothers."

Karl smiled at her like she had just said something very wise and said, "Honey, bring me a shot of Frangelico too!" She smiled back and batted her eyelashes at him, then headed off to get their drinks.

"We need to do this now," Rudy said to his brothers. "Addy is alone in the old man's house."

Karl added, "She told me that she hopes to go back to Edmonton tomorrow. Heinrich, call her right away and say you are flying in tomorrow and hope to see her. She will stay for you."

The barmaid came back with three beers and a shooter, and her tee shirt pulled down to reveal even more of her cleavage.

Karl's eyes zeroed in on her bust and she wasn't in a hurry to leave the table. Rudy set his Coke glass down hard and Karl jumped and glanced at him, but then Karl immediately turned back to ogle the barmaid. She jiggled her boobs at him and then walked away.

Karl smiled like this was the best day of his life. He lifted his beer towards the Frangelico and proposed a toast, "To Adelheid, the best sister we ever had." He watched his brothers lift their pints of West Coast brew and click their glasses together as if sealing their oath.

"To Addy," Ricky said with tears in his eyes.

"May she burn in hell," Rudy chimed in.

Karl's smile reached his blue eyes as he swallowed the golden-coloured liquid. Ricky made a face like he just swallowed skunky-tasting horse piss, but he never set the beer stein down. And a look of determination settled across Rudy's face that made Karl wonder what scheme his giant brother pondered.

Ricky didn't like anything about Karl's plan. The way he saw it, his cell phone call would link him to his sister's death. If he used a payphone, Addy would wonder why he called from BC. And that is not to mention that he would be the one who actually murdered her.

Call it natural causes all you like, Ricky thought, *but Karl wants me to look Addy in the eye and then cause her death. And then there are the 'what ifs'. What if Addy won't eat what I offer? Would I let Rudy pour hazelnut extract it down her throat? Would I stand there while she pleads for me to call the ambulance?*

"It is too noisy in here," Ricky said to Karl. "I'll call Adelheid from outside."

Ricky stood up to leave and saw Karl nod for Rudolph to follow him. *So this is how it is*, Ricky thought. *The manipulator sends his pit bull to keep me in line. So I do the dirty work and I get framed for it. Or maybe both Rudy and I take the blame and Karl walks away with the entire fortune.*

Rudy towered over him in the parking lot like Hercules glaring down at a schoolboy. With shaking hands, Ricky took out his cell phone.

"Don't you warn her," Rudy threatened, "Or I will kill you first and then I'll kill her."

"I want the money as much as you do, Rudy. Do you really think Karl will keep his end of the bargain?"

"Call her now!" Rudy screamed. Several people looked their way and Rudy glared at Ricky like it was his fault.

Addy did not recognize the number, but the call display said, 'Ricky'. She answered on the third ring. "Hi, Ricky. How nice of you to call."

"Hey, Sis. I told my boss that my father had a heart attack and she gave me a few days off. There is a flight your way tomorrow morning. I'd love to see you."

"I was planning to go home tomorrow, but there is so much unfinished business that I'll have to stay at least one more day, so your timing is perfect. I'm staying at Dad's house. There is lots of room here so if you can manage it, I'd love it if you would stay here with me."

"It sounds a little frightening, but you and I under the same roof would be like the good old days. If only they were good."

"Give me a shout when you are in and I'll come to get you. Are you calling from your cell phone? You could text me when your plane touches down."

"I'll do that," Ricky said and hung up.

Rudolph escorted Ricky back into Hooters and to their table at the back. "We're on," Rudy said to Karl.

Ricky watched them smiling and acting like best buds. And both of them kept their eyes glued to the barmaid's bust, and they weren't staring at the image of the owl on her white shirt. This time the edge of one of her nipples showed.

"Excuse me," she said with mock modesty as she tucked it back in and wiggled her boobs at them. "For you boys, they just want to jump right out."

Tuesday morning started with a bang. Adelheid sat up in bed with fright and asked, "What was that?" Then she realized Jack wasn't beside her.

She tossed on her mother's plush white housecoat and hurried down the stairs. She didn't find Jack in the great room. She took the short hallway to the kitchen, but he wasn't there either. Addy went out the far side of the kitchen and dining room into the long hallway. Then she saw the studio door propped open with a chair, and the studio lights on.

When she peeked into the studio, she could see the open and badly dented metal office door and the shattered wooden doorframe. The handle of Rudy's sledgehammer leant against the doorframe. She walked tentatively to the office door and blamed the cold marble floor for the goosebumps that covered her body.

From the broken doorway, she could see Jack standing by the desk in an office the size of the living room in her house. He stood there only in his underwear. Chunks of the doorframe covered the floor. He gave her a weak smile.

The desk and chair were identical to the one in the front office, only this one held two computers. A chest-high shelf held another computer. Shelves of photography books and DVDs lined the walls. The back wall was a menagerie of backup hard drives arranged in bins alphabetically, all labelled with names and dates. Film editing equipment covered the huge worktable in the centre of the room.

"It is 5:00 in the morning!" Addy exclaimed. "What on earth are you doing, Jack?"

"I found the door code," he replied, pointing at Rudy's sledgehammer near her feet amid splinters of wood. "You don't want to see what's in here."

"Show me," she ordered in a voice that did not sound excited. She walked hesitantly into the room, trying to avoid putting her foot down on debris.

Jack picked up a DVD off the shelf and showed Addy the cover picture. It showed Addy's father having sex with a young woman who might have been 20. Addy grasped the top of her housecoat with her right hand and pulled it together near her throat.

"I guess your father was not content just filming porn," Jack commented. "He wanted to star in it."

"After what he tried to do to me, I never believed that my father remained faithful to my mother. Yet it still shocks me to see all this," she said as she looked at shelves full of DVDs. "But, Jack, this really could have waited until after breakfast."

"I heard something," Jack answered.

"Jack, you are often a man of few words, but your explanation is nowhere close to a complete and logical explanation. What do you mean you heard something?"

"I woke up because it felt like someone stood in the doorway of the bedroom. Of course, I did not see anyone. I just convinced myself I must have dreamt it, and I closed my eyes. Then I heard the hardwood creak. So I got up quietly and snuck to the doorway. I did not see anyone in the hall or on the stairs so I checked out the library and games rooms, and the other bedrooms."

Addy listened, wide-eyed. She nervously glanced over her shoulder into the studio and then moved closer to Jack.

"I crept downstairs and went room to room as quiet as a mouse," he said. "I expected to find someone around every corner but didn't see anyone. As I walked down the long hall, I decided I wouldn't bother looking in the studio because the door automatically locks. And then I wondered if it really was locked. So I tried turning the knob."

"And it was unlocked!" Addy exclaimed, alarmed.

"No. It was locked. But when I tried the knob, I heard something run away from the other side of the door."

"You heard it too! I'm not crazy. Something stood on the other side of the door and ran when you tried to open the door. Now you tell me if it sounded like a raccoon."

"It sounded like a barefoot child. It sounded like Riley when she runs," Jack said. "So I quickly unlocked the studio door and ran set to set to see where it hid. I found nothing. And then I wondered what hid behind the office door, so I used the sledgehammer door opener."

"And I can guess the rest of the story. There are no barefoot children hiding here. Just a lot of porn. Horrible, ugly, degrading trash. How come my father had to be like that? How come he expected me to clean up his mess?"

"I'll get the shred truck to come back today. We are almost done."

"I'm Adelheid Penner," she said as an introduction to the two ward staff members at the desk. "I'm Hans Ulfert's daughter. I heard that you transferred my father from 6D to this ward this morning. What room is he in?"

"Hello, Mrs. Penner. We heard from intensive care that you would come by today. Your father is in 6110. That is on the left."

"Thanks," she replied, and she walked down the hall in her black Lulu Lemon jogging pants, yellow body-hugging tee shirt, and strappy yellow leather sandals.

Hans Ulfert half sat and half reclined on the hospital bed. His left eye looked like a slit while the right eyelid drooped and leaked.

"I'm here at last," she said as she walked in.

"Adelheid," Hans said and held up his left arm towards her.

She refused to take his hand. "I wanted to see you face to face one last time. I wanted to look you in the eye when I tell you that I will never forgive you for what you did to me. You were in the wrong and you knew it. And then you punished me for it. Soon, you will burn in hell."

Tears trickled from Hans's left eye. His left arm shook, still reaching towards his daughter. "S... sorry... Adelheid," he managed to say with great effort.

"I'm not Adelheid. I'm Heinrich," he said. "The son who walked into the church to use the bathroom because you didn't come right back like you said you would. The son who went into the sanctuary to see what made the noise and found you socking it to the church secretary right on the stage. You were going at it like rabbits right underneath the picture of Jesus."

Hans's mouth hung open in shock and drool slid from the right side of his mouth.

"I was eight and didn't even know what you were doing. But you made me pay. You told everyone you found me jerking off in front of the picture of Mary the mother of Jesus. I didn't even know what jerking off meant."

Hans started to say something, but Ricky cut him off. "Don't you dare tell me you are sorry! You had years to apologise. Instead, for years you made me sit beside you in adult church. You wouldn't even let me go to Sunday School

120

for fear that I might say something. You robbed years of my life and made me endure constant humiliation."

Hans tried to form some words and Ricky cut him off again. "And that was not the worst part. You lied to Mom about me over and over. You purposely kept us apart. You destroyed every relationship I had with family. I hope you die soon. The flames are waiting."

With that, Ricky turned and walked out. Tears poured from his eyes as he walked by the nurses' station.

Ricky wore dark sunglasses and a ball cap as he left the hospital ten minutes later. His heart pounded against his ribcage and he wanted to run, but he willed himself to stay calm, at least on the outside. A yellow cab pulled in to drop someone off and Ricky wanted to flag it, thought better of it, and then hurried down the street and through an alley. Two blocks later, he boarded a city bus.

He texted Addy, 'Sis, arrived at the airport. I'll catch a cab. See you soon.'

She replied back, 'Jack can pick you up.'

"Oh shit!" Ricky exclaimed. He texted back, 'Spend time with your man. I'll taxi it.'

It took him 35 minutes and a transfer to get to the airport. There he took his overnight bag out of a locker, redid his makeup in a hurry, took off his falsies, changed his clothes and brushed his hair. Then he texted Rudy and Karl, 'Change of plans. Husband is with her. Leaving the airport without R. I'll see if I can find a way.'

He flagged a cab and the driver put his suitcase and overnight bag into the trunk. When Ricky got in, he said, "Thanks for taking me. The taxi driver before you saw that I was gay and refused to take me. That is a human rights violation!"

The Lebanese driver was flabbergasted. "Did you get his name? Or the cab number? My boss will fire his ass."

"No," Ricky replied. "I couldn't believe it. Then someone hopped in and off he drove." Ricky spent the cab ride to his father's house telling the driver stories of the prejudice he'd experienced.

Karl arrived at the Foothills Medical Centre as Addy walked out. She looked towards the cab he was in, and then hurried down the street. *Just like my sister*, he thought. *She has access to the old man's money, yet she parks four blocks away in a residential neighbourhood so she doesn't have to pay for parking. At least I didn't have to talk to her before we kill her.* He carried the backpack with his clothes and toiletries across the street to the Nightshift Pub and drank a couple of beers. He just ordered his third when Heinrich texted him.

So Jack is here? A wrinkle, that's all, Karl thought. *The result will be the same. I guess it is time that I put these chess pieces in motion.* Karl chugged his beer, paid his tab and jaywalked across the street to the hospital.

At the information desk in the atrium, he asked, "Which room is Hans Ulfert in?"

"Room 6110. That is on the sixth floor and in the A section. Look for signs when you get off the elevator."

Seeing his father shocked Karl. Not only was one side of his father's body paralysed, but his face looked grey. "I'm here, Dad," he said. His father did not respond.

Karl's plan was simple. He would be visiting with his father in the hospital while Heinrich murdered Adelheid. The nursing staff were his alibi. *Rudolph will make sure that she dies*, he thought. *If Heinrich chickens out and, no doubt he will, then Rudolph will freak out and kill them both. It is a win-win! Rudolph ends up in jail. Heinrich and my sister die. And I get the money.*

They took separate planes to avoid suspicion. That was Heinrich's idea, and he arrived first. He'd wait in a coffee shop for Rudolf to arrive. They'd cab it to Rudolph's place and Heinrich would continue on alone to the old man's house. Rudolph would follow in his truck and wait just down the street.

The way Karl explained it to his brothers, he would take a cab to within a few blocks of the German castle, walk down the street and join Rudy. When Ricky got Adelheid to eat or drink hazelnut extract, Heinrich would text Rudolph. Rudy would drive to their father's house and Karl would stand guard in the driveway.

The last thing Karl said to Rudolph before he flew out of Vancouver International Airport was, "If you don't hear from Ricky within an hour of him arriving, just show up at the door. Then kill them both."

"But, Karl," he argued, "You already said that the cops would come straight to me."

"Then make sure you have an alibi," Karl said condescendingly. "Get your latest plaything to vouch for you." And Karl grinned.

Rudolph stepped into Karl's personal space. Karl's nose would have been against Rudy's chest if it wasn't for Karl's potbelly. Rudy glared down at him and hissed through gritted teeth, "I ought to…"

"You ought to what, Rudolph?" Karl asked calmly. "Beat the crap out of me? Smash my brains against the pavement? Don't be such a dummkopf. You lay even one of your Gorg-sized fingers on me and the cops get the package!"

Rudy huffed and puffed and swore. His face coloured like a first-day-in-Jamaica sunburn and his hands clenched and unclenched like he was pumping up an air mattress. But he never raised his hands and Karl refused to step back.

"Don't push me," Rudolph threatened.

"I own you," Karl said to him firmly as he stared up at Rudy's bearded face. "You will do everything I ask. Everything."

"And you'll be there to cover my back?" Rudy asked, sounding doubtful.

"Oh yes. I'll be watching you."

Rudolph turned and walked away and Karl breathed a quiet sigh of relief. It gave him an adrenaline rush to push Rudolph. And he could get away with it.

When Karl still lived in Calgary, he stopped by his dad's house to check on things while his parents were away. He walked in on Rudolph socking it to some young thing. The girl was obviously drugged. One might call it date rape except the girl was too young to be on a date.

Karl snapped a picture with his phone and pocketed the Rohypnol vials off the dresser. Then he ran for his life. Rudolph begged him to destroy the evidence. When that didn't work, Rudolph threatened him. Only once.

"If you ever threaten me again, I'll go straight to the police," Karl told him. And, until today, Karl never actually threatened to use the evidence he hid away.

Karl re-read the text from Heinrich and said, "Shit. Shit, shit! This is going sideways."

Rudy wandered around the Calgary airport trying to find Ricky. Then Ricky texted him that Jack was with Adelheid, and he would leave on his own.

Rudy texted back, 'Wait for me.' Ricky did not respond.

"Now what the hell am I supposed to do?" Rudy said out loud.

A woman with a multi-coloured suitcase case on wheels looked up at him and said, "Luggage pickup is one floor down. Just follow the signs."

Rudy took a cab home and did not feel happy about it. He planned to stick Ricky with the fare.

Raven met him as he ducked to come through the front door. "I'm so glad you're home, Rudy. I'm having contractions. My water hasn't broken so this might settle down, but who knows. Maybe I'll have the baby tonight."

"Oh shit!" Rudy exclaimed. "Now?"

"Yes," she answered excitedly. Then she grimaced with a contraction. "At first I was terrified of going into labour but, after being pregnant for nine months, I can hardly wait for this to be over." Raven no sooner said that when she felt wet between her legs and did the pregnant waddle to the bathroom.

Rudy stood in the doorway, not sure what he should do next when he heard the native-drum ringtone of Raven's phone. He walked in and picked up the phone from the coffee table. The call display read, 'Bowness Coin'.

"Hello," he answered.

"I'm sorry. I must have dialled the wrong number. I'm looking for Raven."

"She is busy at the moment. Why are you calling?"

"Are you her husband? Are you Rudy Big Bear?"

"Yes, I'm Rudy."

"This is Norman Paplinski from Bowness Coin and Antiques. As you know, I bought a couple of sheets of coins from Raven, but I understand that you have inherited quite an extensive collection. Perhaps I could help you catalogue it. Then, if you decide to sell any of it, you could…"

Rudy hit the end call button.

Raven came out of the bathroom with only her top on. She held a bath towel between her legs. "My water broke, Rudy!" she exclaimed excitedly. "I'll put on some dry maternity pants and then we need to get to the hospital." She turned and walked down the hall.

One step from their bedroom door, Rudy's giant fist smashed into the back of Raven's head. Her feet came off the floor as she flew forward into the room.

She landed facedown with a thud on the floor, her head almost touching the bedpost.

Rudy grabbed her around the ankle and dragged her unconscious body down the hall like a seal that had been clubbed on the ice. Rudy left a trail of Raven's blood and water down the hall, through the living room, and out the front door.

Rudy stood on the crooked front step and tossed Raven towards the street like a bag of garbage. Her body flew three metres before it slammed into the dry and dandelion-covered front lawn. Then she bounced and somersaulted twice and ended up in a mostly naked heap.

Rudy grabbed Raven's overnight bag from just inside the front door and Rudy tossed it at her. He never gave Raven another glance as he slammed the front door and then, with determined steps, walked around the front of the house to the back yard. He kicked the pit bull hard and it cowered behind an oil-covered and half dismantled Ford super-duty engine.

As Rudy pulled his truck out of the driveway and backed into the neighbour's fence, he announced, "Now I am ready to kill someone."

The hospital called at 12:03 p.m. "This is the Foothills Medical Centre. Am I speaking to Adelheid Penner?"

Addy could tell by the tone of voice that the reason for the call was not good news. She braced herself, swallowed, and answered, "Yes, this is Hans Ulfert's daughter."

"Your father has taken a turn for the worst. His blood pressure and oxygen levels are dropping."

"I'll be right there," she replied and hung up.

She texted Ricky, 'Where R U?'

'Almost at the doorstep.'

'Dad has taken a turn for the worst. We'll head to the hospital as soon as you arrive.'

'Leave without me.'

'I'll wait.'

A minute later, a yellow cab pulled into the driveway. Ricky paid the driver and got out. He stared up at the castle walls and then at the gigantic front door. He shook his head in disbelief.

Addy noticed that Ricky looked pale. His hair was longer than the last time she saw him and he had it pulled back and tied with an elastic into a small ponytail. Addy thought that it made his face look masculine. He wore blue jeans with bling on the back pocket and a blue shirt.

She chuckled because she wore blue jeans with bling on the pocket and a mint-green tee shirt. Addy hugged Ricky and he hugged back. Tears spilt from Ricky's eyes and fell on Addy's shoulder. "It will be over soon," he comforted her.

"We better get going then. It would be a shame for you to come all this way and have our father die before you get there," Addy said.

"Really, Sis, I have a headache and would just as soon stay here. I came here to see you, not him. Besides, I don't think I have anything to say to him."

"Maybe he needs to see you. Maybe he needs to deal with how he treated you."

Tears welled up again in Ricky's eyes, he nodded and said, "Yes. He really should have to face up to how he treated both of us."

Jack carried Ricky's pink suitcase into the house, set it down in the great room, and locked the inside door. He set the alarm and closed and locked the castle-like outside door. Jack crawled into the back of the compact rental car so that Addy and Ricky could talk. Jack's felt crammed in like a Great Dane sitting in a Chihuahua's basket.

They could have taken his SUV, except the gas gage read empty.

The ambulance crew strapped a long spine board onto Raven, carefully immobilized her head, and lifted her into the ambulance. Immediately, an attendant placed an Ambu bag over Raven's nose and mouth and squeezed the ball to push air into Raven's oxygen-deprived lungs. He counted to eight and squeezed the ball again and watched Raven's chest rise and fall.

Raven came to as they lifted her into the ambulance. She started to scream and then passed out. When she woke, she felt like someone had taken a meat cleaver and hacked up every part of her. The ambulance swerved and her scream drowned out the wail of the siren.

"We've got you, ma'am," the ambulance attendant assured her. "We're getting you to the hospital as quickly as we can."

She felt a contraction begin and, as it grew stronger, darkness closed in from her peripheral vision until she saw only a pinprick of light. Raven got the distinct impression that she stood on the high-diving board at the swimming pool, only someone turned out all the lights. She quickly got down on her knees and held each side of the board as she backed up. Her feet fell off the end of the board. Then, in terror, she crawled forward.

She crawled less than a metre when she reached the end of the board. "What?" she exclaimed as she tried to turn around. At that moment, she discovered the board beneath her shrunk to only a half metre square. She still felt it shrinking as her hands moved closer together. When the diving board contracted to the size of a dessert plate, Raven toppled forward screaming as she fell into the blackness.

Rudy drove to his father's house. He didn't have a plan, but that didn't bother him. "I'm screwed already," he told himself. "Screwed all to hell. Let's hope my shithead brother goes through with his end of the deal. He'll feed Addy something to kill her, and I'll stop Jack from taking her to the hospital. Or maybe I'll just kill them all." The thought of it made him giddy with adrenaline.

Rudy noticed the GMC Terrain in the driveway as he passed by. Jack's, he presumed. "It is a good tall-person SUV with lots of headroom, but not a tall person like me." For his own truck, Rudy custom-built a tall cab and seats with a low profile so he'd have enough headroom. He flipped a U-ey and parked just down the street. He downed another couple of steroids with Coke and waited for Ricky to text or call.

When they arrived at the hospital, Ricky did not want to go in. "Now that I'm here, I don't know that I can face him."

Addy took his hand. "Come on," she said. "I'll be with you. Besides, Dad is a pathetic shell of the man he used to be. You have nothing to be afraid of."

Ricky thought, *You and I have every reason to be afraid.*

On the sixth floor, Addy introduced herself to the staff at the nurses' station in section A. "Hello. I'm Adelheid Penner, Hansel Ulfert's daughter. What room is he in?"

The charge nurse gave her the oddest look and replied, "He is still in 6110. I'm glad you came back. He is slipping fast. And your brother is with him."

"Rudy? I thought the hospital banned him," Adelheid said to Jack.

Ricky led the way to the room. "Karl!" he exclaimed as he walked in. "What are you doing here?"

"The same goes for you, Heinrich," Karl shook Ricky's hand, gave Addy a quick hug and then shook Jack's hand.

Addy noticed that Karl smelled like beer.

"He is not doing well," Karl said nodding towards his father. "I had a feeling I should come so I took the day off and flew out here. I had no idea he was this bad. You should have let me know, Adelheid."

"I never said he was doing well," Adelheid replied defensively. "I told you that he had a heart attack, a stroke, and a brain aneurysm. Oh yes, brain surgery, too! What else needed to happen to your father before you thought it was worth taking a trip to see him?"

Jack put his hand on Addy's shoulder and said, "We are glad that you are here, Karl. And you too, Ricky. Your father does look much worse than yesterday."

"Did he say anything to you, Karl?" Ricky asked.

Karl still glared at Adelheid as he answered, "No. He never said a word. His eyes are closed most of the time and, when they are open, I don't think he knows I am here."

An alarm rang and a nurse came in and checked the machine and the oxygen mask. "This is not good," she said. "We have the oxygen turned up to full, and still his levels are dropping. We'll need to put him on a ventilator so I'll need you to clear the room." And she dashed out.

Addy took her father's hand and said, "Goodbye, Father. I don't judge you. Ich liebie dich."

Ricky's mouth dropped open in disbelief. His face turned red and he stormed out of the room. When Addy stepped into the hallway, Ricky demanded, "How can you say that to him? Hans Ulfert is a tyrant and a liar and a manipulating bastard."

"He is worse than that, Ricky. You don't know the half of it."

"Then how can you say that stuff to him?"

"You and I spent our childhoods being judged by him. We had to earn love. And even when he should have loved us based on what we did for him, he withheld it. I'm not him, Ricky. I don't want to be anything like him. I choose not to be."

"You're a fool," Karl said from behind her. "You think that you can swoop in here after all these years, tell the old man what he wants to hear, and somehow he'll put you back into his will. I'm telling you right now that I won't let that happen."

"I don't want his money. I'm not you Karl. And you can choose not to be like our father."

Ricky's phone pinged and he read the text from Rudy, 'Is she D?'

Ricky replied, 'No. Old man took a turn for the worse. We're at the hospital. Karl is here.'

'WTF?'

'My guess? Karl set us up.'

Karl took his hateful stare away from Adelheid and saw Heinrich texting. "And you! Do you think, because you show up, the old man will somehow have a change in heart and put you back in the will? You won't get a penny if you are waiting for him to die."

Ricky heard the threat. "Screw off, Karl! I don't know what scheme you have going, but I'm not going to get caught in your game. I won't let you manipulate me. Not ever!"

Karl's mouth hung open speechless. He stormed out of the hospital and jaywalked to the pub. He ordered a pint and texted Rudolph, 'H needs to D 2.'

At Foothills Medical Centre, they rushed Raven into an operating room. First, they took the baby by Caesarean section and then they started with x-rays almost before the doctor finished the last stitch.

Raven roused enough to remember the utter terror of falling off the diving board into the black abyss, knowing that any second she would hit the water. As the seconds stretched into minutes, it felt like her heart would break out of growing fear... every second compounding how hard she would hit the water... every second knowing her baby would drown.

Then it dawned on her that she didn't feel air rushing by her. "I must have hit the water and blacked out," she told herself. Then she held her breath in the pitch black at the bottom of the pool. She wanted to swim to the surface but, when she tried to move, her head hurt like a chain saw buzzed through it. Her neck hurt like someone tried to chop her head off with an axe. Way down deep inside, her uterus hurt. She knew she no longer carried her child.

I must have hit my head on the bottom of the pool, she said to herself, and she felt the air bubbles float up past her face. *I must have delivered my baby underwater. I need to find him.* With that thought, she inhaled lungs full of water and even her semi-consciousness went black.

The doctors screwed metal pins into Raven's skull and attached the cage that would hold her neck stretched and her head immobile for the next year. With luck, her shattered C2 and C3 would grow back together as vertebrae.

127

With luck, her spine might not be permanently damaged. With luck, someday she might play with her son.

When Karl came back from the bar, he found Ricky and Addy still by their father's bedside.

On the sixth floor, east wing, Hans Karl Ulfert looked up at his children as they said goodbye to him. He did not know why they said those words. "I'm fine," he reassured them. "My mind is finally out of the fog. I can think again. I'm sure the hospital staff will let me go home now." But his children did not seem to hear him.

"Adelheid," he called. "No daughter should ever have a father like me." She did not reply, but she wiped a tear from her cheek.

"And Heinrich. There is no excuse for what I've done. But I am what I am." Heinrich did not respond, but looked worried.

Hans sat up in the bed and said, "I need to go home now." Then he stood, pushed his way between Karl and Jack, and walked towards the door. He looked back over his shoulder and saw Adelheid, Jack, Karl and Heinrich still gathered around the hospital bed.

"Good," Hans told himself. "I need to get home before they come to visit. I have to make sure Adelheid doesn't find the secret." He sighed as his heart suddenly filled with a lifetime of regrets, and his spirit left the room like cigarette smoke whisked away by a strong wind.

They stood around the bed when they heard a sound leaving their father like the wind moaning through an abandoned prairie farmhouse. They watched Hans Karl Ulfert die.

Karl started blubbering like a baby. Addy suspected the several beers Karl downed in the hour that he spent away had something to do with it.

"We should let Rudy know," Ricky said calmly. "Does anyone have his cell number? We need to warn him not to do anything stupid because our recently departed father is not around to bail him out."

"I don't have it," Addy said. "I only have his landline."

"Karl?" Ricky asked. "Will you let Rudy know it is over?"

Karl glared at him. He did not answer Ricky, but pulled out his phone and sent a text. 'The old man kicked it. Like usual he fucked up everything. But congrats! You're a millionaire.'

Rudy laughed as he pulled out onto the hill-top road and started heading home. "I've got Karl's coins and I'll get 25% of Hans Karl Ulfert's estate."

He did not laugh for long because, almost immediately, he saw flashing lights behind him. He pulled over hoping to let the squad car pass, but it pulled in behind him. Rudy rolled down the window and turned off the engine.

The officers carried their pistols as they approached him, one on either side of his truck. Rudy raised his hands. He knew the drill.

"Keep your hands where we can see them and step out of the vehicle," the officer on his side of the truck ordered in a firm voice.

"How the hell am I supposed to open the door with my hands raised?" Rudy asked.

"Step out of the vehicle!" the officer repeated as if saying it louder made it logical.

"I could if I was Jesus. But I need to open the door. I am going to lower one hand so I can do that."

"Keep your hands where I can see them!" the officer screamed.

"Then I guess you better open the door for me then, you stupid shithead. Go on. Be my servant and open the door. I dare you to."

"Step out of the vehicle," the officer screamed in a rage.

"Make up your mind, asshole," Rudy screamed back. "Do you want me to keep my hands up or do you want me to open the friggin' door?"

The police officer from the passenger side of the truck came around, opened the custom-made, extra-large door, and jumped back.

"That is more like it," Rudy said to the officer that had been shouting at him. "Your partner is the smart one." Rudy stepped out and stood towering over the officers. "I'm out. Now what?"

"Turn around and put your hands behind your back," they both yelled at once.

"No damned way! If I turn around, you'll shoot me in the back!"

The officer closest to him sprang forward and slammed a fist into Rudolph's stomach with all his might. Rudy never even flinched and the officer bounced off him like he'd hit a wall.

"You punch like a girl. I owe you one," Rudy hissed. "And you won't be standing when I hit you."

Backup arrived seven minutes later. They couldn't get handcuffs around Rudy's massive wrists so they zip-tied his hands behind his back. One zip tie for each hand and one to hold the two together.

"Does this mean that I am under arrest?" Rudy asked as he snapped the zip ties just by flexing his muscles.

The officers that just arrived stared dumbfounded at the other officers.

"We didn't get around to telling him that," the one explained.

The other said, "You are under arrest for aggravated assault on Raven Big Bear."

At that moment, an officer noticed Rudy's phone on the dash of the truck showing an open line to 911.

Addy said to Karl, "Come with us to Dad's house. There is beer in the fridge and lots of empty bedrooms. I'll order in some pizza or Chinese."

Karl looked at Heinrich and flashed an evil smile. He turned to at Addy and said, "Yes, I'd like that. I'll ask Rudolph to join us."

Karl texted Rudolph, 'Wake at the old man's house. Now's our chance.' Rudy did not reply.

Addy drove. Karl sat in the front and Heinrich sat in the back seat with Jack. Jack's knees were up in front of him and Addy already pulled her seat was as far forward as it could go.

"Where is your minivan?" Karl asked Adelheid with a sneer in his voice. "You always drive a minivan."

"At the impound lot," Jack answered for her. "Addy found out that it is illegal to drive with a cracked windshield."

"And I got a ticket to boot," she chimed in.

"Stupid cops," Karl exclaimed. "They towed your car for a crack in the windshield?"

"Well," Addy replied, "The windshield looked like a big spider web. I got caught in a hailstorm. I should have known better."

"So what happens now?" Heinrich asked.

"Normally, I'd just pay the impound fees and get the van back but, because of the hail, the insurance company…"

"No," Ricky interrupted. "I mean with the old man. Will they do an autopsy and then we have the funeral?"

"There won't be an autopsy," Addy replied. "When someone dies in the hospital from a diagnosed medical condition, their body goes straight to the funeral home. Well, after a family member confirms that the deceased is their loved one. One of us will have to do that tomorrow."

"We were all there when he kicked the bucket," Karl complained, "And we still have to do it?"

"I guess it is the law," Addy answered. "Any volunteers?"

Karl stared out the window and Ricky stared at his hands.

Jack said, "Karl, ask Rudy if he'll do it. Addy has been dealing with your dad's stuff for a few days already and she really could use a break." He knew the second those words spilt from his mouth that he should have chosen his words more carefully.

"What do you mean she has been dealing with stuff?" Karl demanded of Jack. And then he turned towards Adelheid. "What stuff are you taking? The will leaves everything to me and Rudolph! Everything!"

"Take it easy, Karl," Addy replied trying hard to stay calm and concentrate on driving. "Dad asked me to get rid of his porn collection." She could tell by the look on Karl's face that he knew his father collected pornography. "So you knew about it?" she asked.

"I came across some photos in his darkroom once," Karl answered. "Not his usual nudes."

"Did he know you'd seen them?" Ricky asked.

"Yes," Karl admitted. "I got anything I wanted from that time forward." Karl dropped the sun visor, looked at Heinrich in the makeup mirror and grinned.

More than anything, Ricky wanted to reach over the seat and strangle Karl. Tears rolled down Addy's cheeks.

"Your father was a piece of work!" Jack stated.

"Yes," Karl replied. "A real son of a bitch. But he left us millions! Correction, he left me millions." And Karl laughed.

Addy regretted inviting Karl over to the house. She wished she could toss him out of the car… while it was moving. She felt relieved when they finally got to the house so she could put some space between them.

Karl stood right behind Adelheid and watched as she put in the door code and turn the key. Then he held out his hand and demanded, "I'll take that. The house is mine so hand over the key."

Jack stepped in between them, forcing Karl to move back. Jack stood 10 centimetres taller than Karl, and Jack's muscles rippled. Jack demanded, "Do you even know what the will says, Karl? For all you know, your father gave the house to charity. Until the reading of the will, Addy is in control. If I hear one more ugly demand from you, you can go spend some of your new millions on a hotel room."

Karl swore, grabbed his cell phone and stomped towards the fountain in the courtyard. He texted Rudolph, 'Where R U???'

When he turned around, he realized that the others had gone into the mansion so he rushed through the open castle door. He never got to see Addy put the code into the inside door, but he went in right behind them. Then Karl ran room to room to see if he could spot anything missing.

While he did this, Jack took a bottle of wine from the temperature-controlled wine cooler in the dining room. He opened it as Addy got crystal wine glasses.

As Karl came panting down the stairs, he saw below him Addy and Ricky sitting side by side on the antique love seat drinking Bordeaux. Jack held a German beer in his hand as he sat on the arm of Hans's favourite armchair.

Karl stormed up to Addy and glared down at her threateningly.

"So what did I steal, Karl?" Addy asked. "Tell me what is missing. And I suppose you went through my stuff in the end bedroom?"

"The door to the studio is locked!" Karl yelled. "You are hiding the stuff in there!"

"Quite the opposite. That door automatically locks. But I'm sure you already knew that. You've been in there before."

Addy turned to Ricky, "Join us, Ricky, for a tour of Dad's studio so that your brother can quit worrying about something he thinks he lost that is more important than grieving for his dead father."

Addy led them down the hall and punched the code into the wide door. Jack purposely stood in Karl's way and went in first. The lights popped on.

"This place is amazing!" Ricky exclaimed as he walked in. And his voice echoed off the walls. "Look at all the sets!"

Karl rushed into the main studio, saw the twisted office door. He whirled around to look at Addy and screamed, "What the hell? …You owe me for a new door and doorframe, Adelheid!" He ran into the studio office and came back out a few seconds later. He looked around the office and demanded, "Where is all the stuff? Return it right this moment or I'm calling the police!"

Jack walked up to him and explained, "Addy followed your father's directions. She got rid of a mountain of porn."

"In case you hadn't noticed, he's dead!" Karl screamed in Jack's face. "I'm in charge now. And I want everything back. Now!"

Jack grabbed Karl by his collar and dragged him out of the office. "I warned you," Jack said. "It is time for you to leave."

"Screw you, Jack! You are nothing but a gold-digging farm boy. You can't throw me out. This is my house!"

It surprised Addy that Jack didn't deck him. Instead, Jack grabbed the belt at the small of Karl's back, hoisted him onto his tiptoes, and marched him down the hall, through the great room, and out the front door. The whole time, Karl screamed obscenities. Jack tossed him onto the paving stones.

Addy threw Karl's backpack towards him. Truth be told, she threw the bag at him, but she missed.

"I'm calling the police!" Karl screamed.

"Please do," Ricky said. "I'm sure they would like to hear my perspective on things."

Karl ranted like a madman as he picked up his bag and headed to the street. He texted Rudolph. 'Where R U? I want them all dead. Now.'

On Wednesday morning, rookie Detective Boyd Wiebe made his first stop of the day. "Another stupid case," he complained as he parked his unmarked car and put the police business sunscreen across the inside of the windshield. "It's obviously domestic violence. At least that is what it looks like. So why does DCRT need me to confirm this?"

The sergeant of the Domestic Conflict Response Team called him the previous evening and said, "There is something really off about a case that just came so I am sending it your way, Detective. Do me a favour and help put the perp behind bars."

Before coming down to the hospital, Boyd reviewed the little information available in the police report. A passing motorist found a 17-year-old woman unconscious and half naked on the lawn. The ID the police found in her suitcase indicated her name is Raven Big Bear and she lived at the address where they found her. She is pregnant. The police arrested her boyfriend, Rudolph Ulfert, in the snob-hill area. His rap sheet included a string of assault and rape charges, yet he never spent time in jail.

He must have a very good lawyer, Boyd thought.

First, the detective talked to Raven's doctor.

"I see battered women come in here every week," the doctor said. "The typical injuries are broken noses and broken jaws. Sometimes I see smashed eye sockets. And there are often defensive wounds like broken fingers or broken arms. This one is different."

"Different how?"

"The patient has no facial injuries other than a bit of a grass burn on her cheek, and no injuries on the front of her body. The back of her skull, just where it meets the neck, is one massive contusion. My guess is that she was hit from behind and never saw it coming."

"I understand that they found her on her own front lawn, right next to the sidewalk. Just to be clear, is there a possibility that a car hit her or a bicycle?"

"Detective, other than the bruising and scrapes on the front of her body, her injuries are similar to what you might see in a rear-end collision where a person's head is whipped back over the seat. You'd expect whiplash and possible fracture of C3. Only in Raven's case, the blow threw her head forward and up. The force stretched her muscles and her spinal cord, shattered C2 and C3 and pulled C1 away from her skull."

"A blunt force injury?"

"Yes, but not likely done with a weapon. There were no marks from the edge of something hard. The skin wasn't broken either."

"A punch?"

"Perhaps. But it would take a very powerful punch. The person would have to be a boxer. More like a kung-fu kick. And did I mention that she was in labour when it happened?"

"My notes said she was pregnant, but not how far along, or about labour."

"Her water broke. It might explain why she had no pants on. We delivered her baby boy by Caesarean before we could set her neck."

"So the mystery is how she ended up on the front lawn."

"My best guess is that she someone dragged there. It would explain the grass in the scrapes."

Detective Wiebe mulled this over as the doctor lead him to Raven's room.

The contraption that held Raven's head reminded Boyd of a birdcage crossed with a medieval torture instrument. Blood seeped from around stainless-steel pins that held the cage to Raven's shaved head. A childhood memory of a Frankenstein movie flashed across Boyd's mind. Raven's eyes remained closed. Straps held her body down so she wouldn't move.

The doctor warned him that she suffered a concussion from the blow and a migraine headache from the neck injury. And the doctor reminded him that the intravenous lines fed her heavy-duty painkillers. Boyd really didn't expect any answers.

"Raven," he said softly. "My name is Detective Boyd Wiebe with the Calgary Police Service. Can you tell me what happened?"

"He's going to kill her," she mumbled without opening her eyes.

"Who threatened to kill you?" he asked.

"I fell off the diving board. Baby is at the bottom of the pool. They're going to kill her."

The detective heard enough to know Raven was delirious. To comfort her and end the conversation, he said, "Your baby is safe. No one will hurt him."

"Rudy's sister. Stop him."

As Detective Wiebe walked to his car, he looked at his few lines of notes. *Nothing Raven said made any sense*, he thought. *One thing for sure, she felt afraid someone would kill her. But why did she keep referring to herself as if she talked about someone else?*

Raven felt relieved. Now she could finally sleep. "I never believed Rudy would hurt anyone. I did not believe that he would really kill his sister. I did not want to believe that Rudy ever hurt his exes. And I knew he would never hurt. Then he put me on the diving board," she mumbled. "How else could I have gotten there? Rudy put me on the diving board and then turned out the lights. He wanted me to fall. If he would do that to me, I know he would kill his sister. That policeman will stop him." With that, Raven drifted into a drug-induced sleep.

Detective Wiebe checked for 911 calls placed from the victim's house in the last year. There were none.

When Detective Boyd called the Bowness Division Police station to arrange an interview with Rudy Ulfert, he discovered they already let Rudy out on bail. "How is that even possible?" Boyd complained to the lieutenant in charge.

"He has a high-priced lawyer, and there was some screw up with his arrest," the lieutenant answered. "Mr. Ulfert dialled 911 when he saw the squad-car lights come on behind him so they recorded the whole thing. He filed an excessive-force complaint against one of our officers."

"Roughed him up a little, did he?"

"Hardly. My guy said he hit him under the solar plexus hard enough to bring down an ox, and his fist just bounced off. Apparently, this guy is seven-feet tall and is built like a tank. They couldn't even put handcuffs on him because his wrists are too big. They brought in the paddy wagon to bring him in. The report said that Rudolph Ulfert could take on Hercules, so be careful, Detective."

The detective asked himself, "How does a low-life afford a high-priced lawyer? Is he a drug-dealer? There is nothing to do with drugs on his rap sheet. Yet, one doesn't have a high-priced lawyer if you live in Bowness."

Detective Wiebe drove past Rudy's place, turned right at the end of the block and then drove down the back alley. "The neighbour from hell," Boyd said out loud as he drove by the back of Rudy's yard. A half-dozen different truck engines filled one side of the driveway to the garage. The motorless body of a half-ton truck stood on end, the back bumper on the ground and the top of the half-ton hanging over the sagging chain-link fence into the neighbours' yard.

The few red shingles that remained on the garage roof looked curled and broken. The siding on the garage looked newer than the siding on the house but unpainted for at least three decades. The mix of faded paint reminded Boyd of a very faded tie-dye shirt.

As he drove by the short section of chain-link fence, the detective saw knee-high grass growing around various half-assembled engines that lay strewn across the entire backyard. A tan-coloured pit bull lunged at the chain-link, barking ferociously.

After Boyd drove around the front, he parked the unmarked police car across the street and four houses down. The peeling white paint on the trim around the windows looked like scales on a fish left out in the sun. Yellowed and cracked stucco, coated in glass from broken pop bottles, covered half the house was. Wide tin siding covered the rest and it looked like, many years ago, someone painted it blue, then orange, and then yellow.

No police tape surrounded where they found Raven. *What is there to secure?* Boyd thought. *Just a weed patch in front of a 60-year-old bungalow.*

He just pulled over and parked when Boyd saw a black Lexus SUV coming down the street towards him. The driver obviously hunted for an address. In front of Rudolph Ulfert's house, the driver slowed down to a crawl and checked the house number against the slip of paper in his hand. But he did not stop.

The SUV rolled by Detective Wiebe's car with the driver still looking back over his shoulder at the Ulfert house. A decal with white letters on the driver's door read, 'Bowness Coins and Antiques'.

Hardly three minutes later, a green and white Barrel Taxi pulled up in front of the house. The man that got out looked to be in his early 30s and stood perhaps five-feet eight-inches tall. He had clean-cut, sandy-blonde coloured hair and a noticeable beer gut. The man walked over the uneven sidewalk blocks, up the three steps and rang the doorbell. The pit bull barked unceasingly and lunged at the gate.

When the front door opened, the suspect's body filled the doorway. Then Rudolph bent down to get through the door and stepped out onto the slanting cement steps. Even though Boyd heard that Rudy was big, seeing him step out of the house took Boyd's breath away. The top of the visitor's head did not reach Rudolph Ulfert's shoulders, like seeing David standing beside Goliath.

There is no doubt that this giant could break a person's neck with a single punch, Boyd thought. *And the doctor said that Raven never saw it coming.*

The men on the step hugged and went inside. As Boyd saw the giant stoop down to go through the doorframe, he noticed how similar the two were in face and hair colour. "Not lovers," he said. "They are brothers."

The detective looked down at the notes in his book and read, "They are going to kill her. His sister. Stop them."

"Maybe Raven wasn't talking about herself. Perhaps she wasn't living in fear. Maybe she tried to tell me that her common-law and his brother are planning a murder." Boyd picked up his phone and did an internet search for 'Ulfert, Calgary'.

The first thing that came up was Hans Ulfert Portraits. Detective Wiebe switched the search to images. Many images came up of Hans Ulfert with the rich, the famous, and the infamous. Boyd scrolled down the lines of photos, and then he saw it. A photo taken at a wedding showed Rudolph Ulfert in the back row of a wedding party, towering above the rest. Hans Ulfert stood beside his wife. And the gorgeous bride looked remarkably like her mother.

"God bless the internet," Boyd said. "I've accomplished in 40 seconds what would have taken hours or days the old-fashioned way."

He could now assume that the money for the suspect's lawyer came from Rudolph's rich father. He guessed that Rudolph wasn't in his father's good books or Rudolph would live in a better house in a better neighbourhood. "Hans Ulfert is protecting his son to save his own reputation," he concluded.

And the detective knew Rudolph had a sister.

Boyd called into the deputy police chief. "Sir, I may have stumbled upon a murder plot," the detective said. "It might be easy to disprove if I could track down the sister of someone I am investigating."

"What do you need, Detective?"

"It would help me tremendously if someone could find the name and contact information of Hans Ulfert's daughter. Hans Ulfert is a famous photographer."

Norman Paplinski was worried about Raven. The more he thought about it, the more worried he got. First and foremost, he didn't want to discover that the coins he bought from Raven were stolen. He didn't want the embarrassment of telling his clients that they needed to return the coins he'd sold them. And he didn't want to lose the hefty profit he'd make from selling the coins that remained in his safe.

She signed a paper saying that the coins were hers to sell, he reassured himself. *She gave me her contact information including her address, which is really kind of crazy considering she showed me pictures of at least a million dollars' worth of coins in a pile on the basement floor.*

Norman Paplinski also feared that he caused harm to a young, pregnant indigenous woman. The more he thought about it, the more worried he became. *I didn't see anybody when I drove by the house*, he reasoned. *She probably is in the hospital having her baby.*

However, he couldn't stop thinking about how his phone call ended with Mr. Big Bear. He phoned Raven's number a dozen times since. He'd left messages for her to call him. He even left a message that he had a baby gift for her. She did not respond.

To appease his conscience, Norman picked up the phone and called the police tip line. "This may be nothing so, if it is, then just ignore this. I'm worried about someone. Raven Big Bear sold me something. Oh, nothing illegal. When I called her back to see if she had more… ah, stuff to sell, and her husband answered her phone. He seemed surprised and hung up. I haven't been able to reach Raven since. Could you make sure she is all right?" He read out her address and phone number, then hung up.

For 20 minutes, Detective Wiebe listed questions he wanted answers for and then pondered the possibilities. Sarah, his girlfriend, told him he asked too many questions. She said to him, "Some things are meant to be mysteries. You are not supposed to figure everything out."

He knew for certain that he had not figured her out. They lived together for the last three months, and he still didn't have a clue what made her happy. When he thought he was onto something, then he'd no more of it.

"Do I look like a car to you?" she'd asked him last night.

"Of course not," he answered.

"Then stop treating me like one."

"I haven't got a clue what you are talking about," he replied.

"That is obvious. For a detective, you are pretty dense sometimes. I want to be loved. Cherished. Ravished. When I don't feel that way then I think all you want to do is ride me. I think that I am just a tool for your tool."

Boyd heard the dog barking again and that brought his mind back to the situation. He heard Rudolph yell, "Shut up, you stupid mutt!" But the dog kept barking.

The detective started his car, drove down the street, turned left at the corner and parked where he could look down the alley. He watched a souped-up, custom-bodied, blue Ram 250 with lots of chrome back out of the garage until the back bumper hit the neighbours' broken fence, then it turned the opposite direction from him. It turned left out of the alley.

Boyd drove down the alley and pulled out about a block's distance behind them. The blue truck turned left onto 73rd Street and, after a few blocks, merged onto Bowness Road. The detective stayed a good ways back and followed Rudolph and Karl to the Foothills Medical Centre.

As they walked in the hospital doors, he walked right behind them. Boyd presumed they were here to visit Raven. However, at the information desk, Karl explained that their father had died and they were here to identify the body.

"And what is your father's name?" the woman asked.

"Hans Karl Ulfert," Karl answered.

"And your names please?"

"I'm Karl Ulfert and this is my brother Rudolph."

"Rudy," the big man interjected.

The detective could tell by the way the woman's eyes grew wide that there was a problem. A moment later, the security guard came hurrying from beside the gift shop. He was probably 65 years old, silver-haired, and wasn't as tall as Karl. The rent-a-cop did a double-take when he saw Rudy.

The woman calmly said, "I understand that there is a restraining order against you, Rudolph Ulfert. Sir, could I please ask you to leave the premises?"

Karl glared at Rudy. Rudy shrugged and said to Karl, "They didn't want me visiting the old man. He's dead so what difference does it make if I am here today?"

The security guard begged, "Please, sir. You should leave."

Rudy flexed his arm as he glared at him. The guard shook in his boots. Rudy laughed and meandered to the door with the security guard trailing behind like a stray dog. Rudy called to Karl, "I'll wait for you in the parking lot."

After a doctor met Karl at the front desk and lead him to the elevator, Detective Wiebe approached the information desk. He showed his badge and asked who he might talk to about Hans Ulfert. He still waited at the desk when he saw Karl come out of the elevator and head for the front door.

The doctor walked over to Boyd, introduced himself and said, "Detective, I am sure you are aware that I cannot discuss any of Hans Ulfert's medical information with you without a warrant as it would be a breach of privacy."

"Absolutely," Boyd replied. "I'm actually trying to track down his daughter. It is an urgent matter."

"You need to reach Mrs. Penner?"

"Yes. Would you have her first name and a contact number?"

"They have all that in the brain trauma unit up on 6A."

Up on 6A, the charge nurse gave the detective Adelheid's contact information. Boyd thanked her and said, "I understand there was a restraining order against Mrs. Penner's brother. What happened?"

"That was not in this unit. That was 6D. I heard that Hans Ulfert came in with a heart attack and was recovering nicely. The next day his son comes to see him. I'm not saying that the son was trying to kill him, but suddenly the father has a stroke and an aneurysm while the son is in the room. During surgery, they notice that his left leg is bruised the shape of a hand."

"You don't say?" Boyd commented to keep her talking.

"It is a real shame," she said. "About the father, that is. He makes it through brain surgery and seems to be recovering then, 20 minutes after his daughter visits him, he crashes. His son Karl was with him. He was the one who noticed that his father was having difficulty breathing."

"You don't suspect the daughter of harming him?"

"No, she was sweet. She called first thing in the morning after we moved him from D ward to see how her father managed the move."

Just down the hall and around the corner, Boyd asked the same questions of the staff at the 6D nurses' station.

The ward clerk told him, "Mrs. Penner visited her father every day. Sometimes a couple of times. Her father seemed to do much better after she visited. But don't you think it strange, Detective, that both times the millionaire father has a medical incident, one of his sons is in the room?"

Boyd did find it strange. Undoubtedly, Rudolph Ulfert contributed to his father's death. Proving intent would be impossible. The detective cursed the lag in getting information into the system because he wanted to read the incident report now.

The logical view said that, when a man experiences a heart attack, a stroke, an aneurysm and brain surgery, he might take a turn for the worse. His body could easily fail. Just because his son Karl was in the room is not evidence of foul play though Boyd was curious to know Karl's financial position. And Karl's brother Rudy would certainly benefit from the death of his father.

He again mulled over what Raven had said, "They will kill her." The daughter helps keep her father alive, and the sons want him dead. So maybe they decide to get rid of the sister. "This is a weak motive," Boyd admitted to himself as he walked towards the elevator.

Sarah was everything Boyd's ex-girlfriend wasn't. Not that his ex-girlfriend wasn't sexy. Brenda dressed for sex, always. And she was easy to understand. She liked to drink and, when she drank a lot, they had sex a lot.

Boyd's mother did not like her from the moment they met, which really didn't surprise him. Boyd's parents were very religious so when he took Brenda to his parent's home in Steinbach, Manitoba, for Easter, it did not go well. Boyd's sister described Brenda's idea of Easter Sunday clothes as 'trailer-trash slutty'.

Brenda brought two bottles of wine for Easter Sunday dinner, one red and one white, even though Boyd told her that his parents didn't drink. "They are Mennonite Brethren," he told her. "They don't drink, smoke, dance, or swear. They even think going to movies is a sin."

"Then there'll be more wine for me," Brenda replied.

Boyd might have drunk a glass of Chablis during the turkey dinner except he didn't feel right about drinking in front of his folks. They knew he drank wine so it wasn't like he tried to fool them. He just showed them respect by honouring their traditions. Brenda emptied both bottles and didn't care who she offended.

His mother asked him afterwards, "Do you really want that woman to be the mother of your children?" His mother went on to say that she saw Brenda roll her eyes when Boyd's father read the resurrection story out of the Bible after dinner for family devotions. And, of course, Boyd's mother pointed out that they shouldn't be sleeping together.

As far as Boyd could tell, sleeping together was the point of having a girlfriend. He wasn't with Brenda for the conversation. And, as far as religion goes, he attended the Mennonite Brethren church with his parents until he left home to join the police force. In that whole time, he never saw one miracle. He never saw the slightest sign of anything supernatural. The church was nothing more than a social club for people who wanted to believe that there was some divine reason for the suffering in the world.

At the same time, he had to admit that the Mennonites were good, hardworking and generous people. He had a great childhood, and that was more than he could say for Brenda and many of the people he met.

Until his mother mentioned it, Boyd never thought about getting married or having children. Brenda was his plaything and he was her designated driver and her bank. In hindsight, he wondered if his mother's questions or her prayers caused the whole thing to fall apart. Logic said it would have happened anyway.

Boyd woke up in the middle of the night asking himself, "What if Brenda is pregnant? Would I marry her? Can I see myself with her five years from now?"

His logical mind told him that Brenda was an alcoholic or close to it. She was not the person he wanted to raise his children. He would marry her if she got pregnant, but could foresee them divorced a year or two down the way.

Their relationship ended three weeks after Good Friday. Brenda wanted to go on a bar crawl and he suggested that they go for a walk. She went bar hopping without him. Two days later, she came by with her new boyfriend to collect her stuff. Boyd wasn't heartbroken or angry. He felt surprisingly relieved.

In the year after that, he never went out with anyone. And then he met Sarah Herrera. They met by accident. He was in the robbery investigation unit at the time and rushed down Crowchild Trail to get to the scene of an armed robbery. He came up fast behind her vehicle and turned on the siren. Sarah hit the brakes and started to pull over. The front right bumper of the squad car clipped the rear left corner of the bumper of her Mini Cooper.

To say he felt pissed off was an understatement. He radioed in that he would not reach the crime scene anytime soon, and that was a big blow for someone trying to make detective. And he'd have the accident report paperwork to do. And it would look like the accident was his fault.

He marched up to the window prepared to give the driver a piece of his mind, but when he saw her, he stood there speechless. The young woman behind the wheel took his breath away. Her long mahogany-brown hair cascaded from her shoulders and her long eyelashes framed brown eyes. He stared at her perfect Spanish lips.

"You hit me," she said.

"Um, yes. Are you all right?"

"Yes, I'm fine. It just felt a bit of a bump. Do we need to phone the police?" she asked, smiling.

"How about if I pretend I am one and we can exchange information?"

"Well, you look the part."

"Why did you hit the brakes?" he asked.

"I thought that pulling over is what you do when the police come up behind you and turn on the siren."

"Well, I just wanted to pass you."

"How was I supposed to know that?" she asked. And she waited for an answer.

"I needed to get somewhere in a hurry," he said trying to avoid answering.

"And how is that working for you?"

Boyd realized that this woman threw him off balance. She made him uncomfortable because she asked questions and challenged him to answer. And he wanted to answer. He wanted to see her smile again.

"Not one of my better days," he admitted, and he smiled.

Sarah got out of the Mini Cooper and walked to the back to inspect the damage to the bumper. Boyd noted she wore tight blue jeans, cowboy boots and a Run for the Cure tee shirt. Boyd stared at her shapely body as she examined the paint scrape.

"Can I get your name and phone number, miss?" he asked.

"Do you mean my driver's license and insurance card?"

"I'll need that too," Boyd replied, "but I was wondering if you'd like to go out sometime." He fully expected her to say no. She said yes.

From his car in the hospital parking lot, Detective Wiebe phoned Addy. "This is Detective Wiebe with the Calgary Police Service. Are you Adelheid Penner?"

"Yes," she answered. "Is everything all right? Are my children okay?"

"Sorry to alarm you. I'm sure they are fine. I'm calling about Raven Big Bear."

"I'm sorry. I don't know who that is."

"Raven Big Bear was your brother Rudolph's girlfriend."

"Was? Did Rudy kill her?"

"Does your brother kill people?"

"No. Well, not that I know of. It is just that he frightens me sometimes."

"That is the reason for my call. Raven Big Bear indicated that you might be in danger from your brother or brothers."

"They are not happy with me at the moment. When my father had a heart attack last week, he asked me to take care of a few things for him at his house. My brothers think I am robbing the place blind. Rudy is a real piece of work, but I think that his threats are just a lot of bravado."

"So he has threatened you?"

"Detective, my father died yesterday afternoon. After the funeral, I will never see Rudy or Karl again. I appreciate your concern. And thank Raven for worrying about me, but I am all right."

"Raven is in the hospital with a broken neck. It looks like your brother tried to kill her. For your own safety, don't turn your back on your brothers."

The call shook her and Addy managed to say, "Thank you."

Detective Wiebe wrote down in his notebook, "Possible motive: Brothers think sister is emptying the house."

When he got back to his desk at police headquarters, a phone message waited for him. The forward said, "This came in from the tip line and could be related to the case you are working."

The message followed:

This may be nothing so, if it is, then just ignore this. I'm worried about someone. Raven Big Bear sold me something… oh, well, nothing illegal. When I called her back to see if she had more… ah, stuff to sell, her husband answered her phone. He seemed surprised and hung up. I haven't been able to reach Raven since. Could you make sure she is all right?"

In the mall, Boyd walked up to the counter as Norman Paplinski looked at old coins through magnifying lenses attached to his glasses. The detective thrust his badge out over the top of the coins and watched the store owner's face go pale. "What did Raven Big Bear sell you?" the detective asked.

"I thought that the tip line was supposed to be anonymous," Norman complained.

"It is anonymous until you drive by the crime scene with Bowness Coin and Antique plastered all over your car."

"So there has been a crime?" he stated and his face turned even paler.

"You said in your phone tip that there was nothing illegal in your transaction. Is that still the case or do you want me to get a search warrant?

Norman pulled out his receipt book. "She came in with a sheet of coins on Sunday. She said her husband's father died and left them his coin collection. She said her husband told her to sell some of the coins so she could buy a crib and a highchair. Here," he said as he handed Boyd a sheet of paper. "Here is where she signed to say that the coins weren't stolen and that she had the right to sell them."

The date on the paper read Sunday, obviously before Hans Ulfert died.

"That's it? That is why you phoned her on Tuesday?"

"Well, um, Raven came back on Monday with another sheet of coins. Really excellent coins. The best I've ever seen and like the first ones. I bought those, too, and asked if there would be more. She showed me a couple of photos of a knee-deep coin collection piled up on the basement floor. There had to be a million dollars' worth of coins!"

"And you got greedy?"

"I am a businessman. A couple of clients fought over the coins Raven sold me and they promised to buy anything like that I brought in. So I called, but her husband Rudy answered the phone. And he hung up on me. After that, I never heard from Raven. Is she all right?"

"Not anywhere close to all right."

"I'll need to take your statement. And I'll need copies of your purchases and Raven's statement. I'm presuming you took some photographs of the coins and I want those too. And any coins you haven't sold are now evidence. We will double-check your records. Do I have your cooperation?"

"Absolutely!"

"Is there anything else Raven said about the coins?"

"No, nothing. On Monday, when I asked if she bought baby furniture with the money I paid her, she said no. She said that her husband was away and she needed his truck to hall the stuff."

"And to confirm, on Sunday Raven told you that Rudy's father was dead?"

"Yes. She said that Rudy didn't want to sell many coins because it was his reminder of his father."

Detective Boyd had not left the mall when he called Addy. "Mrs. Penner, this is Detective Wiebe again. Just a quick question for you: did your father have a coin collection?"

"Yes. He collected for years. What has this got to do with anything?"

"And where is this coin collection?"

"It's here in the house in the safe."

"Are you sure?"

"I presume so. I don't have the combination to open the safe. The coin collection will go to my brother Karl now unless my father changed his will."

"Is there any possibility that Rudolph had the combination to the safe?"

142

"Dad would never give Rudy the combination. He didn't trust Rudy. And everything in the safe is supposed to go to Karl." She paused and exclaimed, "Oh shit. No! It couldn't be."

"Mrs. Penner, what couldn't be?"

"When I arrived at the house on Friday, I saw that Rudy had tried to break into the studio. And in the front office where the safe is, the desk had everything pushed to one side like someone needed more room. And I found one of my father's coins underneath the desk. I planned to ask my father about it, but he deteriorated so quickly that I didn't get a chance."

"So it is possible that Rudy stole the coins?"

"Now that my father is dead, perhaps I can get the safe combination from the lawyer and I could find out for sure."

"Please do that, Mrs. Penner. Please do not tell your brothers about this conversation. I have something that I need to. We will talk again soon."

From Bowness Mall, Boyd drove straight to the hospital. At the brain trauma unit, he asked the charge nurse if she noticed anything unusual the day Hans Ulfert died. "Mr. Ulfert's children are a strange bunch," she answered. "But I see a lot of dysfunctional families come in when a parent is dying."

"Could you check the log for the day?"

She smiled at him and flipped back to yesterday's log. "Everything was normal. Mr. Ulfert showed a slight improvement in his blood pressure in the morning. We changed out a bag of fluid after his daughter was in. It was draining too fast. That is the only entry until he started to fail."

"What would cause a bag to drain too fast? Obviously, it was unusual because you wrote it down."

"Sometimes they get a hole in them. It is like the water cooler in the staff room. If the bottle gets a hole in it, then no suction created in the tank, and the water pours out. Even a pinhole in a saline bag could mean that the contents aren't sterile. We write it down when it happens."

"And the saline bag? What happened to it?"

"We'll send it back to the manufacturer so that the hospital gets a refund. It is in a plastic bag in the supply room."

"I need you to bring it to me. It may be evidence," the detective said. "Now I'll need to talk to the doctor that looked after him."

The nurse's face went pale. "Did the family send you here? Are they suing the hospital? I shouldn't be telling you anything."

"No. Quite the opposite. I'm sure the last thing they want is me asking questions."

"What is going on here, Detective?" Deputy Police Chief Burns asked Boyd. "You start out looking into a domestic violence case and come back with a story about an imminent threat to the suspect's sister. Now you are telling me that the sister of the suspect murdered their father in the hospital?"

"I know this sounds far-fetched, and I don't have all the pieces yet. However, if it is true, then someone will get away with murder. If I am wrong, what do we have to lose?"

"You are a rookie detective and I am wondering if you are bored and trying to come up with cases or if you are actually bright and can see past the obvious. I am about to find out. You've got your autopsy."

"Thank you, sir."

"Don't thank me. If you are wrong, I'm going to bust your butt back down to patrolman. And as far as what you have to lose when you tell a family that their loved one might have been murdered, you unleash a world of pain. And if you implicate any family member, you will destroy all trust in the family. Even if someone else confesses to the crime, the trust remains destroyed. False accusations undermine the police service and our society. Everyone has a lot to lose."

Addy rode the elevator to P. K. Parkman, however, this time Jack accompanied her. Marsha met them at the elevator and walked in front of them down the path. She wore a very short, skin-tight red dress. Addy knew Marsha put an extra swivel in her hips because Jack walked behind her.

Jack sipped some 18-year-old Glenfiddich scotch and Addy sipped red wine as Paul Parkman walked into the waiting room.

"Mrs. Penner, how lovely to see you again. And this must be your husband Jack." As he held out his hand to Jack, Paul Parkman did not seem the least bit embarrassed that he had been hitting on Addy just a few days before. Jack shook Paul's hand and Paul said, "I am sorry for the unfortunate circumstances. I like to think of Hans Ulfert as a friend, not just a client."

"Thank you," Addy said. "Besides wanting to know what happens next, I did receive a strange phone call from the Calgary Police Service. They asked about my father's coin collection. Do you know anything about it?"

"Let's talk in my office," he replied and led them down the hallway.

In Paul's office, the lawyer opened up a file folder from off his desk. "Here is a copy of your father's will," he said to Adelheid. "He names you as executor. You have the right to refuse. If you do, your brother Karl becomes the executor."

Addy started reading through the will. What she read so far matched her expectations because of her father's threats.

Paul said, "Let me summarise it for you. Although Alberta law states you can claim up to five per cent of total assets as executor fees, after probate and lawyer fees, of course, your father asks you to waive those fees. His request is not legally binding, so you may claim fees regardless. He did make provision for you to get paid for your time. The will itself states that your father left three-quarters of his estate to Karl and the coin collection. One-quarter of the estate goes to Rudolph. As for you and Heinrich, you may take one photograph each from the house. Your choice."

Jack swore. Addy looked up from reading, startled. It was rare for Jack to ever swear. "Sorry," he said. "I just kind of hoped that he would leave you something."

Addy put her hand on Jack's shoulder and said, "The money was never mine. Why would I want it?"

Paul said, "You mentioned in the waiting area that the police asked about the coin collection. To my knowledge, it is still in the house in his safe. Your father made sure I kept a complete list of his collection and updated it every time he bought or sold something. There is no reason why you couldn't give it to Karl before the rest of the estate is settled. As your lawyer, I would recommend that you have witnesses when you open the safe."

Addy took out her cell, scrolled to her recent calls and hit the detective's number. "Detective Wiebe? This is Adelheid Penner. You called me concerning my father's coin collection. I am with my father's lawyer and he just gave me a copy of my father's will and the combination to the safe. He suggests I have witnesses when I open the safe so I'd like to invite you to be there when I open it."

Addy handed her phone to Paul Parkman. "This is Paul Parkman, Attorney at Law."

"As far as I know, no one else has the combination for the safe." There was a pause then, "Yes, I have a complete list of contents as well as photographs of the contents."

When Addy got her phone back, she looked up the number she got from Karl and called it. "Hey, Karl, I'm at the lawyer's office and just got a copy of the will and the combination for the safe. Dad's lawyer said that you can take the coins now if you want. Why don't you and Rudy come over and watch me open the safe? Jack and I should back there in a half-hour. Ricky is at the house to let you in if you get there before we do. See you soon."

While they were in the elevator on the way to the main floor, Jack asked Addy, "Why on earth did you agree to become the executor? And why forego the executor fee? You certainly don't owe your father anything."

"My father was not a good man. I know that. But he was still my father, and I wouldn't be with you if not for him. The Bible says to honour your father and your mother. It doesn't say to only honour them if they deserve it. So I am honouring my father and my mother by cleaning up a mess."

Detective Wiebe arrived at Hans's house in an unmarked police car 17 minutes after receiving the call. He saw pictures of this castle when he googled Hans Ulfert. He noticed the scars in the wooden-plank front door where EMS had tried to batter it down. He parked in front of the garage doors but did not get out of his car. He backed in so he could watch people arrive.

First, Rudy and Karl arrived. Boyd watched the driver stare at him as the blue Ram 250 turned into the driveway. The giant of a man parked, got out, and glared at him as he walked right to him. Rudy put his giant hands on the windowsill, leant in, and threatened, "This is private property. Get the hell out of here."

Karl grinned, obviously enjoying the show.

Boyd lifted his badge and said, "I'm here to see Adelheid Penner. Police business."

Rudy yanked his hands back from the car like he just touched a hot frying pan. Hatred filled his eyes and he screamed, "She's not here, so screw off!"

Just then, Adelheid pulled into the driveway. She parked in front of the door and then she and Jack walked over to the detective's car. "It is all right, Rudy. This is Detective Wiebe. I asked him to come to watch me open the safe so Karl doesn't think I've ripped off his coins."

Rudy turned to look at Karl. "Karl would think you did, even if you didn't. He'd assume that you took some of them at least. Your brother is a suspicious bastard." And Rudy laughed.

Ricky heard the commotion and came to the door, so Karl went in, followed by Rudy. Boyd got out of his car. Adelheid apologized to the detective, "Sorry that I didn't arrive before my screwed-up brothers. I'm Addy and this is my husband Jack."

"Detective Wiebe," he said as he shook their hands. "I'm actually glad they arrived first."

Boyd sized up everyone. He took mental notes, "Rudy was definitely hot-tempered and dangerous. Karl seems to enjoy watching someone else get threatened. Adelheid and Jack seem like the people you would like living next door."

Inside the great room of the massive stone mansion, Addy introduced Ricky, the small-framed and somewhat feminine-looking brother. Ricky definitely acted nervous in the presence of a police officer.

Addy led the detective down the hall and found Karl and Rudy standing in front of the studio door. "Open it," Karl demanded. "This is my house and I want this door open now."

"To be accurate, the house is part of the estate and the profits from selling it will be split between you two." Addy turned to Ricky and said, "Sorry, Ricky." She turned back to Karl and Rudy. "The layer will set up a reading of the will. After that, I need to get Dad's income tax done and all his bills paid, then I'll get probate, and you two can fight over the house. That will be a year from now at least."

"A year?" Karl demanded.

"Open the studio!" Rudy screamed.

"I'll open it. Not because you threatened. And not because I have to." Addy punched in the numbers as the brothers watched. They rushed into the studio, knocking Addy against the doorframe as they pushed by her.

Just like Karl did the day before, Rudy marched straight over to the broken office door. His sledgehammer leant against the doorframe and he looked over his shoulder at Jack and swore. "Damn you, Jack."

Jack wanted to say, "I beat you to it." Instead, he quipped, "Thank you for providing the combination."

"You still owe me for a new door!" Karl screamed.

Rudy ducked to get into studio two. He came right back out. "There is nothing in here. Where is all the stuff?"

"They emptied the place," Karl accused.

"And what do you think our father kept in there?" Addy asked. Rudy looked at Karl hoping his brother would provide the answer.

"Porn," Jack told him.

"You had no right to touch it. It might have been worth thousands," Karl complained.

"I had every right to get rid of it," Addy told them. "Ask Dad's lawyer. Dad asked me to clean up the house. He specifically told me not to let you have any of the porn."

"How do we know what was in here?" Rudy demanded. He took a step towards Addy and glared down at her as he pumped his fists. "And if it was porn, how do we know you got rid of it?"

"What would I want with porn, Rudy?" she answered calmly as she stared up at him.

"We have photos of the rooms," Jack said. "And we shot video of the shred truck destroying it."

Rudy turned his hate-filled eyes toward Jack like he would kill him right then.

Addy asked, "Are you done with sight-seeing now? I asked you here to witness me opening the safe. If you are not going to be civil, I'll have Detective Wiebe escort you out and the safe can wait until the estate is settled."

Rudy snarled, "I have to wait another year for my share so Karl can wait for his precious coins."

Karl jumped in, "No, you are right, Adelheid. We are here to witness you opening the safe. Rudy can leave if he wants."

"And miss the show? No way!"

Everyone crowded into the office. Rudy stood just inside the door. The detective glanced at the portrait on the wall and then at Addy. "My mother," Addy said to answer the question he did not ask.

"Get on with it," Karl demanded.

Addy opened the folding doors to revel a six-foot Super Fortress high-security safe. First, she put the double-cut key she got from the lawyer into the keyhole and turned it. Then she read the directions out loud as she spun the dials. When she turned the dial to the last number, there was a click. Karl pushed her aside, pulled the bar upward and swung the safe's heavy door open.

Detective Wiebe watched the grin spread on Rudy's face as Addy reached the end of the instructions. As everyone else gasped and Karl swore, Rudy smiled like a schoolboy in an ice-cream shop.

"Where are my coins, Adelheid? Give them back right this second!" Karl screamed.

Rudy chuckled and everyone turned to look at him. "See, Sister, I told you he would accuse you. Now face it, Karl, you pissed off the old man one too many times and he sold his collection just to hurt you."

The safe contained one large brown-coloured envelope with Karl's name on it. Inside was a list of the contents of the safe, the inventory of the coin collection.

Detective Wiebe asked Karl, "Are you saying that there has been a robbery? Do you want to report a theft?"

Karl glared at Addy as he spat out the words through clenched teeth, "Yes, I want to report that someone stole my coin collection."

McCarty touched a button on his phone, lifted it to his ear and said, "Execute the warrant."

Everyone stared at him as he put the phone back in the pouch on his belt. "This office is now a crime scene. Please don't touch anything as you leave. And please do not leave the house until after I talk to you."

Detective Wiebe already had a warrant drawn up to search Rudy's house for evidence of a crime against Raven. But he also believed the coins were there, and they wouldn't be considered evidence of a crime unless someone reported the coins stolen.

As Addy walked out of the office, Boyd said, "Mrs. Penner, can I ask you a few questions?"

"Certainly," she answered.

Boyd checked the hallway to make sure they were alone. Then he stated, "I noticed that the desk has everything pushed to one side as you said on the phone. Why did you mention it?"

"My father never left anything out of place. Even the handles on the coffee mugs all face the same way. Take a look in the kitchen cupboards if you don't believe me."

"And you mentioned a coin. Do you still have it?"

"Yes. I was going to show it to my father..." she choked up and couldn't finish the sentence.

"May I see it?"

"It is in my purse. I'll run and get it," she said, and she left the room. Addy came back in a minute with her purse, set it on the desk and dug the coin out of a zippered pocket.

Right away Boyd noticed the $90,000 price tag. *She certainly isn't trying to steal the coin*, Boyd thought, *or she wouldn't tell me about it.*

"Now please show me where you found it," Boyd prompted.

Addy bent down with the coin in her hand and held it just above the computer cords. "Right here," she said. Then she got worried and stood up and asked him, "You don't think I stole the coins, do you?"

"No, ma'am. I have already solved the case. I really just want to know how he did it."

"Rudy?"

He ignored her question and asked, "Did you ever try to open the safe other than today?"

"No. My father wanted me to get rid of photographs that he did not want the public to see and did not want to fall into my brother's hands. All of us knew that Dad kept nothing but his coin collection in this safe."

"So we won't find your fingerprints on it other than on the dial?"

"No. I never touched it until today."

"And you are sure your father wouldn't give your brother Rudolph the combination number?

"Not in a million years!"

"You mentioned that Rudy tried to break into the studio."

"When I arrived, there was a half of two-litre of Coke leaning against the studio door. I guessed that he tried to figure out the passcode. Later that day, when I got back from visiting my father, I found a sledgehammer leaning on the front door." She smiled and added, "I should mention that I changed the combination on the front door."

"This sledgehammer is the one that your husband used to break down the office door in the studio?"

"Yes. My father was a little paranoid. Even inside the house, he locked doors."

"He hid his porn collection because he would be embarrassed if anyone found it?"

"No, nothing as benign as that. My father produced pornography. He didn't want anyone finding out. Especially my brothers."

"And you knew about this?"

"Not until the day before yesterday. Dad told me to destroy his secrets. He told me not to trust my brothers."

"From what I understand, both you and Ricky get nothing from the estate?

"Not a penny." And she pulled a copy of Hans Ulfert's will out of her purse and handed it to him. "I can't speak for Ricky, but it suits me fine. I didn't have to spend my adult life jumping through hoops to please my father. And believe me, he always set out expectations."

"How was your father when you went to see him yesterday morning?"

"I only saw him once yesterday. I went in the afternoon. The hospital called to say he was failing. I should have gone in the morning." Tears rolled down her cheeks and Addy pulled a tissue from her purse and wiped her nose.

A tactical team arrived outside while Boyd asked Addy questions. He said to her, "You have been most helpful, Mrs. Penner, so I am truly sorry for what I am about to do in your time of loss."

"You are going to arrest Rudy?"

The detective watched her face as he said the words, "Yes. And I am ordering an autopsy on your father."

Shock covered her face. "Tell me that Rudy didn't kill him!" she exclaimed.

Her reaction baffled him. Boyd could imagine his commander saying, "There are huge holes in your theory, Wiebe. You have speculation without any fact. What you've got is nothing more than a conspiracy theory and you are chasing your own imagination down rabbit holes."

He would argue, "But I have witnesses to say that Adelheid visited her father in the morning. I've seen the log. They even describe her down to the yellow shoes. Yet she denies being there."

"At best, you have a theory that someone murdered her father, and you have a daughter visiting her father in the hospital. She had to know the staff would remember her, especially when she introduced herself. She is either very stupid or she is innocent."

Boyd had to admit that Adelheid did not have motive to kill her father. At first, he assumed she might bump him off to get the inheritance. Now the only explanation is that she felt rage at being cut out of the will and saw her opportunity to kill him. He could already hear his commander's question, "If she was cut out of the will, don't you think she would try to get him to change the will. Wouldn't she want to keep him alive?"

Detective Wiebe answered Adelheid, "I'm not saying that someone murdered your father. I just want to be sure there was no foul play because of how Rudolph attacked your father in the hospital. The autopsy results will not come back for weeks, so please go ahead with the funeral. And I would appreciate it if you would keep this between you and me. There is no sense in getting everyone upset over nothing."

"I can do that. I don't want to believe that my brother murdered my father. A week ago I'd have sworn that my brother would never hurt my father. Now I am not so sure."

After Adelheid left the room, Boyd looked around for places where someone could hide a small camera. He admitted to himself that the black and white portrait drew his eyes like a magnet. The beautiful woman in the photograph could easily be the woman who just left the room. He pictured Adelheid naked which was easy to do as he stared at the photograph.

Detective Wiebe gave his head a shake and that is when he saw it. Dust lay over the top of the picture frame except for a small section on the right-hand side. He rolled the office chair from in front of the desk and knew, as he crawled up on it, that he would catch hell from occupational health and safety if they found out he stood on a chair with wheels.

He could clearly see a 2.5-centimetre-wide, square-edged, dust-free piece of the picture frame. He turned his back to the portrait and tried to imagine what a camera lens might capture. *Not enough*, he thought as he jumped down.

With his latex gloves on, he swung the safe door closed. With the open folding closet door at his right-hand elbow, he put his head down near the dial and looked up into the slats in the door. He shined his flashlight between the slats and saw a little smudge of blue sticky tack.

Rudy and Karl dug through the filing cabinets in the studio office when the tactical unit filed into the studio and spread out like a V around the office door. Rudy ducked to get through the office doorway and back into the studio. He glared at the tactical team and knew they came for him. "Really?" he screamed.

Detective Wiebe walked up to him and said, "Rudolph Ulfert, you are under arrest for stealing Hans Ulfert's coin collection."

Rudy turned to look at Karl, obviously more afraid of what Karl thought than the fact that the police came to arrest him. "It's a lie," Rudolph screamed at Karl. Then he pointed a giant finger at Adelheid, "This is all her doing. She is trying to steal our inheritance!"

Karl stared daggers at Adelheid so Detective Wiebe said, "We searched Rudolph's house and found the stolen coins."

"You son of a bitch!" Karl screamed at Rudolph. "All this time, you were trying to screw me over!"

Detective Wiebe shouted over Karl. "Rudolph Ulfert, you are also charged with aggravated assault for your attack on Raven Big Bear. Please come along peacefully."

"Or what!" Rudy screamed.

Three of the men lifted Tasers. The other four lifted sidearms.

Hans Ulfert's funeral took place on Monday morning. Addy picked the oak coffin, the white flowers, and the German hymns. Fortunately, her father purchased two side-by-side grave plots when Wilhelmina died so she did not have to deal with that as well.

Jack helped write the obituary. Addy told him, "I can't say one nice thing about him. Not one."

Besides the date and place of his birth, Jack wrote:

Hans Ulfert loved to travel and had an unparalleled skill at taking amazing pictures that captured the essence of people. He will long be remembered for his booming voice, his generous gifts to charity, and his quirks that made him so unique. He is survived by his daughter Addy (Jack) Penner, and sons Karl (Ursula) Ulfert, Rudy Ulfert, and Ricky Ulfert. He had several grandchildren.

When Addy read it, she exclaimed, "Karl will have a bird!"

"We can always hope," Jack replied.

The police brought Rudy into the church, two minutes before the service started. They did not allow him into the mourners' room with the rest of the family. After the family members filed into the sanctuary, the police led Rudy to the aisle seat of the third row from the front on the left-hand side, across the aisle from where Addy's family sat. Jack sat nearest the aisle, within arm's reach. Addy sat beside Jack, then Riley and Cody. Ricky sat in that row right against the wall.

Two hefty police officers sat beside Rudy and two more sat directly behind him. They never took their eyes off Rudy.

Karl and Ursula and their kids sat in the second row from the front. When Rudy came in, Karl and Ursula shuffled to the right until everyone in the row was smushed together at the far end of the pew. Karl made sure he wasn't within Rudy's reach.

Other than when the police brought him in, only Karl's kids dared glance at Rudolph. The front pew remained empty.

When Boyd arrived, he thought the building looked like a historic church like you might see in Heritage Park. It was painted white with green trim, had a steeple, and stairs with six steps to reach the door. Fortunately, the steps were cement and not the originals.

The inside of the church looked very plain, no doubt typical of the era. The walls and vaulted ceiling were white-painted plaster. Even the three bullet-shaped windows on either side were just plain, clear glass divided by white-painted wooden mutton bars. There were no ornate stained-glass images he'd seen in some churches. A red-carpeted aisle ran straight down the middle over the original plank flooring. On either side, 12 rows of ancient, un-padded pews were perpendicular from the edge of the carpet and butted up against the walls. At most, eight people could sit on each pew. In an alcove like an altar at the front of the church, hung a picture of Jesus on his knees praying.

"This building would be a nightmare to get out of if a fire broke out or if someone went postal during the service," Boyd worried as he watched Rudy fidgeting. Detective Wiebe slipped into the back row on the right side as Reverend Braun made welcoming remarks from a raised pulpit on one side of the platform. Boyd wore the dark suit he bought for attending funerals. Grey-haired seniors filled about one-third of the small sanctuary.

On the way in, Boyd read a plaque in the vestibule that said Trinity Lutheran Church was founded in 1899. From the empty back row, he looked around and joked with himself, "I wondered if any of the attendees today are the original founders?"

Reverend Braun, a bald, middle-aged man in a black suit, white shirt, and black tie, read the scripture, "Jesus said I am the resurrection and the life. He who believes in me will never perish."

Later on, Boyd realized this was the only mention of Jesus at the funeral. A woman sang *Amazing Grace* in German and then Karl climbed the steps to the pulpit to give the eulogy. He felt so nervous, the paper in his hand shook. He started to read what he had written, ended up putting the paper down on the pulpit and said, "Han Karl Ulfert was my father. He married my mother Wilhelmina Fischer and their children are sitting here today to say goodbye to him. He was famous. He was gifted when it came to taking pictures and making money. I will miss his generosity."

Karl came down from the platform and stopped mid-step when he saw Rudy staring at him. Watching Karl try to pass in front of Rudolph unscathed was like watching a mouse scurry past a farm cat. Just as he fearfully took another step, Rudolph lurched forward and four policemen sprang to their feet. Rudy remained seated and laughed. The officers sat down.

Reverend Braun returned to the pulpit and talked ad nauseam about all the good things Hans Karl Ulfert did. He concluded his sermon with, "Hans was a generous, or shall I say extremely generous, contributor to the church, missions, those in need, and to the arts. He will be welcomed into heaven by his loving wife Wilhelmina."

Boyd wondered if everyone else came to the same conclusion from the sermon as he did. "If you have lots of money to give away, then you go to heaven."

With some difficulty, the six elderly men pallbearers carried the heavy casket down the narrow aisle towards the back of the church. The policemen stood and Rudolph got to his feet. Rudy sneered down at Karl's frightened face, glared at Jack and Addy, and then followed the pallbearers. The four officers followed just behind him as there was no room in the isle to have officers on either side of Rudy's massive frame. Karl and his family stepped into the aisle to follow the officers. Jack, Addy, their children, and Ricky filed into the aisle.

The officers planned to take Rudy out of the church before the rest of the attendees, put him straight into a paddy wagon, and have him on the way back to jail before any of the mourners came out. Detective Wiebe knew there would be trouble the moment Rudolph turned to face the back of the church. A smirk crossed Rudy's face when their eyes met.

Boyd petitioned the judge to keep Rudolph away.

"You want to keep a man away from his father's funeral?" the judge asked. Rudy's lawyer insisted that he was no threat to anyone.

Rudy followed the casket until he stood almost even with the back row. Then he swung his left fist at Boyd's head. Boyd threw himself to his right. The wall beside Boyd's left ear exploded as Rudy's fist shattered the lath and plaster.

As the detective fell sideways and slightly forward, Rudy's kick caught him under his hip and flipped him head over heels as if he did a cartwheel down the row. Boyd's feet slammed into the sidewall at shoulder height. His head hit the wall below the pew. Then Boyd dropped onto his head and crumpled down to the floor between the pews.

The pallbearers at the front of the casket just stepped down the first stair when, startled by the crash and the screams, the pallbearers dropped the casket. It slid and bounced down the six steps like a train car sliding down an embankment. As it hit the sidewalk, the casket flipped and the lid flew open. It landed upside down, partially on the sidewalk and partially on the street. The shattered lid laid an arm's length away from it.

Inside the church, the officers immediately behind Rudy kicked him in the back of the knees and brought him down to his knees. Then the other two officers pounced on him knocking him down. As he fell towards Boyd, Rudy made a fist with his giant left hand and brought it down with all his might on Detective Wiebe's thigh.

Ten days later, Boyd's doctor said that he was fit to return to duty. He showed up for work at his usual time on Tuesday. His lieutenant watched Boyd limp in and glanced at the sling on Boyd's arm and said, "Detective, the deputy chief wants to see you. Now."

Boyd wished he put in earplugs. He wished everyone in the building wore earplugs. He knew that, all the way down the street, everyone heard the deputy chief reaming him a new one.

"What the hell were you thinking, Wiebe? You claim the giant is dangerous, yet you show up at his father's funeral. Were you trying to provoke him? Then you sit down where he is forced to walk right past you. Did you think you were freakin' invisible? And you sit where you have no means of escape and no way to protect yourself. Do you have shit for brains?"

Boyd started to answer, but Deputy Chief Burns continued. "You look like hell. What doctor in his right mind declared you fit to come back to work? I suppose you told him you work a desk job? Now get the hell out of my sight. I don't want to see your face for another week."

Boyd was about to say, "Yes, sir," but he saw the look on the deputy police chief's face, so he turned and limped away.

All-in-all, he did not fare badly. The attack broke his shoulder blade, gave him four stitches above his right eyebrow and a bruise that covered his entire thigh. Every officer he passed on the way out of headquarters stopped what they were doing, stood and saluted.

He wasn't sure if he earned their respect because he got the shit kicked out of him or because he survived screwing up without getting fired. The extra week off sounded like discipline but somehow felt like compassion. Sarah would be happy. She told him that morning he was not ready to go back to work.

After school that day, Riley asked Addy, "Why did Grandpa Ulfert give you this picture, Mom?"

"Grandpa didn't actually give me this picture, sweetheart. His will said I could have my choice of any picture in the house. I liked this one the best."

"I like it too!" Riley exclaimed.

The truth was that Addy had no use for portraits of famous people. Sure, she could sell a picture of one of the movie stars, but she had no interest in that. And she could sell the gold picture frame for thousands, but she did not want her father's money.

She gave Ricky the first choice and she knew what he would take. He picked the metre-wide portrait of their mother in the ornate gold frame that hung in the front office. Addy would have liked it but would have to have kept it locked away for her kid's sake. She used her father's debit card to pay to have the portrait boxed, insured, and then shipped on Ricky's flight home.

Riley asked, "What language is this?"

"It is German. Your grandpa left me a clue so that I could unlock a room at his house."

"Why didn't he just give you a key?"

"I have no idea. Your grandpa did some strange things."

"Where are you going to hang this picture?" Riley asked.

The framed photograph still sat on the hallway floor where she set it the day Addy brought it home after the funeral. She had not even moved it when she vacuumed the hallway carpet. The hall really wasn't the right place to hang it, and Addy certainly did not want it somewhere more prominent where visitors would ask about it.

The picture represented her childhood, a time when her father acted like a father, at least occasionally. As a child, she thought she lived in a perfectly normal family so the reminder of her past felt like a connection to at least a little bit of love. The picture also reminded her of how really bizarre her home life had been, and how very warped and dysfunctional her family was and her brothers still are. This picture of a horse in a plain honey-oak frame represented the total of her inheritance from her millionaire father.

Addy lifted the picture and said to her daughter, "I think Black Beauty belongs in your room. When your daddy comes home from work, I'll ask him to hang it for you."

On October 11, 6 days later, Boyd returned to work. He still wore the cotton sling, but the bruises were gone from his face and the stitches from his forehead. When he got to his desk, the detective that took on his workload said, "I have some good news and some bad news. Which do you want first?"

"I could use some good news," Detective Wiebe replied.

"Your workload got lighter while you were away. The brother in Vancouver dropped the charges against the giant that beat the crap out of you," Daniel Hollingsworth said as he braced himself for Boyd's reaction.

"How can that be possible?" Boyd exclaimed. "We found the stolen coins in his brother's basement. Rudolph's fingerprints were on the safe, and we found the video surveillance from his hidden cameras still on his computer. We even found the pencil camera he hid in the closet door!"

"Maybe your boyfriend threatened him."

Boyd exclaimed adamantly, "Rudolph is not my boyfriend!"

"The witnesses said he had a real thing for you. They said you like it rough!"

Boyd flipped him the finger and said, "His brother Karl seemed pretty angry that he stole part of his inheritance. I can't imagine that he dropped the charges out of brotherly love."

"You know what they say, blood is thicker than family squabbles. The stolen coins are still a motive for what the giant did to his girlfriend. You'll get him on that."

"If that is the good news, I'm afraid to hear the bad."

"Burns wants to see you. He said if you showed up to work one day early, I was to march you straight to his office." Hollingsworth handed him a pair of bright orange earplugs. "You'll need these."

Boyd still chuckled as he walked into the deputy chief's office, scrunching the foamy earplugs in his left hand as it rested in the sling. He tried to hide his smile but did not succeed.

"Do you think disobeying your commander is funny, Detective?

Boyd did not answer as he was prepared to hear a tirade without getting a word in edgewise. He stood there staring just over the deputy chief's shoulder at a distinguished merit award. He suddenly realized that Burns waited for his reply, and he quickly answered, "No, sir."

"Did I specifically tell you that I did not want to see your face for another week?"

"Yes, sir."

"And how many days is it since you stood in this office?"

"Six, sir."

"So you do know how to count?"

"Yes, sir."

"So are saying, Detective, that you are purposely disobeying me? Are you trying to tick me off?"

"Yes, sir. I mean no, sir."

"You are lucky the face I am looking at does not look at all like the man that stood here six days ago. That man would be one day early and I would think that he no longer wants to work for me."

Boyd did not know what to say so he replied, "Thank you, sir."

"I hope you are thanking me because I said that you are looking better, not because you think you can disobey me and get away with it."

"Yes, sir."

The deputy chief picked up a brown envelope from his desk and held it up. Boyd wondered if it was his walking papers until he saw that it came from the medical examiner. "I told you that the autopsy on Hans Ulfert was a test of your worth to this force. You do remember that said I would bust your butt if you were wrong?"

"Yes, sir," Boyd said and his heart beat fast as he took the envelope.

"In spite of your ineptness, somehow you spotted a murder. Now bring this one home, Detective. And for Christ's sake, stay out of the way of that giant."

Detective Wiebe opened the office door and was walking out when the commander said, "And Wiebe, give those earplugs back to Hollingsworth. He will need them."

Boyd didn't dare laugh out loud as he headed back to his desk. Hollingsworth asked, "So what happened?"

"Lady Luck is on my side today. Maybe not on yours." And he handed Hollingsworth his earplugs. Then Boyd pulled the toxicology report out of the envelope.

Rudy shuffled into the interrogation room and ducked to get through the doorway. The heavy chain between his feet made it impossible for him to step more than the length of his giant feet. Because no handcuffs existed for wrists or ankles his size, the prison staff wrapped a loop of chain around each ankle and wrists and padlocked them together. A chain ran between his wrists and his ankles so that he could not raise his arms.

Interview with Rudolph Ulfert

Location: Police Headquarters, Calgary, Alberta

Present: Matthew Hennigar, Rudolph's lawyer

Wiebe: "Mr. Ulfert, I have a few questions regarding your father, Hans Karl Ulfert."

Rudolph: "He is in hell. Go ask him yourself."

Wiebe: "When your father had a heart attack, you went to his place and let EMS in. Can you tell me about it?"

Rudolph: "He had a heart attack and I went to his place and let EMS in."

Wiebe: "When EMS left with the ambulance, what did you do?"

Rudolph: "I thought the old man kicked it or would soon so I ate the meal the delivery guy left at the house. No sense letting it go to waste. Then I took Karl's coins."

Lawyer: "There are no charges against my client concerning the coins. Rudolph, I advise you not to answer questions concerning the coins."

Wiebe: "Why did you take the coins?"

Rudolph: "Because my father always made a bid deal about how special Karl was. Karl could do no wrong, and the old man never let us forget it. Taking the coins was an f-you to them both."

Lawyer: "Rudy, I strongly advise you not to answer questions about the coins."

Wiebe: "You hate your brother that much?"

Rudolph: "More than you could know."

Wiebe: "He must not feel the same way about you. He dropped the charges."

Rudolph: "Like he had a choice."

Wiebe: "The hospital put a restraining order against you. Did you attack your father?"

Lawyer: "Don't answer that."

Rudolph: "He started thrashing. I grabbed his leg to keep him from falling out of the bed. It is in the police report. He was having a stroke or something."

Wiebe: "Raven said that you were out of town on Sunday and Monday. Where did you go?"

Rudolph: "I went to Vancouver."

Wiebe: "Isn't that where Karl lives?"

Rudolph: "Yup."

Wiebe: "What were you doing there?"

Rudolph: "Deciding if I wanted to move there once the old man croaked."

Wiebe: "Did you see Karl while you were there?"

Rudolph: "We went for beers."

Wiebe: "You went for beers with the brother you hate?"

Rudolph: "He was buying."

Wiebe: "Did anyone in your family have reasons why they'd like to see your father dead?"

Rudolph: "Who didn't? He was a son of a bitch. We all had reason to hate him. Adelheid most of all. If I were her, I would have killed the bastard years ago."

Wiebe: "Why do you say that?"

Rudolph: "Ask Addy."

Wiebe: "I saw your sledgehammer at the house. Why did you want to break into the studio?"

Lawyer: "Don't answer that."

Rudolph: "My old man kept everything locked. He was paranoid. I figured if he died, I'd want to see what he kept hidden before Karl got it all."

Conclusions/Speculations/Questions

Rudolph Ulfert admits that he stole the coins and that he went back to the house to break into the studio. He indicated that Adelheid had the motive to kill her father. He hates his brother Karl, yet goes to see him. Why?

Detective Boyd Wiebe visited Raven Big Bear that afternoon. The room stank of disinfectant and Raven's unbathed body. A cloth covered her eyes to block the light.

"You're looking better," he said as a hello. "I'm Detective Wiebe. I spoke with you just after your surgery." The truth was that she looked pretty much the same, only thinner and blood no longer seeped from the metal pegs in her head. Her black hair was growing back as stubble across her skull.

She lifted the cloth and squinted at him. "I'm sorry," she replied. "I don't remember you."

"You told me not to let them kill her."

"Did you stop them? Is Rudy's sister okay?"

"You were drugged up and in a lot of pain. I was not sure I caught what you were telling me, but I followed up anyways. Adelheid is fine."

"Good. I've never met her, but nobody deserves to die."

"Tell me about the coins."

"Rudy stole them because he thought his father was dying. When I passed on the message from his sister that his father was recovering and would come home, Rudy became very upset. He knew he'd be caught and his father would write him out of the will."

"And you took some of the coins?"

"I sold some so I could buy a crib and a highchair. Rudy kept promising, but never came through on anything."

"You do realize that you are admitting to selling a stolen property?"

"Yes."

"So what happened the day you were hurt?"

"I was having contractions and Rudy arrived home just as I was about to call a cab. Then my water broke and I ran to the bathroom. I don't remember anything after that."

"So why did you tell me that they were going to kill Adelheid?"

"Karl phoned Rudy to say that his sister was trying to get back into her father's good books. He said she was making a grab for the money and wanted her father to cut all the brothers out of the will. Rudy went ballistic. He said that they would kill her when he came back. Then he left for Vancouver."

Conclusions/speculations/questions

Rudolph steals the coins and then discovers his father isn't dying. He will be cut out of the will. He goes back to the house to find something to blackmail his father with, something hidden in the studio. He cannot get in, possibly because Adelheid changed the door codes. He goes to the hospital and threatens or attempts to kill his father. The motive is money and not getting caught.

Karl and Rudolf conspired to kill their sister. Why? She was not in line for any money. Karl set it up. What does he have against her?

Interview with Adelheid Penner

Location: Police Headquarters, Edmonton

Wiebe: "Thank you for coming in, Mrs. Penner. I have a few questions that I wanted to ask you."

Adelheid: "Questions that you could not ask over the phone? Do I need a lawyer?"

Wiebe: "You are welcome to have a lawyer with you, although I don't think you will need one."

Adelheid: "Is this about my father?"

Wiebe: "Yes. But before we get into that, I wanted to say that you have great shoes. My girlfriend would be jealous."

Adelheid: "Thanks. My mother had a thing for shoes. Before my father died, I had one pair of high heels, some loafers and a couple of pairs of running shoes. Karl was in a generous mood after you arrested Rudy and he gave me 20 pairs of brand-new shoes from my mother's closet. That wasn't nearly all of them. She had over 100 pairs. Lucky for me, I have the same size feet as my mother."

Wiebe: "My girlfriend is crazy about the colour yellow. Do you have any yellow shoes? Did your mother have any yellow shoes?"

Adelheid: "No, I look ghastly in yellow. I don't have anything yellow. My mother and I shared the same skin tones. She wore nothing yellow either."

Wiebe: "My girlfriend loves yellow. So you have no yellow sandals or summer shoes? No yellow tee shirts?"

Adelheid: "Yellow is just not me."

Wiebe: "Tell me about the morning your father died. Where did you go and what did you do?"

Adelheid: "I woke up to the sound of Jack smashing down the office door in the studio at 5:00 a.m. Then we spent a couple of hours hauling pornography out to the garage. After that, we ate breakfast. Luckily the shred truck could come in the morning. It arrived just before 10:30 and we shredded everything by 11:00."

Wiebe: "So Jack stayed with the shred truck while you visited your father?"

Adelheid: "I never saw my father until the afternoon. I stayed at the house to make sure every speck of porn got shredded. Besides, Ricky called on Monday night to say he was flying in. We planned to go to the hospital together when he arrived."

Wiebe: "You mentioned the pornography previously. Why was it so important to get rid of a porn collection?"

Adelheid: "Not only did my father produce porn, but he also starred in it. He asked me to get rid of it for him. I think that having the heart attack scared him. I think he wanted to be free of it in case he died."

Wiebe: "Why you? Why not ask Karl or Rudolph?"

Adelheid: "I think it was because I didn't care about the money. He knew I would do what he asked without trying to blackmail him."

Wiebe: "Your brothers would do that? They would blackmail your father?"

Adelheid: "In a heartbeat. Karl and Rudy have been blackmailing each other for years. At the hospital, Karl gloated that he blackmailed my father. And with all the crap that Rudy put Dad through, I wouldn't doubt that he held something over him."

Wiebe: "For the record, are you in line to receive any money from your father's estate?"

Adelheid: "Not a penny other than what I get for the time I spend settling the estate. Two of my brothers get everything. Ricky and I receive nothing. Well, we each got a photo."

Wiebe: "So what did you do after 11:00 a.m. when the truck left?"

Adelheid: "Just before 11:00, Ricky called to say that he arrived and would take a cab over so Jack and I took a quick shower. Then I poked through business files and Jack destroyed a computer that Dad used to edit the porn."

Wiebe: "Rudolph mentioned that you had more reasons to hate your father than the rest of them. What did he mean by that?"

Adelheid: "My father was not a good man. He was controlling and demanding. When I didn't do everything he wanted, he told lies about me."

Wiebe: "Then why were you helping him?"

Adelheid: "In spite of how he treated me, he was still my father."

Wiebe: "So why did Jack break down the office door?"

Adelheid: "Uh, well, I think he got tired of the time we wasted trying to figure out the clues my father left to discover the door codes."

Wiebe: "So why the games? If your father wanted your help, why didn't he just give you the door codes?"

Adelheid: "I think he wanted the help, but that meant I got to see into his sick mind. I like to think that the game was his psychological way of slowing me down so that I didn't discover all of his secrets at once."

Wiebe: "So what time did Heinrich arrive?"

Adelheid: "Just after noon. Later than I expected. He said that he checked his carry-on bag then had to wait for it. Then a cab refused to pick him up so it took a little longer to get to the house."

Wiebe: "So he went with you to the hospital and you took him to your father's room?"

Adelheid: "Kind of. The hospital told me that they moved Dad to 6A, the brain trauma wing. That is just the next hallway from where the cardiac unit is, but I had no idea what room he was in. Besides, I needed to introduce myself to the nursing station. We stopped there, and then Ricky went ahead of me to the room."

Wiebe: "I noticed that you seemed to be closer to Heinrich than to your other brothers. How is your relationship with Karl?"

Adelheid: "Karl is so much like my father it is scary. Maybe I keep him at a distance because of it. Other than for my mother's funeral and now with my dad's, I really have nothing to do with him."

Wiebe: "Did you have a big falling out at one point?"

Adelheid: "No. I left home before Karl turned 15. We've hardly spoken and, whenever we do, he tries to control me. I think that is what he hates about me. I don't let him get to me."

Interview with Jack Penner

Location: Edmonton Police headquarters

Wiebe: "I'm trying to get the timing right on everything that happened the day your father-in-law died. But before we get to that, can you tell me if Adelheid has any yellow shoes or sandals. My girlfriend is crazy about yellow, and I was thinking about buying her yellow shoes."

Jack: "Addy doesn't wear any yellow. No dresses, shirts or shoes."

Wiebe: "Addy said that she went to see her dad on the morning he died. What time did she leave for the hospital?"

Jack: "That is not possible. The shred truck arrived at 10:30 and she didn't go anywhere before that. She must have the days mixed up."

Wiebe: "So she didn't leave you to shred things while she visited her father?"

Jack: "Her father was doing better the evening before, although he looked awful to me, so Addy wasn't in a rush to see him. Besides, on Monday night, Ricky phoned to say that he was flying in and would arrive in the morning."

Wiebe: "It sounds like you did some heavy-duty shredding. What company did you use?"

Jack: "Shred-X. Their machines can shred hard drives."

Wiebe: "From what I gather, Hans Ulfert was not a very nice man. How would you describe your wife's relationship with him?"

Jack: "Distant. There were years where they never spoke. Only when Addy's mother was dying, did they get back into contact. I think they spoke twice on the phone since the day of her mother's funeral."

Wiebe: "Rudy said that Adelheid had more reasons to hate her father than the rest of them. Could you tell me what that is about?"

Jack: "Rudy said that? Oh my God! Maybe he saw the recording."

Wiebe: "What recording?"

Jack: "Addy's father tried to rape her when she was 16. Addy said that it happened at his old studio and that her father filmed it. Apparently, after that, he made her life hell until she left home."

Wiebe: "When did you learn about the assault?"

Jack: "Just a couple of days before her father died. Addy told me while we were cleaning out mountains of porn."

Wiebe: "Addy said that on the morning her father died, she awoke early when you smashed down the office door with a sledgehammer. Why did you do that?"

Jack: "Um, I thought I heard something. Addy heard it a couple of days before and I thought it must be a raccoon or a squirrel in the studio, but I never found any sign of animals when I looked. But that morning I heard it too."

Wiebe: "Let me get this straight, you smashed down a locked door in the studio because you heard something while you were in an upstairs bedroom?"

Jack: "Yes. Maybe I just felt tired of the torture that Addy's father put her through. Maybe I just wanted his manipulation over."

Wiebe: "So you did not find what made the noise?"

Jack: "No."

Wiebe: "Did you find the recording Adelheid's father made of his assault on her?"

Jack: "No, but we found hundreds of recordings of Hans Ulfert having sex with various women. We were not hunting for the recording. By that, I mean that we did not play any of the videos or look at every label or picture. We just destroyed everything."

Wiebe: "When I was at the house, you mentioned to Karl that you took pictures and videos of you shredding the pornography. Did you record shredding the pornography on that Tuesday?"

Jack: "Well, not all of it of course. Just short clips throughout. Addy wanted to be able to prove to her brothers that we destroyed everything we took out of the house. You met them. You saw what they are like."

Wiebe: "I'd love to see those recordings."

Jack: "I'll send you the whole works if you'd like."

Wiebe: "Yes, please do as soon as we are done here."

Jack: "You've got it, Detective."

Wiebe: "On Tuesday, when you took Ricky to see his father, did you notice anything strange?"

Jack: "The whole thing was surreal. First, Ricky flies here to see his father then complains that he has a headache and doesn't want to go to the hospital with us. I get it. Hans Ulfert acted more than cruel to him, but Addy persuaded him. And then, when we get to the hospital, the staff was rude. Then we find Karl in the room. You'd think if Karl was flying in, he'd let his sister know."

Wiebe: "What do you mean the staff were rude?"

Jack: "Addy introduced herself and asked for her father's room number. The nurse acted annoyed like Addy should know without asking."

Conclusions/speculations/questions

The sexual assault is motive for Adelheid to kill her father. Perhaps festering anger at being cut out of the will, but she does not appear angry or resentful. Hurt maybe because she is asked to deal with stuff without being recognized as a daughter.

She was not forthright in saying that her father assaulted her. Why would she be? Either she is hiding motive or she is embarrassed to talk about it. She is evasive about why Jack smashed open the office door.

Jack's answers confirm hers. Either they are well rehearsed or they are telling the truth. I'll verify with the shredding company and through the videos. Jack was definitely hiding something concerning the office door. He admitted that he just found out that Adelheid's father sexually assaulted her. This is a possible motive for murder. Maybe the two of them planned this out and carefully arranged the alibis.

Interview with Karl Ulfert

Location: North Vancouver police station

Wiebe: "Karl, I'm trying to piece together the events the day your father died."

Karl: "She killed him, didn't she? That is what this is about."

Wiebe: "Who killed him?"

Karl: "Adelheid killed my father. I knew it!"

Wiebe: "Why would you say that? I thought she went to Calgary to take care of your father?"

Karl: "Women are always after the money. She was pissed that he wouldn't change his will and she killed him. All her sanctimonious words about not being like him, and she is playing all of us for fools. I saw her leaving the hospital. Then she comes back an hour later acting all surprised that her father is failing."

Wiebe: "When did you see her?"

Karl: "I arrived at the hospital around a quarter to 11:00. She walked out the front door and straight towards the cab I was in. Then she turned right and walked down the street."

Wiebe: "You'd swear in court that it was her?"

Karl: "I know my sister. She walked by 20 feet away. Yes, I'd swear."

Wiebe: "What was she wearing?"

Karl: "A yellow shirt, black sports pants, a Blue Jays ball cap and sunglasses. (Chuckle)"

Wiebe: "What is funny?"

Karl: "Nothing really. She wore her hair through the back of the hat like a ponytail. I just realized that my screwed-up brother wears his hair the same way. What a fruit!"

Wiebe: "Rudolph?"

Karl: "No, Heinrich."

Wiebe: "Rudolph came to Vancouver on Sunday before your father died. Did you see him?"

Karl: "We went to Hooters for beers."

Wiebe: "Why did he come here?"

Karl: "I think he considered moving here once he got the old man's money."

Wiebe: "Are you okay with that? He stole your coins and you seemed pretty ticked. I am surprised you dropped the charges."

Karl: "He is a piece of shit, but he is my brother."

Wiebe: "And Adelheid? How is your relationship with her?"

Karl: "We are not close. She always did her own thing regardless of what my father said. She didn't care if she made him happy. Fortunately for her, my mother doted on her."

Wiebe: "At the hospital, you saw your sister, but you did not let her know you were there. Why was that?"

Karl: "I wanted some alone time with my father. I didn't want my sister interfering."

Wiebe: "Rudolph said that he came here to discuss how the two of you would kill Adelheid. Why did you want her dead?"

Karl: "God, what a loser! All the 'roids he pops have scrambled his brains. Seriously, Detective, Rudolph can kill a person with a single punch. Why would he talk to me about violence? Addy is a strange one, but she is still my sister."

Wiebe: "I understand that you will receive three-quarters of the inheritance. I take it that you had a good relationship with your father?"

Karl: "It wasn't hard to follow his desires. And the result is that I get most of the money. Adelheid is a fool. Did you know that her kids never saw their grandmother until her funeral? They never knew what a great man their grandfather was. They never got one penny from him. He showered us with money every time we visited... tens of thousands of dollars."

Conclusions/speculations/questions

Rudolph and Karl's answer align about Rudolph's visit to Vancouver. However, it is hard to imagine. Perhaps Rudolph warned Karl about what questions I might ask him. But why would he unless the two were hiding something?

Karl stood to gain from his father's death and he was there when his father began failing and the nurses discovered the leaky IV bag. Maybe he killed his father and now implicates his sister. He does confirm Adelheid was at the hospital before him. Hospital staff confirm as well.

To add to her motive, Hans Ulfert kept Adelheid's mother away from her. Adelheid may have been jealous that Hans showered Karl and family with money and that Karl and Ursula had a good relationship with Karl's parents.

However, Adelheid has an air-tight alibi. Not only do I have the video she shot on Tuesday morning, but I also have the testimony of the shred-truck operator. He said she was fanatical about not letting a single piece of pornography remain and watched every second. She even checked the bins at the end to make sure nothing remained in them.

Karl did not seem flustered at the question about planning to murder Adelheid. He is a great liar. An innocent person would have acted horrified.

Interview with Heinrich Ulfert

Location: (via video conferencing) Service de Police de la Ville de Montreal

Wiebe: "I have a few questions concerning the day that your father died."

Heinrich: "She didn't do it. Addy didn't kill him."

Wiebe: "I never said your father was murdered."

Heinrich: "He was. And Addy didn't do it! She loved the old man. God only knows why. He was the most abusive, evil person you could imagine. And a master liar. I'm not sorry he is dead."

Wiebe: "So why do you think someone murdered him?

Heinrich: "For the same reason you know he was murdered. Someone put poison into his IV bag."

Wiebe: "How do you know this?"

Heinrich: "It wasn't Addy."

Wiebe: "Who was it then? Did you murder your father?"

Heinrich: "I wish I had thought of it. I would have done it for her. I can't say I didn't imagine it a few times over the years, but I'm glad it worked out the way it did. I am still able to look my sister in the face."

Wiebe: "What time did you arrive in Calgary?"

Heinrich: "A few minutes before 11:00."

Wiebe: "And what time did you arrive at your father's house?"

Heinrich: "Just after noon."

Wiebe: "What took you so long?"

Heinrich: "I hung around the airport for a little while, trying to steel my nerves before having to face my father. I told my sister I had to wait for my bag, but I travelled only with the carry-on. When I finally did decide to go, the first cab I came to refused to give me a ride."

Wiebe: "Did you file a complaint?"

Heinrich: "I complained long and loud to the cabbie that did take me."

Wiebe: "You obviously were not close to your father. Why did he cut you out of his will?"

Heinrich: "My father was a master at destroying lives. He knew how to cause the maximum amount of emotional pain. I'm not just talking about being hurt by him. No, my father would find your weak spot and then manipulate you for years. He deserved to die."

Wiebe: "Go on."

Heinrich: "From the time I was eight, he kept me away from my mother. He used me to manipulate her and her to manipulate me. All this because I saw him having sex with the church secretary. Karl would have blackmailed him. I didn't."

Wiebe: "So your father cut you out of the will."

Heinrich: "Understand Detective that I never was in his will. There was never going to be money coming my way. He just said I was cut out so that my brothers would do as he said out of fear. He sacrificed me so that Karl and Rudy wouldn't turn out independent and brave like Addy."

Wiebe: "You really love your sister."

Heinrich: "She was like a mom to me. She loved me as a kid and loves me the way I am now. She is better than all of us put together. No matter what anyone says, I would never hurt her."

Wiebe: "Who would accuse you of trying to hurt her?"

Heinrich: "Believe me. I would never hurt her intentionally."

Wiebe: "What is your relationship with your brothers?"

Heinrich: "I hate them. They are scheming and evil."

Detective Wiebe watched the recording three times before he saw it. In the very last frame, after Heinrich was told he could go, he reached for his sunglasses and hat. A Toronto Blue Jays ball cap.

Conclusions/speculations/questions

Heinrich had the motive to kill his father: the abuse as a child and his love for his sister. He knew that his father was murdered. He could have heard this from Adelheid or speculation from Karl. However, he knew how someone murdered Hans Ulfert. Heinrich was adamant that his sister did not do it.

Heinrich looks similar to his sister in size and face shape. His hair is almost identical in length and colour, down to the highlights. He arrived at his father's house later than expected. Perhaps he wore the sunglasses and ball cap at the hospital to make people think he was his sister. But he called it poison. Perhaps he did not know what he injected. Perhaps he got it from someone?

He swore he would never hurt Adelheid, and then added the word 'intentionally'. He claims his brothers are evil and scheming. Karl is known to blackmail. Rudolph is known to threaten. Was Heinrich coerced into a scheme to kill his sister and decided to save her by killing their father? Or did he pretend he was her so she would get the blame?"

Sarah felt more than annoyed. She was steamed. When Boyd suggested they go to Vancouver for the weekend, she jumped at the prospect of a romantic weekend away. She hadn't pictured them spending Saturday evening at Hooters. And this was their second Hooters.

She knew what would happen next, the waitress would come by and hit on her man. He would smile like his live-in girlfriend was not sitting beside him and order a glass of red wine for her and a pint of beer for himself. And he'd stare at the barmaid's bum as she walked away.

When they left the hotel that morning, he said, "Let's go sightseeing." What he meant was driving around a residential district in North Vancouver looking for an address. When he found it, he parked across the street for 20 minutes. He never spoke a word as he poured over his notebook again and again.

At least after that, they went to Stanley Park and walked the Sea Wall until the rain forced them indoors.

The barmaid came back and batted her eyelashes at Boyd while she set down his beer. She put the wine down without even glancing at Sarah. She clearly knew where her tip came from.

"What is your name, sweetheart?" Boyd asked. Sarah decided that she would never let Boyd use that expression on her. Ever.

"Julie," she answered as she leant forward to give him a good view.

"Julie, I was wondering if you could help me. I'm a detective and this is my assistant. I'm trying to track down a guy that comes in here. You see, his father died and left him a pile of money."

Sarah thought, *Now I am his assistant. I'm nothing but arm candy while he works.* She watched Boyd unfold a page with a photograph of a wedding party and a picture of Karl Ulfert.

The barmaid's eyes got big. Pointing to the picture of Karl, she said, "That is Karl. He comes in here all the time. He tells all the girls that his father is a millionaire and, someday, he'll get all that money. I thought he was stringing bullshit just to get us in bed with him."

She turned towards the back section of the bar and called, "Cindy, come over here for a second." And she turned back to Boyd. "Cindy waited on Karl and the giant a month or so ago."

The woman who came over wore the same Hooters' uniform, short orange shorts and a white scoop-neck tee shirt. However, Cindy left a lot less to the imagination.

"Apparently, Karl really is getting a whack of money!" Julie exclaimed.

Cindy grinned ear to ear. She turned to Boyd and asked, "Are you a lawyer or something?"

"No, a detective. I'm trying to track down Karl and his brother. The big guy. Apparently, the lawyer has the wrong addresses." And Boyd showed her the 12-year-old wedding photo.

Sarah thought, *Boyd is a damned good liar. It probably helps him with his job, but it makes me wonder if I can trust him.*

Cindy said, "After Karl came in here with the giant, I spent the night with him. He's only been in a couple of times since. I wanted to try on his brother to see if all his parts were giant-sized, but he acted way too scary. He wouldn't let anyone sit in the tables close to them, like they were having a secret conversation."

"Did you ask Karl what it was about?"

"Yes. He just said that he would be the only one that would inherit his father's money."

"Did he mention his sister?"

"No. I didn't know he had a sister. But his other brother, the small one, was kind of femmy if you know what I mean."

Boyd just about came out of the chair in excitement. "His youngest brother was here?"

"Yes. He bolted from the table and barfed before he got to the can. Really strange since he was only drinking orange juice. And when he came out, some biker guy wanted to fight him, but the giant brother stopped him like swatting a mosquito. Our bouncer shit himself thinking he might have to do something."

"Did you notice anything else strange?"

"Well, there was no love lost between them, yet they were together. The giant insisted he only drank coke and the little one said he only drank organic juice, yet Karl ordered them beers. And they each drank a pint, making grimaces the whole time. Karl laughed about it that night. He said that they had to do whatever he said."

"That is strange," Boyd commented.

"And one more thing, Karl ordered a shot of Frangelico and left it to sit on the table untouched. He really likes his booze so that is strange. When I cleaned off the table, I also found two hazelnuts. When I asked Karl about it, he told me that it was his way of saying that he was nuts about me."

Cindy turned to Sarah for the first time and said, "I don't know what it is with men, but they have no concept of romantic."

"You can say that again!" Sarah exclaimed.

"When will Karl get the money?" Cindy asked. She practically danced with excitement.

"It will be at least a year," Boyd answered. "Maybe even two. They have to settle the estate and do his father's taxes."

When the barmaids left the table, Boyd picked up his cell phone and dialled Adelheid Penner's number. She answered on the second ring.

"This is Detective Wiebe. I'm sorry to interrupt your evening, Mrs. Penner, but I have a quick question for you. Does your family have a toast that they do with Frangelico? Or perhaps a tradition they do with hazelnuts?"

"I'm deathly allergic to hazelnuts. I had an allergic reaction as a kid and I still carry an EpiPen. Hazelnuts and hazelnut liqueur were never allowed in the house when I lived there, although things might have changed after I left. Why are you asking?"

"I'm working on a puzzle and random bits of information can help connect the pieces. Thanks for the information." And he hung up the phone.

He turned to Sarah and said, "I'm done working. Now let's go celebrate." They left Hooters without finishing their drinks and Boyd drove to Le Crocodile, a French restaurant on Burrard Street. Sarah was surprised that he had a reservation and she felt underdressed.

"You should have told me," she complained as the maître d' led them to a table.

"You really thought my idea of a good time is an evening in Hooters?"

She was going to say yes, but they arrived at the table and the maître d' pulled out the chair for her and put the white linen napkin across her lap when she sat down. He no sooner left when the waiter arrived at the table. "My name is Yves. Can I bring you a drink while you decide on supper?"

"Bring us a bottle of Charles Heidsieck," Boyd replied.

"Ah, champagne. Is this a special occasion?"

"Yes, I am having dinner with the most beautiful woman in the world." Sarah blushed.

Sarah ordered the lobster bisque as an appetizer and B.C. Salmon as her entrée. Boyd ordered escargot and then prime rib on the bone. For dessert,

Sarah ate crème brûlée à l'orange and Boyd enjoyed the tiramisu that came in a cup made of chocolate.

As they walked out of the restaurant, Sarah said, "I've never seen you drive after having more than one drink. Should we get a cab?"

"I already ordered one," he replied as he pointed at a white carriage with two white horses was parked in front of the restaurant. Boyd led her to it and the coachman opened the door for her.

Sarah leant on Boyd's shoulder with a blanket pulled up to her neck as she watched the night lights. It had been the most amazing and romantic evening of her life so it seemed out of the blue when Boyd asked her, "Do you know why I dragged you along with me while I worked?"

"Because you're a workaholic?" she ventured.

He laughed. "Quite possibly. The truth is that I'd rather have you near me than away from me. I also wanted you to see what I do."

"Like lie through your teeth?"

"Yes, exactly. When I am working a case, it drives me. It consumes a lot of my thinking. And I twist the truth or lie outright to get people to give me information. I wanted you to see me like that so I could promise that I will never lie to you."

She did not have a clue why he said that so she replied, "Okay. Thanks for telling me that."

"I thought it was fun having you with me today, but you looked like you would rather be anywhere else."

"I thought you didn't have a romantic bone in your body. I asked myself why I was with you."

"And now?"

"Tonight has been so special; I wish it would never end. I love you, Mr. Detective."

"Then marry me," he said as he held a diamond ring.

2nd Interview with Heinrich Ulfert

Location: Service de Police de la Ville de Montreal

Wiebe: "I have a few more questions for you."

Heinrich: "I gathered that because I got dragged into here for questioning. And you showed up in person."

Wiebe: "Do you have any yellow shoes?"

Heinrich: "Several pairs."

Wiebe: "And a Blue Jays baseball cap?"

Heinrich: "Yes."

Wiebe: "I checked with the cab company, and the driver distinctly remembers picking you up and taking you to your father's house. However, I discovered that you didn't fly into Calgary from Montreal. Why were you in Vancouver?"

Heinrich: "Karl lives there. He asked me to come for a visit."

Wiebe: "What did you talk about at Hooters with Karl and Rudy?"

Heinrich: "Karl told us that Addy was taking all the money. He asked how we could stop her."

Wiebe: "Why would Karl ask you that? My understanding is that you aren't in line for any part of the inheritance."

Heinrich: "Karl said he would share his inheritance with me."

Wiebe: "Does Adelheid trust Karl?"

Heinrich: "Not in the least."

Wiebe: "Does Adelheid trust Rudolph?"

Heinrich: "Not as far as she could throw him. (Chuckle)"

Wiebe: "Does your sister trust you?"

Heinrich: "Absolutely. I've never given her reason not to."

Wiebe: "How will she feel when she discovers that you went to Calgary to kill her? Will she trust you after she finds out that you were going to put hazelnuts into her food or drink?"

Heinrich: (crying) "I had no choice. Rudy said he would kill me if I didn't poison her. He was going to beat her to death if I refused to do my part."

Wiebe: "Is that why Rudolph waited in his truck a half-block from your father's house?"

Heinrich: "Yes."

Wiebe: "Tell me about your first visit to the hospital."

Heinrich: "I don't know what you mean."

Wiebe: "Why did you introduce yourself as Adelheid to the hospital staff?"

Heinrich: (gulp) "I thought there would be a restraining order to keep me away. Ask Addy, she'll tell you what our father was like. I knew that Addy waited for me and wouldn't have gone to the hospital yet, so I went to see my father disguised as my sister."

Wiebe: "So did you kill him to save your sister's life? Or did you kill him and hope your sister would go to prison for it?"

Heinrich: "I was trying to protect her. She should never have come under suspicion. That was accidental."

Wiebe: "Heinrich Ulfert, I'm charging you with the murder of your father, Hans Karl Ulfert, and with conspiracy to murder your sister, Adelheid Penner."

Addy could not believe it when Detective Wiebe told her the news that he arrested Ricky for the murder of their father. If that wasn't bad enough, he added, "Heinrich confessed that your brothers planned to murder you the day he arrived. If it is any consolation, your father's death may have saved your life. Heinrich may have been trying to save you."

Addy felt like someone punched her in the gut. Her mind felt numb and she could not find any words to respond. She pressed the end-call button without saying goodbye.

"What can I say when I find out that my brother is a murderer? How can I take in the knowledge that my brothers want me dead? More than just wish I was dead, they actually planned to murder me? And for what? It is not as if I get the inheritance and my brothers would only get money if I died. They have nothing to gain. What did I ever do to make them hate me that much?" she asked Jack.

Correctional service transferred Ricky to Calgary for Ricky's arraignment the day after Remembrance Day. Addy took the day off school and drove down to Calgary. Addy thought her brother looked broken as they brought him into the courtroom. He glanced at her and gave a weak smile.

The judge said, "Heinrich Burkhardt Ulfert, you are charged with murder in the death of your father, Hans Karl Ulfert. How do you plead?"

"Guilty," Ricky answered. "I did it to save my sister."

"Do you understand the gravity of pleading guilty?"

"Yes."

"And to the charge of conspiring to kill your sister, how do you plead?"

"Not guilty, Your Honour."

"On the confession of your guilt in the murder of your father, I sentence you to ten years in prison. On the charges of conspiracy to commit murder, a trial date is set for March 17th of next year."

The whole thing lasted less than three minutes. As Addy left the courtroom, she hurried to catch up to Detective Wiebe. "He didn't do it," she said to him. "Ricky didn't kill my father."

"He confessed to it, Mrs. Penner. I get it that it is hard to believe a family member could do such a thing, but you heard him. He did it for you."

"Ricky is a terrible liar. He may want me to believe that, but it isn't true."

"He confessed and he pleaded guilty. Unless some new evidence comes to light, your brother will remain in jail."

Boyd hoped that Ricky would plead innocent, not that he thought Ricky didn't commit murder. Boyd wanted to find out the missing pieces in this puzzle and a trial might bring things into the light.

Addy didn't attend the trial in March. Detective Wiebe phoned her and told her, "Heinrich gave details of the conversation with Karl and Rudolph. Your brother wanted Heinrich to put hazelnut oil in your food or drink. Rudolph would park around the corner and come in to prevent you from using an EpiPen or calling 911. Rudy threatened to kill you and Heinrich if your youngest brother did not go through with it."

"They wanted it to look like a severe allergic reaction," Addy said.

"The barmaid testified that she saw Rudy threatening Heinrich at the table. She also testified that Karl said that his brothers had to do whatever he said. The Hooters' security guard said that he saw Rudolph threaten Heinrich in the parking lot and made him place a phone call."

"The call Ricky made to me to say he would arrive the next morning."

"When asked why he didn't phone the police when he got out of their sight, Heinrich said that they would have known and killed him. Heinrich said he planned to warn you in person, but when he found out that Jack was with you, he knew you were safe, so he went to the hospital."

"So if Ricky was trying to protect me, why did he dress like me? Was he trying to get me arrested for killing my father?"

"The judge asked that too. Heinrich answered that his plan wasn't well thought out. But the texts he sent to your brothers confirm that he begged them to leave you alone. The judged dismissed the conspiracy charges against him."

"What about Karl and Rudy? Will they be convicted?"

"It is hard to say. Karl has no criminal record so even if he is convicted, he may not serve very much time. We'll find out next week. Rudy's trial is the end of next month."

On Monday of the first full week in April, Jack and Addy made another trip down to Addy's father's house. It was spring break week, and it actually felt like spring. The new minivan's thermostat read 18 degrees Celsius. They left Edmonton right after breakfast, and both Riley and Cody fell asleep before they reached Red Deer.

They brought the kids along, but it wasn't a vacation. Jack was on a mission to compile the papers so the accountant could finish Hans Ulfert's taxes. To do that, Jack needed to find the business and charitable donation receipts. Once the accountant filed his taxes, the lawyer would take care of most everything else and they could walk away from anything to do with Addy's father.

In the months since the funeral, they spent hours sending out death notices, and change of address notices for the bills that still needed to be paid, like for the utility bill for the house. They put stop-payments on automatic withdrawals from everything from charitable donations to magazine subscriptions. Every time they thought they were done, another annual renewal notice arrived.

They went through Hans's client lists and let them all know that Hans died. They received many anxious calls from clients who wanted assurances that their private photos would remain that way. Addy complained to Jack, "Taking care of my father's affairs is like having a full-time job."

This was their third Calgary trip since Christmas, and Addy hoped it was the last. She hid her tears from Riley and Cody as she unlocked the dented front door.

"It's a castle!" both children shouted.

Addy cried because her children never set foot in their grandparents' house, and now they saw the house, but not her parents. She also felt glad that Riley and Cody had been to the farm dozens of times to spend time with Jack's parents. Unfortunately, that thought did not dull her pain. In fact, it made it worse because she knew what could have been.

The apple tree in the front landing was without leaves or buds and Addy wondered if it died over the winter from lack of water. The kids still thought it amazing to have a tree in the entrance. Jack assured Addy that it hibernated.

After the funeral, Addy rescued the goldfish from the fountain. All but one still swam in a bowl on their kitchen counter.

Inside her father's house, the kids ran around like puppies after a bath. They threw paper aeroplanes off the balcony, played tag in the studio, and gathered up all the kid's books they could find. Addy wished her mother could have seen it. She rejoiced that her father didn't see it because then her children would have learnt of Hans Ulfert's temper.

They ate an early supper at Krueger's Wiener Schnitzel Haus and the owners made such a fuss over their children that Addy almost felt embarrassed. Almost. After that, Addy and Jack took the kids to a Disney movie at Cinema Odeon Westhills.

At 10:30 on Tuesday morning, Riley still slept so Addy went into the bedroom to check on her. Riley opened one eye, saw her mother and pulled the covers over her head.

"What is the matter with you, sweet pea? You are always an early bird. Cody said that he missed you jumping on his bed to wake him up this morning."

Riley got up and gave her mom a bleary-eyed hug and wandered to the room's ensuite.

Jack sorted through paperwork and computer files all morning while Addy packed her father's clothes into garbage bags to take to the Salvation Army thrift store. She felt glad that her children were elsewhere in the house because she found condoms in several pockets and pornographic pictures in some of the dresser drawers.

Around 1:00 p.m., Cody watched his mom make salmon sandwiches. Addy stirred in chopped up green olives and mayonnaise, just the way her mother used to. When the mushroom soup was almost ready, she said to Cody, "Go call your dad and your sister to come for lunch. This house is too big for me to call them with my small voice."

A few minutes later, Jack came into the kitchen. Cody returned a moment later without Riley. "Where is Riley? Isn't she hungry?" Jack asked.

"She is sleeping," Cody answered. "I called her, but she didn't wake up."

Addy's face registered concern as she said to Jack, "After we are done lunch, I'll go check on her. Maybe she is coming down with something."

At 2:00 p.m., Riley still slept. Addy sat on the edge of the bed and put her hand across Riley's forehead. She didn't feel feverish. Addy shook her gently and said, "Riley, you've been sleeping a long time. Are you feeling okay?"

Riley yawned and sat up. "I'm just tired, Mom. Me and that girl played for hours last night while you were sleeping."

"What girl?" Addy asked, thinking that Riley must still be half asleep.

"Lam. The girl who lives in the basement."

"It sounds like a fun dream, sweetheart, but this house doesn't have a basement."

"Lam says it does. She said that Grandpa Ulfert left you clues to find it."

At hearing those words, a cold chill swept over Addy. In her head, she screamed, "God, no! Not more secrets!" Out of her mouth came the barely audible question, "Was she barefoot?"

"When Lam and me run around barefoot in the studio, it echoes off the walls. It sounds really cool, Mom!"

"Lam and I," Addy corrected her to hide from her daughter that, inside, she shook with fear.

Addy held Riley's hand as they walked through the open studio door. Jack wedged a doorstopper under it to keep it open the day they arrived. Addy almost hyperventilated by the time they reached the office door. Jack sat at the computer surrounded by papers spread out everywhere. Several files remained open on the computer screen.

Riley pointed to a wallet-size black and white picture tacked to the pegboard above and behind the monitor. "That is her, Mom. That's Lam. She is from Vietnam."

Jack looked up at the decades' old photo and then at Addy with questions in his eyes. Addy's face looked pale and frightened.

"We need to talk, Jack," Addy stated seriously. "Riley is going to play outside with Cody. They are not coming in until we call them."

She turned to Riley and said, "Not until we call you. Got that?"

"Yes, Mom," Riley said obediently. She didn't think she was in trouble, but her mom used the school-teacher voice on her, so she knew not to ask questions.

"Then be sure that your brother keeps his coat zipped up. Go now." And Addy turned Riley towards the door and gave her a gentle push. "And pull the stopper from under studio door. I want that door closed."

Once the studio door slammed shut, Jack asked alarmed, "What is it? What is going on?"

"Her," Addy answered as she pulled the photo off the pegboard and looked at the back. There was nothing written on it. "When I saw this photo the first time, I thought she must be one of the orphans our family supported. Over the years we must have had 20 foster children through World Vision. My dad was fanatical about helping the less fortunate."

"What does that picture have to do with anything?"

"Riley said she spent most of the night playing with this girl."

"She was dreaming. That's all."

"Jack, Riley said that the girl came to her bedroom and woke her. Does that sound familiar? Then Riley said they ran around barefoot in the studio."

A chill ran down Jack's spine, but he did not want to believe what he heard. "This is insane! There is no way a child could live alone in this house. And there is no way she could go unseen. Besides, this picture is from years ago. This girl would be our age now."

"Riley said the girl told her that she lives in the basement. And before you tell me there is no basement, she told Riley the reason I had to use clues to open the doors is so that I would know how to find the basement."

"I don't believe it!" Jack exclaimed. "I don't want to believe it but, for your sake, we'll look. We've taken almost everything out of here. How will we find clues?"

At the same moment, they both said, "The photographs!"

Addy pulled out her phone and the looked for anything out of place in the pictures she took of the studio office. They almost gave up when Jack exclaimed, "Kids' books." There, in the picture were six children's books on the top shelf on the back wall. "Why would your father have children' books in his office? That has to be it!"

"Cody and Riley took them out of here yesterday. Now they are with the other books on the floor in the great room."

"Give me your phone so I can bring you the right books," Jack volunteered.

Jack hadn't reached the studio door when a girl's voice asked Addy, "Are you the Mother?"

Addy whirled around to see a thin Asian girl standing right behind her. The girl looked to be perhaps 10-years-old. Her straight black hair hung past her waist and she wore nothing but a thin, faded-green cotton dress. She had a very pretty face and big eyes.

"Are you the Mother?" she asked again in her Vietnamese-accented English.

"Yes," Addy answered. "I am Riley's and Cody's mom."

"I don't like mothers," the girl stated defiantly. "My mother sold me to Hans Ulfert for $50. Will you sell Riley? I hope not. I like Riley."

Addy tried to convince herself that she hallucinated. She glanced towards the studio door, hoping she'd see Jack coming back. "I won't sell my children," she told the child. "I am sorry your mother sold you."

The girl asked, "Did Hans Ulfert buy you from your mother?"

"No. My mother did not sell me." Addy glanced towards the studio door again.

"Are you waiting for the man? I don't like men. Hans Ulfert hurt me. He put his man part in me. Many times. He said if I cried, he wouldn't feed me. He said we had a contract. If I did my part, he would feed me. Does your man have a contract with Riley?"

Tears rolled down Addy's cheeks as she said, "I am so terribly sorry that happened to you. Men should not do that to little girls. It was a very evil thing that my father did to you."

"Does your man do the very evil thing to Riley?"

"No. Jack is a good man. He does not hurt Riley."

"Your father was not a good man. He wanted to do the very evil thing to you the night he got back from Vietnam. I begged him not to."

These words hit Addy like a sledgehammer. The thing she didn't want to think about, the thing she didn't want to believe was true. Her father molested children.

"Riley said that your name is Lam. Is that right?"

"Lam Trinh. I'm from Long Xuyen, Vietnam. Hans Ulfert promised my mother that he would make me a famous model and that he would send me to university. He said I would make lots of money and I could take care of my mother in her old age. Your father lied."

"How old are you, Lam?"

"I'm 11. You were 11 when I first saw you. Now you are the Mother. Why didn't you stay 11?"

"Because I wanted to be old enough to leave home."

As Jack walked across the studio, he said, "I think I brought the right ones."

When Addy turned back to talk to the child, Lam was gone.

Jack took one look at Addy and asked, "What happened? You look like you've seen a ghost."

"I just talked to one."

Jack brought the books, but they didn't know what to do with them. They went around the room looking for anything that might give them a clue. Finally, Addy said, "Let's put them back on the shelf in the order they were in the picture to see if it means anything."

Addy read out the order of the books and Jack reached up and put them on the highest shelf. They stared at them for a few moments and Jack asked, "Miss Drew, do you see anything that will solve this mystery?"

Addy smiled, but her heart shook with grief. "No, all I see is children's books. And they are in the wrong order."

"Your OCD is kicking in again, Nancy."

"That's it!" Addy exclaimed. "I hate to admit it, but my father knew I was a little obsessive-compulsive like him. The books should be in the order that a child would read them."

She dragged over the white folding step stool from behind the door, climbed the three steps, and rearranged the books. Then they spent several minutes trying to spell words using the first letter of the titles. They tried reading the titles as a sentence. Suddenly Jack said, "Wow!"

"What? What do you see?"

"I see books in the right order. We don't know if there is a basement and we are rearranging books that we don't know are even a clue. We are trying to invent meaning out of random book titles. Face it, Addy, a child could read these in any order."

"You're right, Jack. Well, except about the basement. I didn't read these in the order they are now. Some of these books were given to my brothers. *Charlotte's Web* and *The Lion, the Witch and the Wardrobe* belong to me so I read them first. My mother gave *The Velveteen Rabbit* to Karl. Then I read *The Secret Garden.* I read *Bread and Jam for Francis* when my mother bought it for Ricky."

Jack ended up holding a few of the books as Addy rearranged the ones on the shelf. When she put Ricky's book down in the last spot, there was a discernible click. "A weighted release," Jack exclaimed. "Very ingenious."

Addy scrambled down the step stool and moved it out of the way. Jack grabbed a shelf and pulled it towards him. A section the size of a low door swung out into the office. Behind the shelf unit, they found an empty, two-metre square room with a low ceiling. Grey coloured, indoor-outdoor carpet covered the floor.

Jack bent down and stepped in. He examined the walls and the ceiling, but it was obvious that there were no false walls or hidden doors. "There is nothing here," Jack comforted Addy. "Whatever secret your father kept here is long gone."

Addy did not look comforted by Jack's conclusion. He followed her gaze to a corner of the carpet that looked slightly curled. Jack grabbed that corner of the carpet and lifted it to look underneath. Then he backed into the office dragging the carpet.

On the floor of the secret room, they saw a metre-by-metre-square, stainless-steel door without a handle. Near one edge of the door, they saw a panel the size of a slice of bread. Jack put his finger into a Loonie-sized hole in the panel cover and slid it to one side to reveal a keypad.

"Not again!" Addy cried.

"Now what? Do you have any ideas?"

"Lam, I could use some help here," Addy said to the air but heard no reply.

"Jesus, we could use your help," Addy prayed out loud.

Jack started to say something, but Addy waved her hand at him as she shushed him. "I'm thinking," she said. Starting with the most recent ones, Addy pondered all the clues and the patterns her father used to come up with the clues.

Jack started to think that Addy had gone into a trance when she suddenly said, "Use what you least expect! Jack, the PIN for the debit card was 212B, Sherlock Holms house number. The note from my father said to use what I least expected."

"There are no letters on debit machines. So you figured out that the letter B was for number 2."

"No, it is number 1. The A is zero."

"So how does this help you?"

"What word would you least expect my father to use as a code?" Jack shrugged. Addy squatted down and pushed 0, 3, 4, 1, 1, 7, 4, 8, 3. Adelheid. The lock snarled, clicked and one side of the door lifted on hydraulics like the lid of a coffin in a horror movie.

They could see the top two galvanized-steel stairs. Below that, the steps disappeared into blackness. A dark fear gripped Addy unlike anything she had ever known, and she turned to run. Jack put his arm in front of her, hugged her shaking body, and said, "We've come this far. Let's end this today." And he stepped down.

Suddenly the lights popped on. When Jack's head was even with the floor, he looked up at her and asked, "Are you coming, Nancy Drew? Or is this a mystery you will let your assistant solve?"

Addy's heart beat like a drum in her ears as she stepped down onto the first stair. Her head felt dizzy. It felt like she purposely stepped down into hell. "I don't know why I am doing this, Jack. I don't want to find out any more of my father's secrets. I really don't want to know."

Goosebumps covered Addy's whole body before she started to descend and, as she climbed down the steep steps, the cold basement air made her shiver down to her toes. At the bottom of the stairs, she found herself at the end of a long hallway.

The unpainted concrete wall to the right was the back wall of the house foundation. Wire-mesh-covered florescent lights on the concrete ceiling provided mediocre light for the unpainted grey concrete hallway floor. The long pea-soup green wall to her left made the basement feel very industrial. They could see three unpainted galvanized-steel doors and doorframes.

"The Mother says you are the Good Man," a child's voice suddenly said. Jack jumped and whirled around. A pretty Asian girl peeked out at him from behind Addy. Addy put her hand on the child's shoulder and moved her forward so that they stood side by side. The girl squeezed herself against Addy as if looking for protection.

"Jack, this is Lam. She is 11." Jack's eyes looked as big as saucers and his mouth moved as he hunted for words.

"The Mother says you don't do the very evil thing to Riley. She says you don't have a contract with her. The Mother says you are the Good Man."

Jack's mouth still hung open. Finally, he managed to ask, "Do you live down here?"

"It is very lonely. I want to play. Where is Riley?"

"She is outside, dear," Addy said smiling down at her. Addy ran her fingers through the child's long black hair as she explained, "I didn't want Riley to see what is behind those doors."

"I don't want to see either," Lam said as she took Addy's hand and led her past Jack. She looked up into his eyes as if trying to see into his soul as if she hunted for some proof that Addy judged Jack's character correctly.

Jack followed them down the hall. His head told him, "You are dreaming," but his eyes told him he was awake. Addy held the hand of a pretty little Vietnamese girl who skipped along beside her in the skimpiest green cotton dress. She wasn't wearing panties. Lam looked exactly as Addy had described her.

As they passed the second industrial-type door, Lam exclaimed, "You are famous, the Mother. Did Hans Ulfert send you to university? Did you make lots of money and support your mother?"

"No, Lam. Hans Ulfert did not keep his promises to me either." The girl hugged her around the waist as they walked.

Like the two doors they passed, the third door was closed, but not locked. "This is your room," Lam said with excitement, sounding like a child showing off her home to a visitor. "Go in."

Addy's right hand touched the doorknob, but her hand shook so badly, she couldn't turn the knob. Finally, she took a deep breath, turned the handle, and pushed the door open. The room in front of her looked pitch black and Addy backed into Jack.

"Don't be afraid of the dark, the Mother. Hans Ulfert isn't here anymore," Lam comforted. "Hans Ulfert is never coming back." And Lam took Addy's hand and dragged her into the dark room. The lights came on after two steps.

The room looked like a warehouse. Fluorescent lights hung on chains from the unpainted cement ceiling and lit white-painted, windowless walls. In the shipping area, they could see metal-topped tables piled with boxes, packing tape, weigh scales and postage machines. On the back wall, the pull-up door stood open on a small freight elevator that obviously could be used to haul things up or down from the floor above.

On the wall to their left, they saw a galvanized-steel roll-up door for taking pallets or boxes from room to room. On the wall beside the door hung a control with a green button to lift the door and a red button to put it back down.

On the unpainted cement floor in the centre of the room, Jack counted two rows of eight pallets. On each of the 16 wooden pallets, Hans Ulfert stacked waist-high rows of hardbound, coffee-table-style picture books. The books were stacked five by five across and at least 36 deep.

The books on all the pallets looked similar with cream-coloured dust jackets with a large picture of Addy in the centre. Each pallet held books with different cover pictures. Addy immediately recognized the picture on the books on the pallet closest to the door.

"This is my baby book, Jack. But why does my father have so many of them?" she asked as she picked one up and showed Jack her picture. "That is from when I was one. He made a book for my mother every year."

"I thought your father never called you Heidi?" Jack asked.

In shock, Addy read her nick-name on the cover then flipped the book open and the colour drained from her face. She flipped a few more pages and let the book fall from her hands. Jack picked it up off the floor and saw images that were not pictures a normal person would take of their one-year-old.

Addy went to the next pallet. The cover picture on the book called *Heidi at Two* showed her smiling mischievously. She flipped it open, and the page it opened on had images of Addy naked and on her hands and knees crawling away from the camera. The pictures were shot from ground level and focused on her genitalia. She closed the book without turning pages.

She walked to the next pallet and picked a random page in *Heidi at Three* and one side of the page showed her naked and sucking on an English cucumber. The other side showed her licking it with a mischievous look in her eyes. Addy dropped the book like it burnt her hands.

Down the row, Lam sat on a pallet swinging her legs. "The Mother at 11," she said holding up the large book.

Addy bypassed the pallets of books in between and took the book from Lam's hand. The cover showed Addy asleep in bed. She opened to the first photograph and, as she turned the pages, she realized it showed a photograph by photograph documentation of how her father undressed her the night he got back from Vietnam. The last photograph, taken from right above her, showed her legs spread and her father's penis at her opening.

Addy vomited. She wretched and wretched.

Lam hugged her and said, "He didn't do the very evil thing to you. I screamed. I screamed and screamed and he stopped. He told me I was not allowed to follow him home, but I always did so I could see you. I felt very lonely in his studio except when you came. There are more books," and she dragged Addy towards the next pallet.

Heidi at Twelve. She remembered the photoshoot where the cover picture came from. She wore nothing but a pair of her mother's red high heels and they were too big for her. Her father told her how to stand. She could hear him saying, "Don't you dare tell your mother you were wearing her Pradas. It is our little secret that you are all grown up."

Addy never opened the book. She went to the last pallet. *Heidi, Sweet Sixteen.* Several of the photos could only have been taken through two-way mirrors or with hidden cameras. There were a few pictures of her in the shower, on the toilet, and in her bedroom. Most were from the final photoshoot she did in the old studio with her hair done up and her makeup on.

The second last photo showed her father behind her cupping her breasts. The final photo showed him naked, turned on and reaching for her.

"You are a famous model, the Mother. Hans Ulfert sold thousands and thousands of your books. My room is the next one. I am not as famous, but come see my books!"

Lam led Addy out of the far room and down the stark hall. Jack followed close behind and Lam looked over her shoulder and said to him, "You chased me down the stairs. You smashed the door down. I thought you were the bad man. I thought you wanted to do the very evil thing."

"I am sorry," Jack answered. "I thought that you were an intruder."

"What is an intruder?" Lam asked.

"Someone who goes where they don't belong," he replied.

"Then I met one," she answered sadly. When they reached the second door, she announced. "This is my room."

Jack opened the door. With her right hand still in Addy's hand, Lam grabbed Jack's hand with her left hand and nudged him in. The room was much narrower than the other but just as deep. Four pallets of books were neatly parked against the right-hand wall.

Lam let go of them and skipped over to the first pallet. "That is me before Hans Ulfert bought me," she said, pointing to the front cover of the books on the first pallet.

Addy picked up the book and flipped a few pages. The images showed her father molesting Lam. Both Addy and Jack wept.

Lam said, "When it came time for him to go back to Canada, Hans Ulfert did the very evil thing to me many, many times. Then he took me for a boat ride. He said that I couldn't go to heaven because the Jesus would never forgive me. He said the Jesus would burn me forever."

"Jesus is not like that," Addy said through her tears. "He loves children."

"That is what the shiny people with wings tell me. But I won't go with them. I don't want to burn forever."

"Jesus won't burn you for what an evil person did to you, Lam. What my father did to you was not your fault."

"Hans Ulfert said that I was evil. He tied an anchor to my foot and threw me over. After a long time, he pulled me up, almost to the boat. When he could see me in the water, he cut the rope."

Addy sobbed. Jack held his stomach like he might hurl.

"Is the Jesus the Good Man like Jack?" Lam asked.

"A much better man than I am," Jack answered. "He gives us a home in heaven with lots of children to play with. We don't ever have to be lonely or afraid again."

"Riley sings the Jesus song when we run around in the studio," Lam said as she wiped tears off Addy's cheek. "You used to sing the same song when you were 11 before you became the Mother. Do you still know the Jesus song?"

"There are many Jesus songs," Addy answered. "Which one does Riley sing?"

"*Black and white*," Lam answered. And she smiled a beautiful child-like smile.

Addy sat on the pallet of books, lifted Lam onto her lap and tried hard to control her tears as she sang, "Jesus loves the little children, all the children of the world. Red and yellow, black and white, all are precious in his sight. Jesus loves the little children of the world."

Even Lam's eyes smiled. "I would have liked it if you were my mother," she said to Addy, and Lam hugged her like she would never let go.

Finally, still with her head against Addy's breast, Lam said to Jack, "Take care of the Mother. She needs the Good Man. I never had a father, but if I could choose one, I'd pick you."

Jack got down on one knee and Lam hopped off Addy's lap and threw her arms around Jack's neck and kissed him on the cheek.

When she let go, she said to Addy, "Say goodbye to Riley for me. I am going with the shiny men now." And she disappeared.

The room suddenly seemed twice as dark and twice as oppressive. Addy hugged Jack and they both cried.

They walked to the last pallet and Jack picked up a book. He opened it from the back and held the book so Addy could see. The second-last picture showed Lam in a boat, wearing only a thin cotton dress, with a rope and anchor tied to her foot. The last picture showed a dead girl under the water with her black hair fanned out in the current. Hans Ulfert's hand held the rope tied to Lam's ankle.

Addy threw herself into Jack's arms and sobbed. "He really did murder her," she cried. "How could he kill such a sweet child?"

One more door remained and neither of them wanted to find out the secret behind it. They felt shaken and broken and filled with horror and grief as they

181

walked down the hall towards it. Jack tried to put on a brave front as he asked, "What could possibly be worse than what we have just seen?"

This big room contained only two pallets of books. An orange pallet jack sat under the farthest pallet. They were afraid to see the pictures, and Addy said, "I can't do this. You look, Jack."

"Oh my God!" Jack said when he saw the pictures on the book covers. "That is Angelika!"

When Addy called the kids into the house, she saw Cody leaning over the edge of the fountain. With his left hand, he hung onto the foot of the statue of a nude woman for balance, and with his right hand, he tried to scoop koi out of the circular pool. Riley examined the flower gardens for any sign of spring.

When they reached the entryway, their mother said to them, "I want you to take all the books you've sacked up in the front room upstairs. Stay in one of the bedrooms and read to each other. Your dad and I have to talk to the police for a little while so we need you to stay upstairs."

Cody said, "Okay."

"Cody, you need to take your turn reading to Riley. Got that?"

"Yes, Mom."

Riley asked, "Are you okay, Mom?"

"Yes, I'm fine. We just need to clean up a mess that Grandpa Ulfert left."

At headquarters, Addy's phone call interrupted Detective Wiebe as he ploughed through the paperwork. "Detective Wiebe, this is Adelheid Penner. I'm at my father's house and came across something you should see." She said little more than that, but the tone of her voice indicated that she felt distressed, so he dropped everything and headed over to the house.

Jack met him at the door. "We found a secret room, well, much more than a room. We'd like your advice on what to do next."

Jack led the detective into the great room. Addy sat on the loveseat, and her red and puffy eyes made it obvious she had been crying. She stood and said, "Thank you so much for coming by, Detective. It is all so overwhelming and I wanted someone I knew seeing this first."

With that Addy led the detective to the studio door, across the studio and into the office.

"I would have never guessed that there was a secret room behind the shelving unit, but this is hardly a crime," Boyd said.

Then Jack lifted the carpet to show the hidden door. He punched in the code and the door lifted open. "After you, Detective. The lights will come on."

Addy followed them down. When she stepped off the bottom stairs, she explained, "Behind each door is a horrible secret. The far one has to do with me." And she led him in down the hall.

He noticed her hand reached for someone, and then she pulled it back to her side.

Addy opened the door and Boyd took it all in as he walked over to a pallet and picked up one of the books. Although the cover picture showed Adelheid as a schoolgirl, someone would not hide that kind of book in a dungeon. He said to Addy, "Pardon me, Mrs. Penner. I really don't want to look inside this, but it is obvious that you called me here because of this. Do I have your permission to look?"

"It appears that many people already looked without my permission," she answered. "Guessing from a glance at his records, my father sold tens of thousands of these books over the last couple of decades."

Boyd opened the book in his hand and quickly closed it again. "Are all of these like this?" he asked.

"I only opened a couple of them. There is one for every year until I was 16."

"The Child Exploitation Unit is dedicated to tracking down perpetrators of child porn," Boyd said with compassion in his voice. "I'll need to get them involved. It may be uncomfortable."

"We figured as much," Jack replied. "That is why we called you. We need someone who can vouch for us."

"I hate to ask, but what is in the next room?"

"Come see," Jack said.

Addy opened the door but refused to go in. She started to sob and ran to the stairs. Jack wondered if she would keep running.

The detective walked in and saw the pallets. "Who is this?" he asked Jack. "Who is Little Lamb?"

"Her name is Lam Trinh. She died 25 years ago in Vietnam."

"Your wife must have known her," Boyd said.

Jack opened up the back of the last book and handed it to Boyd. "He killed her. Addy's father used her and then killed her. Then he sold the images of his crime."

"How do you know this?"

Jack ignored the question and said, "What we really need you to see is in the last room."

Addy had pulled herself together and waited for them in the hall at the door nearest the stairs. She opened the door and led them in. "This is my father's most recent victim," Addy said as she pointed to the picture on the cover of the closest book. "That is my niece Angelika. Karl's daughter."

Throughout the basement, police discovered thousands of barefoot footprints. The Special Victims unit tried to identify what child Hans Ulfert kept down there.

Detective Wiebe asked Adelheid if she knew anything about the footprints. She answered, "Lam Trinh's ghost." The detective looked skeptical so Addy said, "Ask Riley." And then she just smiled a motherly smile and started humming a Sunday-school song he vaguely remembered from his childhood.

Riley told him, "Lam is from Vietnam. She lived in the basement. She wasn't afraid of the dark. She said she was 11 the same time Mom was 11. We ran around barefoot in the studio. Mom said Lam went to heaven to be with Jesus."

Jack told him, "She was the cutest little thing. She called me the good man. Lam saw more evil than any child should know in a lifetime, yet she was still sweet." And he choked up and could not say another word.

To confirm Riley's story, the police dusted the floor of the studio. They found footprints from two girls. Riley's prints matched one set but did not match those in the basement. The other set from the studio matched those in the basement. There were places in the studio where the mystery girl's footprints overlapped Riley's.

That night, Boyd told Sarah the ridiculous story the Penner's told him about the ghost of a girl murdered in Vietnam 25 years earlier living in a secret basement in Calgary.

Sarah asked, "If you had three witnesses to anything else, would you presume you had a true version of the story?"

"Yes, but they are talking about a ghost!"

Sarah restated what she told him months earlier, "There are things in life you will never figure out. Some things are meant to be mysteries."

"There are no such things as mysteries. Only missing clues," he replied.

They went together for eight months before she slept with Boyd. And it was six months after that before Sarah moved in with him. He was a great guy. And handsome too, buff and muscular, a cop's cop.

If he had a flaw, it was that he wanted everything to be logical. Everything had to have an explanation. He didn't get emotions at all. And he didn't believe in God.

"I'm not an atheist," he told her once. "There might be a God. I've just never seen any proof."

She had seen proof. She was living proof.

Sarah smiled, glanced up and said, as if speaking to the sky, "Here goes." She took Boyd by the hand and led him to the living room. "I have something to show you that might have something to do with the so-called ghost." She ran to the closet and took down an old picture album. She sat down by Boyd and told him a story.

"When I was four," she explained, "my parents lived in Homestead, Florida, just south of Miami. We used to go for picnics to the everglades. I got lost. A fisherman found me five days later."

"Five days? I'm glad he found you," Boyd answered.

She showed him yellowed newspaper clippings behind plastic in an old photo album.

Hunt for the missing girl called off for the night

This afternoon, four-year-old Sarah Herrera disappeared from her parent's picnic site in Everglades National Park. "It appears that she either fell into the water or was taken by an alligator. Park rangers and volunteers combed the area. As the sun sets, the hope of finding her dwindles," Clint McCoy, the search coordinator, says, "As heartbreaking as it sounds, no one is to go into the glades at night. At the best of times, the everglades are extremely dangerous. Nighttime is when the gators are hunting." Search efforts will resume when the sun rises.

Missing girl still not found

At the end of day two in the hunt for four-year-old Sarah Herrera, the only sign of the girl missing in Everglades National Park was a single sandal found floating in the alligator-infested water. Search Coordinator Clint McCoy says, "Over 100 people searched the area where Sarah went missing. As we go into the second night, the hope of finding the child is all but gone." The search coordinator has confirmed that the search and rescue helicopter that flew the previous night using infra-red detection will not be deployed tonight.

Search called off for girl missing in the everglades

At noon today, search efforts were officially called off for four-year-old Sarah Herrera who disappeared while on a picnic with her parents. A spokesperson for her family issued this statement, "One moment our baby girl helped carry things to the picnic table, and the next moment she was gone. Our deepest thanks go to everyone who put their own lives at risk in order to hunt for Sarah. For all your thoughts and prayers, we are grateful."

"They declared you dead?" Boyd asked alarmed. Sarah nodded and flipped the page in the album.

Fisherman finds the missing girl alive days after the search is called off

In what everyone is calling a miracle, Sarah Herrera was found by a snook fisherman five days after she disappeared in the everglades. "I couldn't believe my eyes," said Carlos Mendoza. "At first I thought I was looking at a bird or an animal swimming because she was wading towards me through water that came up to her neck. Then I said Holy Jesus, this is the missing girl. I was terrified that a gator would get her before I reached her. I pulled her up onto my boat as fast as I could."

Mendoza placed an excited call to 911 and told them where to meet him. While they waited for authorities to arrive, Mendoza shared a ham sandwich with Sarah. The girl was found 17 miles away from where she disappeared. The girl suffered many insect and leech bites but otherwise appears unharmed. Her parents were notified that their daughter was alive during the memorial service for their daughter at Sacred Heart Church.

Boyd set down the newspaper clippings and said, "Wow! That is quite the story. I can see why you think there some higher power looked after you. Don't take this wrong. I'm overjoyed that you survived, but you were lucky. Very lucky. In a thousand other lost child stories, the ending is not good."

"You don't get it," Sarah replied, "because you've never been to the glades. The alligators are everywhere. The authorities wrote me off as dead when my mother told them she heard me scream and saw gators swimming everywhere.

The authorities only continued the search in hopes that they would find some of my clothes to show my parents. And then there are the snakes," Sarah said, and she shuddered.

She looked past Boyd as if she searched for something a long ways away and said, "I remember it like yesterday. Mom faced away from me as she lifted a quart sealer of home-made lemonade out of the green Coleman camp cooler to pour into ice-filled clear plastic cups. Dad was down on one knee behind the car splitting firewood with a hatchet so he could build a fire to cook the hotdogs.

"I helped my Mom carry things from the trunk of the car to a weathered old picnic table underneath a couple of gnarly pine trees. I carried the paper plates with both hands, but then tripped over a tree root. The breeze sent one of the plates rolling on edge between the Brazilian-pepper bushes and down an animal trail towards the swamp, two metres below the picnic site.

"I chased the paper plate down the steep bank and stopped when my toes reached the water. The paper plate floated away on the brackish water like a sailboat in the breeze. That is when I saw it. A huge Burmese Python lay stretched out along the water's edge, sunning itself, its nose only centimetres from my foot. The snake's four-metre-long chequered body looked as big around as a telephone pole. Its black tongue darted out and tickled my ankle at the same time its body pulled itself towards me into coils that spilt out into the swamp.

"Its dragon-sized head rose from the ground as the front of the python flowed into the path between me and the top of the bank. Its head rose above me as if deciding if it could swallow me whole. Its black tongue flicked out and slapped my cheek and then the snake's head hit me with the force of a wrecking ball, knocking me into the water.

"In an instant, the snake's coils wrapped around me and squeezed the air out of my lungs. But at that moment, a five-metre long alligator clamped its deadly jaws over the snake's head and swam for deep water. It dragged me along like a dolphin caught in a fishing trawler's net.

"After what seemed like an eternity, the snake tried to wrap itself around the alligator. For a moment I rode on the alligators back as the snake's coils fell off me. I sucked in the air before the alligator dived.

"Then a blow from the alligator's tail propelled me up to the surface where I caught another breath of air. The python and the alligator rolled over and over in the water right beside me and the waves washed me to the shore. When I say shore, I don't mean the shallow grassy bank of a prairie lake. Shore on that small island was a wall of tangled mangrove roots like twisted jail bars growing down from the trees above into the water, and rooted in the mud below. With slippery hands, I pulled myself up unto the sun-bleached roots. Then I saw a dozen alligators swimming towards me.

"Somehow I managed to crawl up onto the mangrove roots and scrambled to my feet, but the tree trunk stood between me and shore. I needed to step root to root to get away from the water. With my left hand on the tree trunk for balance, I tried to step where the next root joined the tree. But my feet were wet and I dropped into a narrow gap between the roots.

"As I fell, a giant gator threw itself at me, open-mouthed. Its teeth caught some of my hair as I fell into a cage made of roots. Under the tree, the water was only as deep as my waist, but I sank up to my knees in the soft mud. The gator tried to crawl in after me, but only its closed snout fit between the roots, its nose millimetres from my face. With its powerful legs and claws, the alligator tried to tear apart the roots above me and chunks of mangrove root fell on me. Then it dove into the water and tried to find a way to get at me, but the strong roots protected me.

"I was in a jail-like cell the size of a shower stall. The mangrove roots were as big around as my wrist. Where they reached the waterline, five centimetres of water separated them. Above me, they came together like the arches of a Russian cathedral, well, except for the gap where I fell in.

"Snake blood filled the water and the gator left. Then I could hear my mother's agonized screaming from somewhere not too far away and I called to her. Immediately, the alligator came back. Smaller ones came too. The big gator tried to get at me again through the gap at the top of the mango roots so the smaller alligators went back to fighting over scraps of the python.

"The gator's nose came a little farther down this time and its mouth opened about a little. I ducked down until the water covered my mouth and I prayed to Jesus to rescue me, but I didn't dare call for help. Salt-marsh mosquitoes swarmed around my head and bit every spot of skin where the water washed off the mosquito repellent my mother slathered on me. Did you know salt-marsh mosquito's bites feel like a hornet sting?"

Boyd answered, "No. I didn't know that. What happened next? How did you escape?"

"A search boat came by a couple of hours later, although it did not come close because the big gator's upper body covered on top of the mango roots. I watched from underneath it as a man scooped one of my flip-flops out of the water with a net. The gator above me snapped its jaws at them and hissed.

"I called to them, but they could not hear me because of their boat's outboard motor. The water all around the boat looked like it boiled from all the alligators so the men left quickly. Although they officially searched for me the next day, when they found my sandal, they gave up any hope of finding me alive.

"Night came, and I've never known a blacker night. A couple of times I fell asleep and water engulfed me. I woke up coughing and choking, and then the gator would try again to get at me. At one point I heard a helicopter coming my way and, for a moment, a spotlight lit up the gator above me. And that was it.

"When I thought that I couldn't possibly stay awake any longer, the gator left and an arm reached in and pulled me out. At first, I thought my father found me, but a stranger pulled me out. He carried me on his shoulders across the water and down the shore away from the picnic site."

"Wait a second!" Boyd exclaimed. "You're saying someone lifted you out and then carried you on his shoulders through the alligators?"

"Yes. They were all around. He told me it wasn't safe to stay in the mangrove roots any longer. I don't know how long he carried me because I fell asleep. I woke the next morning in a heron's nest, three metres off the ground in a scrubby white mangrove tree on a small island."

"So someone rescued you but didn't take you to authorities. He left you in a bird's nest?" Boyd asked in disbelief.

"Yes, the first of the handful I slept in. He lifted me into nests at night and down in the morning. Then we walked hand in hand or else he'd carry me through the deep water. He told me which plants I could eat and pointed out poisonous ones. He said he was my angel, and I believed him."

"Your angel? He sounds more like some nut case living in the swamp! He heard you were missing, found you and abducted you," Boyd argued.

Sarah answered, "I don't expect you to believe me, although it would be nice if you did."

"You were four. At four you think everyone is like your parents. Everyone is your friend," Boyd stated bluntly. "Your angel was a pervert and you are lucky you escaped."

"I didn't escape. On the morning of the fifth day, he told me that a fisherman would come to that spot. He told me that the man was a good man and I would be back with my parents that day. About a half-hour later, I heard the boat coming. The angel told me to walk straight to the boat, and I did. I never looked back and never saw the angel again."

Boyd shook his head. "For whatever reason, the creep decided to let you go," he stated. "Even if I made the leap of faith to believe your story about the angel, it doesn't make any sense. If an angel did rescue you on the first night, why wouldn't it just take you to your parents? Or at least to a place where you would be found? You obviously believe in the supernatural, but it is just your mind coping with the horrors of being lost."

Sarah smiled. "The angel gave me a message to pass on to you."

Boyd did not believe it but asked anyways because Sarah's smile always made his heart melt. "Uh-huh," he replied.

"The angel said that when the man I was going to marry heard my story, I was to ask him a question. It never made sense to me, but I never forgot it."

Now Boyd felt afraid. He said to himself, "If I screwed this up, then my relationship with Sarah will end. To make matters worse, it would fall apart over a make-believe angel from 20 years ago."

With trepidation, he asked, "OK, what did the angel tell you to ask me?"

"Where are the fingerprints?" she asked. She could tell by the look on his face that the question hit Boyd like a freight train.

Boyd had not told her that, although there were thousands of footprints, they did not find a single child's fingerprint in the basement.

Karl looked haughty and proud as he walked into the North Vancouver police station. Ursula looked nervous and frightened. "The judge threw the conspiracy case out, Ursula," Karl reassured her. "We have nothing to worry about."

A sergeant led them to a counselling room and offered them coffee. A few moments later, three detectives came in. Karl recognized Detective Wiebe. Immediately, Karl rose to his feet and threatened, "You have no right to harass us like this. I'm calling my lawyer!"

The other detective said, "I'm Detective Ray Schmyr of the Vancouver Crimes Against Children unit. This is my counterpart, Detective Len Fabrik from the Calgary Police Services' Violence Against Children unit. You need to hear what we have to say. Detective Wiebe is here because his research uncovered what I am about to show you."

Ursula stared down at her hands. Karl's mouth hung open and tears welled up in his eyes. "Crimes against children? Whose children?"

Detective Ray Schmyr opened a file folder and pulled out a letter-sized photo and set it in front of them. It showed the photo from the front cover of one of the books. "Do you recognize this child?" he asked.

"That is Angelika!" Karl exclaimed, obviously alarmed. "Where did you get this?" he demanded.

Ursula began to weep.

"And what about this person?" Detective Schmyr said as he set down a picture that showed a man's head and bare shoulders. It was obviously cropped out of a bigger picture.

"That is my father," Karl answered. "But why doesn't he have a shirt on?"

Ursula sobbed loudly as she wrung at her hands.

"For the record, you confirm that this is a photograph of Hans Karl Ulfert, your father?"

"Yes, but what has this got to do with anything?" Karl demanded.

"There is no easy way to tell you this. Your father molested your daughter over several years."

"I don't believe it! It is not true!" Karl pointed at Detective Wiebe and yelled, "This is your doing! You are trying to drag my father's name through the mud!"

Boyd pointed at Ursula and calmly replied, "Ask her."

Karl turned towards Ursula and demanded, "What does he mean?"

"I found out the day your brothers came," she sobbed. "Angelika told me that Grandpa made her a woman. She told me that she was already a famous model and someday she'd be rich and could buy a horse."

Detective Schmyr asked her, "Did you report this revelation to the police?"

"The police? You've got to be kidding! He molested my baby girl!" Ursula shrieked. "Two hours after she told me, I boarded a plane to Calgary. I killed the bastard the next morning." She turned to Karl and said, "Why your shithead brother claimed he did it, I don't know."

"How did you do it?" Boyd asked, remembering the medical examiner's report:

The subject had high levels of medetomidine in his liver and blood.

189

Medetomidine is an anaesthetic used in veterinary clinics. In Canada, it goes by the name Domitor and is approved for use on dogs and large farm animals. Levels in the subject were sufficient to shut down lung function.

Ursula answered, "I put enough Domitor in his IV bag to knock out an elephant."

"Where did you get the anaesthetic from? Domitor is a restricted substance."

"I am a distributor for veterinarian supplies. I pulled a syringe, bottle of Dom and a uniform from an order going out the next day. When I delivered the broken bottle to the vet, he signed that the bottle was broken and the contents spilt. Then I put in a claim with the company that supplied it."

"So how did you get by the nurses' station without being seen?"

"Did you know the nurses don't even look up when the cleaning staff go by with a bucket? The other hospital staff are beneath them. It was the perfect crime to rid the world of a horrible, child-molesting bastard. I boarded a plane for home an hour later. Karl was out humping some bar slut and didn't even know I was away. Then Ricky screwed the whole thing up."

Conclusion

Angelika gave the police details of her contract with her grandfather. From what police gather, Hans Ulfert groomed her from the time she turned two. He went from praising her, taking nude pictures of her, and then to having her star in movies. He often had access to her while her parents took day trips to Banff or Jasper. Angelika still goes for therapy twice a month.

When they told Ricky that Ursula confessed, he told Detective Wiebe his side of the story.

"I said my piece to my father and walked by the nurses' station crying. I went into the women's bathroom to blow my nose and redo my mascara. As I walked out, I saw Ursula step out of the elevator with a yellow hospital bucket in her hand. She carried it. She did not wheel it like the hospital staff do.

"She wore a blue uniform similar to what the cleaning staff wear, except there was a puppy embroidered on the top left shoulder. The look on her face showed pure hatred and I thought that she came to speak her mind to my father like I did. So I waited for her. She came back out of the room not 30 seconds later and I knew she killed him, so I ran down the stairs.

"Then it dawned on me. I showed up at the hospital as my sister and then my father dies. Addy would get the blame. Or I would get the blame. I didn't know what to do so I hurried back to the airport to establish an alibi for myself. I didn't kill him so why should I go to jail?

"Then you show up and ask me what my sister would think of me when she finds out that I planned to kill her. So I confessed to killing my father so Addy would know I tried to save her. Then she would still love me. I never killed my father, although I wish I had."

The jury convicted Ursula of murder and the judge sentenced her to five years in prison. The case was airtight and the evidence conclusive. They released Ricky from jail the day after the sentencing.

In spite of testifying about the brothers' meeting at Hooters, Cindy, the barmaid, moved in with Karl the day the police arrested Ursula. Cindy discovered quickly that Karl spent a lot of nights out, but she stayed for the money that would be his. And hers. She is not a good mother to Angelika, Torsten and Ulrich.

The police destroyed hundreds of books from the photographer's basement. From Hans Karl Ulfert's meticulous records, they were able to identify over 3,000 paedophiles worldwide. Raids are still ongoing. So far, the police have identified dozens of young victims. It will take years to go through all of the leads.

Boyd married Sarah on New Year's Day. They went to Florida for their honeymoon. As part of their adventures, they hired a guide to take them on an airboat tour of the everglades so Sarah could show Boyd where she was lost for five days. Boyd saw where the snake knocked Sarah into the water, where she spent her first night, and where the fisherman found her. Boyd lost count of how many alligators he saw that day.

When the accountant totalled up the estate, Hans Ulfert owned $47 million in assets. Karl got 75% and Rudolph got 25%. Rudy will be out of jail in three years. Only Karl showed up for the reading of the will. Addy refused to take an executor fee which pleased Karl.

Karl got his father's coin collection, even the coins Raven hid in the box in Rudy's spare bedroom. The collection means nothing to him.

Fortunately, Rudy's punch didn't completely sever Raven's spine and, on her son's second birthday, Erik's foster mother brought him to Raven's community-living apartment for a birthday party. The doctors have confidence that someday Raven will be physically able to look after her son.

Raven sued Rudy for child support, for suffering and injuries, and for what the doctors agreed will be permanent debilitating pain. The judge awarded her 3 million dollars. Rudy's lawyer is fighting the ruling and Raven still has not received a penny.

For her 12th birthday, besides a cell phone for emergencies only, Addy gave Riley the *Modern Adventures of Nancy Drew*. Riley remembered her mom's story about tracking down the clues at Grandpa Ulfert's house, so she decided to see if she could decipher her grandfather's German handwriting on the back of Black Beauty. As she struggled to lift the photograph off the nail, the picture dropped.

That night at supper, Riley asked, "Mom, is it hard to learn German?"

"Some of the sounds are guttural and it takes a bit of practice. If you want to take German at school, I can help you practise."

"And I could teach you Plattdeutsch," Jack said to annoy Adelheid.

"No Low German!" Addy stated emphatically, and Jack winked at Riley.

"Well, I don't really want to speak it. I just want to read Grandpa's message on the back of Black Beauty."

"It said something like, if you want to play the game, you need to watch closely so you know what to do next."

"And what do the numbers mean?" she asked.

"What numbers?" both Jack and Addy asked at once.

Riley led them to her bedroom. The broken picture frame lay face down on her bed. "Sorry, Mom. It fell when I tried to lift it down. I'll pay for a new frame from my allowance or babysitting."

Neither Jack nor Addy heard Riley's apology because they concentrated on reading the precise German handwriting written in pencil on the back of the actual photograph.

"Adelheid, long ago we made a contract, but I never paid you your commission. The account with my ill-gotten gains is in the Scotia Bank,

Nassau, Bahamas. It is yours now. Imagine it as a coffee tin full of coins. Don't tell your mother or your brothers. The password is what you least expect. I have done evil that there aren't words for, so I know I won't see you in the afterlife. You are rid of me at last. Hans Karl Ulfert."

The account held over 68 million U.S. dollars. Over the next year, Addy and Jack started the Lam Trinh Foundation for Sexually Exploited Girls. They built and staffed the first shelter and orphanage for girls in Long Xuyen, Lam's home city. The year following, they built two more orphanages in Vietnam and drew up plans to expand into Cambodia. The foundation's goal is to build safe places for girls around the world.

Addy and Jack never used a penny of the money for themselves. They still live in the same house in the Jackson Heights area of Edmonton. Out of her teacher's wages, Addy paid for a new frame for Black Beauty, which still hangs in Riley's room.

Addy has not seen any of her brothers in the last three years. It may be a few years yet before she will feel comfortable being in the same room with them. If ever.

Ricky sold the gold frame that surrounded his mother's picture. With the proceeds, he paid for a sex-change operation.

Boyd Wiebe believes in God. He named his daughter Faith.